ALSO BY PETER HANDKE

THE
MORAVIAN
NIGHT

THE MORAVIAN NIGHT

A STORY

PETER HANDKE

TRANSLATED FROM THE GERMAN BY KRISHNA WINSTON

FARRAR, STRAUS AND GIROUX   NEW YORK

Farrar, Straus and Giroux
18 West 18th Street, New York 10011

Copyright © 2008 by Suhrkamp Verlag Frankfurt am Main
Translation copyright © 2016 by Krishna Winston
All rights reserved
Printed in the United States of America
Originally published in German in 2008 by Suhrkamp Verlag, Germany,
   as Die morawische Nacht
English translation published in the United States by Farrar, Straus and Giroux
First American edition, 2016

Library of Congress Cataloging-in-Publication Data
Names: Handke, Peter. | Winston, Krishna, translator.
Title: The Moravian night : a story / Peter Handke ; translated from the German by Krishna Winston.
Other titles: Morawische Nacht. English
Description: New York : Farrar, Straus and Giroux, 2016.
Identifiers: LCCN 2016002079 | ISBN 9780374212551 (hardback) | 9780374715618 (ebook)
Subjects: | BISAC: FICTION / Literary.
Classification: LCC PT2668.A5 M6713 2016 | DDC 833/.914—dc23
LC record available at http://lccn.loc.gov/2016002079

Designed by Jo Anne Metsch

Our books may be purchased in bulk for promotional, educational, or business use. Please contact
your local bookseller or the Macmillan Corporate and Premium Sales Department at 1-800-221-7945,
extension 5442, or by e-mail at MacmillanSpecialMarkets@macmillan.com.

www.fsgbooks.com
www.twitter.com/fsgbooks • www.facebook.com/fsgbooks

10 9 8 7 6 5 4 3 2 1

Grateful acknowledgment is made to the Federal Chancellery of Austria for its generous support of
this translation.

THE MORAVIAN NIGHT

I

EVERY COUNTRY HAS its Samarkand and its Numancia. That night, both places were here with us on the Morava. Numancia, located in the Iberian highlands, had at one time been the last refuge from and bulwark against the Roman Empire, while Samarkand, whatever it may have represented in history, became and remains legendary, and will still be legendary when history is no more. On the Morava, in place of a fortress we had a boat, to all appearances a rather small one, which styled itself "hotel" but for quite a while now had primarily served the writer, now the former writer, as a dwelling. The HOTEL sign merely provided cover: almost anyone who inquired about a room for the night, a cabin, would be told "No vacancy" and sent packing. Such inquiries, however, hardly ever occurred, and not only because the boat always anchored in places along the river to which no proper roads led. On the rare occasions when someone did find his way there, it was because of the "hotel" sign beckoning at a great distance through the darkness, across the fields bordering the river: MORAVIAN NIGHT.

The boat was not really anchored, merely moored to trees or pilings, and in such a way that the hawsers could be loosened quickly and easily—whether for a quick getaway or simply for pushing off without any fuss, for maneuvering upstream or downstream. (After many years of sand and silt buildup, not entirely the result of war, during the period in question long stretches of the Morava had become quite navigable again, all the way to the sources of its southern and western branches, thanks to a flourishing and—almost—universally recovering economy that was spreading even beyond the borders of our country, previously reduced to the most wretched backwater of Europe.)

On the night when we were summoned to the boat, it was tied up between the village of Porodin and the town of Velika Plana. Although Velika Plana lies closer to the river, the summons came from the riverbank on the Porodin side, far from the bridge linking the two towns, and as a result we zigged and zagged, each of us wending his way separately from the village, turning now left, now right, along cart tracks that switched direction from one field to the next. Since all of us happened to be in Porodin or nearby villages, on various farms, we, the friends, associates, distant neighbors, collaborators of the former writer—each of whom had been his traveling companion on one leg of his journey or another—soon formed a convoy of sorts, in cars, on bicycles, on tractors, and on foot, the latter making as rapid progress cutting across fields as those in vehicles, who had to follow bumpy tracks that kept veering away from the destination on a course to nowhere that soon petered out. Even those on foot, with that glowing MORAVIAN NIGHT sign seemingly just a hop, skip, and jump away, would unexpectedly happen upon a deep canal that forced them to make an abrupt turn, only to find themselves facing an impenetrable thicket that forced them to turn off again.

Why had our boatman chosen to make the Porodin area, of all places, his residence? We could only guess. Some surmised that it had to do with a story told all through the Balkans between the wars—it had always been either wartime there or "between the wars": apparently a peddler had been killed by a local resident, for which the entire village had done penance ever since on the anniversary of the murder. Others believed that he had moved there because of the Morava, to be able to gaze out at the river, especially its shimmering bends, one just upstream, the other downstream. Still others speculated that it had to do with the many crossroads and forks in the good-sized village, where he simply wanted to sit on the terrace outside one of the little Balkan taverns, watching flocks of sheep grazing as far as the eye could see, a glass of the cloudy, iron-rich local wine in front of him.

It was long past midnight. As if by previous agreement, we had gone to bed unusually early, and were already fast asleep when the summons reached us. Yet instantly we were wide awake. Not a moment of bewilderment or confusion. The wake-up call had come in a number of ways, but mainly by mobile telephone. One or two, however, heard a messenger knock on the barnyard gate or toss a pebble at the window—one little knock or a single little stone was enough. And one of us, opening the door to find the procession assembled outside, told the others that as he had lain in his bed in Porodin with the curtains open as wide as they would go, he had been startled out of his sleep by the seemingly imperious flashing of that neon sign far off in the meadows along the Morava, and the next person claimed to have been jolted awake by a signal sounding more like that from a seagoing vessel than from a houseboat. Jolted? Maybe so. But it had been no ordinary jolt. And however it happened, the rousing had taken place without words. And one way or the other: each of us felt as if the summons had seized him by the scruff of the neck, at once roughly and gently. The telephones had beeped only once. And one of us, who answered a fraction of a second before the ring, with the kind of presence of mind one has only when one has been fast asleep, heard nothing but a very brief, almost inaudible laugh, sounding to him, on the threshold between deep sleep and wide-awakeness, all the clearer, and that meant, without words: "Get up!" The laughter was melodic, and it was not the laugh of our friend on the boat but unmistakably that of a woman, which, however, came as no surprise to the person thus summoned. Nothing surprised him at that moment, nor did anything surprise him as he then made his way across the fields and the fallow stretches—despite the highly fertile land along the river and the all-pervasive new economy, the untilled areas continued to expand—all the way to the MORAVIAN NIGHT. Nothing surprised us, any of us, in that moment of waking long before midnight. And likewise in the hour that followed, as we hobbled and wobbled over sticks and stones: not a flicker of surprise. The prevailing sensation: that of great freshness, coming both from the night air outside and from deep inside us: an all-encompassing freshness.

Those who went on foot reached the boat first. Those with vehicles, even bicycles, had had to abandon them long before they reached the banks of the Morava; it was impossible to make headway in the increasing tracklessness, with more and more drainage ditches and thorny thickets. The hikers, accustomed to the dark, had little trouble finding gaps and crossings, while the drivers and bikers had to grope their way forward, night-blind after switching off their headlights. This description gives the impression that there must have been many of us, quite a large number indeed, a convoy. But that was deceptive: we merely seemed numerous as we made our way across the river valley by night. There were not more than six or seven of us, corresponding, so to speak, to the hours stretching ahead, the episodes, the chapters of the night, until morning. The season: not long before the onset of spring. The date: not long before Orthodox Easter, which that year, in contrast to earlier practice, had been aligned with the pan-European Easter, as was supposed to be done for the foreseeable future. Moon phase: full. Wind: gentle night breeze, stronger down by the river. Fields of clouds drifting slowly from west to east. The first summer constellations, which for a brief hour toward night's end made way for a glimpse of Orion and a few other winter constellations.

Contrary to one expectation or another, the former writer received us alone on his house- and escape boat. Contrary likewise to various expectations or fears, he looked healthy and, as might have been said in an earlier time, hale; no spring chicken exactly, but steady on both legs (whereas during his years as a writer a typical habit of his had been to shift his weight from one leg to the other, although that "meant nothing; all the people in the village back home did the same, from childhood on"). The way he stood there quietly was reassuring, especially after all the things one or another of those summoned had heard about his tour, his *daura*, in some stages of which he had been fleeing, in others wandering aimlessly, in others courting death, and in still others running amok on his native continent of Europe.

On the other hand, it accorded with the general expectation that the host seemed not especially elated to see his guests arriving. Not so much as the whisper of a greeting could be heard from the silhouette visible up there by the railing under the invitingly glowing MORAVIAN NIGHT. Not even the hint of a wave to beckon our little band, by now gathered one and all on the brushy riverbank, onto the boat. True, down by the water lay a kind of plank that connected the boat to the land somehow. But it was so narrow, and furthermore angled so steeply, that we teetered precariously as we made our way up it, as if on a chicken coop ladder, dropping onto all fours, one behind the other, as the plank shuddered and we kept sliding back. Obviously he did not reach out to any of us to heave us onto the deck, let alone welcome us. Perhaps also noteworthy was that he initially left us alone on the boat for a long time, only later coming to join us, appearing from god knows where.

Although he had had us summoned, it seemed now as though we were disturbing him. Not only did our arrival not please him; it actually displeased him. He resented it. We were undesirables, interlopers, river pirates. We had expected such a reception, to be sure, were accustomed to this apparent lack of hospitality, contrasting so harshly with the tried-and-true Balkan tradition. Nonetheless, that night we were offended, especially when his first words after a long, rigid refusal to speak chided us for

7

our "servile punctuality," our "predictability." And the next thing he did was to switch off the neon sign, leaving us in total darkness on the boat for a while. And likewise the Balkan music, which admittedly had lured some of us on board, fell silent. In its place nothing but the skull-splitting frog chorus from the vegetation along the Morava, which would go on all night, the only other sound being the howling of the trucks on the expressway near Velika Plana, it, too, persisting un-abated through the night: the long-distance freight traffic, not only to Turkey and back but also from continent to continent, roared by with-out a second's letup.

Once our eyes had adjusted to the darkness, some of us discovered something unexpected about our host: he was swaying his head to the squawking of the myriad frogs and accompanying the distant thunder-ing and roaring of the tractor trailers with a humming that seemed in-tended to convey a melody. This was new to us because we knew no one more sensitive to noise. Hadn't this sensitivity escalated to the point that a sudden gust of wind, no matter how gentle, had been enough to make him jump as if an enemy had laid hands on him? And had he been joking when he said again and again that he had given up writing out of a growing dislike for noise of any kind? As time went on, he had come to experience every sound as a racket, as noise, malevolent noise. Even music? Yes, music, music especially, that of Claudio Monteverdi as much as that of Franz Schubert. And after the whistling of wind and the rustling of leaves, once two of his favorite sounds, which had always filled him anew "with an inchoate love," eventually his third-favorite sound had also become repellent to him—the rhythmic and melodic scratching of his pencil in silence. Could a change in his attitude toward the world of sounds be the result of his participation in the Interna-tional Congress on the Acoustics of Silence and Sound, to which, as one of us who had accompanied him there knew, one stage of his tour had been dedicated?

We who were summoned to the boat that night were all men; again in conformity with our expectations, he told us to remove our shoes, as one would before boarding a seaworthy yacht. But supposing a woman had been present, no matter who, he would not have hesitated to issue this order. He spoke, however, in an oddly soft voice, different from his usual soft voice. Although we were all trusted friends of his from way back, not all of us grasped immediately that he meant this soft speech to be contagious. To some he had to whisper insistently, "Shush, shush!" At that it became clear to each of us that the prohibition on resonant voices was neither a foible on our host's part nor a point of etiquette, but a response to danger. Suddenly we all became aware of the danger, though not its specific nature. We felt it: the danger of *danger*. Not that all of us began to whisper like him; we fell silent. We became completely silent, from one minute to the next. And in that silence we realized that the cessation of the music, like the extinguishing of the MORAVIAN NIGHT sign, had had a hidden significance: both had signaled danger. We stood motionless on the strip of deck by the door leading into the so-called reception area; from there on one side one could enter the "salon" or "restaurant," on the other side the cabins or hotel rooms, which in actuality, like the "restaurant," served the boat's owner as living, sleeping, and watch areas.

What we smelled next was not danger, however. It was the smell of the Morava, as it had smelled for millennia on April nights, when—or so we imagined—the snow began to melt in the southern and western mountains from which it flowed; this smell, at least in our imagination, was something that had persisted through the ages—at most a hint of another smell seemed mixed in with it: maybe that of iron rusting away deep in the water, iron from all the bridges destroyed along the river's upper course (it goes without saying that they had long since been rebuilt, joined by more and more new ones, including those for the high-speed trains)? maybe from the constantly puffing-up bodies of the hordes of frogs in the reeds along the banks? More likely from the frogs; hadn't each of us kept in his nose the smell that even a single frog's warty skin deposited in my hand when I caught him?

Unexpected—or perhaps not—a hug from the boatmaster. One

after another we received a wordless, tight, prolonged hug, accompanied by the obligatory mutual three kisses on alternating cheeks; how could it be otherwise? And the door to the enclosed area was held open for us, as if by a bellman, and likewise that to the salon or lounge, as if by a master of ceremonies. The salon was heated by a crackling fire, welcome on that April night on the river. Amazing, a fire like that on a boat, but as previously mentioned, nothing surprised us that night, as almost nothing had for a long time, especially nothing involving our faraway neighbor. This fire, sometimes blazing, sometimes just glowing, provided the only illumination for the rest of the night. And it was sufficient, and thanks to the windows all around the salon we could look out, at the Morava on one side and the floodplain forest on the other. It probably upset no one that various features of the room could only be guessed at; nor did it interfere with the course the night took—more likely the opposite.

One could only guess, for instance, at the face and figure of the woman who later unexpectedly joined the group. She slipped in from the open deck after the guests, left alone by the boatmaster, had been standing around the salon indecisively, feeling keenly the absence of their host. The tables seemed to be set, but each for only one person, or was that impression deceiving? Group or no group: no sign of anything resembling a dinner table. Each separate table was also markedly at a remove from the next, forming in relation to it, and likewise to all the others, an angle that from the outset did not merely render any kind of grouping more difficult but also made it more or less impossible. Of course we could easily have pushed the tables together to create a dinner table of some sort—straight, diagonal, curved, semicircular, L-shaped. But we knew our host, and his mania for not tolerating the slightest displacement of anything in his home by anyone else, only too well; had one of us dislodged a single possession of his, whether a book or just a chunk of brick, by less than "half an inch" (he liked to use old nonmetric measurements) from its appointed place or merely given the object a tiny spin—and by the way, there was no way to recognize that it was in "its place"—the result would have been a tongue-lashing in comparison to which a rap on the knuckles would have seemed almost like a caress.

The woman guided the guests, one at a time, to the separate tables, where they then sat with their backs to each other or at least half turned away, in a pattern suggestive of being abandoned and scattered at random—at least initially they felt a kind of estrangement. This feeling was soon forgotten, however, in our being attended to by the unknown woman, and in another way, incomparably more pleasing, in our intuiting her beauty as she moved among the tables in the dim light, describing circles, spirals, and ellipses. We had all long since lost the habit of being waited on, and by now were generally loath to accept it. We did not like having anyone get close to us; we wanted to take care of ourselves! But to be waited on by such a beauty, or by beauty altogether, that was something we could accept. And what seemed beautiful to us about this stranger, this somewhat shadowy woman, was primarily her hips, which in fact could be seen clearly from time to time, between light and semidarkness. Their curve harmonized with the movements she made in the course of attending to us, no, anticipating our needs, yes, anticipating. These hips struck us as beautiful? Her beauty manifested itself in them. Surely the entire woman, the entire human being there, had to be equally beautiful. And the beauty of those hips radiated kindness. In the curve of her hips beauty and kindness became one. The unknown woman's hips were the seat of kindness, with nothing more necessary.

A question, then, unspoken, when, after his brief disappearance, familiar to us from other meetings, the boatmaster expectedly unexpectedly reappeared and lent the woman a hand between galley and salon and among the tables; he and a woman: what was that about? No one, or at least none of us, his chief associates since he had settled on the boat on the Morava, far from his country of origin and also from his earlier home, had ever seen him in the company of a woman. And if someone had, he had immediately made it clear that he had nothing, nothing whatsoever, to do with the woman. She just happened to be with him, for technical, financial, or other reasons, and her gender was irrelevant. He seemed embarrassed to be caught with a woman, and he went out of his way to show how unconnected, how inconsequential this other person was to him. It was a random person—another person, that was all. He deliberately moved away, and if he spoke to her in our presence, his tone was businesslike, and he emphatically and repeatedly used the formal mode of address. And when we left, he saw to it that the woman departed before us, or at least at the same time.

Some of us thought he feared we might jump to conclusions; perhaps he wanted to avoid having any conclusions drawn about himself, let alone about his relationship or nonrelationship to a woman; wanted to prevent anyone from forming an image of him, from putting any image of him in circulation ever again. Others thought he was afraid of women altogether. "He's scared of them!" said one, and a second went so far as to say, "He's terrified of them, terrified to the core." And didn't such a fear, or terror, haunt some of his books, although his time as a writer was now quite far behind him, the emotions of his early years a thing of the past? Yet hadn't the tour through Europe over the last few months—as we knew from hearsay—been motivated at least in part by a need to escape, to escape, in fact and in particular, from a woman, an escape very different from the one that had once caused him to start writing?

Not that he and the unknown woman there in the boat's salon appeared as a couple. But there was an easy familiarity between the two of them, at least so long as they were tending to the guests, serving the meal and pouring wine for them. We were not merely his guests, we were their guests. Apparently the two had experienced something that had brought them together. But what? Evidently, too, it had not been only a momentary experience, a brief episode. And if brief, if momentary, then in a different time dimension, where neither brevity nor length held sway, but rather some third element. They seemed to assume the role of accomplices during that first hour of the night on the boat, devoted as it was mainly to eating and drinking, with hardly anything said, let alone recounted. Nothing more natural than that the stranger should display a dancer-like quality in the calm way she passed back and forth through the swinging door to the galley and circled among the various tables. But that the man, too, whether in front of, next to, or behind her, joined in, becoming something like her dance partner, this man of all men: that was amazing. True, they were dressed in no way alike, he more in "Western" style (if that term has any meaning nowadays), and she, as one could dimly make out, more in "Balkan" style. Yet each outfit looked coordinated with the other. A woman and this man complementing each other so naturally: that was something none of us would have expected. Much less his providing a woman with a home, as seemed to be the case. And one or another of us remained skeptical all night long.

And what did they give us to eat? Since it was still too early for Easter lamb, what else but catfish and carp from the Morava, accompanied by salads whose main ingredient was cabbage, *kupus*, flavored with caraway, and potatoes baked in the glowing embers of the fireplace, and before that aspic, *piktija*, made from fish and also wild hare, accompanied by flat bread, freshly baked, and followed by sheep cheese from those sheep grazing as far as the eye could see on the hills beyond Porodin, drizzled with Montenegran olive oil, which, thanks to United Europe, had completely shed its former taste of rancid motor oil and, according to the label on the bottle, could be classified as "toscanissimo." And as a beverage they poured us wines from the southern plains of the Morava—from vineyards in Kruševac, Aleksinac, and especially Varvarin, long since in Burgundian, Lower Austrian, and Californian hands but allowed to retain their old vintage names: "Emerald," "Ruby," "Onyx," "Exhaust," "Market Hall," "Melencholija," "Bridge Cider"— and even wine produced more to the south, far from the Morava, in what was earlier Kosovo Polje, and generally labeled "Bordeaux-quality," was still called "Blackbird Field." Only "Rakija," once the most indigenous brandy, no longer existed, at least not under that name; but on no account were brandies to be drunk that night in any case.

At a certain moment the issuer of the invitation had joined the rest of us and eaten the evening meal, also alone at a table. The beautiful stranger, however, stayed in the half-darkened galley, in a throwback to an almost vanished Balkan custom, emerging only later to clear the tables wordlessly. Through the bull's-eye window in the galley door anyone who got up from his table could glimpse her, when her work was finished, perched silently on a stool in the niche by the stove, motionless but not rigid, her hands folded quietly in her lap. But soon after the meal the boatmaster got up and began to pace back and forth in the salon. With the tables standing every which way, hewing to a straight line was hardly possible, so he snaked among them, first erratically, later smoothly, and eventually keeping to the same path back and forth, back and forth. It was as if he had no intention of ever stopping. He had opened all of the salon's doors and windows, and as time wore on the rest of us began to feel chilled to the bone.

After he had finally aired out the space to his satisfaction, he continued his pacing for a while—except that now he went backward, backward upstream and backward downstream. When at last he seemed ready to sit down, one of his shoelaces had come loose, and having tied it, he resumed his pacing, back and forth, backward, as if there were no help for it. And a second time he was already seated when a log in the fireplace did not explode, no, but must have been insufficiently seasoned, for it began to sizzle and hiss, sounds akin to a whining or whimpering. And the third time he was not only seated but was already straightening his back, turning his head to the nocturnal horizons and at the same time surveying the circle of guests, and had just taken a deep breath when—no, it was not that one of our mobile telephones rang, not even that someone's stomach growled (how could it, after such a meal?), but merely that a breathing became audible, a very, very soft breathing, in preparation for pure listening (perhaps precisely that became an obstacle?)—and once more: see above. So apparently the master of the house was not cured of his noise sickness after all, even though he had given up writing for good? Perhaps in the meantime the sickness had even intensified and now interfered with his speaking, as it had earlier with his writing books? The slightest, most innocuous sound, when it reached his ears, could constitute a disturbance, seal his mouth, constrict his throat, snatch away his speaking breath? And even a sound that anyone else would have perceived as open, friendly, plainly well disposed toward the speaker, a sound, the sound, signifying selfless anticipation, yes, unconditional assent, promptly stifled his breathing, assumed material form as a blockage in his windpipe? Yet he had rather sturdy ears—with multiple ridges surrounding the auricle, providing concentric fortifications, as it were, ears seemingly made for hearing—proper listening organs.

What finally induced the former writer to remain seated after all, to speak, to tell his story during that nighttime hour on the Morava, was danger. Before it showed itself, I think he would have perceived a disturbance even in our holding our breath. Danger? He might have merely imagined it, or had he perhaps seen signs that were in fact no such thing? Signs? Suddenly, from the trans-Balkan expressway a searchlight raked across the meadows on the other side of the river, so powerful that it could hardly come from the tractor trailers—which in any case all had to drive straight ahead (the highway had no curves in that section)? And here, on our bank, at the moment when this light swept across the trees and bushes lining the river, it silhouetted a figure, that of a woman, who seemed to be aiming at the boat, as if with a weapon, yet empty-handed, and making faces that mimed the sound of shots, several in quick succession, yet inaudible? Imagined danger? Signs that were nothing of the sort? Whatever the case, I think it finally prodded the former writer into speaking, made him loquacious, or caused the story to speak. Was that figure out in the fields actually a buck, roaring in the night, as if in a rage and at the same time piteously? The owl that now hooted: was it a real owl? (A strange time, when one felt one had to add "real" and "actual" to so many words.) He ignored both sounds, and likewise the crash as something in the galley fell to the floor, the squeaking when one of us shifted his chair, someone's coughing, the kind of coughing produced only by Balkan tobacco, even if it had long since found its way into all the world brands.

Yet he was not the one who began the story of his so-called tour, a story that would be interrupted time after time, then continued at another spot on the river, and would finish, as day dawned, on another river altogether, no longer the Morava. The first sentences were spoken, on the urging of the boat's owner, by the person among us who had set out with him in the beginning. "You tell it. You start." Once the story had got under way, the former writer chimed in. For the duration of several sentences the two of them spoke in unison, or almost. If they contradicted each other at all, it hardly had to do with content, more with the use of one word or another. Yet it must be said that these few clashes, inconsequential for the most part, pertaining to minor details, nothing of note, were waged with an apparently obdurate insistence on principle, with each party fiercely defending his version; when it came to individual words, the host was adamant, in that respect probably still considering himself an authority whom no one in our circle had any right to question, in spite of his having abandoned writing as a profession.

From the moment the first speaker uttered his introductory phrases, the host seemed to be taking notes, apparently only a single word each time. It had been so long since the rest of us had seen him spontaneously pull out a pencil and jot something down. The action seemed almost involuntary, for every time he quickly put his writing instrument aside. Yes, was he embarrassed to be seen doing this?

That was how the recounting of the stages or stations of his tour continued all through the night: he signaled those who had accompanied him during the phase under discussion to begin, and he? he picked up the thread as soon as they provided an opening. In between, for one or two sections, especially those in which he had been particularly active, he would tell the other to keep on talking, and hearing the two voices from a distance, during these moments and transitions, one might well have mistaken them for a conversation, a dialogue, a harmonious one, well suited to such a night on the river—but (see above on the main speaker's niggling over words) from one moment to the next an irritable, almost shrill, choleric tone would erupt: Was someone yelling bloody murder on that boat? Would the first shots ring out any minute? How could that quiet murmuring be swept away so suddenly by such yelping? (Which lasted so briefly that from a distance one might think one had been mistaken—had it perhaps been just a parrot screeching on board?) And what else could one have heard from a distance? All through the night the vowel sounds the trees along the banks made in the wind, and the sounds the storyteller on the boat made in harmony with them, like a response, an addendum. The trees' vowel sounds? Basically nothing but an ah—ah—ah, again and again . . .

Some stages or chapters of the tour the boatmaster recounted without a second voice. The stages in question involved stretches during which he had found himself cutting across Europe alone, the case especially during the last phases before our rendezvous near Porodin, the starting as well as the end point (point?) of the journey. In that stage no eruption of sound interrupted the flow of the narrative. The voice of the solitary speaker became not only softer and softer but also smoother, yes, and then completely smooth. It also trembled. Was that possible, to be soft and tremulous at the same time? Yes, it was possible, a soft, tremulous, smooth narrative flow, far from resonant, yet close to it? And did this tremulousness stem from what had happened to him as he traveled on alone, or from the current, changing, real or imagined threats? Or from both? What struck us listeners as most important, to be sure, were the current threats: were he to be jolted out of his equanimity, he, and we with him, would be done for, as a column of mountaineers trying to cross a glacial fissure on a bridge of snow and ice would be if the person in the lead shifted his weight for so much as a second. And during that night his tremulousness infected the rest of us: the tremulously soft-spoken storyteller was surrounded by his tremulously silent listeners. And as day broke, when on the boat, now in motion, colors began to emerge, eventually we, too, felt responsible for any threat hanging over us, saw such a threat as almost justified: for was it anything but a provocation, and a dangerous one, at least at this particular time, that the owner had not only equipped his *Moravian Night* with an outsized flag from a long since disbanded or disgraced country but had also painted the entire vessel, from the hull to the very top of the funnel and from stem to stern, in those ominous colors? Did he want to see his houseboat as an "enclave," as a self-proclaimed extraterritorial refuge? Did he refuse to acknowledge that such enclaves had long since been banned? That anything of the sort, any "enclave mentality," was totally "unacceptable"?

He created more and more obstacles to his undertaking, or imagined them, which amounted to the same thing. Without these obstacles or challenges that night of storytelling would have been meaningless. Under no circumstances, however unpleasant, could he dispense with them, as he gradually, not immediately, became aware. He had to keep to his circuitous route (which did not mean that the circles, or even a single circle, had to close). During these hours, during this time, something was at stake, for heaven's sake—who knows what? He appeared ever more determined, ever more defiant, ever more undeterred; ever closer to a kind of fanaticism. It seemed then as if nothing, nothing at all, could put a stop to the undertaking. Thunder and lightning would have merely heightened its intensity, likewise the onset of fever, an injury, a blow to the head, a collapse of the ground beneath his feet. It was a fact that in one way or another this night-long speaking eventually had such a powerful effect that not only the speaker but also we, his listeners, felt closer to taking action than ever before.

There was something, however, that could have brought the night-long speaking to a screeching halt, from one moment to the next. He had no need to mention it. The rest of us recognized it without words. This one thing, one single thing, could have made him instantly forget the earthshaking expedition he had experienced. And it became clear to each of us at his own table when later that night the woman, the stranger, showed her face in the galley door's window. The story at that point also had to do with her, and she had emerged from her corner, probably to listen. And what became clear to us? That for the sake of this person, if she were in need, in truly dire need, if she had to be rescued, he would abandon not only the current tour but any imagined or actual storming of the gates of heaven. This one person in need of rescuing took precedence over the tour. At that moment we did not yet know, or had at most intuited, that on the contrary it was the young woman who had rescued the man, and not merely "as it were," and not merely "so to speak."

Although the former writer did not explicitly say so, the journey had begun as an escape; in the beginning, and later on as well, though less unambiguously, it was a kind of flight. And this flight—how assiduously he avoided the word!—was an escape from a woman. That woman: at the time he did not know her in person, did not even know what she looked like, did not want to know. What he did know was that the woman was his enemy, his mortal enemy. She made that plain, and there was no way to turn a deaf ear or a blind eye to that. If it had seemed at first that her enmity was directed at him as a writer, at his writing, it became evident later that the woman, this complete stranger, hated not merely his way of being but the very fact of his existing, his very existence. Once he had stopped writing, her letters—initially those of a single-mindedly hostile reader—expressed her satisfaction at having played a part in "getting you to shut up at last." But then the letters did not stop coming; on the contrary, they became more numerous, one a day, then several a day. And as seemed to be usual in such situations: even after the former writer moved to another country, an entirely different one, to the boat here on the Morava, she soon, very soon, obtained his new address, and . . . There seemed to be no escaping certain people. She had a sixth, even a seventh or ninth, sense for tracking down this man on whom she had fixed her sights. And not in a lifetime would she let him be, not in her lifetime. She would neither rest nor let him rest until he faced her for a showdown that he could only lose, even were he to win it.

The rest of us wondered what accounted for such hatred. He had no explanation either. But he did not want to know. He did not need any explanation; the question did not arise for him. In his childhood it had already become obvious to him that he attracted hatred, groundless hatred. And since then he had accepted this fact. This was how it had to be. The more groundless, the more self-explanatory, not that he accepted the hatred without defending himself. His entire previous life—whether in this role or that or whichever—had been dogged to a greater or lesser extent by inexplicable haters. By men as well as women, who would one day disappear somehow or other, or run out of steam, or, as sometimes happened, even make amends.

He was used to these haters. But eventually this last one in the series took even him by surprise. Such persistence on the part of the woman in question, accompanied by steady escalation from one act of hatred to the next, was something he had not experienced earlier. It began to affect him after all, or to wear him down, the more so because in the last few years all his other enemies had fallen silent, whether because he lived so far away, because they had forgotten him, or for some other reason. Wear him down? Yes, in that the woman had found her way into his dreams and become the main character in them.

And this she achieved by switching from letters to signs and symbols. Another writer, ah, so long ago, had once told him that his favorite letters from readers were mere signs. Or rather, his preferred visitors were those who left nothing behind but signs, at a decent distance from his house: a feather in the hedge along the path; a hazel or whitethorn stick carved by the reader and left leaning against that same hedge; a bottle of wine; a bag of nuts. But the signs left by this woman were not nice at all. By light of day they might seem trivial—a dead baby hedgehog at the foot of the gangplank, a baby bird speared on an acacia thorn, a snake in a canning jar among the dill pickles, one of his books (a book he himself considered a failure) dipped in liquid manure, its pages smeared and stuck together, or merely a few beheaded flower stalks from the riverside, or perhaps just one, a tiny one. These trifling items, however, took on much larger significance in his dreams, with the unknown woman calling the shots.

How did he even know it was a woman, when none of the letters, written in a clear, decisive hand, were signed? He knew, just as the other writer immediately knew whether a bag of nuts or a feather had been left by a male or a female reader. Did he also have an idea of how she looked? (A question shouted by a pushy listener.) "Her face came to me clearly in a dream." "And how did it look?" "In no way as ugly as the woman, the reader, in the story by Stephen King, I think, who takes the writer hostage when he happens to fall into her hands, and eventually wants to kill him. Quite beautiful. Actually beautiful. Downright beautiful."

Escape? It was probably an exaggeration to characterize his setting out on the tour as an escape. One day or one night he had simply had enough of all the evil or horrid signs left in front of, behind, next to, by, or under his houseboat on the Morava. He wanted to breathe. Besides, the trip had been planned for a long time, and this sense of being hemmed in had perhaps provided the necessary impetus. So if not escape, at least a sort of capitulation, which, as one of us flattered him, "isn't really like you"? No. He wanted to face up to her, or, on the contrary, had been burning the entire time to make her face up to him—except that this person did not show herself, refused to let herself be seen. And he toyed with the idea that they would finally meet precisely while he was traveling. And what exactly did he have in mind? To kill her. He would kill this woman. Really? Yes, really. Absolutely. And why? Because she had pestered and persecuted him for all these years? No? Then why? Because—because in one of her letters, no, not just in one, in all of them, she had insulted his mother. No, not merely insulted, but called into question, no, doubted, no, besmirched her memory—and she had escalated this besmirching through her signs. On his tour he would confront the woman and kill her. No, not with his own hands, but with the help of a killer, a female killer, a hired killer. He himself would not touch the woman. To hell with her.

A few stations on the tour had been planned in advance. In addition to his (still uncertain) participation in the aforementioned conference or symposium, or whatever, on the topic of "Noise—Tone—Sound—Silence" (or such) in a godforsaken village in the Spanish Meseta, not far from the ancient settlement of Numancia, destroyed by the Romans long before Christ, he intended to look in on his brother in Carinthia, who had been ill for a long time; also to stop in to see his former colleagues Gregor Keuschnig and Filip Kobal in villages nearby, who, in contrast to him, had not yet sworn off writing; to circle around the birthplace, in the southern Harz Mountains, of his father, whom he had never known and who had been dead for a long time; to roam the island in the Adriatic where, as a very young man, he had written his first book, working almost entirely outdoors, in the blazing sun. But one station or another, one direction or another, would also be left to chance, to whatever came up along the way and might give him ideas. What came would come. It came as it came. "As chance would have it," as people said, and not only back home.

Yet he also planned to be back soon in, and on, his *Moravian Night*. But what did "soon" mean? Some of us felt his absence had lasted far too long. Others, however, had the sense that hardly a month, indeed not much more than a week, had elapsed between his departure and his return. To me, for instance, it seemed as though both his departure and his return had occurred only yesterday. I, on the other hand, felt the former writer had left me alone all winter, while to me, yet another friend, it seemed like a whole year. And what did "yesterday," "winter," "year," "a long time," "a short time" mean? To the boatman or traveler himself it seemed during the night in which he narrated the story of his departure, or had someone else narrate it, as if he had "just then" taken his small suitcase, after locking up the houseboat rather carelessly, then stood on the gangplank, which he then "locked up" as well, and teetered down to the bank of the Morava, yes, as if he were just in that moment teetering there, on and on; as if he had "just now," while crossing the Semmering by train, encountered the person, the near-child, reading an old book, who looked up from the book and immediately recognized him, even though it had been a long time since anyone had been able to "recognize" him, and how; as if "just then," lying in a woman's arms by the Atlantic, he had realized in a terrifying moment, yes, a moment of terror, who his unknown enemy was and what her face looked like.

So he had returned to his point of departure "in no time"? "In no time" from A to B, from B to C, and so forth: had driven, walked, stumbled, roamed? Had been on the road "in no time"? Which time, which tense, which type of time was the operative concept for the former writer's round-trip? First of all: no "round" form of time, just as the trip itself had in truth not been a trip, and certainly not "round." The operative concept was all times at once, together, intermingled, juxtaposed, parallel, running in opposite directions, canceling each other out, crossing. And primarily, most prominently, connecting, uniting, and obliterating all these times, tenses, and types of time were the seconds that came into play now and then, and not merely the seconds of terror, not merely the seconds of terror and being terrified. Second of terror. Second of pain. Second of sorrow. Second of joy. Second of horror. Second of love. Second of patience. Second of letting be. Second of taking pity. Second of taking heart. Second of inhaling. Second of exhaling. When it came to the condition of being on the road as well as telling the story, seconds were the appropriate, the vital, the natural measure of time. (Some other measure would have been operative for the enumerating and reporting.) Not minutes, not hours, and also not, definitely not, tenths and hundredths of seconds: only my, your, his, our, your, their moments, the quivering, crackling, alarming, reassuring seconds. The seconds that mean both what comes after something, what follows it, as well as the primary thing, the thing that precedes it, that combines what precedes and what follows. Praised and feared be the second.

The first second was rather slow in coming on his tour. For a long while each hour resembled every other, each day resembled every other, each moment passed like every other. And for a while that was fine with him: although no seconds pulsed and darted through him, at least there were moments, one after another, at a steady pace, as seemed normal for any departure. The single cup he had left standing on purpose, unwashed, on the table in the boat's galley. The single map that he then removed from his luggage, having decided he would try to find his way without technical assistance. Likewise the pair of shoes, and the one book (of two). Then blowing, as on every other morning, on the ship's bell, oversized, with its massive, heavy clapper, in actuality a bell from one of the churches farther to the south, where it was no longer needed: the daily attempt to make the clapper swing and strike the bell with a mere breath, a gentle puff—if he succeeded, it would signify something, something in his imagination. Something important, indeed earthshaking—but once more nothing, his morning and departure breath too weak—the only effect being that, as on every previous morning, the clapper's bracket gave off a tiny whirr, audible probably only to him. And then, from the bank of the Morava, a glance over his shoulder at the entire boat, which by now, in the course of an entire decade, had become his *domovina*, his little house and home, with the thought—or was it a premonition? no, premonitions had no hold over him, for either the future or the past, but only for now, for the moment, for the present—with the thought, then, that he would never return from this tour to the boat here. Wasn't this one of those aforementioned seconds, a quivering one? And again no: the thought did not dart through him, caused him neither sorrow nor pain. In the meantime such thoughts came to him daily, even if he simply went shopping in Porodin for half a day, even if he simply disappeared for an hour into the floodplain forest, the *luka*, to collect firewood or do something else; came to him just as much as before the great departure. His refuge glowed blue-white-red at his back, and from bank to bank the ceaselessly pulsing streaks of the Morava shimmered, and again that could be his last glimpse of them, and—? All right. Whatever.

I was the one friend of his who did not live farther upriver or down-river but directly across from the river in Porodin. My farm, or rather my late father's farm, was located there, if hardly operated anymore, and likewise, outside the village, was located my, or rather my father's, vineyard, which I would have liked to keep running, if only it had not become life-threatening to do so, as it has become for all of us in Poro-din to use the land beyond the ever narrower village limits, since, well, you know since when. Our only outlet was a sort of corridor to the Morava, which was the route I took to pick him up on the morning of his departure, on my tractor, which thus had something to keep it busy for a change. The man on the boat had at one time done a lot of driv-ing, or so he said, but since his accident in Alaska, which he described to us in the same words almost every time we saw each other, he had stopped driving. Wearing his hat and long coat, with his suitcase on his knees, he looked on the tractor rather like a refugee or evacuee, this impression reinforced by his facing backward, his eyes fixed on the river landscape. Was he looking? Not really.

I had suggested that I drive him—he seemed not to object to the tractor—to Velika Plana, on the other side of the Morava, roadblocks be damned, checkpoints be damned, and even farther if he wished, and why not all the way to Belgrade? But he wanted to take the bus from Porodin, the one daily bus, and also the only one that went anywhere outside the enclave. Our bus station no longer existed, and neither did any proper bus stop or stopping place—and how should it, after all, when the bus did not arrive from anywhere, and always simply parked overnight, after returning in the evening "from out there"? Its parking spot: not the village center, wherever that had turned out to be, or in front of the church either (at least the church had been left us, though with almost indescribable additions—of which more later, perhaps), but in a rear courtyard, in rear courtyards that changed from one time to the next. "Towns with rear courtyards," you say, "yes. But a rural area with rear courtyards—where do you find such a thing?" It did exist,

25

there in the Wallachian village of Porodin, where behind the former farmhouses one courtyard bordered on the next, one rear courtyard extended farther into the fields than the next, some of them as long as freight trains and as wide as a highway, some of them with patches of lawn and flower beds, finally merging into orchards, lined on both sides by cow, sheep, and chicken sheds, barns, equipment and machine sheds, except that most of them had long been neglected, like the fields beyond, or stood empty, or had collapsed and been torn down, so that most of the rear courtyards had become enormous dumps, rutted, muddy, hummocky—but where else could our enclave bus have parked?

On the morning of departure, it seemed to me that the entire enclave had gathered at the debris-filled depot. Yet only a few of those present were travelers. As happened every time, these few were given a big send-off, not only by their relatives but also by their neighbors, more distant ones rather than closer ones, than ones who lived next door. The gathering made a positively cheerful impression on me, perhaps because of the huge amount of luggage, stowed in a trailer, not so much satchels and suitcases as crates, which I imagined as containing equipment for the various acts of a traveling circus. In addition, beds, wardrobe chests, and mirrors were being loaded, looking more like found objects than heirlooms (there had been nothing, at least of that sort, to inherit here for a long time, had never been). Patches of snow formed a pattern in the courtyard, so it must have been winter, the beginning of winter or the end? never easy to tell in our region. The crowd was so dense that these patches were promptly compacted, along with the tracks of doves and sparrows from the previous hour, when the courtyard was not yet serving as the bus station. "And nonetheless you could see traces of birds' toes here and there," the retired writer intervened in my narrative. "Retired writer?" Who posed that question? He could have been the one asking, too.

Of the few passengers none was in a hurry to get on the bus, whose engine, as always, had probably been running since the first rooster crowed—if it were switched off, it would not start again all day, or at least not until late in the afternoon, and that would mean no departure today; any trip on the bus in the dark, the bus of the enclave, held dangers quite different from those of the daytime, even with police protection. But what a racket our bus made in that dump (and how black the fumes puffing out of the tailpipe, known in German very appropriately as the *Auspuff,* "and"—here the former writer intervened again—"by your Balkan loanword from the German, *auspuh* "). It was a racket that increasingly incorporated and absorbed other rackets, the rattling and chattering of the imperfectly closing rusted doors, the clinking of the windows—as if about to shatter, all of them with radiating cracks and loose in their frames—the passengers' possessions crashing against each other in the trailer. Added to all that was the racket, alternatively the noise, alternatively the din, made by the enclave inhabitants as they shouted to each other, tried to outshout each other. (From my time as a guest worker in Germany, I have retained a few common turns of phrase, such as "alternatively," also "notwithstanding," "granted"—adopted from my friend—"including," "be that as it may," "gross income," "clearance," "seemingly.")

Seemingly a racket like that did not trouble the former writer. Perhaps he even sought it out. Why else would he linger in the crowd, in as little hurry to board as all the others? I seldom saw his eyes glow, ever more rarely with the passage of time. But in this situation they glowed. Still, no cries of joy of any sort from the crowd. These were no rejoicers ("rejoyers," the boatmaster offered as a variant). The people there had to shout to make themselves heard amid the gradually escalating din of departure; every second person, at least every third one, was actually yelling. Yes, here and there you could hear loud talking, bellowing, shouting. But the underlying tone—if at top volume, then at a different kind of top volume—was a pervasive weeping, penetrating everything, yet not at top volume at all, the more quiet the more pervasive, the weeping of the children. And on closer inspection it also became apparent that not a few in the crowd, yes, maybe the majority, were neither shouting nor crying but were silent, not only at this moment but for quite some time already, and would remain silent for some time to come.

But what accounted for the glowing eyes? During that night on the boat on the Morava, the time came when in place of me, born and bred in the enclave, the host picked up the story. (As for me, I merely added comments here and there to round out the story of the departure, now taking place at long last.) Yes, a profound sorrow was present in this rear-courtyard throng, a great sorrow. Squeezed in among the others, he felt his heart breaking, yes indeed. At any moment he might fall down dead, quite possibly with his forehead impaled on the jagged bottle neck poking out of the debris. And at the same time, yes, the very same time, his heart, this very heart, opened up to him, took on palpable form, and bled as it had not bled in "an eternity," or so it seemed to him. He did not feel as if he were hemmed in by the crowd but rather free in its midst, free as a result of it, freer than he had ever been in all the years, whether alone or with us, his friends, on the river, wide as it was in some places, on the boat, which no turbulence ever rocked.

He, so dependent, or so he thought, on distant horizons, presumably greatly in need of them, rediscovered in this crowd the advantages of narrow horizons, close ones, more than close. In fact, and in his narrative he emphasized the word "fact," it was a rediscovery, a recovery. Everything had begun for him, long ago, with close horizons. It did not have to be his mother's face—as he recognized, and not only after the fact—which often came too close and tended to block out larger vistas. Closeness could also be found, for example, in the so-called "eyes" in the wooden floors of his house, or the knots in the planks, wide ones, that came together to form a ship, a term whose etymology— just think of it!—goes back to the concept of a hollowed-out tree. Closeness could also be found in the heavily scarred chopping block in the shed, with the ax buried deep in the wood and bloodstains that had seeped into the grain from the many chickens beheaded there. It was in the large fungus gathered in the woods, attached to a piece of wire and stuck into a bonfire outside the church at Eastertime. When you took it out and swung it through the air, it would glow red-hot. It was in the kernels of corn when you husked the ears, especially on those occasions, rare ones, when the kernels were not yellow but red or black.

Close horizons like those, whose peculiarity was that they were experienced neither as close nor as distant, but simply as horizons, as something to be seen, something that offered itself to be seen, as something with which you came face-to-face (a phenomenon not to be taken for granted, at least not by him): they had been constituted in those days almost exclusively by objects, by things. No matter how intently he focused his memory—a long, long pause in his narrative—it did not yield a single close horizon made up of human beings, not a soul, either whole or in part. At most he could think of animals, and usually only very small ones, such as a frozen bee that one wanted to try to revive by blowing on it, a daddy longlegs, lying dead in a dusty corner of a room. There were also larger ones, alive, perhaps in the eyelash line above a cow's eye or the curve formed by a horse's back.

For a long time, human closeness, the proximity of human beings, other than his mother, had meant not horizons to him but rather a sense of being surrounded. This was the case with individuals, and he felt still more surrounded when a number of people approached him at once. Even at a certain distance he had the sensation of being confined, trapped, and one (he kept slipping into this "one" perspective) became completely encircled, fenced in, hogtied, in a crowd. The first human horizon he had encountered, before all eye, ear, and lip horizons, was a girl's genital area, still hairless: the act of looking, admiring, being drawn in (without touching), feeling a sense of belonging, continuing to look. Didn't all that deserve to be called a horizon, whether close or distant?

Later, in the course of time, such horizons turned up now and then, including in a crowd, amid pushing and shoving, indeed often under precisely such conditions, and a couple of times even when he was hemmed in. It did not have to be at a soccer game or among tens of thousands leaving a rock, or some other, concert. In a crowded train human horizons could take on more monumental proportions than any Monument Valley; there were other situations, too, in which one horizon after another would become visible, or sometimes one horizon would give way to another. Such a situation might arise if one were caught up in the close quarters of a funeral procession for some unknown person, caught up unintentionally the first time but more intentionally with each succeeding time; or it might be in a subway car into which the passengers were packed so tightly that only the most shallow breathing was possible, like that of fish taking their last gasps while being transported in crates. Such a horizon might consist of the line of a person's neck a hand's breadth from one's eyes, or hair literally standing on end in the crush. At such moments the gill-breathing could be supplanted by deeper and deeper breaths, a breathing for which one did not need to inhale; a breathing so deep inside one's body that it seemed to create its own air in there; a breathing that did not originate with oneself.

A mistake, as he now realized: that was what his search for wide horizons had been. A mistake? An erroneous pursuit. A sickness, because more and more, day after day, hour after hour, he had focused exclusively on finding such horizons, and not only since he had moved onto the boat in this land so foreign to him. It was no longer an avocation but an addiction. How could he have forgotten that the Great Horizon never let itself be seen from the outside, from way out there, even at the most distant distance? And above all never when he intentionally looked for it? That it emerged at most in a particular proximity and then took shape internally, and often could remain there long after the moments of proximity, as Goethe had reputedly continued to see certain afterimages on the inside of his closed eyelids months later.

Didn't horizons in the midst of the crowd around him dart through him now, in the form of guidelines, and wasn't that therefore the first quivering second, before he properly got under way? No, these lines communicated themselves to him only gradually, first one, then another, and so forth, all in, oh, such a gentle symmetry, as the waves of a strangely still ocean there in the Balkan interior, a classic interior. It was less the weeping, or the earsplitting bawling, in the crowd that allowed him to rediscover the "decisive" horizons (his term) than the silent waves emanating from an unfamiliar brow line close to his shoulder, a cheek line, a neck line. "It fled, and the heart bled." (We let him get away with that sentence, not his usual style.)

He was the first, then, to board the bus. Yet he was in no more of a hurry than the others. Delaying, postponing, retarding had become almost second nature to him (perhaps starting during his time as a writer, when he felt increasing urgency to turn everything into a narrative—following what model?). Three times he had hugged me, quite spontaneously, something new for him, and so warmly that it was as if he were hugging not only me. And then I could see him sitting in one of the windows, one of the cracked ones, as I would have expected, in the back, also as expected, and in the only row of seats that faced backward. He was staring intently, also as was to be expected, yet neither at me nor at the crowd below, which was gradually calming down and here and there risking a laugh and even snatches of song, but rather at part of the garbage-strewn courtyard that quite obviously offered nothing to see. How predictable my friend was. And in the end, shortly before the bus departed—which happened without warning, like so many other events in our Balkans—I caught sight of him again, jumping up from his seat and, as I could guess, mechanically digging through all his pockets, according to a deep-seated habit, in search of a pencil and paper, apparently without success. So did he want to write something down again after all? Had he forgotten that his skin broke out in a rash if he touched a piece of paper, especially a blank one, and sometimes even if he merely heard paper rustling? That he had broken all the pencils on board and had thrown them into the river?

Now the former writer resumed the storytelling, and would carry it on during the next nighttime hour without a second voice, for on the bus and also for a considerable time after the bus ride he had traveled unaccompanied. It was true: he had involuntarily groped around for writing materials, but not to write something down. It was a sudden urge to draw. To draw? To trace contours, merely to sketch them, or to reinforce them wherever an opportunity to do so presented itself. Presented itself? Yes, presented itself. Or no, to discover the contours in the process of drawing them—for that reason any kind of photographing would have been completely out of the question. Did he feel an urge to draw the people outside the bus? (He asked himself that very question.) The line of a cheekbone here, of a chin there, of a thumbnail over there? And again no: it was the contours of things that interested him, as they had when he was a child. But that rear courtyard: Wasn't it empty, except for the bus? What was out there to draw? The backs of the seats in front of him, every one of them torn or slit open? The brackets for ashtrays, the ashtrays themselves all missing?

And again, no: the debris-strewn space suddenly appeared not as empty as it had seemed at first. The huge block of stone in the farthest corner of the former farm was in reality the last intact structure of those that had once rimmed the courtyard—the sheds, the stables, the barns, the wine cellar. It was the hut where at one time the local brandy had been distilled. The stone block formed a dome that rose out of the debris, leaving an opening into a hollow space with just room enough for a still and—how could there not be one here in your Balkans—a bench, short and narrow, but nonetheless.

The bunker, which was how he viewed the hollowed-out block, stood there without the large glass bulb filled with clear brandy. But the bench was still in place, at worst a little askew. This bench, and above it the stone dome, demanded to be drawn or sketched, if only with a last pencil stub, which was actually better, and if only on the back of a sales receipt, also better. And since neither one nor the other turned up, he traced the contours not on the bus's windshield but in the air. He felt carried away, knew he was carried away at the sight of that bench in the former brandy-distilling cave, shimmering in the early morning light. Carried away? Did such raptures still happen nowadays?

Being carried away was certainly not the same as losing touch with reality. To be carried away in this fashion did not mean being torn away from the world, or, as far as I am concerned, from the present. How real everything (everything?) appeared in this rapture, not only the bench, not only the structure. That was it. That is it. That will have been it. This form of being carried away whisked things into their proper place. People, too? That was an entirely different question, not to be answered, or at most to be answered during a general rapture, in another time. One way or the other he would have liked to revise or correct a sentence from his days of writing things down: "Only when engrossed do I see what the world is"?—"Only when carried away do I see what the world is." Might that now become his new profession?

That lasted all of one moment, though an immeasurable one. But it was enough time for the stone cave with the bench to become populated. Not that flesh-and-blood people took their seats there, or at least not those who had disappeared into the long-ago past. Rather it was conceivable human beings whose presence filled the empty dome, a virtual gathering place, so to speak (no, not "so to speak"), yet such a tiny one that it could hardly hold two or three people, a conceivable togetherness that had nothing to do with the structure's earlier purpose, namely settling down and sampling the *rakija*—though perhaps that could happen, along with one thing or another; who among you would object to that? At the moment, however, there was no aroma of brandy. No songs rang out from the cave as if from the depth of the years, and no crisp, colorful peasant figures celebrated the Ascension before icons, as in a film flashback. This was no flashback, and these were no hallucinations; the rapture offered nothing of the sort, but rather? See above. Furthermore there was nothing rustic in this, hm, glimpse of a tableau— which otherwise inspired the thought: "Land ho!" Land? What kind of land?

The bus jerking backward. Slowly, slowly, to make sure the trailer did not jackknife. The sound of the engine in reverse: on the one hand threatening, on the other as if threatened. (If he had a consistent goal in mind for his tour, it was to pay attention to sounds, to reflect on them, to compare them, to translate them.) The trip began with jerking, which was to persist for a while longer, especially for the stages taking place in the Balkans. Balkans and jerkiness: for him those two went together, and he almost felt something was missing when, on days spent only on the boat on the Morava, the jerks did not come—not the case, however, now, during the night in question.

Much waving outside in the debris-strewn area, with little response from inside the bus. How few passengers there were in comparison to the crowd seeing them off. And not a glance outside; if one of them did look, it was a blank stare. But most of the passengers, as soon as they had taken their seats, were preoccupied exclusively with themselves, including members of couples or families, each individually unwrapping a packet of food, biting into an apple, taking a swig from a bottle, chewing on fingernails, starting to work on a crossword puzzle, a Sudoku (even in the Balkans, even in Porodin, the days now began with Japanese number puzzles), and one—yes, are my eyes not playing tricks on me?—even opening a book; no, not the former writer himself.

No residual effects from the recent crying and sobbing, not even a sniffle; and the eyes so dry, positively hyperdry. Because no one blinked? No eyelid movement could be detected? Or perhaps after all: in the one person who was reading a book, very rapid eyelid movements that caused the observer to doubt whether that person was reading at all, or whether it was real reading, the kind of reading that he at least would define as such. He, he would not read, not yet. For the time being he would read no book, and, listen to this, during the entire tour no newspapers: another firm principle, this one, however, relating to refraining from doing something. A single principle involving doing, not a few for refraining from doing something. Would he be able to follow through?

The backward jerking happened so slowly that the crowd outside, all together, could keep up with the bus, providing an escort. The crowd still ran alongside after the rear courtyard had finally been left behind, on the narrow side street that led past the Porodin church to the major highway and thoroughfare, still called "Magistrale" on the old maps, as even the most wretched arteries in the Balkans used to be called (the term now long since out of use). It was not only because the access road was so narrow that the bus continued to crawl, jolting along, though no longer backward. It was important to be on the alert, especially as they neared the church, for things other than the sides of buildings, trees, or parked vehicles. In truth this stretch had neither houses nor trees nor vehicles, and it was not even an alley but a mere passageway, a passageway that took shape only as it was traversed in that particular jerky fashion through an apparent no-man's-land surrounding the church (which bore no resemblance to a village church, a common phenomenon in the post-Pannonian lowlands). Apparent: this no-man's-land was actually a cemetery, its grave mounds so small that they hardly protruded above the grass, their plaques, if they had any, just a hand's breadth above the ground. That might still correspond to the old burial custom in the Morava region, but it was certainly not the old custom to bury the dead in the middle of the village, next to the church. In this region the cemeteries had always been located outside the village, often very far outside, surrounded by semiwilderness, beyond the last cultivated fields and meadows, not seldom on the crest of a hill, the graves easy to mistake from below for weathered chunks of limestone. So was this a new custom, introduced or simply evolved in the course of the general homogenization? No. It was out of necessity that the deceased of Porodin were buried in the middle of the village, around the basilica, rather than outside in a former vineyard. It was simply not possible to do otherwise. The old cemetery was completely destroyed, and any gravestone installed up there would have been smashed to bits the very first night, any fresh grave mound, no matter how shallow, leveled. And this dire situation had not existed only since yesterday. The sole burial place still possible, the churchyard, had become packed with graves during the enclave years; if Porodin was a village, it was a large one, densely populated, indeed overpopulated, as a result of all the refugees from the surrounding area, whose—what is it called—"death rate" was considerable. The apparent grassy no-man's-land at the center of the village was a graveyard, with the burial mounds cheek by jowl, so the crowd escorting the bus tiptoed through it, twisting and turning, more meandering than walking, their arms raised to help them keep their balance and not make a false step, which created the image of a mass prancing, much like traditional round-dancing. And the bus likewise twisted and turned, making its way across the remaining free space at the speed of a walk. Maybe as soon as tomorrow this terrain would be impassable. But then the bus would in any case be departing from a different rear courtyard.

Having finally lumbered onto the Magistrale, the bus would not have been prevented from picking up speed; the road was deserted. At first, however, the bus slowed down even more, if possible. Some of those escorting it, and not only children, had climbed onto the running board and the trailer. One scrambled onto the hood in front. It was an old-style bus, from the middle of the previous century, which had once seen service as a postal bus in Austria, long before the advent of automatic doors, tinted windows, and adjustable seat backs; a donation from the neighboring country after the last war, the postal horn symbol from that other country still on the sides, not painted over, the only recent addition being the word "Porodin," but unmistakably clear, and in Cyrillic to boot: ПОРОДИН.

Then, from one moment to the next, without any warning, acceleration. The running-board riders and their comrades seemed to have been expecting it. They nimbly jumped and rolled off to the side of the road. And not a few among the crowd picked up their pace as well, running, sprinting, storming along beside the bus. It took the vehicle quite a distance before it could leave them behind. Billows of diesel fumes, some of which also seeped into the passenger compartment, obscured the view of the last few pursuers, though not so completely that one could fail to notice that as they ran and leaped they were also grieving, and with them the entire crowd, soon out of sight. Before he gave up the chase, one of them executed a somersault on the road's cracked asphalt, and then another, before he, too, dropped back, the last one to do so, and performed a *salto mortale* (wasn't that the soccer star—even villages, even enclaves, had their stars—of Porodin?). Yes, that was possible: high-jumping, somersaulting, performing a *salto mortale* out of grief, a sprinting, leaping procession of grief. It was a wild grief, expressing resistance where resistance was futile, and for that reason all the more unconstrained.

In the bus he was the only one with eyes for all that. The people for whose sake all the others had run after the bus with such a fervor paid no attention. They remained intent on biting into their apples, causing a crunching, squeaking, and gnashing; they stuck their earbuds into their ears and turned up the volume on their music devices so high as to drown out any melody, singing, or instrument, also drown out any beat to which others might have tapped their feet. Nothing made itself felt but a rushing sound, permeating everything, inescapable all through the bus, despite the roar of the engine; having solved the first puzzle, they ostentatiously turned the page to the next; they combed their hair thoroughly; they picked their noses; one after another they stuck cigarettes in their mouths (though without lighting them); they incessantly tapped on their mobile telephones (just to pass the time); they munched sunflower and pumpkin seeds as well as their own fingernails (that, curiously enough, drowning out the engine); and one of them popped a toothpick in his mouth, in addition to the cigarette.

How he wished they would feel grief, too. Would act inconsolable, hopelessly distraught. Why didn't they hurl themselves to the floor, or onto their stomachs in their seats, why didn't they slit open the backrests with their fingernails instead of biting them, or at least pound the seats with their fists? How he wished they might be a different sort of company, one worthy of his journey. He almost went so far as to order them, with a stern expression, to behave as he imagined they should: if only they, the couple of them who were leaving their village forever, would take each other in their arms, or even just put their hands on each other's, exchange a few words, however inconsequential, cozy up to each other, the couple of them. But no, each sat there on the bus alone, silent and stiff, except for one up front, diagonally across from the driver. And what this one jabbered, incessantly and at the top of his lungs, also in no respect matched the solemnity of the moment, resembling instead the prattling of someone the former writer recalled from his bus rides as a child, in a bus almost exactly like this one, who always sat or stood next to the driver and for the entire trip would bombard not only the driver but also the entire bus, all the way back to his, the school-boy's, seat in the rear, with nonsensical chatter, with changing content but always at the same volume and equally unavoidable. In those days the role of the jabberer had usually been assumed by a woman, whereas today it was a man—though that was nothing new—and quite an elderly one, too. The tone of voice, the incessant chatter, even the laughter—when really there was nothing to laugh about?—filled and battered the auditory spaces now just as they had for an eternity.

That these passengers paid no attention whatsoever to him, who rather affectedly turned his head now and then to observe them: that he did not exist for them was fine with him. What was not fine with him, however, was that their comportment clashed with his conception, or his will? his ideal? his idea?—his sense of a narrative based on all he had just witnessed. Ah, you and your damned neo-Balkan inadequacy, obtuseness, mediocrity. Things had not always been this way, had they? At one time no voices more animated, no eyes more wide open, no ges-tures more inclusive than could be found among you. What had hap-pened to your eloquent gaze, your eloquent shaking and rocking of heads, your eloquent sighs? It was not even necessary for someone to turn up with a *gusla*, fiddling a tune on its one string that pierced one to the bone, and singing to that accompaniment a centuries-old tragic heroic ballad.

No sign indicating where the village of Porodin ended, one of the last enclaves in Europe, barely tolerated, and one that stretched mile after mile, "werst after werst" along the road. Did it end at the point where not even a dog still panted along beside the bus? Or where the first of the barns out in the fields lay in ruins, where the first vineyard huts had been burned to the ground, or at least charred? Where, despite the fertile pastures, neither sheep nor cows were grazing, and certainly no pigs skidded through the muck from one fenced orchard to the next? (Orchards still there, but abandoned, and the fruit, whether in early winter or early spring, still clinging to the trees everywhere, unharvested.) Where no road sign was not pockmarked with bullet holes, painted over with death's heads, smeared with threatening slogans, in Roman, not Cyrillic, script?

Perhaps the most obvious indication of the crossing from the enclave into the other realm: way out on the Magistrale a second police or military-police vehicle joining the one that had been serving the bus as an advance guard from the time it left the village center, this new vehicle bringing up the rear, so that the bus was now traveling in a convoy. (It was from that moment on that he, the solitary traveler, began to see the passengers and himself at certain moments as "we," and thus also referred during that night to "us.") We had unmistakably left the orbit of Porodin when the exits from the Magistrale, leading to side roads, even to (former) wagon tracks across the fields, were now blocked by tanks. And where there were no tanks, the barriers consisted of coils of a particularly tough barbed wire, apparently hard as steel, alternating with tank traps. The tanks' muzzles were all extended, aimed not at the highway, still almost deserted, but at the chain of hills on one side, the river valley on the other, where the absence of human beings and anything else was total. Constant waving of hands from the tanks' hatches, not so much friendly as impatient: "Move it! Keep going! Step on it!" And in fact the convoy sped up, or perhaps it merely seemed so to us.

The former writer now experienced something that would recur now and then in the course of the tour: looking back in the direction from which they were coming, he saw the bus from the outside, from a furrow in a field, with the driver, the emigrants, and himself silhou-etted in the windows. They all appeared in profile, thus hardly differ-entiated from one another. Through the window, its cracks resembling a star or a spider's web, he saw his own profile, facing backward. And all of a sudden, still in the view from outside, the windows of the bus steamed up, the vapor on the inside, from them, from all the passengers, so dense that all at once, while the profiles did not disappear altogether, they became shapeless blobs. Involuntarily he used his sleeve to wipe away the steam, which was no illusion, none at all. From one moment to the next the panes had steamed up. And he was the only one who wiped and wiped—after each wipe a fresh coating formed. And his glance, then, again over his shoulder, at his fellow passengers: how rig-idly they sat there, the impression of rigidity reinforced by those jackets, once worn throughout the country, now only in the enclave, of coarse, stiff leather, that reduced men as well as women to boxy shapes. The prints of a cat's paws on the back of one of the jackets: was that something he was imagining, or a pattern, or did they really come from a cat that had stepped on the jacket? And on another jacket's back, a dog's paw prints? And on a third traces of a wolf's paws! He jumped up and slid open the vent in the roof of the bus, a gesture familiar to him from rides in that same postal bus when he was an adolescent: how the sky shone blue once the vapor had dissipated, what a mild blue (which he transformed in his narrative to "wild"). And again he could see the bus from that distant external perspective, with the profiles of all those inside once more distinct, and curiously enough a thought now came to him unbidden, in these very words: "Have mercy on us."

Then a side road, actually just for tractors, which was not blocked by either a tank or coils of barbed wire. Why did the bus turn off here instead of continuing on the Magistrale? No one posed that question, however, including him, as if during his years in the Balkans he had lost the habit of asking questions, or at any rate mostly; in these parts hardly any question did not sound like prying. The bus was moving very slowly now, rumbling along no faster than a walk, although no obstacle was in sight. The increasingly rocky landscape, untilled and treeless, was bare far and wide. They were leaving behind the river valley and the highway that cut through it and heading up into the southern hills, still in convoy with the police cars, one leading the way at a distance, as a pilot, so to speak, the other close behind the bus, the three vehicles, seen from the outside, wrapped in a single cloud of murky yellow dust, which, despite the slow speed at which they were traveling, billowed massively skyward in that uninhabited waste, at the same time confined to the convoy, wrapped around it, while on all sides the atmosphere remained that much clearer. No, there was no longer any reason to fear mines; all that belonged to the distant past. What slowed our bus were the many curves in the road, rather puzzling in this uncultivated terrain, as well as the narrowness of the tractor tracks, left over from the time when the fields had grown crops and were lined on both sides with old irrigation ditches, now without water, but clogged here and there with rusting machine and car parts, tangles of rags and plastic bags, animal cadavers either rotting or reduced to skeletons, and in between, not infrequently, jumbled crosses from graves, wreaths that could be mistaken for automobile tires decorated as if for a wedding, sections of car antennas with bows on them (which actually did come from weddings), rubber boots buried upside down, and, above all, the rubble of houses and cottages. Unexpectedly—"well, not so unexpectedly"—he interrupted himself during the Moravian night, something resembling a settlement. If this was a village down in the hollow, it was one fundamentally different from Porodin. Not just that it was built in a huddle rather than strung along a road: the styles of the houses were different, so different that it was like being transported suddenly not merely to a new country but to a far-off unfamiliar continent. Were these farmsteads, or more likely forts? If forts, then not surrounded by classic palisades but rather by stone walls higher than any imaginable palisade. The forts' interiors, almost entirely roofed over, were hidden from view, even from the crown of the hill, which was where the settlement in the hollow first became visible.

An unknown continent, toward which the bus convoy was rolling, even more hesitantly, if possible? Yes, and furthermore, or at least so it seemed to him, the stranger to these parts, a forbidden one. And that was as it should be. Above all, no questions. But the fellow passengers, too, natives of this entire country, expressed through their heads, retracted at the sight of the hollow, the sense of something like an illegal border crossing. Even without changing seats—which they did do, after all, as the bus entered the village down there—they seemed to edge closer together. The nibbling of pumpkin seeds, the gum-chewing, stopped. Or, in the case of one or two of them, it intensified, just as the puzzle-solver suddenly worked more furiously and the book-reader followed the lines in his book more intently. The majority, however, fell into a shared state of bated breath. And now he got up from his seat in the back, moved forward to join them, and likewise held his breath.

Bated breath, which at the same time involved looking out. Yet no one looked out when the bus, still groping its way along the narrow tractor track, reached the farms or forts with their windowless walls and probably padlocked gates, in which, one after another, peepholes opened, then closed, if possible even more quickly. Those in the bus were looking, not at what was right before their eyes—at times the bus almost scraped the walls—but at the gaps between the buildings, and then at the ruins there, which, overgrown with brambles and weeds (not the useful kind), were so difficult to distinguish from the uneven ground that to the unaccustomed eye they became identifiable as ruins only as the bus passed gap after gap. (And the gaps distinctly took up more and more space, until the end of the village turned out to be one big gap, one expanse of ruins, hardly recognizable anymore.)

Unaccustomed eyes? No, not theirs, not those of his fellow passengers. They knew what they were seeing. And they were seeing something entirely different from what was there, in many places almost swallowed up by the earth, perhaps more to be intuited than still to be seen. And their eyes focused, more often than on the ground, out through the gaps into the empty countryside, to the slopes of the hollow and up to the top, where there was nothing, nothing at all. Down in the village not a single being out in the open, not even animals, whether dogs or chickens. Or only the sparrows that whizzed back and forth in front of the bus—always a calming sound—or, untroubled by the heavy vehicle rumbling past, bathed in the dust, also in patches of snow.

It was no longer a track on which the bus traveled uphill after the settlement ended, it was a steppe, trackless and increasingly steep. When would the bus finally stop? No, no questions. And then it was standing still, aslant on the ruin-strewn slope, yellow against grayish brown. All out!? No need to make that explicit. Were they, and he with them, asking no questions, now headed uphill on what must have been a path at one time? Hardly any traces of it, but the matter-of-factness with which each of them in the little band of pedestrians set out across and up the steppe allowed one to sense where it had been. Apparently the old path had taken a serpentine course, a wide-looping one. Possibly it had been intended for the transport of heavy loads; walkers without packs would have taken a more direct route to the top, snaking in less leisurely fashion or heading straight uphill, as did the military policemen providing security up ahead for the procession.

Providing security? Yes, indeed; for upon arriving at the top, we found ourselves surrounded by them as if by sentinels, posted at the four corners of an empty field that formed a plateau high above the village in the hollow. Submachine guns at the ready, aimed not at us but away from us in all directions; and the plateau ringing and crackling with two-way radios. Was there a connection with the figures far below, who, little by little, in ever more rapid succession, emerged or actually swarmed out of the fort-like farmyards, which had previously seemed uninhabited, and closed ranks as they headed uphill, the vanguard halfway up already?

Except for him, the bus passengers seemed to notice none of what was taking place around them. Or if they did, they had no eyes for it. The only thing for which they had eyes was their destination, located on the farthest edge of the empty field. They stayed on course toward it, undeterred by the uneven ground, and it was clear that he had to follow. The sun shone warm in the southerly blue sky, almost hot. Underfoot the withered herbs, wild thyme and rosemary, gave off a summery smell. Eyes only for their destination? And how. Even down below, while they were still on the bus, their demeanor had changed at the sight of the hilltop. After all their earlier corpse-like staring, their eyes suddenly came alive, even if only for a hasty, almost surreptitious glance. And now, as they hobbled and stumbled toward their destination, with one or another of them tripping and falling now and then, their gaze became completely open and unabashed; no fall could deflect it from its goal.

But what was the destination? No, he still did not ask, not even himself. Clearly the edge of the square field, now turned to steppe, the verge of the wilderness, was as empty as the rest of the field, at most somewhat rockier, as such edges usually are. Whatever the case, this strip at the end of the field was the destination. The entire group, except for him and the bus driver, who had come along, squatted in a circle around a spot where, other than grass, rocks, and brush, there was nothing to be seen. One after another they pulled out of briefcases, handbags, and plastic bags various items to eat and drink and placed them in the circle, all this taking place smoothly and with gestures as practiced as those in a Balkan shell game. Then the various items were unwrapped, if necessary, and organized: cookies and waffles removed from their packages, chocolate bars slid out of their foil, cheese taken out of its wrapping; apples were added, also oranges, one or two bananas, even a couple of homegrown kiwis (the enclave was not that distant from the rest of the world); and the caps of the beverages were loosened slightly.

An odd picnic, for which all of them remained in a squat, no one sat down, let alone ate or drank; and at which in broad daylight a candle was lit; and at which, after no word had been spoken for a long time, in fact since they got off the bus, no, even longer, since they turned off the Magistrale to the village, now weeping broke out among these emigrants, entirely unlike that of the crowd that had accompanied them in the morning: a weeping from which one wanted to turn away at once, whether to the sky, or to the earth, or to nowhere at all, just turn away; for which one felt responsible without being to blame or having any urge to blame someone else; a weeping that challenged one to take responsibility.

Wanting to turn away from people weeping in this fashion did not signify closing one's ears to them, did not signify failing to absorb these tones, each and every one, or failing to let them imprint themselves on one's consciousness. It did not mean consigning these people to their fate, the earlier nose-pickers, nail-biters, belchers. Or did it? Or did it? Was being forgotten, being ignored perhaps the kindest thing that could happen to these people, whimpering here in this deserted place? And they themselves wanted it this way? No. They wanted nothing, and certainly not anything from someone like him. They were beyond wanting anything.

As the weeping continued, on and on, the driver shared with him, quietly, the story behind it. Before the last war, the village in the hollow had been inhabited by two peoples, and those crouching in the circle here were some of those who had been driven away after the war, let's call them the Wallachs. Now, for the first time since the end of the war, some members of this former second people had returned to their region, if only for a visit, and the first time would also be the last. And this spot was where their graveyard had been located. Not a trace of it left. Or perhaps there was: the couple of darker, marbled chunks of stone among those indigenous to this place and the Balkans, the lumps of white limestone jutting out of the reddish eroded soil. According to the driver, these were the only remnants of a grave, all that remained of the burial ground on the plateau high above the village, long since and probably forever inhabited by only one people. The, hm, driven-out and now actually resettled people were crouching at a distance from the ruins of the grave marker at a spot where nothing was left. In approximately this location, the driver continued, during the war one of them

45

had witnessed several members of this people being surrounded by a group wearing masks that suddenly burst out of the underbrush and dragged them off, never to be seen again. (He, crouching behind a nearby grave, had gone unnoticed.) The ambush had occurred during a festival celebrated by his people that called for visiting the dead and bringing them food and drink, while the living sat down on a special bench at a special table—of those not a trace either—and joined in heartily; this cult of the dead or the ancestors constituted a main feature of their religion, still strenuously observed at the time; each tribe preserved the memory of its dead going far, far back, and thus one feast day, or at least one feast hour, by the graves led to the next. Yet traditionally this practice also signified danger, and more acutely in wartime: feast day and crime, feast day and betrayal, feast day, decisive battle, and defeat all went together "for us."

And now the survivors were visiting what was left of the cemetery, bringing food and drink. But how could it be—without the ancestors' graves, and also graves for those who had disappeared, who had not yet been declared dead and whose corpses, hm, if indeed they really were dead, were decomposing somewhere else, probably unburied? No questions. It was as it was: the survivors, those who had escaped and gone away, were crouching where, according to that one witness, a father, brothers, a sister, an uncle, aunts had sat shoulder to shoulder, and then, a few moments later, were gone, dragged away by the masked men into the underbrush.

The candle placed in the middle of the victuals kept going out, extinguished by the wind on the plateau, or something. How about crouching down with them? Heaven forbid. They were weeping so loudly into that empty space, completely unabashed. Perhaps the weeping of the men was not quite so unrestrained, especially that of one man, broadshouldered, with a, hm, low forehead, who in the bus earlier had glared in all directions as if on the verge of perpetrating murder and mayhem; the weeping emanating from him was more intense than a child's, when, after screaming and screeching, bawling and whining for help, in the realization of being totally lost, nothing remained but this one long-drawn-out, high-pitched wail, much higher than the others', and likewise much softer than that of the others, the women. There was no help to be had. And as if in confirmation, as one of those crouching moved some fallen branches aside to make room for a new candle, out shot a snake, awakened from its winter paralysis and set in motion by the burning sun, but it did not strike, merely slithered away, after whipping into view, into the grass of the onetime burial ground, with a rustling that came not from any rattles but from the snake's skin rubbing against the brush. And for the group there in the grass the moment when the snake darted forth had not existed, or it did not count; not one of them reacted in any way. And for him, the bystander, the command to keep his ears open remained in effect. Listen: the creaking and squeaking of all those stiff black leather jackets, together with the continuing chorus of wails, together with the moan of grief passing from one to the other. The bleating of sheep down below in the village and the bleating of a hawk overhead in the sky.

Then, as if nothing had happened, back down to the bus, in silence. In the meantime a crowd had gathered around it, so large that these people could not possibly all come from the village? Yes, they could, this many and even more, thousands lived there, though on ordinary days most of them could be neither seen nor heard. But this day was no ordinary one, for anyone, on one side or the other. Yes, in contrast to the crowd that had gathered for the departure from the enclave, there were two sides here, and the crowd belonged to the other one. The crowd seemed neither angry nor hostile. The military policemen did not need to hold it in check. The gathering kept its distance without even one weapon's being drawn. All the members of the crowd completely expressionless as they took in the little band from the bus. They in turn, without making any move to board the bus, gathered in front of it, appearing rather relaxed, and returned the others' gaze, but as if among the thousands of faces they were searching for a familiar one here and there. And a number of them succeeded. That was clear from a glow in their eyes, a strange glow, certainly not a happy one, and the glow was not returned in any way by the other side. General wordlessness, as the one group strolled back and forth in front of the yellow bus with its Cyrillic lettering while the other, the children included, remained almost motionless, if possible not even blinking. This crowd looked almost beautiful in its silent, wide-eyed symmetry, also in contrast to the jerking and jumping, the flailing and floundering of us visitors, caught in the trap of their gaze. And then, with us back on the bus, as it started up and pulled out, a single motion in the crowd, which greatly outnumbered us, the motion of one individual. One of us on the bus, seated by a window, had suddenly waved, as if it were nothing, as if nothing had happened, as if nothing had ever happened. Unquestionably the wave was not meant for the crowd, for the horde, which is what it was now after all in the moments of departure, pantomiming in unison taking aim with guns and firing, alternated with an orchestrated blowing of kisses, accompanied by a sardonic grinning, as if on command—but meant for a single person in their midst. The former writer, following the direction in which the waver, male or female, was looking, managed to make out who it was. Was it obvious that the wave was intended for a child? No, he would have been no more surprised to discover it was for an older person or an adult. The waving was aimed, yes, aimed, at a child, whether coincidentally or not. And the child, almost hidden in the throng, waved back. He had realized that he was meant, he alone. And what a waving it had been!

During that night on the Morava boat, our host interrupted his story. The event he had been describing seemed to have happened long ago, and at the same time it was taking place again. And thus he shifted from the paster-than-past and the past, after a pause to catch his breath, into the present. What kind of a waving is it, actually? The child from the other people, the "enemy," does not react right away, and then only with his eyes. He does not know what to do. He feels ashamed. The whole thing is embarrassing. He blushes. He would like to look away.

He would like to get out of the situation altogether. Yet he also does not want in the slightest to go away. He would like to blow a kiss like all the others, to the woman waving from the bus. He would like to stick out his tongue at her, stick out his tongue until his whole face is contorted. For a quivering second that is not merely possible but is about to occur, as the very opposite is also not merely possible—otherwise this second would not quiver, and with it this child on the other side of the dividing line, quivering all through his body, without the quivering's making its way to the surface and becoming visible to any of the bystanders.

This quivering remains confined to the inside but takes hold all the more powerfully, a quaking deep within that makes an eruption unavoidable. Any minute now it will happen. And now it is happening. And this eruption takes the form of the child's waving back, a hardly noticeable gesture. The little stranger waves almost imperceptibly, also entirely unobtrusively, no, that is not the word, but rather? tenuously, yes, that is the word. Unlike the woman on the bus, he does not make any move to wave, does not raise his arm. Rather he lets his arm droop, alongside his body. His arm droops down to his knees, as a child's usually does. And the answering wave appears as the mere jerking of a finger, a brief, one-time reflex like the reaction to a hammer tap on the knee, which bobs slightly.

So teeny-tiny is the wave, no, that is not the expression, so— secretive. And it is "in fact," "really" (see above) a wave, not a reflex. For a reflex the motion of the hand is too slow, even if the curling of the finger occurs only once and is so slight as to be almost imperceptible. And the little hand does not move automatically, but rather reflectingly, no, reflectively; as slowly as reflectively; hardly noticeable is this curling of the finger, but it emanates from the entire body. And the former writer apologizes to his listeners on the boat for this "close-up"— but only in this way could that second be conveyed, and he owed it to himself and to the others to convey it, especially to the child listening to him in his imagination, perhaps long since not a child anymore. Or actually still a child after all? And what did "actually" mean? "If things were as they ought to be."

Back to the side road where, after the detour into that wasteland, a large crowd lined the road, motionless on both sides except for various obscene gestures, and back onto the Magistrale. Over-the-shoulder glances by the occupants of the bus, for one last time, then for one more last time, and yet another last time. In the meantime the solitary traveler had taken a seat among them and, instead of imitating them, looked around at all of them. Unlike in school buses, where, as he knew from earlier observation, the pupils, or at least the younger ones, always sat way in the back, as if in obedience to some law of physics, usually leaving the front seats empty, these emigrants were crouched—yes, it was as if they continued to crouch as they had in the vanished cemetery, and it seemed as if that had been long, long ago—in the front, near the driver, all in a heap, as it were. As expected, once the bus was back on the broad Magistrale, they reverted to their earlier preoccupations or attitudes. Puzzling over numbers in Sudoku. Spitting into a checkered Balkan handkerchief. Spooning food out of a tin canteen (which somewhat resembled a military helmet). Except that these actions (including someone's snoring) produced no mere sounds of one kind or another; they created reverberations that, even when they came intermittently, yielded a kind of harmony, a fleeting one, for perhaps an hour. And another constant feature could be seen in their hands, those that were idle. ("Ah, here come the hands again!" the storyteller interrupted himself.) These hands were resting on people's thighs or were thrust between the seats as if doing something indecent, something that had developed a life of its own, yet remained completely still, at most vibrating along with the bus. All of them had their palms facing up, forming bowls, empty ones, and it seemed to him—an effect probably created by the vibrations—that something was being weighed in the bowls, a bird, to be specific, a more-or-less small one. Live weight? Dead weight? An image and a question that would stay with him on his tour.

Then a dog was running alongside the bus, in the middle of the Magistrale, spray-painted, or was that a coincidence, in the former national colors. It ran and ran, refusing to give up, and was eventually taken on board for a stretch, without further ado.

Later the first larger settlement, located along the highway, which wound its way through it. And there the first rock was thrown at our bus, which had to slow down on the curves and thus offered an easy target. At first the storyteller did not know it was a rock that struck one of the windows sharply. It sounded and felt like a vigorous blow from a fist, hitting not only the window but the entire bus. Yet the passengers did not react, and neither did he. The glass, a special kind, did not shatter but was merely nicked, with delicate cracks radiating from the point of impact. One question, "Was that a rock?" and in reply a nod, just a brief one; the others seemed to find the incident not that unusual. On the next curve another rock, and a third as they were leaving the settlement (earlier called Malishevo, but meanwhile, under the reorganization, Malisheva, all the short *o* endings having been replaced by *a* endings, fuller in appearance and in pronunciation).

And so it went as the trip continued, through the reorganized country, from settlement to settlement, despite the escort vehicles in front of and behind the bus, yet without ever amounting to a hail of stones. Each time only a single rock crashed, clinked, or clattered against the glass of the "Steyr Diesel" or the whatever-it-was-called rust bucket from postwar Austria, and perhaps leaving, but also perhaps not, yet another dent. In any case, from a certain moment, or stone throw, on, the trip took place accompanied by a kind of constant expectation and premonition that were something other than fear, and nonetheless, to quote the storyteller verbatim, "not entirely without." A couple of stone throws after the first one, and then a few stone throws later, they were no longer just stupid child's play.

Yet it also seemed as though the rocks were all on the small side, certainly no large chunks. Although all of them hit the bus squarely, the most pronounced effect remained the unexpected suddenness of the crash every time, impossible to anticipate no matter how one braced oneself for it. And for a long while there was no glimpse outside the bus of one stone thrower or another. No matter how intently one—or only he—scanned the surroundings: no one to be seen, either before or after the rock landed. Not once did a stone come flying when one expected it, thinking *Now!* and *Now!*, for instance when, from one settlement to the next more and more groups of youths gathered along the road, apparently informed in advance of the passage of the extraterritorial bus; no, not one of them bent down, or so much as moved, even grimaced; all that could be seen was their silent, dark, wide-eyed staring—veritably iconic (though they would have objected to such a characterization). In addition, the driver, who had cranked up the window on his side as if for no particular reason, now turned on music, loud, completely un-Balkan music, without rattling harmonicas or short-tube trumpet blasts, music that could not possibly provoke anyone; instead it was the long-distance echoing guitars from the "Apache" instrumental piece, the most universal sounds imaginable, while he, the lone passenger, felt as though he had already heard these same Apache guitar chords accompanying his ride to school years before on the same bus as now.

Moments of absentness while the music was playing, accompanied by the dwindling and disappearance of expectation. And out of just such absentness he then saw the next stone-thrower, and after that, because he now knew how to look, the next one and the next. All of them were children, and for the most part so little that the stones they threw suddenly seemed disproportionately large, so little that—if there had still been anything that provoked astonishment—it was astonishing how sure-handedly they all, without exception, set about their work. They squatted in the dust along the Magistrale, seemed to be playing, and perhaps really were playing in earnest, each of them alone, engrossed in his play, and apparently unaware of the bus approaching. And nonetheless each of them hurled his rock without any windup, popping up from the dust without one's being able to see the object coming, let alone follow its flight through the air, and almost at the same moment one saw the child squatting again, playing. Was it the noise of the engine? The bright yellow, caught out of the corner of their eye? Yes, one child after another snapped to attention upon glimpsing something out of the corner of his eye. But it was not really the yellow so much as the gray-blue lettering on the yellow surface. Each of the children was still too young to be able to read the script of his own country or nation, let alone the foreign Cyrillic script. But what they did know, or instinctively grasped: in the form of this script, no matter how bleached and blurred it was, the letters half blending with the yellow surface, it was the enemy approaching, and this enemy, they knew reflexively, before any thought or decision could register, had it coming—and pow!

The bus picked up speed. No more music. Dusk. It would not last long—they were still in the south—and it was clear that the driver was not the only one in a hurry to get to the other side of the border before dark. Yet the acceleration in no way resembled flight. The settlements, and with them the hurled rocks, lay behind us. We were driving through a no-man's-land, apparently interminable, no lights anywhere, as if depopulated once and for all. The acceleration resulted rather from impatience and, even more, as the storyteller recognized when he moved to the front to sit next to the driver, from anger. And there it also occurred to him that when the first rock had hit the bus and later as well, until he caught sight of the little children, he had pictured the stone-thrower or the organizer as his unknown enemy, the woman; the idea haunted him that she was on his trail, hot on his heels.

The noises made by the bus, by the engine, now increasingly sounded like expressions of this anger. Only the words were missing—otherwise every feature of an angry outburst was present. The driver let the engine rise to a howl, let it bellow, screech, drone, spit, grind its teeth, howl, sing off-key, growl (yes), threaten, and all this rhythmically, with a steady beat that harmonized with the angry quivering inside him and resembled an instrumental prelude, now really comparable to the first notes on the thick plaited string of the Balkan *gusla*, a merely apparent cacophony, in which, if one listened more closely, the sounds were kept distinctly apart, easily recognizable individually, and at the same time giving rise to each other, yielding a rhythm. An anger at once wild and controlled, even playful, issued from the engine and from the entire bus, too, both of them furnishing the driver with instruments for his overture, and the equally rhythmic flashing on and off of the head-lights' high beams, not necessary on the completely deserted Magistrale, formed part of the performance. Soon words and a voice would be added, and it did not have to be a singing voice.

And that in fact happened. But no, this was not the voice of a *gusla*-player, breaking forth suddenly, from deep inside the breast cage, fill-ing the space. The words came from the driver's lips, half under his breath and not directed at any audience. If the storyteller had not intuitively moved close to the driver, they would have remained incomprehensi-ble, indeed inaudible. There was also no rhythm to what he said, no coherence, and accordingly, as he opened his mouth, the noise of the engine went back to normal, becoming hardly noticeable, and at the same time the high beams stayed on. Nonetheless it was anger being articulated, a specific anger, even if the man beside him had never before heard such gentle, no, childlike expressions of anger. For one thing, the effect resulted from the curiously high-pitched tones, all of them head tones, in which the angry man spoke, half under his breath, the sound contrasting to the massiveness of his body. And then it was a type of an-ger in which the angry speaker, and in this case it was no contradiction, made noises with his lips the way small, very small children sometimes do, and the succession of lip sounds accompanied his imprecations, curses, expletives with something like a melody.

The bus driver's anger was vocalized as follows: "They have always hated us. They got everything they wanted, and still they hate us. More than ever. In more of a blind rage than ever. More blindly than ever. They have their own country now. They are a nation now, like the Lith-uanians, like the Catalans, like the Transnistrians, like Cisnilians, like the Valley Kalmuks, like the Mountain Slovenians, like the Danube and Mekong Delta Autonomians. They are a national people and, now that their great dream has been realized, a one-people state, they still hate us, what remains of the second people, which has no state of its own, hate us as if we remnants were the national people instead of them. And they need not even teach this hatred to their children. It simply gets handed down, from generation to generation, from gene to gene, long past blood feuds and wars. Your hatred of us became baseless ages ago and has taken on a life of its own, if indeed there ever was a basis for it, but no, there never was a basis. It has become not your national consciousness but your life force. Ha, life. Your state merely provides a vehicle for living out your hatred, protected by your national boundaries, your flags that signal hostile intent, your anthems that are anthems of hated. Your hatred for everyone who is not of your nationality, for everything that is not the nation. You derive no pride from your nation, only legitimation and perpetuation of your hatred. And in that respect you typify all nations nowadays, you are the quintessential modern nation, the new form of nation. Nation and hatred go together. Ha, these parents and grandparents—who not only did not energetically dissuade their children from hating others, hating us, but on the contrary passed the hatred on to them—should never have been allowed to become a nation, such a nation. Ha, such parents and grandparents, tribal chiefs and clan leaders, politicians and teachers, star athletes and poets—to whom it never occurs to whisper in angelic voices, yes, angelic voices to your little children, just learning to walk and hold on to things, and to drive out of them with utmost concentration of energy the rock-throwing gene, to smoke out the rock-throwing instinct, to whisper away the hate-pounding drum from their little ears, reaching into the deepest recesses of their brains—never do they, never do you have the right to a nation of your own. But nation or no nation: your hatred never ceases."

Here the driver fell silent. The end of his angry outburst, uttered half under his breath. He did continue, however, after a pause, though in a different tone and louder, almost in song, introduced by a humming in which the opening bars of "Apache" could clearly be heard: "But what of it. Let them declare each of their hay sheds a national hay shed, or, for all I care, every marker of a property boundary a national border marker, every little rock-thrower a national icon. I am stateless, and proud of it. I was always stateless. And hope to be stateless always. Apache, Apache. No proof of nationality and no passport, and my only anthem is Apache, Apache. No travels tempt me, and you can keep your free world. Stateless persons of all lands, stay where you are and what you are. Apache, Apache. Foreign countries: leave me alone. No more getting up early and standing in line for a visa, for no matter what country. Apache, Apache. Staying for all time on my reservation, where the eagle flies, but not on a national crest. Taking pride in my reservation, where the silhouette of a jaybird in a pine tree does not compel me to think: Ah, our national bird. Being content for all time with our reservation, where in school the question never comes up on tests: What is our national flower? Apache, Apache. Bear droppings in the sunset. Love after midnight. Gray-blue on yellow. Dogs' barking does not interfere with the clouds' drifting. All paths lead to the mill. Better to be alone than to sit together in discord. Vinegar tolerates only its own eels. You'll dance for the worst ape when its time comes. He who knows himself knows his master. May you live or die: Hello, my love, adieu, my love."

Night had long since fallen when the bus finally crossed the river (had we heard right? Ibar? Abar? Sabar? Samar?), the river that after the war had become the border. It was a border without checkpoints and without barriers, and if it was guarded, then unobtrusively, downright secretively, on both sides. Nevertheless it was a border in the fullest sense, and like none before it. What had appeared earlier along an interminable stretch to be a far-flung no-man's-land became for the few moments on the bridge an intensely concentrated one. The same passengers who had not reacted in the slightest to all the rock-throwing now involuntarily ducked. In the water, fast-moving but not deep, under the bridge, neither especially long nor especially high, which one good spurt of gas was almost enough to speed the bus across, pipes stuck up out of the darkness that were not necessarily to be mistaken for stove pipes or the exhaust pipes of threshing machines. And both on this side and the far side of the river, in the dim light of the few intact streetlights in this border town, stone buildings could be glimpsed whose only distinct feature was their ruined and vandalized state—with the exception of one house or another on either side that was not simply unscathed but actually glowing inside and out, festively, and also peacefully, illuminated, surrounded by a tended garden like something out of an Oriental fairy tale: despite the time of year, roses in bloom, artificial waterfalls cascading over miniature artificial cliffs, torches lining winding paths of white sand, and through the rattling of the bus one almost thought one could hear, from inside the villas, the sound of shepherd's pipes and lutes.

As if in a countermovement to their ducking, some of the emigrants rose from their seats once the bridge and the no-man's-lands on either side were left behind. It looked as though they were getting ready to disembark, once and for all. Yet they still had a long journey ahead of them, through the night, with a different driver, across several borders of various sorts, as far as Belgrade and then perhaps on another bus or by train to Budapest or Vienna by way of Novi Sad, and some of them on to Copenhagen, Lyon, Seville, Porto, one of them perhaps by plane to Canada, but primarily they would be traveling by bus, for there were bus lines connecting even the smallest town in the Balkans with the rest of Europe. Only the bus from the enclave of Porodin had Belgrade as its last stop.

But then at a hotel, in the city that had been split in two by the war, everyone got off, if only for the supper scheduled to be served there. The only ones leaving the bus for good were the driver, who would wait here for the bus to return the following afternoon, and the solitary traveler. He decided then and there to spend the night in the hotel, the only one in this part of the two-people town, a border town far from every other border marked on maps. There were plenty of rooms available;

in fact he was the only guest; the driver would find lodgings elsewhere—perhaps because he really had no passport, or did not want to show one? The hotel room, under the eaves, looked out on the bridge, distinguishable almost only as an even darker darkness down below in that dark town. On the far distant horizon the outlines of the slag heap belonging to the local magnesium mines, out of operation for many decades now. No more profit could be made here, ever again? A chunk of slag began to roll and struck another with a sharp retort audible far and near, that was how deserted the border town seemed.

He ate the evening meal at the table with the passengers who would be resuming their journey. He had been invited to join them. They seemed disappointed that he would not be coming along. Listening to him that night on the boat, we nodded, for we knew how they felt. How could he leave them to their fate that way, not even witness it? Surely they had realized with time who he was, at least not a complete stranger or a reporter in disguise, and at any rate certainly not their enemy. If they felt disappointment, they did not voice it, however. One after another, they simply showed him hospitality, nothing more. The hotel restaurant might have been the emigrants' very own dining room (so expressions like "very own" still existed?), and they wanted him to feel at home there, as their guest. Although there were no actual festive touches, such hospitality had something festive about it, and not merely because they had passed that long day together. A festive mood emanated from and around the table at which they ate and drank quite quietly, the food and beverages served by the emigrants themselves, who brought them from kitchen and cellar as if they had been cooked or pressed by them personally, as the hosts. And as the boatmaster described the individual dishes in that border-town evening meal, ah, how long ago that was, we who had been invited for his Moravian night, although we had just been served delicacies by the unknown beauty and had eaten our fill, all of us at our tables found our mouths watering, and we experienced a kind of longing to drink the same wine as the company gathered in the hotel had drunk that night, notwithstanding that it would soon be named not for a sparrow but for an eagle.

After the meal he saw them back to their bus. It stood there, yellow, in the deceptively silent border-town night, under a tree (here, too, no provision had been made for a parking place). The tree was a linden, recognizable now in winter by its straight trunk and the unique, regular perpendicular lesions in its light-colored bark, and at the same time by its foliage, which in disregard of the season almost all remained on the branches, though withered, as if this linden, *lipa*, were too old and/or too weak to shed its leaves, or/and there were no wind where it stood. Up to this moment the emigrants had asked him as little as he had asked them. But now, as the first of them was getting back on the bus, he paused on the running board, making the others hold up, too, and said, looking back over his shoulder, which made his leather jacket creak, something that could just as well have been an observation as a question: "You're an attorney(?)." And already the next one was saying, likewise: "You used to be a farmer(?)." And likewise a third: "You come from an island(?)." And yet another: "You're a widower(?)." And another still: "You have no father(?)." And then one more: "You are homeless(?)." And then one more: "You were once a soccer player(?)." And one more: "You have money(?)." And: "You're not a man of the times(?)." And: "You're a sharpshooter(?)." And: "You're a misanthrope, brother(?)." And: "You're not a foreigner(?)." And at the very end: "You're one of us(?)."

As the bus pulled out, a woman suddenly began to sing. This was no highway music like "Apache," and also no song of the Magistrale. It was singing from the depths of the Balkans. Was there really such a thing? Yes, for instance in this voice now. Notes held so long that after a while the voice sounded like an instrument, and yet remained, note after note, a voice, voice and instrument in one. And what was perhaps more remarkable: it was not this particular woman who seemed to be singing— she briefly showed her face at the bus window, completely impassive as the singing became loud and grew louder, her mouth hardly open even a crack—but rather someone else, a third person, more invisible, above her? below her? next to her? behind her? Yes, behind her, far, far behind her. The woman had had a rather old face. And how youthful the voice was.

He did not wish he were on the bus with them; for the time being he had had enough of buses, even that one marked with the postal horn familiar from his early years. And nonetheless, as he stood there alone under the nocturnal tree, with the diesel fumes still in his nostrils, an unfamiliar loneliness overcame him, a sensation new for him after all these years of his earthly sojourn (the expression he used). It was painful. No, it was a momentary ache, although he knew he was still in the emigrants' company. The ache of desolation? No, of abandonment. Momentary? No, for a second. It was that quivering second which, ache or no ache, along with the other quivering seconds produced the sense of existence, or indeed of the earthly sojourn, for the first time on his journey.

He wished to be not on the emigrants' bus but away from these Balkans, the Balkans with these border towns without specific borders, the Balkans of the thousand invisible borders, each and every one malevolent and bitterly hostile, from valley to valley, from village to village, from brook to brook, from manure pile to manure pile, the Balkans where little children threw rocks, where people blew kisses full of scorn, where garlic made vampires even more bloodthirsty. He wished he could get away from these gloomy Balkans to metropolises festooned with lights, bustling with sonorously honking taxis in skyscraper canyons, with bridges on which every pair of lovers was something like a peace symbol, located on rivers where weddings, baptisms, and business deals were celebrated on boats, where people just celebrated, for no particular reason, maybe on a boat with imitation paddle wheels like a Mississippi steamer called the *Louisiana Queen*. And simultaneously he wished he could get away from these Balkans to those other Balkans he had experienced so often in earlier years, as profoundly as no other region on earth, for instance on his houseboat on the Morava, wished he could be back on his *Moravian Night*, the journey be damned.

For now, however, he just wished to be in bed. It had been a day full of adventures. Of course (an expression he seldom used), he needed such days. But the adventures he had had on this first day of his tour were not the kind he wanted. He had also found it difficult to describe them to us. Earlier, too, during his time as a writer, it was an entirely different kind of adventure that had excited and inspired him. What kind of adventure? A different kind. Only such adventures suited him. Only for those did he feel driven to find the right language. Thus it did not trouble him that after all the day's fairly unwelcome adventures the sheets on his bed were ripped, holes had been burned in the one towel, and the radiator remained cold. He even found it appropriate. After the day he had just had, these things signified peace. For bedtime, he opened the skylight as wide as it would go and looked out toward the invisible bridge. He thought he could hear the river rushing, and from the half-buried tank muzzles came a drumming and a ringing, as if from a brook shooting over a cliff. O, language! How it bloomed in the gardens of the absent and the dead, how it bloomed and bloomed. If, God willing, he were to make his way back from his tour, he would cross this deserted bridge to gradually close the circle. The bridge would be his point of return. (That, too, was not to happen . . .) The Incas are not extinct. Sursum corda!

The last sentences our host had spoken he had addressed more and more to himself, murmured to himself. It seemed as though the rest of us were ceasing to exist for him. Did he need a premonition of danger for storytelling? But this, too, was a danger, one entirely different from the one he urgently needed. He was at risk, now as always before, of losing consciousness of others, and the result, instead of speech leaping across the gap to us, was his solitary murmuring and finally falling silent, including toward himself. Whether as a writer or anything else, he represented his own greatest threat to himself. Which of us would get him to stop, like a high-wire artist who begins to wobble and must stop before taking the next step? And how to get him to stop? By inventing a threat, an external one? Painting in imaginary colors one of those dangers that would jolt him, or perhaps merely tickle him, out of himself?

2

~~~~~~~~~

~~~~~~~~

~~~~~~~~

BEFORE HE RESUMED telling the story, speaking clearly once more, as we were accustomed to his speaking, and also expected—sometimes more, sometimes less—he thought out loud about the nature of time. Time had always been his problem, or, translated back into Greek, something "thrown in his way." We had often heard him begin to muse on the subject, with a deeper sigh, if possible, on every occasion: "Oh, dear, time . . . ," "Ah, time . . . ," "Ha, time . . ." And on every occasion he had got bogged down in his so-called basic problem, and that is what also happened now, to our relief and his as well. He said something like this: "No, time was and is no problem for me, but rather an enigma. In being, in this one life we are given, at the beginning a pure enigma, the purest enigma, the enigma to end all enigmas, the enigma pure and simple, and then, in time, no, counter to it, a terrible enigma, the euphemism for death, or also merely for boredom, boredom with myself and my not knowing what to do with my time. In my one life, in being, time either passes far too quickly or far too slowly for me. In storytelling, however, in my other life, time seemed from the beginning until now, and now, and now, a fertile enigma, no, enough playing around with the term: a splendid enigma. In one life anxiety-producing, in the other splendid. In storytelling, too, I don't know how to deal with time. But there I also feel, or intuit simultaneously, that time, precious time, is on my side; so long as my storytelling is on the right track, I am moving in, no, am standing solidly on time. And the result, it seems to me, is that in narrated time, in distinction to clock time—which for me in everyday life all too often amounts in one way or another to mandatory time-calculation—instead of the overweening, generally imposed or prescribed dates, I find forms or even mere formulas for time with whose help I can play, no, leap, yes, investigate, and forget the generally accepted measures of time. 'Last summer . . . ,' 'The following winter . . . ,' 'When the war broke out . . . ,' 'When my sister was still able to speak . . . ,' 'A year later . . . ,' 'Shortly before Pentecost . . . ,' 'At the beginning of Ramadan . . . ,' 'The morning of the following day . . . ,' 'The evening of the third day . . . ,' or simply, 'And then . . . and then . . . ,' or even just, 'And . . . and . . . and . . .' Time in storytelling: a splendid enigma? Or a problem after all, but a splendid one? Or no, a fantastic one? A liberating one? A soothing one? O, time . . . Listen up, you times there! What do you think?" Whereupon, not unlike him, each of us at his table in the salon of the *Moravian Night* fell to shaking his head, which produced little more than a humming here, a muttering there, a hm-hming, a throat-clearing, nose-blowing, sighing—nothing that would have moved the boatmaster to continue his story. What did succeed in doing so, finally, was a pop, a mighty one, in the galley, even if merely caused by a bottle's being uncorked, or perhaps not? No, that was it! A moment later, as had happened earlier that evening, a bottle was poured for us by the mysterious woman. Our host, easily startled as always, without being anxious (note the distinction), had jumped at the sound, as the myriad frogs in the reeds along the Morava had fallen silent for a second (and a bit more), along with the owl out in the meadows, whose constant hooting could be anticipated from one hoot to the next, and likewise all the dogs barking separately off in Porodin had uttered an unmistakable nocturnal yelp for a moment. But then came his voice, all the more quiet and deep, if also now and then, no, for short stretches, somewhat tremulous, and what he said, as mentioned, clear, sometimes more so, sometimes less. "On the evening of the following day." "A good while later." "After many more river crossings." "Then beyond seven mountains." "Within three days' walk." "In one hour by car." "Before takeoff." "During the next leg of the flight." "On a stormy morning." "In the middle of a storm." "In the hour of his death." "At the time of the snow melt." "And then . . ." "And then . . ." "And then . . ."

A good deal of time had to pass on his tour before he no longer felt drawn back to the boat on the Morava. During the first period, when he was alone again after the long bus ride in the company of others, he not only counted the days but also the hours, and occasionally even the minutes: ah, another one gone, finally. The first few nights, during moments when he was half-awake, he thought he was back in his familiar bunk and cabin. All the more alien, then, his actual surroundings, different night after night, so alien that they did not even give rise to astonishment. And it took more than just a couple of nights in such unfamiliar settings before he stopped missing his own bed. And not until he had got lost, walking or riding, several times did any random place to sleep suit him, so long as he could stretch out. And he had to be on the road a good while before the moment came when he thought: "Now the adventure is about to begin!"

For a long while the former writer continued to roam hither and thither across the Balkans. Although he sometimes moved in a straight line, it was as if he were going in circles. In the middle of early spring, winter returned with a vengeance, and then from one day to the next it was as hot as in midsummer, while above the snow-covered Dinaric Alps an autumnal blue sky shimmered, and that same evening a snowstorm might blow in from the east, complete with thunder and lightning.

Then all at once the Balkans were behind him. Relief. What a relief. But what revealed that one had left the Balkans? Was it the sea air, the first clumps of wild thyme or rosemary, a laurel bush, a palm tree, the only one initially, as Ivo Andrić described it in recounting his youthful journeys from the inland valleys, away from the mountain-cold Drina, to the Adriatic, or the Jadran, as it was called in his language? Yes, that, too. But it became even more evident from things that after a while no longer turned up everywhere, and then not at all—were absent as a result of one's no longer being conscious of them. No longer in the Balkans, on the Balkan peninsula: that came from inside one. From behind this limestone outcropping no one would suddenly jump out, gun at the ready. No decapitated ram would be found rotting by the roadside, its head stuck on a fence post nearby after having been ripped off the living animal with bare hands, the horns, however, carefully sawn off. No more Muslim grave steles standing in the bleak karst, as if abandoned forever, the half-moon emblem on them long since undetectable (or was it, after all?). None of the dried-up well shafts, rock fissures, or other abysses along the way still served as reminders of one Balkan people or another who long ago, during one of many wars, had installed their transmitters deep inside, or into which they had been hurled by members of the enemy people. Or it was simply that all the sidelong looks were absent, the stepping aside that preceded aggressive shoving, the frequent spitting, the refusal to return greetings, the mocking laughter at an old woman when her umbrella broke in a storm, someone's turning away however often one tried to catch his eye. Away from the accursed Balkans: one's eyes free, one's ears free, one's nose simply nostrils now, a great sigh of relief, as if even one's pores and even one's oral cavity were nostrils.

Although he was headed toward the Adriatic or Jadran, it was less in a westerly than in a northerly direction. The destination: that island where, long, long ago, he had tried to write a—he hesitated at the word—

66

book, his first. And why did he hesitate? Because, he answered the rest of us, in the meantime it had become customary, among writers themselves, to use the term "book" for something that was only on its way to being one; every manu- or typescript, every computer printout was immediately, often after only a few pages, referred to as "my book," supplied with covers that made it look from the outside like a finished work. No, he said, a book was a book was a book, and to him it was something unique, or at least something very rare, powerful, wondrous, something fallen from heaven, so to speak, no, without "so to speak."

The island he described to us during that night on the Morava boat went by the name of Cordura in his story, though in reality it had another name. Cordura had been his name for the island even long ago, inspired by a Western whose title had been *They Came to Cordura*. Incidentally, for the other stations of his journey he also used place names different from the ones by which they were customarily known, or he left places nameless. Either he borrowed a name from elsewhere, somewhere else entirely, or he distorted the actual names, either out of obstinacy or, more often (so it seemed to us), out of fondness for the place. The people he encountered, on the other hand, almost all went unnamed, with the exception of those already mentioned and introduced to us, Filip Kobal and Gregor Keuschnig. And with those exceptions, no first names either. Even his brother appeared consistently as "my brother." Names had no relevance was his oft-repeated refrain, and not only during the night in question. Toward the end of that night, one name was mentioned after all, or let slip, a name that had relevance aplenty.

A ferry transported the abdicated writer to Cordura. In the decades after his book-writing attempt, the island, located just offshore, had been connected to the mainland by a very long causeway. But on the day he reached the coast, the causeway was shut down for some reason ("take a guess!"), and so the ferry was back in operation, the same ferry, or at least so it seemed to him, as long ago. And the same dog as long ago sniffed at his leg during the crossing, and it was also the dog that during the departure from Porodin had been the last living creature to run behind and alongside the bus, refusing for a long, long time to give up the chase. And the same bread baskets as years before were stacked up, still warm. And the same wind was blowing, the very one, not merely one just like it, and in this wind his hair, which over the years had thinned somewhat, felt exactly as it had back then.

In the intervening years he had never been back to Cordura. Stepping off the ferry, and then standing stock-still, at most turning his head now and then, he recognized nothing at all. Yet in reality the harbormaster's building, a centuries-old structure built of karst limestone on a marble foundation, appeared to be the same, just as the fishing boats were pretty much the same ones, and likewise the "let's say" Venetian church tower atop a rocky mound, along with the obligatory stone lion.

For an entire summer he had gone into town almost every morning and evening, first to purchase bread and fruit, then to sit around or go to the movies, and now, although hardly anything significant had changed, the place had become unfamiliar, as if he had never set foot there. Was this really Cordura? Was it actually near here that as a very young man he had wanted to refocus his life, on his own, single-mindedly, no, single-handedly, come hell or high water, or come whatever?

It was midafternoon, in spite of which things were humming in the harbor, which bore the same name as the island. On the fishing cutters the catch was being dumped out of the nets and sorted into baskets. The spectators were primarily children on their way home from school. No tourists. Either it was not the right season, or in contrast to before, no tourists came anymore? The natives, not a few of whom were perusing the skimpy island newspaper as they walked along, or in one case reading a book, saw and recognized each other out of the corners of their eyes, and there was a constant exchange of greetings, sometimes out loud, sometimes with a mere wave. Outdoors, in front of a bar near the water, stood a jukebox, silent; impossible to tell whether it was glowing from inside or from the low-angled sun. It, too, seemed to be the same one as long ago, yet it remained strangely insubstantial, or at least was not the same object as before. Almost the only objects that seemed substantial were the dead or dying fish, and the sounds they made as they landed in the baskets, a slapping underlined by the thwacking of bodies rearing up one more time and a crackling in the container for shellfish and crusted creatures, for spider crabs and shrimp, and in between the scrabbling of those still alive, and, almost inaudible, in a third container the feeble movements of perhaps the one polyp still alive in the dense heap of lifeless ones. By comparison, even the fishy, seaweedy, oceany odor that he was breathing in, much more powerfully, it seemed to him, than the last time he had been there, struck him as insubstantial, no, completely devoid of substance, ethereal. Despite all the bustle, it was an empty world that wafted toward him from this island of his first book, and this emptiness, rather than welcoming him as it usually had in the past, repelled him; resisted him. An impulse to turn back, to the ferry, to the mainland? Yes, but turning back was out of the question. And then came something like a contrary impulse, emanating from the sight of a shark lying on a cutter's deck, a not very large shark, its white belly turned up, its rows of teeth equally white, almost milk-tooth-like, the shark eyes closed, as if on purpose: long ago, when he had swum far out into the sea after writing, calls had reached him from the shore that sounded like "Seadog! Seadog!" He had paid them no mind and simply swum farther, and only later, when he looked in the dictionary, did he discover that "seadog" was the local term for shark.

Then, having arrived in the writing village of long ago, far from the town of Cordura, he did not recognize anything either. Earlier, as he walked, a sense of familiarity had returned with some of his footsteps, familiarity with the landscape, the road, the island wind, and, in another way, with his own gait, with his own body, as if the longer he walked the more he fell into his previous footsteps, footsteps of air, as if he were filling with his current body the airy outline of his long-ago body, and as if that were creating a single body, beyond past and present, a body as solid as any could be. His walking had become a striding, his striding a measuring, and added to that the great sky over Cordura and above him. "Cordura and me."

The lack of recognition that followed turned out to be entirely different from what he had experienced in the harbor. In fact the village no longer existed. When telling us this part, he avoided the term "fishing village" altogether and spoke instead of a "village where a few fishermen lived," and his room there "way back when" had been rented not in a "fisherman's house" but in a building described in a detailed and roundabout fashion as a "stone cottage without electricity where one got tangled at night in nets," and so forth, which, however, as one of his listeners interrupted, amounted to the same thing as a "fisherman's house," whereupon the storyteller merely corrected him briefly with "No, not the same thing!" Whatever: the house in which he had spent the nights that summer, with the Adriatic visible from the skylight in his room, was no longer standing, and likewise the couple of other houses in the village had disappeared. The emptiness there was real and physical, not "virtual" (although he spoke the latter word as if the whole thing were a game). The thing that had remained most present to him all this time, the tree standing among the stone cottages, in whose shade he had sat at a small kitchen table and typed day after day: in its place a bare patch. And even if he was mistaken about the exact spot: nowhere else in the vicinity could another tree be seen, or even a trace of one. No village, to say nothing of "fishermen." Instead, built partway out into the ocean and onto the cliffs, a sort of marine center, glassed in, and closed at the moment, or altogether. And yet this was the village with the tree— whose botanical name he did not know, although he insisted it had been a plane tree—and thus he took up a position, and planned to stay awhile in the empty space in what had been the village center, where the waves, as close as before, were audible as a mere lapping, also just as before.

On the way to his first book—it would be some time before it deserved that name—he had also had his first girlfriend there in the island village. This girl was the first person he, the would-be writer not much older than she was, had betrayed, and along with the young woman his future book, though in a different sense. As a traitor to what he had undertaken, what he was writing, what he intended to accomplish: this was how he already saw himself in those days every time they kissed or just walked hand in hand, and he looked into her eyes, and that is how he saw himself now, sitting there alone in the void, under a rather lowering sky. As a traitor to the dreamed-of book, daily to be dreamed anew—and also to the girl? More as a swindler. "Ah, so torn!" was what he exclaimed that night on the boat.

Yet it was a grand summer, "possibly," as he, who otherwise did his utmost to avoid superlatives, found himself bursting out right after that remark, "the grandest in my life." He had recognized the conflict early on, yes, the incompatibility, even unsuitability. But in those days he enjoyed the back-and-forth. The sweetness and, yes, the exaltation of merging with the other person's body, then spending hours alone at the table, where word after word demanded something of him that he merely intuited, but soon thereafter, and after that again and again, and soon daily, experienced against a backdrop of unmistakable, palpably merciless menace. Only both experiences, precisely because of their incompatibility, gave him for the first time something like a sense of completeness, a sense of life. In later years that would change. Eventually he could find no pleasure in the conflict between being obligated on the one hand to practice the profession of a writer, or recorder, and on the other being a lover or a loved one. It was a form of guilt. It was culpability. The two together were criminal. Either-or.

The abdicated writer got up and paced back and forth, then in a circle, in the former village square or writing place, or whatever he had decided to call the empty space. ("Where did you leave your suitcase?" the pushiest member of our group interrupted him. "At the Hotel Cordura," he replied.) He had never felt a calling to write, and certainly not before that summer. If there was to be a calling, it had to come from him, from him alone. He had to try to discover his calling, and—

this at least seemed like a sign, the only sign he had received in his life, as he had already sensed when taking leave of childhood: perhaps this self-determination could be accomplished through writing.

The former writer continued to pace back and forth and around in a circle, and eventually also backward. The lapping of the Adriatic. The ever-present island breeze. Oncoming dusk. Writing? What had that meant to him? Primarily an escape. An escape from what? From so-called reality? From the heavy hand of reality? From the world? The demands of the world? No. Or yes. If opening one's mouth, having to speak, being told "Come on, out with it! Tell us!" constitutes such a demand of the world, he did feel impelled to escape from it, and not by falling silent but rather by writing things down. He, who during the Moravian night just talked and talked, had resorted to writing in order to get away from all the damned jabber. Damned? To him, yes, at least in his early years. Yet he, the villager, hailed from a region and from a clan in which orality was almost the only medium of communication, and if the written word played any role, it always evoked the suspicion associated with anything official, governmental, or it took the form chiefly of numbers, of calculations. But there was no need to look beyond him and his person: it was his very own orality from which he wanted to escape. It was his own voice. It was not only that others usually found his voice too soft—"Speak up, please!" He himself did not want to hear his voice, and not only because it was so soft, or thin, or tremulous: he had only to hear himself speak and promptly he did not want to go on speaking—he had a deep reluctance to hear himself speak, and in his early years, and not those alone, when he did speak, even to himself, his own voice constantly got in the way. But when he was writing, ah, how he could forget himself, at least for a while, and not such a short while. Oh, the damned echo of speaking. Oh, the echo of writing. (Yet during our Moravian night he seemed to have forgotten himself completely while speaking, and the rest of us forgot with him that it was him—even forgot from time to time that there was a voice to listen to.)

His landlord and landlady back there in the island village had probably never read a book. At least there was none to be seen in their house, not even one about fishing. Certainly they had never had any contact with an author, let alone one like him, who was writing a book before their very eyes, and outdoors, too, where they also did their work. At first they laughed at him amiably, then they were astonished at him, and by the end of the summer they actually expressed admiration for his activity, probably also because of his persistence, which matched theirs, and his refusal to let anything disturb him, whether noises—radios, tractors—or smells, beneath a sun from which at certain times of day no leafy shadows could offer protection. When an occasional bad smell wafted in his direction from the rotting fish heads and innards, he held his handkerchief over his nose and went on typing, using one finger of his free hand, and the same thing toward evening when the cows, having eaten their fill in their island pastures, passed through the village on the way to their stalls, not a few of them quite bloated and relieving themselves in an endless succession of farts, billow after billow of a stench that challenged him not to lose his sense for rhythm, images, indeed all feeling, as he chose his words. What an undertaking. A grand summer.

A challenge, however, not only from the outside, but also from the inside, an inside that was entirely unlike him and his person. Challenge? Demand. Order. Law. A pretentious concept? No, the proper one. As he wrote, and in that which he was writing, the "book," a law was at work. It had begun to manifest itself with the first sentence, and in the course of the writing it became all-encompassing. And what did it express? Affirmation, no, assurance, and on the other hand, no, on the contrary, a threat, no, a menace. And the law was absolute. It brooked neither omissions nor exceptions. And with what did it threaten him? Punishment? What kind? The menace, absolute though it was, remained unclear. But what was clear: there would be, or again on the contrary, there would not be, a verdict, no, a conviction. And "on the contrary" meant: if he violated the law. And how would the violation become apparent? Heavens, it would be obvious the moment it happened. It would be branded on him, then and there. And it would burn inside him until the final judgment was pronounced.

The menace sprang to life inside him in response to seemingly small, trivial factors: all it took was a fleeting irritation at the heat, at a wind gust that flipped over the paper in the typewriter, making him type the letter he was about to strike on the back instead of the front of the page, and the whole undertaking would be called into question, and with it he himself. Anything that began with *un-*, such as a touch of unhappiness over something, a vague uneasiness, an unfriendly response he caught himself making—that was enough to bring on the sense that an unnamed sanction was imminent, and how! Especially dangerous was unkindness, not merely in his actions but also in what led up to them and followed them, when he was standing in line to be waited on in a shop in Cordura, or waiting to buy a ticket at the cinema and chafing inwardly at those ahead of him. From the beginning he had lacked patience and could picture himself as an infant shrieking if his mother's breast was offered a fraction of a second too late, or even if the sun, for which he was constantly on the lookout (or so his mother had told him), refused to emerge from behind clouds. This lack of patience, or, to use another term, lack of self-control, had been his worst character defect until those months on the island. Up to the Moravian night and probably long after, it formed part of his problematic relationship to time. How would he, who became downright mean in his lack of patience, ever manage to produce a book, the fruit of tranquillity combined with patience, the fruit of having time, which, as he began to learn there, was the most noble of feelings? A summer fraught with danger. A summer of adventure.

If he wanted to become a writer, then the kind of writer of whom, so he felt or daydreamed, at least sporadically—he liked to use this word, riffing on the name of the twenty-four Greek islands in the Aegean—he could find traces in himself, he had to steer clear of everything. "Steer clear!" he had admonished himself in the preceding years whenever, driven less by curiosity than by his own lack of affiliations, he had participated as a student in meetings of a political party or some other kind of party. Exhibitions, concerts, and readings to him also seemed like party gatherings from which he should keep his distance—which he did not do consistently, "to my shame." (He did not consider going to the movies a party activity.) And even with someone "of the opposite sex" he saw himself as engaged in a party activity. And belonging to a party was not for him. He would either miss a scheduled meeting on purpose or he would keep hoping the other person would not show up, or he would find an excuse at the last or next-to-last moment to avoid being alone with the other person.

With the girl on the island it also turned out that he felt he had to swindle his way out of being a couple. As he saw it, being with her sometimes meant just going through the motions, on his part at least. His desire to fly the coop actually accorded with the way the two of them had met. One evening he was sitting in a, hm, sporadic gathering of island villagers on a bench constructed around the tree that marked the village center—that was how big around it was—when suddenly a hand thrust itself into his. And he? His hand, which, as he later thought, embodied the whole of him, jerked back, "not exactly as if it had been stung by one of the island's tarantulas, but almost!" He knew immediately whose hand it was, although it was dark and the girl was facing away from him, seated on the other side of the tree trunk. Yes, he had jerked away, and almost at the same time, as if in response, something unfurled in him that was greater than him and transcended him, his attempt to free his hand was contradicted in the very way that movement occurred, a nameless, boundless, and enormous ecstasy, to describe which, during the night on the boat, he paraphrased a sentence by Gustave Flaubert—instead of "The moon rose; tranquillity crept into his heart," "She chose me; ecstasy entered his heart." Accordingly he revoked his jerking away; this once there was still time, but on future occasions, when it happened to him with this woman and later with others, no longer. His inconstancy was no longer forgiven, either by these lovers or by the one intended to be his one and only, whom he had not seldom cheated on, indeed betrayed.

In the meantime he was washed up as a writer, or almost—another word he used repeatedly, whether involuntarily or intentionally—almost to his relief. For some time now he had been feeling almost liberated. He no longer needed to swindle, to betray. He had been released from the law, that terrible sweet law. A good thing, too, that the village he had known no longer existed, not one house, not one tree. So had he been hoping for a memorial plaque? Whatever the case: as he paced back and forth and in a circle in that empty spot (he had soon forbidden himself to walk backward), his one thought was: lovely emptiness, my legacy. And then, in that nothingness-times-two, something suddenly overcame him, no, overwhelmed him, that was different from longing or desire, and this was, far from all living beings, a powerful hunger that was at once a physical hunger and a hunger for air. He was gripped by a kind of hiccupping that remained bottled up. Could he allow himself this kind of hunger now? On the spur of the moment he shed his clothes and swam out into the ocean, this time not as far as at the time of the shark, to live, for life. Whereupon the person in our group who, during that night on the Morava, interrupted our storytelling friend with factual questions whenever he began to portray his own interior world as a universally valid exterior world, did so again, asking this time, "Wasn't the water too cold? I hope you didn't step on a sea urchin? And what did you use to dry off? And how did you get back into town?" Whether he received an answer or not, these questions did not upset anyone. They fit the occasion.

Back in the town of Cordura, never mind how. Evening. Time now, as long ago, for going to the movies. Except that the movie theater no longer existed; it had been turned into an auto repair shop. The ticket booth fronting the street was still standing, complete with its window and the revolving drawer for money and tickets, next to the open garage door; the booth served as a storage area for lubricants, paint cans, and so forth. He tried to swivel the drawer, and it worked. He placed a coin in it and gave it a push. From the old church tower came the call to evening Mass, the bell sounding tinny and toneless, just as before. The Mass refreshing—very different from earlier—and that matched all the experiences he had gathered in the meantime with Masses celebrated on islands. It seemed to him as if there, in contrast to the mainland, something additional floated in among the words of the liturgy, and besides—this, too, a difference—a service on an island had nothing to prove. No particular faith had to be defended against evil foes or hostile brethren. No drawing of distinctions was grimly celebrated. Like other island churches, this one was no bulwark against such forces. These churches were not outposts of the one true Christian faith. Although the church door remained closed during the Mass, one increasingly felt as if one were out in the open, and despite its still being winter, the ceremony could almost have been accompanied by a chorus of swallows, as its tuneful tangent. It seemed fitting that he, a stranger to the place and to the country, should be urged, just before the "*introibo ad altare Dei,*" to join in and read the lesson, taken that evening from the Psalms, and that he, who for a long while now had avoided any sort of public appearance, should agree without hesitation, even though his pronunciation revealed that he came from beyond the border. "Why the tumult among nations?" So was this still Dalmatia after all?

Night. The island corso, which in the absence of a proper main street involved circling around the square down by the harbor. A walking, walking, walking that seemed to involve everyone. Without the succession of words, images, and actions from earlier in the church, without the sentences from the Gospel, the kneeling for the transubstantiation, the procession to the altar for Communion: Would this movement have seemed as harmonious, flexible, inviting, inclusive? Would a similar impression of inclusivity, for once entirely unintentional, for once nothing but peaceable, have arisen? Obviously the whole thing was an illusion—the Mass just another movie. But for a while this kind of movie gave pleasure: "Count me in." With one churchgoer or another in the tavern, all drinking whatever one drinks there, yet remaining church-goers for a while, and he with them.

So it came as no surprise, and certainly not as a disappointment, when the harmony ended abruptly. And with this "abruptly" some features of the Balkans broke over the jetty, features from which this island world had purposefully distanced itself long ago, if indeed it had ever been party to them. Suddenly a concentrated form of Balkanness mani-fested itself in shouts, blows, curses, spitting, baring of gaps between teeth. But that the person being shouted at, etc., turned out to be him, who had been taking part unobtrusively in the corso, that came as a sur-prise. It caught him off guard, struck him, at least, as an assault, while the others walking in a circle probably saw it differently, as more harmless.

Only in retrospect did he realize that the shouting was not merely an exclamation but actually contained his name, or one syllable of it. And he at first interpreted the poke in the back, forceful though it was, as accidental, and when it came again, even more forcefully, as a friend's greeting that had simply taken this form out of enthusiasm, a greeting from one of us who happened to be on the island and had recognized him in the crowd. But when he turned around to look at the presumed friend, he saw a woman in rags baring her teeth at him—see above, gaps between teeth—and she spat at him and began to intone a litany of curses thor-oughly worthy of the Balkans: "You dog without a tail! You seadog without fins. You sun-worshipper in the dark. You flat-footed praying mantis. You bead of sweat in the empty grave. May the brimstone but-terfly fuck you. May the firebug fuck you. May the sultan's cook fuck you. May your mother fall out of the pear tree, so even if you fuck her you won't be able to bring her back to life . . ."

Now he recognized her as the beggar he had seen earlier huddled by the entrance to the church. She had looked up when he dropped money in her cup, but not to thank him; she wanted more. And when he gave her more, she insisted on even more, with an imperious gesture, as if demanding tribute. The spot by the church seemed to be her regular post; it was as if she had not moved from there, under the porch roof, since time immemorial. Like the homeless in large cities, she was surrounded by piles of bulging plastic bags, and clearly the stench that spread in all directions for a considerable distance came less from the bags than from the woman herself, half sitting, half lying there, with trickles of piss, some already dry, others still damp, forming an unusual kind of sidewalk art around her. Her colorless hair, pasted to her skull as if baked on in a layer of fat, short on one side, barely reaching down to her ear, hip-length on the other side, and heavy, as if it were hanging in a net. Amid this colorlessness, her face deep red, chilblain red, and the cheeks free of wrinkles, smooth, stretched, shining, in fact, just like a chilblain; one wrinkle and one only on her forehead, but almost delicate, as if she had been born with it, with hardly any depth, hardly furrowed, only lightly incised, also not continuous, not extending all the way across, looking as it must have when she was a child.

And this wrinkle enabled him to recognize her as someone else, while she continued to curse him. Yes, it was she, the very one, the island girl from the summer when he was writing his first book. Even before he was sure, her name popped out of his mouth—a name that, as previously agreed, has no relevance here—not as a question but as an exclamation. Before he knew it himself, the word knew it for her. And she at once stopped her cursing, and her redness became redder. Yes, it was she. And for the duration of this second—yes, it was a long second—her whole face, not only the broken wrinkle on her brow—became recognizable as that of the young woman from his long-ago experience, her long-ago experience, their shared long-ago experience, gentle and full of grace. Then, as abruptly as she had started shouting at him before, she wheeled and disappeared into the corso.

Later that night he came upon her again. He had searched for her. She was not by the church door. Only the plastic bags were still there, but looking more like props for a scene in a film, used some time before and left behind. One of the bags was empty and was blowing back and forth over the cobblestones in the faint night breeze. In the stillness all around the sound seemed particularly gentle to him, and he resolved to take note of it for the upcoming symposium on noise to be held in the Spanish Meseta: as he listened, he even believed he could make out a kind of instrument, tones rising and falling, cadenzas. And he noted: "Hearing as seeing."

Where he eventually found her? In one of the taverns down by the harbor, and at first he was not at all sure that she was the same homeless person. Not that she seemed transformed. But she had "dolled herself up," to use an expression current at one time in the region where he had grown up. She had put on a long dress with a colorful pattern that made one think of a local island costume, even though such a thing probably did not exist, and her hair seemed more or less restored to its original shade, the uneven sides pinned up in the back to form an almost classic coiffure. Her red face: was it powdered white? or was this her natural pallor, reminiscent of those Egyptian statues of couples, which always showed the man's face bronzed while the woman's was swanfeather white?

Yet this was still the local vagrant, wasn't it? At any rate she circulated as such among the tavern's tables, and when she paused, which she seldom did, and spoke to the seated guests—he was standing too far away to make out what was said—she had the air of someone voicing demands, even though no outstretched hand could be seen. In the course of her continued circling, she repeatedly passed him at the bar, in a cloud of salty perfume, but paid him no mind. She had already said to him all there was to say? He no longer existed for her? And perhaps she had not recognized him as her first man but as the person on his way to evening Mass who had refused to give her what she was owed?

For his part, he resolved not to let her out of his sight during this hour of the night. That was his duty now. That much he owed her. Now and then she went to one of the windows and stood there, her hands clasped behind her, gazing out at the dock and perhaps beyond. The light flashing at intervals into the taproom did not come from a lighthouse. It was heat lightning far out over the ocean. As time wore on, whenever the woman exchanged words with people at one of the tables, she came to resemble, from a distance, the proprietor, keeping an eye on things all evening and checking on her guests' well-being. The only person she avoided was him. At most a glance came to rest on him now and then, as if from far away, a fairly somber look that brushed him or swept over him, and each time that happened, he recalled in that second the first time they had been together, and how she had lowered her eyes, which had been looking into his, to rest on his body, and how a wave of heat had surged through him, the boy he was then, and now? And he remembered, as she made her rounds, the way she had seemed always to be waiting for something, watching for something. The way she bustled around, straightened and tidied things, gathered up decks of cards, set up chess pieces for a new game, smoothed out crumpled lottery tickets, then smoothed them again. And no one except him was paying the slightest attention to her, although in that small space she was by far the most active. Actually none of those she addressed answered; if someone seemed to be doing so, in fact he was talking to someone else at the table or someone behind her, at the next table. And then, as he stood by the bar, at one point he found himself pulling out his notebook, hardly used anymore, as if to record all these small details, a habit he had long since given up. Secretly, secretly, as he had done in the past, he opened it under the lip of the bar and then hastily put it away again, without first needing to feel his former lover's eyes on him.

In the end he followed her out onto the square by the harbor, by this hour past midnight deserted. He had always felt the urge to follow someone or other unobserved, not in order to ferret out some secret— just because. When it looked as though a discovery or a revelation was about to occur, he would instead turn and head in the other direction. He had a horror of sneaking up on or shadowing a person. So, too, on this night he ducked into an alley the minute he saw her, in a flash of heat lightning, awkwardly kicking off her stiletto heels at the edge of the square and, almost falling in the process, putting on a pair of slippers, clearly scuffed, and having done that, bunching up her long dress and crouching down. What to do? He did want to do something, something for her. He knew from earlier, however, from his earlier life, so to speak, that every time he had done something for someone, it had only made things worse. At most his good deeds had held disaster at bay for a while. The best thing was not to get involved. To let whatever was going to happen happen. Let it be: that had become part of his law for himself. And yet. And yet.

A large dog followed him back to the Cordura Hotel, the same dog that had run alongside the bus, the last living being to accompany it as it departed from Porodin. But hadn't the mutt back there been much smaller? one of us chimed in. No, it was the same one. And the dog and he stopped in front of a relief sculpted on a wall, from the period long before the Venetian winged lion. It was an intertwined spiral from the Carolingian, Langobardian, or possibly Illyrian period, or some other historical or prehistorical period. He urged the dog to translate the symbols for him, and the animal then spelled out something like this: "There is no such thing as a happy love, and heat lightning will not produce a thunderstorm, and the water in the harbor is all deep, and it is far to Numancia, and you will not die in peace, and you kissed each other amid the farting of the cattle, and one time she had the name of a cherry, and he who is enthroned in heaven laughs, and the dew will be salty the next morning." And in the end the dog was speaking in the voice of the woman, no, the delicate voice of the girl from long ago: "Did you not know—did you not wish to know it to this day? I was carrying your child under my heart, and you, you killed it, and me with it."

At this point in the account of his tour of the continent, our host suddenly stopped speaking and jumped up from his seat. He turned his head this way and that, peering into the darkness around the boat and sniffing the air. Without a word, simply by means of gestures and then actions, he managed to transmit a sense of danger to the rest of us. Although the frogs had probably not fallen silent until he jumped up, he took pains to create the impression that it had happened moments earlier. He put his finger to his lips, tiptoed hastily onto the bank of the Morava, unfastened the hawsers from the trees with the help of the young woman, the stranger, and, dragging her behind him as if they were fleeing, dashed almost without a sound back onto the boat, already beginning to drift slowly downstream, and, without starting up the boat's engine, grabbed the helm and steered, as if holding his breath— whereupon we hardly dared to breathe either—as close to the bank as possible, through dense reeds and shrubs growing in the water, and when the boat had traveled a few stone's throws or spear-casts or rifle-lengths farther, he finally tossed overboard, at the spot where the reeds grew thickest, a proper anchor, as if close to the open sea.

There, with the boat hidden in the reeds and at the same time away from the bank, he continued his story. I, the only one of us who had known him from childhood, had admired even then his knack for conjuring up, for the rest of us village children, dangers and prickly situations that were perhaps not even real—or were they? At any rate he, becoming more and more seduced by his own imaginings, came to believe them himself, and was in turn infected by the fear of his listeners, who even before him anticipated, wavering between fascination and panic, the imminent bombing raid or the return of the Turks, now, now, or the flood about to sweep over us ("and now . . . and now . . . and now!"). I heard from his brother, who was considerably younger, that the bedtime stories he would tell, always in pitch darkness, with the kerosene lantern blown out and later the lamp turned off, usually merged into a kind of live reportage describing something scary that was taking shape outside in the darkness and coming ever closer—until the reporter perching on the edge of the bed, who had earlier playfully struck a match from time to time to scare the smaller boy, would break off his account and fall silent, both brothers now frozen with fear as they awaited the calamity about to strike. Bedtime stories? After that a good night was out of the question, yet the next evening the little brother would wait eagerly for the voice out of the darkness.

I myself recall walking with the future writer, to the distant monastery church, I think it was. The road was actually just a footpath, one stretch of which led through dense shrubbery. It was probably not summertime; I have no memory of heat. But from one moment to the next my friend stopped dead in his tracks and began to talk about snakes. No sooner had the word occurred to him than he already saw them: "There! And there! And there!" He pointed and pointed, shouted and shouted, and sure enough, I saw snakes, too. Snakes everywhere: there were not only loads of them crawling in the undergrowth; some were also darting their tongues up in the branches that arched across the path, and the boughs were bending under their weight. He started to run, with me close behind him, and as we ran I saw with him, who continued to point and shout, snake after snake, springing from bush to bush at eye level with us. (So there was such a thing as leaping snakes, not only in dreams.) Although after the tunnel we were safe, it took only a gray piece of bark in the grass and an exclamation of "Look!" for us to see it start moving and swerve to avoid it. And even now I can see the gray snake there, and also the snakes from before flitting through the air: I saw them, I see them.

During that night on the Morava, many years later: so many dangers were thinkable here and now, and all of them bona fide and at the same time unspecified, and none of us wanted them to be specified, or if at all, only the way the boatmaster did it before he continued his story: he said he had let the boat drift into the reeds to escape from the tax-evasion investigation, the pan-European one. Just as during the previous week the date had been announced for the forest-debris collection, for this week the night for pursuing tax evaders had been set, corresponding to the film *The Night of the Hunter*, where Robert Mitchum lurks under a starry sky on a riverbank, waiting for the boat carrying the children whom he plans to overpower; so the bank of the Morava was swarming with thousands of nocturnal pan-European tax investigators.

3

~~~~~~~~

~~~~~~~~

~~~~~~~~

THE SYMPOSIUM ON noise and sounds was supposed to take place in a conference center located out on the Spanish steppe, at the foot of the round hill where Numancia had stood in pre-Roman times. No settlement in the immediate vicinity, only a few farmsteads, long since abandoned. The road leading to the center was passable only in a Jeep. And then no trace of a "center." The building looked more like a small round hill at the foot of the large round hill, its baby, so to speak, also matching its coloration, a mixture of rock, lichen, and sand. The construction seemed to be intended primarily as a kind of camouflage, perhaps similar to that of military installations, which, especially from above, in a bird's-eye view or such, were meant to look like features of the landscape—yet on closer inspection turned out to be very different: the building material, each component the opposite of stage scenery, the stones not painted tar paper but granite, as solid as any on the Meseta;

the chimneys no mere slits as in a simulated charcoal-burner's pile, and the numerous irregular gaps in the mound all thickly glazed—the architecture obviously aimed for durability, and if meant to withstand a worst-case scenario, then not the kind associated with war. What a surprise upon entering: the dome of stone and glass, its foundations anchored in the ground of the steppe, enclosed one of the old farmsteads, the largest in the area, all of whose components, with their different functions, had been largely preserved in their original order and even their original forms: the main house, the hired hands' quarters, the barns, the stables, the corral.

When the former writer arrived there, it was a dark, clear day, of the sort he wished all the remaining days during his tour would resemble. How had he reached the place? In a rented Jeep. And did he still have his small suitcase with him? Yes, and it had straps attached to one side, so it could be used as a backpack. And had he taken an airplane before this? This question from the chronic interrupter among us he did not answer. The light around the two round hills of Numancia was wintry, so did he wish it would also snow? No. Snow had provided for and guided him often enough in his life, thank goodness, and this time, he promised the interrupter in that night of storytelling on the Morava, it would not snow during the rest of his story; not a single flake would fall.

"Symposium?" The prospect of hearing about one, whether it had anything to do with Plato's or not, made us rather grumpy. We pictured a symposium as a sort of—what was the word?—"roundtable," with movers and shakers, dignitaries, experts, or assorted role-players from all over the world, dressed in suits and ties and each of them with a lapel pin representing some distinction, the tinier the pin the more distinguished, all these gentlemen with earpieces for the simultaneous translation, the event taking place in a bunker located between somewhere and nowhere, protected by special security details, likewise from all over the world, and the participants seated at a more-or-less round table, and for three days giving the world, *urbi et orbi*, an example, but of what no one knew, and showing people like us the way, to where no one knew, and besides, each of us, or at least those of us on the nocturnal boat, wanted to strike out in his own direction—see the small tables standing at the oddest angles to each other in the salon, each with only one occupant, and each turned away from the other, at least slightly.

But as the boatmaster continued his tale, he soon changed our minds. Those who came together at the foot of the round mound of Numancia, under the banner of noise, might be experts, but above all they were victims. And whenever these victims spoke up, they did not speak of something they had survived, something they had put behind them. They were permanently damaged by the noise, the tumult, the racket, which by no means had to be exclusively the din of war; these were people with incurable wounds. A quieter place for the symposium could hardly be imagined. Their persisting symptoms and especially disorders were, as the discussion leader, apparently the only uninjured one, the only healthy one among them, kept repeating, "phantomatic," but that, as the victims likewise kept repeating, made it "no less real." And he, the former writer, what did he say? What was his contribution? He said nothing, said not a single word during the entire symposium, at least not at the table, had come only to listen. How could that be: hadn't he indicated at the beginning that he had been invited as a participant? Wasn't he contradicting himself now? Well, if he was, he replied, in the course of the night he would take the liberty of contradicting himself, perhaps rather often.

He was one of the observers, one of very few, and the only one from farther away. The two or three others—of whom only one remained by the end—all came just for the day from the provincial capital far below in the river valley carved into the steppe, given lasting fame by the poplars and nightingales invoked in the poems of Antonio Machado, and from time to time also by the soccer team known as FC Numancia. And if he had not been invited as a participant, who had made him aware of the conference? In fact it was one of the two or three from that city, "let's call it Numancia as well," a poet, "another one," whom the former writer knew from much earlier when he was working on his prose there. That had been long, long ago.

Symposium? A strange roundtable, perduring three days and three nights. ("Perdure" was the kind of word that sometimes slipped out, cut off as he had been for a long time from contemporary usage.) He had been drawn to major cities, away from his rural Balkans. And now an even more remote location if possible, somewhere, to borrow freely from a pair of place names familiar from the old days back home, between the "Inner Wasteland" and "Outer Wasteland." No: as he listened to the participants, he became part of a metropolis, more so each day, in the fullest sense. That had less to do with the fact that the speakers had journeyed there from all corners of Europe. They formed a center for him, even without the conference, for another reason. And besides, by no means all of them came from capital or major cities. One of them was a "shepherd," or at least introduced himself as such. Another described himself as a troubadour, a third as a former Carthusian monk. The one who had come from America—the only one from a different continent—presented himself as an Indian from a reservation; whether a Navajo or an Apache our host did not want to say.

The impression of a metropolis there at the foot of the godforsaken round mound of Numancia emanated more from the shared, sometimes complementary, sometimes contradictory, problems, misfortunes, as well as fortunate encounters and adventures, with noise, sounds, tones, or silence, of which the roundtable participants spoke one after the other and more and more all at once. Probably the most strikingly adventurous case from an outsider's point of view was that of a man from the suburbs who had attacked his "noise neighbor," as he called him, with an iron pipe ("I could easily have gone after seven to seventeen others; the authorities should issue noise licenses like gun licenses") and who had been punished by being locked up in a soundproof isolation cell for a year. But the former writer, and, as he thought, the rest of us along with him, did not want to hear at length about such an adventure, let alone stories about neighbors, since people hardly had neighbors anymore, and even the word had gone out of use in its primary meaning.

What the reports had in common: noise, racket, the din at home and the noise abroad—by now there was no longer any difference. And that was true both of the decibel level and of something the group found equally worth reporting, and that was the fact that all of them had become just as sensitive to noise abroad as at home, just as noise-sick, noise-crazed, homicidal. They had found much the same explanation for the noise volume, generated equally by natives and foreigners: because there were hardly any foreign countries left and accordingly no borders, the majority of, no, pretty much all the former foreigners, wherever they turned up, which was usually in groups nowadays, behaved beyond their former borders much the way, no, just the way they did at home at all unhallowed times; so that business about the noise made equally by natives and foreigners was not quite accurate. Ah, the days when Italians, even in groups, had moved so quietly and sensitively through foreign cities, and when you heard them speaking: what a delicate melody. Ah, the times when the Spaniards . . . had tried so tentatively and conscientiously to express themselves in one foreign language or another. Ah, the times when the Asians . . . had not laughed so uproariously in foreign subways or had at least held their hands over their mouths when they laughed.

No common explanation was found, however, for the fact that the noise affected one just as harshly outside one's familiar surroundings, in unfamiliar places, where one was visiting, was allowed to be visiting, as at home. That one wanted to scream and demand that it stop, whether in a Portuguese bar or a Scottish pub or a Czech beer hall. That beyond the former borders, where one was merely a guest, one imagined shoving the first helmeted champion engine-roarer one encountered off his motorcycle just as one would at home. One participant explained this inner resistance to noise, in any setting whatsoever, by pointing to the noise level, the same in any setting whatsoever: for those one might call the noise-sufferers there also no longer existed any distinctions, any borders or thresholds. Another person said, no, the domestic or local noise had made him so sick after a while that even in the most faraway corners of the world his ears reacted not like those of a traveler, a guest, an invitee, but incurably as those of someone ill. And yet another commented, no, he had been ill, all of them here had been ill much earlier, spiritually ill, maybe even born with a spiritual deficiency, a mysterious one, as yet unstudied—and it was as a result of this illness that noise had become such torment to him, to the others, or sounds previously entirely harmless were experienced as noise attacks, as witness the way newborns in all countries now winced and went into convulsions when their pacifiers fell on the floor—how long had this been going on?

They also agreed that for some reason even the most delicate sound could suddenly assault one raucously and that silence itself could swell at times to a roar, from which one wanted to take refuge in an actual racket. Just as certain images refused to let one go, even when one was far removed from them in time and space, a noise one had experienced as evil and hostile could persist inside one long after it had fallen silent in the outside world. People no longer experienced silence. The buzzing one had heard all day long continued buzzing during the night in one's dreams. The clang of metal on metal pursued one into the desert. "The rumbling, screeching, crashing, ringing, banging will never cease," sang the itinerant musician—whose hearing, in his own words, was "completely wrecked"—at the farewell party on the third day, "the noise gobbles up my love."

Those attending the roundtable were not noise-sick from time to time, but once and for all, permanently. And in what other ways did this sickness express itself? One of them, for instance, experienced even the most tender music as malevolent noise and covered his ears at the first measures of a piece by Mozart or Schubert, explaining that not long ago these very notes had been employed strategically as part of an attack on his country of origin: all the soul-stirring sonatas and lieder had been deployed not for the sake of the silence that would follow—what more could music accomplish?—but to unmask the music of his country as culturally worthless, and also to unmask his country altogether; since then, anything soul-stirring of which he had previously been fond pierced him to the quick before the first suggestion of the first notes could be heard, and sent him fleeing. Another man flinched at the slightest breeze. Another took cover if a button on his coat brushed against a door handle. And another whipped his head around at the creaking of his own shoe. Far off a pheasant rattled, a coot hooted, and a bicyclist sounded his bell to force one to get out of the way, or a stranger clipped his nails menacingly as he sat nearby. As a fisherman tossed his line into the water, it sounded like a ferocious dog barking. In the rushing of a mountain brook one heard not the fairy-tale voice of long ago but the blabbing and nattering of talking heads on television the world over. A small pencil dropped—such a charming sound once upon a time—and one started, likewise at the drop, no, the crash, of the softest grape hitting the ground. The former Carthusian monk reported that the shuffling of the other monks, obeying the rule of silence, had given him suicidal thoughts. A jay cawed, and a "jogger" sniffed back his snot. The kinds of things that had once simply made one prick up one's ears, like a leaf landing in a puddle, the rustling of heads of wheat, the popping of jewel weed, now caused one to flinch.

Taken all together, the fundamental characteristic of this noise sickness was a loss of space. People's sense of space became muddled. Things heard from a distance attacked one physically. Noises inside the body threatened one from outside. A rumbling deep below the street resounded from high above. A helicopter buzzed on the horizon, and one batted at a wasp. It could get so bad that one backed away from the rumbling in one's own stomach. One might think that in the course of those three days the Indian would have got used to the sounds of this continent—yet on every walk he took out into the local European steppe, the bubbling of a spring or a trickle in the grass promptly transported him back to the glug-glug-glug of booze going down the throats of his fellow tribesmen, and whenever he made the rounds of the barns and stables, the former corral, the chains hanging everywhere—almost impossible to avoid—brought back the rattling of the chain that his own brother back home had swung menacingly as he staggered toward him.

Who was to blame for their illness? They themselves—on this, too, they reached consensus—were not to blame. At one time or another, for all of them perception of what was going on in the world had primarily taken an auditory form: "Listening—hearing—tuning in": this formulation offered by the former itinerant musician. Even as a child, the noise-deranged shepherd, *pastor*, had dropped everything to run to the edge of the woods and sit there quietly, listening to the trees rustle, hour after hour, and he would have given up every game and every book for that, and would still do so—if in the meantime everything, including the leaves' rustling, had not become evil in his ears. "I was intent from head to toe on listening," the itinerant musician sang. And the defrocked Carthusian monk responded, "The fact that from a young age and from the bottom of my heart I was intent on listening means that my soul was healthy. Ah, give me a lovely sound, and my soul will be cured."

No one and nothing else was to blame for their condition either: on that point, too, they achieved consensus (although one or the other at first continued looking for people to blame—for instance, or so it seemed, the great mass of people impervious to noise, of those deaf to any racket, "the ones who are really sick," "the ones who were sick from the beginning, who, oblivious to their own sickness, made the rest of us sick"). If not to blame, at least they were responsible. One member of the group commented that noise and racket had always been there, but increasingly, ever increasingly, the suddenness, the assaultive quality of the world's noise had manifested itself as evil, as destructive. So many contemporary phenomena were veritable noise mines that could explode from one moment to the next. What in earlier times the sound of chalk scratching on a blackboard or a fingernail scraping a windowpane could do to one's hearing by now could be done by almost anything. "Noise lurks in all things," sang the itinerant musician. "The asphalt whispers, the carpet rattles. The lovers whisper, the headphones pound. There's lisping at the Busento, crashing in the Himalayas."

He, the observer, found it notable that the group discussed all these things in an almost cheerful tone, not loudly but also not too softly. The voices remained low-key. During the presentations none of the noise-sickness was perceptible—except at those moments when the conference center's own facilitator intervened: at the sound of his voice, obviously trained, sonorous, mellifluous, and deliberately calming, all the participants noticeably cringed, and one face after another lost its composure. Not that they covered their ears. But you could see their knuckles turn white as they struggled to maintain control. Beads of sweat appeared on not a few brows. No, they were not laughing to themselves. The facilitator's voice was torture to them. It was pain that brought on that sweat—during that night on the Morava he almost caught himself saying "literal" pain-sweat.

Worth noting was something else that became clear to him as the days passed: that group at the foot of the mound of Numancia suffered less from noise and racket than from sounds that at one time had been associated with peacefulness, with reassurance, with healing, with exaltation. Things they had made a point of going to hear when they were children, and long after that, things that, no matter how remote their location, made them feel connected to what went on in the world: these things they could no longer tolerate: the trickling of water, the roaring of wind and rain, the rustling of snow falling on the branches of wintry bushes. Even crickets breaking the silence by chirping from their holes in the ground now struck them as an attack by the omnipresent hostile harshness (or they experienced the chirping, more innocuously, as the creaking of their own knees), as did the flapping of a butterfly's wing, now at one's right ear, now at one's left, a sound normally inaudible. All it took was words like "trickling," "rustling," "rushing," "rattling," and the like, and each of them experienced "spiritual anguish" in his own language, not to mention that "murmuring," from which in earlier times, after neither thunder nor a storm's roaring had yielded any such thing, had allegedly issued the voice of God. It was not merely that all the sounds that had once been so delicate affected people as soulless; now, instead of having a healing effect, they were actually soul destroying. The murmuring, of one kind or another, constricted one's chest and intensified one's anguish, and instead of the warm feeling caused by a bird's fluttering or the humming of a lone bicycle's tires on a country road at night: uncannyness. "Ah, all the reassuring sounds, where have they gone?"

The former monk vowed to silence posed the question, and he was the one who seemed to speak most among those in the circle. He had left his Carthusian monastery because he could no longer bear the silence, his own and the others', the communal silence. "Once we had a factory of stillness there, and buildings of silence stood there. But as the years passed, it became a false silence, false stillness. Probably we should not have constantly looked into each other's eyes. But after a while I no longer noticed the others in the cells next to mine or out in the fields. If I did, it was as coughers, pew-rockers, sandal-scuffers. Our Great Silence was a hoax. Instead of unifying us, it divided us, at least to my ears. Instead of helping me meditate, in the end all it led to was a heartless cocking of the ears. We were setting no good example for the rest of the world. More and more I would have preferred any clattering of machines or cars roaring by with radios blaring infernally loud music to our pretentious silence toward one another, pleasing neither to God nor to anyone else. And do you know where, in my anguish, I sometimes managed to find that other silence, the kind for which I still pined? No, less in the kitchen, while I was baking bread, or in the monastery's vegetable garden, than—how should I put it?—in that quiet spot: the monastery toilets. There, after the worship service with its interminable Gregorian chants that spilled out of both my ears, I could finally take a deep breath and sense a bit of the *veni, creator spiritus*! I looked forward to the weeks when I was on bathroom duty, and would not have minded being the bathroom monk, so to speak, till the end of my days. The rushing there was the old rushing, just as the trickling was the old trickling and the stillness truly a Great Stillness. Has my hearing turned me into a misanthrope? Or into a lover of the world?"

On the last evening, the sound and noise discussants invited the two or three auditors to join them for dinner, though not to participate in the conversation. At the end of the final day, dining was the only thing on the agenda. The dishes and drinks had been provided by the members of the group, by now used to working collaboratively; the facilitator had made himself superfluous and sat there silent, relieved of his role and not at all unhappy about that. And another phenomenon that the invited guest and future storyteller found worth remarking upon: the way in which these racket-sufferers seemed not only to tolerate but actually to enjoy the racket they themselves made as they cooked and served the meal. The louder the proceedings, the more cheerful they became. The screeching of a knife as it slit open a box of wine bottles: let it screech. The more a food processor's whine filled the room, the more their eyes shone. The earsplitting sound of an electric knife slicing the lamb roast through to the bone: no problem. Merry though their noisemaking might be, nothing resembling music emerged from the sounds. Each participant was making a racket just for himself, not responding to someone else's racket. For music, even the harshest kind, there would have had to be some common rhythm. Besides, no matter how one tried, one could not coax any beat or drive or pounding, or whatever one might call it, out of the sounds made by the modern machines they were using, whether small or large, in this respect perhaps different from the machines of a century ago, the locomotives, jackhammers, etc. Nonetheless they all seemed to come together for a while in a sort of homey noise, a sort of life noise. The noise of life, as opposed to the silence of the grave? Brotherly noise? Yes, brotherly noise did exist.

The racket-making lasted only a short while. In the course of the evening meal, although initially tongues had clicked and glasses had pinged, a stillness arose in which hardly a slurping or smacking could be heard, let alone a gurgling—for the Indian's sake. To the auditor, and even more to the melancholic poet from Nueva Numancia seated next to him, it sounded like a melancholy stillness. Everyone around the table would have to return the next day, and each of them alone, to a life-killing world of noise, from which there would be no escape. They would go home to wither away or suddenly run amok. The noise had a system, and was a system, one that had long since girdled the globe, and the islands of stillness here and there, whether in Europe or elsewhere, were nothing but propaganda, or a commercial offering, a product, or a come-on for a packaged travel deal. And the noise system was indestructible, and the only defense one still had against its overwhelming power was simply to run amok, something that "for good reason" was "flourishing" all over the world, except that those running amok always attacked the wrong targets—the "right" ones kept out of sight or did not exist at all, or at least not in flesh and blood. Only so long as the sufferers were eating and drinking together were they in safety, albeit a tenuous one.

At the end of the evening meal, there nonetheless arose from the shared silent, concentrated melancholy, far from any running amok, a kind of resistance, which spread through the assembled company, whereupon one indicator after another emerged for a party, albeit one marking a parting forever. It began when the minstrel, or someone, tapped his glass with his knife, perhaps unintentionally. No one was expecting any speeches. No need for anyone to fall silent in the circle, already silent. On the contrary, other tones and notes provided a kind of response, at first sporadically, then in a sequence, increasingly rapid and eventually syncopated. After a while someone, let's say the former monk, who in any case had involuntarily risen from his seat, launched into a speech, which was then taken up and continued by the shepherd, let's say, and so forth, until in the end every diner had spoken briefly, each time in harmony with the previous speaker, so that soon it did not matter who was speaking.

And this communal speech by the noise-sufferers, in which one or another of the auditors also participated, went more or less this way: "I don't believe in the Big Bang. If it had occurred, I would dream about it. But I do believe in the Original Sound. For I have dreamed about it. No, that's a lie. I've dreamed about Original Sounds, plural, one and then another. I not only dreamed about them but heard them in broad daylight, and I was perhaps never more awake. And I have heard the Original Sounds as a voice. Yes, the flapping of a butterfly's wing, even if by now it's nothing more than that: at one time it tuned me in, once upon a time, at least. Or the splash of that one dewdrop long ago, a splash on the margin of audibility, and then, at an interval, once I was tuned in to it, another drop at the same great interval, landing, let's say, on a piece of firewood, on pebbles in the gutter, on the sidewalk, always in the same spot, until I heard the dewdrops as the regular tick-tock of an unheard-of clock, which at the same time became audible in the inner ear. And similarly, at least in those days, the morning opening of window shutters in the neighborhood as one of those Original Sounds. Likewise the rattling and clattering of morning trains and buses passing in quick succession. Likewise distant shouts of 'Goal! Goal!' Likewise cries of ecstasy or other emotions from the next room. And of course actual voices as Original Sounds: the voice of my dying sister on the telephone. The voices of abandoned children in the night (and also during the day). The voice of the woman, awakened from a deep sleep, that rekindled my love. The voices of old men talking in their sleep, like those of little children. Original Sounds used to mean impressions that would remain in one's ear forever—or so they promised. In one's ear? No, in one's heart, where they had first echoed, corresponding to the Original Sound before all Original Sounds—so similar after all to that voice in a dream that once woke me as I have not been wakened before or since. Was it you calling to me? No? Or you? Not you either. But it was a call. At times I even heard a murmuring, nowadays a word in disrepute, as such a voice, as one of the Original Sounds, and similarly a certain whispering. And a certain hammering? Yes, that, too. And one or another booming, roaring, rushing, shrilling, drumming? Well, why not, and so long as the sound accompanied an action—something was being fabricated, moved along, transported—and the sounds were not set in motion for their own sake, fruitlessly, without any product, set in motion and immediately allowed to idle by millions of completely innocent noise devils, every second backyard and garden patch filled with howling and roaring, against which even the sturdiest sound barriers could not prevail, in contrast to which the racket on the loudest factory floor sounded positively soothing, as an oasis of peace. You noise-devils, who instead of hooves have steel plates on your soles and no ears poking out of your leisure overalls, not a trace of ears. Ah, the one sound, the one tone that would silence all the evil ones, that would absorb them, transform them, causing them to fall in step like a marching band. Ah, the days when my hearing could transform the sound of a pinball machine into an oriole's song. Ah, the time of transformative hearing. Except that by now almost the exact opposite is the case: a jay's cry seems to be imitating aluminum foil being ripped. In the call of a magpie I hear my father's drunken hiccupping, and in a blackbird's trilling his embarrassed whistling the next day. When I hear a sparrow chirping, I reach for my telephone, or is the sparrow imitating the telephone? And is the screeching of a falcon imitating a referee's whistle, or is it I who am . . . ? Wing-flapping? A trapdoor being pushed open. And there are also some sounds, and perhaps there have always been, that no Original Sounds can transform, with which nothing can or ever will be accomplished. A tournament could accomplish something? Impossible. The Distant Sound? The Distant Rumble. If a tournament were possible, it would have to be noise against noise, combating their noise with another, a good noise. But what would that be? And how? And where? Holding a shell to one's ear and hearing, instead of the alleged rushing of the sea, a shrill whistle inside one's skull. Give us this day a different noise, and tomorrow as well. In the current noise I have come close to losing my soul. The most destructive thing about this noise is that against my better instincts I am forced to identify the noise-generators with their noise . . . A single lovable sound, and my soul will be healed. Secrecy: show me the place where you are hidden."

The following morning, a general exodus from Numancia. But by no means all the roundtable participants set out for home. Some of them had apparently decided overnight to stay together and, usually as a couple, to strike out in a third, unfamiliar direction—if indeed there was such a thing. The former writer and the local poet also joined forces for the time being. Actually they did not budge from the spot, but instead kept their rooms at the wasteland conference center. (The interrupter on the boat: "Was the heating adequate? Was there anything left to eat and drink? How much did the room cost?")

Only now, alone with him, did the former writer really concentrate on his old friend, a process no doubt helped by the daylong hike they took together through the steppe, a kind of circling, in which the spirals grew smaller as evening drew near, with the last one consisting of winding their way up to the top of the mound, a relic from prehistoric Numancia, the sparse traces of which were preserved down in the museum of New Numancia. The poet—to avoid having to refer to him this way time and again during the night on the boat on the Morava, the storyteller called him "Juan Lagunas"—looked exactly the same as when they had met a quarter of a century earlier in the provincial capital. But his appearance was not, and had not been at that time either, the appearance of a living person, or at least not that of an ordinary living person or mortal. It was as if he had spent the entire time closed up in a glass coffin, and his youthfulness, even the rigidity of an apparent corpse, had been preserved, along with the pallor (no, not parchment-like quality) of his skin (of which more will be said shortly). His eyes likewise rigid, except for rare, tiny movements, almost imperceptible, this feature, too, unchanged since far back in the previous century, the eyes black, glass orbs almost without lashes and lids, a black without any gleam or sparkle, glass of a sort that would seemingly never mirror anything.

Yet he still gave the impression of being uniquely present, and expectant in a way that none of the others whom the traveler encountered were. Expectant of a conversation partner. And when he found one, as in the current circumstance, he expected, yes, veritably demanded, that this partner focus his questions and answers exclusively on him, Juan Lagunas. And when he himself spoke, he played on words, almost to the point of being aphoristic, for example in the saying he offered one member of the roundtable to take with him on his journey: "This is a time for stillness, and a time for noise"—speaking with motionless lips beneath the rigid black eyes, in a voice that might issue from the belly of a mummy, no, not from any belly or any internal organ, but likewise not from air of any sort—the same voiceless voice as twenty-five and more years earlier.

At the time, Juan Lagunas had been the only person with whom our host, still a writer in those days, had any regular contact during the weeks he spent in Nueva Numancia, working on another book. The poet, barely grown-up, with a packet of self-published and self-printed chapbooks under his arm—that business with the chapbooks had not changed—had stopped him on the street, and from that moment on there was no question of evading those eyes, at least not for the next hour, and for an additional hour here and there in the course of the month. They always met in one of the bars on the Plaza Mayor, and unlike during their present hike through the steppe, when the poet was the only one speaking all day long, at that earlier time the poet had still asked questions about various things; to the object of those interrogations it seemed like "everything." What was the name of his native village, so far away? His mother: had she been beautiful? The name and home of his first girlfriend? How large a royalty did he receive when he sold a book? Had he really been pursued clear across America by a woman? Cypresses along the Missouri: did they exist? And his brother: had he actually worked in an Oregon sawmill? And seriously, had he met Johnny Cash in Atlanta?

When questions were directed at Juan, however—such as what he lived on, what plans he had, whether he wanted to stay in Numancia— no answer was forthcoming. He was the one asking the questions, just as now on the savannah he was the only one allowed to speak. He embodied and represented a law before which the other person had to bow.

During their previous infrequent encounters, the other person was not only the writer, the stranger to these parts. Once or perhaps twice a third person, likewise young, joined them, though he remained silent—not clear whether he was even listening. He merely had to be present, as a squire, an escort, for Juan, the local poetry authority. An authority, however, who made no impression on the crowd in the bars, filled to bursting every evening. Did people ignore him on purpose? No, they simply did not notice him. The girls especially, invoked so often in his poems, gazed right past his shoulders, broad though they were, and past his rather large head, without so much as registering him, their attention unmistakably focused elsewhere. And he seemed accustomed to this treatment and had a spot off in a corner, not as an observer—that role he left to the other man—but with his eyes fixed solely and steadily on his companion and on the wall. But, as he let slip in parting, he would show them! Someday, although he did not actually voice this thought, they would realize who he, Juan Lagunas, was. Someday their eyes would be opened and they would fall in love with him, passionately, boundlessly—no, only one of them, the one.

Thus far he had remained alone. Even his squires, his escort, he no longer had, not one. He still wrote poetry, publishing one chapbook a year. Some of his poems still evoked young women. But for him, the poet, they were now out of the question. In the meantime he had come to see that it was his fate to remain an outsider, and not merely with respect to the world of women. Not a single person in the whole wide world—and Nueva Numancia remained the whole world for him—cared one bit about him, despite the fact that when his yearly chapbook appeared, for a few days a photo of him was displayed in the window of the town bookstore with the caption "Our Local Poet." If people had largely overlooked him earlier, now they perceived him as a nuisance, and not just in his imagination. In spite of everything, he had become something of a public figure, not only because of his picture in the window but also because of the local newspaper, yet no one had read what he wrote. People recognized him on the street, but unlike with a singer familiar from television or a famous soccer player, they had no idea of what he actually did. The profession of poet no longer held any associations for them, neither an image nor a sound. Even Antonio Machado was nothing but a name to most people, but because that name turned up almost everywhere in the town, it not infrequently aroused irritability, as witness the defaced poems that still hung in some of the taverns. And Juan, his successor, his only one, now made the streets unsafe day after day, and people protected themselves by either turning away or giving him a look that expressed disapproval of his profession, of which those fellow citizens knew only the name and which, since he also practiced it in solitude and secrecy, they thought must threaten their existence. He was their secret enemy.

"And the people of Nueva Numancia are not entirely mistaken about that," Juan Lagunas commented during the hike through the steppe. "I began with love poems, addressed not only to women or to one woman in particular, but by now I write almost exclusively poems of loss. Just as I'm an outsider, the others, my fellow residents in the pueblo, are outsiders as well. That's how I see them, hear them, capture them in poems: as they are now, in comparison to earlier. A horde surrounded by black dust: that's what my pueblo has become, and concealed within the black dust is a *lamento* and a memory, which I want to revive with the lash of a whip."

His poems did not sound much different: a quiet raving. Except that this raving hardly captured anyone's attention these days. It was as if he, the melancholic, had to do penance for the high spirits of the poets who had gone before him, whose works were now read only in schools, and who, in the face of current circumstances, came across as heretical or at least irresponsible. These days neither poetic high spirits nor appropriate melancholy meant anything or moved anyone. Did the poet's calling still exist? Or did those who insisted that it did make that claim out of pretentiousness? Wasn't it significant that even Juan's mother—with whom he still lived, occupying the very room he had had as a child—had always urged him not to be so stubborn, to open his mouth and speak up, and when he presented her, his only confidante for these many years, with his poems, she had received them with an anguished expression and later, without any pretense, simply refused to listen to him read them aloud? ("No more poetry readings, please. I, too, as a listener, have sworn off all poets' readings, the melancholic as well as the high-spirited ones, especially the latter.")

And his fellow hiker on the steppe would not have been able to come up with answers to his questions either—which Juan Lagunas did not expect in any case. The man of prose was also filled with uncertainty when it came to the role of poets in the contemporary world. Yet he was certain that at one time in his life he had needed the poetic moment, more intensely than anything else. There were poems that, teetering on the brink and to be read only in a faltering voice, a solitary voice that could not be made audible, poems without rhyme and without a preestablished rhythm, had called him back from his own brink or precipices into the midst of life—back to prose—to writing prose. "As with painting, so also with poetry." And for a single poem of that sort he would have forgiven any contemporary poet for his actual or presumed pretension to that status, more than forgiven. And to that extent writing poetry, regardless of whether it was a profession or not, could still represent a status?

"At one time," Juan Lagunas then said, "we had a fatherland: we could name things. You see, there were names for everything, names for every moment in life, also for recurring moments. We could name the mother, and the son, even God, but this time is past, never to return; never again will we be able to name the days, the twilights, and the dawns. We lost the names, lost this fatherland, lost that village. Our life is empty now. We're buried alive, our eyes fixed on the heavens that we can't see anymore. And never again will we encounter a woman and be able to speak with her about our lost fatherland. All that remains is to wait for the nights and arrange meetings with our ancestors. When all the dead begin to speak: then we will be able to name life again, the poem in the depths of the night like a snake that hibernates, waiting, its slanted eyes almost closed, for the spring and the sun on its skin."

And, lo and behold, suddenly Juan switched to prose. And only a poet could become prosaic in this way. And in the process he acquired a voice, and what a voice, between screaming and screeching. "I'm a social problem. Every year a few more weeks on a locked ward. The only woman in my life was my mother. I never fucked a woman." ("¡Jodido!" he bawled in his native Spanish.) "I would even have done it with a cow. Fallen in love with her like, if I'm remembering this correctly, one of the feeble-minded men who haunt the pages of your William Faulkner's novels. With my beloved *vaca* I would have wandered the steppe day after day, mounting her from time to time, staring her in the eye, her head with its blond curls over the forehead quietly turned to look at me, and in her long, extra-quiet bovine eyelashes not the slightest quiver. And do you know what my mother said to the asylum warden the last time? 'Why don't you keep him, for good!' I can't even sew on a button. I can't even polish my own shoes, let alone cook something for myself. Not even the shepherd's crumbs, *migas del pastor*, the only poor people's dish around my Numancia, am I capable of brushing from the table into my wooden poet's, no, beggar's, bowl. Emperor, king, nobleman; bourgeois, poet, beggar. I secretly beg some people to give me money, in return for a copy of a poem. And if someone does give me some spare change, it's only so he won't have to take the poem. I beg my mother for money, too, every day before I go out. If I wouldn't be completely lost without her, I would have done away with her long ago. Every Sunday afternoon I put my hands around her evil old throat. And now she is dying, my mother. What will become of me? Maybe when I go home this evening, to our apartment in the projects on the edge of Nueva Numancia, she will be lying in her coffin already, the coffin she has cried out for from time to time, in my presence. The sound a coffin makes when it lands at the bottom of that hole in the ground is no laughing matter. Will be no laughing matter. Will have been no laughing matter.

And if I know her, she will have darned my socks before dying. She will have cooked a batch of *olla podrida*, of stew, enough to last me for a whole week, on a low flame. She will have pressed my father's suit, of English worsted, from the area around Manchester, double-breasted, with wide pinstripes and mother-of-pearl buttons and particularly deep trouser cuffs, of the type that have come back into style, will have pressed it with the heavy old flatiron, heated on the stove, and a damp cloth, and the creases, sharp but not knife-sharp, will have allowed her to forget death, my father's as well as her own. Yes, my poem lies: I can name things, all sorts of things. But what I can name and speak of, I am not capable of doing. And I don't want to do it either. It's my job to name things, not to act. It's not my job to act. I'm a poet, and it's my job not to act, not to be an Olympic champion, but also not to be a cook, a greeter, a night porter, a travel guide, a wood- or steelworker, a landscaper, or a pimp, a firearms dealer, a cotton-picker, a pipeline-layer, a laundryman, a shoelace-threader, a locksmith, a dining-table-finisher. Not a person of action, no way, no how."

But wasn't it a sort of action after all when Juan Lagunas finally turned on his companion, striking him in the chest with his fist, and not gently, either? For that moment it was as if the other man embodied the poet's actual or imagined nemeses and mockers in his native town, from the beginning to the present—no, from before any manifestations of hostility and disrespect, those who in his view lived wrong and whose way of life disgusted him in a way for which he had no use in his role as a poet.

Thus he attacked his companion as, at the end of the day, the two steppe-hikers stood atop the mound of ancient, pre-Christian, Celtic-Iberian Numancia. During his first stay in this region, the former prose-writer had met Juan Lagunas only in town, *intra muros*. He had always been alone when he ventured beyond its boundaries. Now, during this second visit, it became clear that the poet had never set foot outside his city. The soil of the steppe beneath his feet was unfamiliar. He stumbled repeatedly, stubbed the toes of his shoes against the chunks of weathered rock lying here and there, and got his legs tangled even when nothing was there to trip him up, only short grass, sand, and the wide expanses. He raised his knees where no objects needed to be stepped over and dodged a bull that was actually a cow, and not one nearby but far off on the horizon. He also kept expecting a path where none was necessary. Trackless steppe? The entire steppe, even if here and there it offered small obstacles—narrow rivulets, a rotted fence—was one big path, easy to see. Even the sound of his own footsteps seemed to make him uneasy. Whereas his fellow hiker revived an old pleasure upon hearing the sand crunch underfoot, grass stems from the previous year and the years before crackling as his ankles brushed them, cushions of moss, still damp with the morning dew, sighing—all of which was and remained a new music to his ears, one that made his entire being fall silent and listen—the poet did not pause for a moment in his daylong monologue to listen, let alone fall silent. Even when his attention was called to the rustling of pebbles as they brushed against each other, to the constantly varied concert produced by dried reeds, at most he gestured impatiently and continued spewing out his town talk, undeterred by his own stumbling and the absent sidewalks. The many-voiced concert of the steppe meant nothing to him.

A cold wind, signaling the imminent onset of night, whipped around the two men atop the mound of ancient Numancia. From the new Numancia far below in the bend of the river rose mist, spreading like a reservoir over the already darkened steppe. Despite the desolation of the scattered farms, the smell of wood smoke grew stronger and stronger. The smell came from underground, beneath the site of the old fortress, long since vanished but at one time besieged for years by the Roman Empire's legions. The men were standing atop a special charcoal heap. They did not speak. Juan Lagunas, too, kept silent as a matter of course. A dog circled them. It had been following them all day, and the narrator of the Moravian night wanted it to be the same dog as the one in Porodin, at the beginning of his tour, although now the dog was as large as a calf, with a dachshund-like belly that sometimes grazed the gravel of the steppe: the padding of its feet had sounded exactly like that of the little mutt of the enclave.

The wind, too, without specifically swirling or changing direction, now gradually seemed to be wafting in from another era. The smell of wood smoke was joined by that of damp animal coats and sour milk. Inside a stockade fence, for the benefit of local tourism an attempt had been undertaken to reproduce the pre-Roman settlement, complete with cave-like thatched-roof huts and alleys that also served as sewers. By this late hour the attraction was long since closed. But the Numancia that now surfaced was different, entirely independent of the imagined or reimagined one. It produced no image, nor could anything be heard: neither pots clattering nor battle cries ripe for a film portraying antiquity, nor any other hoopla. Even the olfactory hallucination was gone in a jiffy. What gave this Numancia substance had been the wind. No matter whether now, in this early-evening hour, it blew in a vacuum: for a few moments, no, for a prolonged second, a Numancia had burst forth in a way that no reconstruction and no historical account could conjure up or put within grasp. Numancia lived. And in what respect did it live? As what? As a sudden intimation. As a lasting intimation. As an alternative present. Who had had the insight at one point that ideas were deeds and should be treated as such? And weren't intimations, or at least intimations of this sort, perhaps also facts that one ought to perceive in their physicality, as living matter in the full sense—as a particular network of arteries?

Nightfall, coming on suddenly—this was the south, after all. The dog, which continued to circle the two men on the mound, broke into wolflike howls. And the poet from New Numancia howled in sympathy. The man beside him, who since his stay in the provincial town had been a faithful reader of his poetry, realized that the poems, without once mentioning the name, all dealt with the vanished Numancia. If he constantly cursed the present town and all towns of the present day, and wished to see them destroyed, he was actually conjuring up the earlier or alternate-reality settlement. What he called "pain of absence," in which the "music of distant parts" was no longer to be heard, for which he blamed "the thieves of illusion," with their "sharp thorn, stabbing our veins"—these images evoked his dream, his intimation, his idea of a different or differently conceivable Numancia. He prayed for that Numancia. He begged for it. He howled for it to the now dark horizons, so furiously that the dog fell silent. Something like a stench billowed from the poet, the stench of a—no, of desolation.

The man beside him had always felt love, if at all, for a lost soul, whether actually lost or lost only in his imagination, and always just one person, never more than one—for a single lost person. His love had sprung, without exception, from the fervent desire to save the person in question. The few times he had fallen in love had gone hand in hand with this thought: "This woman wants to be saved by me, by me and me alone." Even writing books, at the time when he still saw himself as a writer, had always been triggered by the need, yes, the need, to rescue someone, and one day it had become clear to him how he wanted to die: either at his desk, in the middle of writing something, or while trying to save someone, for instance from a burning building or from a firing squad.

But when it came to this Juan Lagunas, there seemed to be nothing more to be saved, and apparently the man also expected nothing of the kind. And besides, our host had hardly anything to say about the outcome of his various rescue attempts. But at least he drew the howling poet to him and stood cheek to cheek with him until he fell silent. The lost poet's skin was not merely cold; it was completely lifeless. Not a pore that exhaled anything or responded in any way to the touch of the other cheek. It was reminiscent of an Indian mask into whose cheeks mice had gnawed their way, a mask supposed to represent a human being "in the process of losing his soul." And nonetheless this seemingly dead skin expected something, and with it, palpably, the entire person there in the darkness. He was expressing a demand. He was still entitled to something from the other man. And if he received it, he would make further demands. He would not let him leave, ever again. And if the other man left him, that would be called betrayal. It would mean: So you are leaving me in the lurch, like everyone else. And would he, at that moment still his partner (or "pardner," as in Westerns), in fact leave him in the lurch, without further ado, just as he had eventually done with everyone else? He had had to do so if he wanted to save himself? And would do it again this time?

The night turned out to have no stars. The poet of Numancia claimed to be unable to see in the dark, "like my mother." So the two of them descended arm in arm from the mound to the steppe, the dog going on ahead, as if to sniff out the path. From all around them, near and far, came a monotonous tooting, a sort of croaking, though an octave higher, you might say, and also emanating more from the air above than from any ditches below, while each individual note formed a layer in a sound horizon that receded into the darkness. Juan, his arm hooked into his companion's, unexpectedly took a hop, then another, and so on all the way down the hillside. It became a dance, and not the dance of someone lost and done for. And he, the storyteller, could not help dancing along with the poet, suddenly vivacious. Yes, he, despite his lack of night vision and all, now showed himself to be in the best of spirits. And it was probably not true that he could find his way around only in his familiar haunts in town: taking his cue from the scents that rose from beneath his dancing feet, he named the plants or herbs that gave them off: "lavender," "thyme," "poppy," "globe thistle" ... His wailing earlier on the hillcrest: it seemed now as if he had actually gathered strength from it and were drawing on it to get himself in the right mood. "Ah, my dear old nightmares," he said at the bottom of the hill, his voice now both calm and resonant: "Up to now you have always saved my life, roused me at the last moment from the sleep of death. Nightmares, my guardian angels."

In front of the convention center in the semiwilderness, unlit and closed for the week, Juan Lagunas made a rattling noise with something:

his car keys. So the lone Jeep parked on the edge of the gravel trail belonged to him. He promptly unlocked three doors: one for himself on the driver's side, one for the storyteller next to him, and the third in the rear, for the large dog, now silent once more. "It's going to be a night of owl calls," he remarked before starting the engine. How would he drive without night vision? On went the headlights, no problem. (But was he really unable to see in the dark?)

During the drive to New Numancia he asked the passenger beside him a question, one the man had heard more and more often in the course of his life: "Are you still writing?" Under different circumstances the answer had always been "No," and initially it had spared him from having to say more—for those asking the question all took it for granted that he had stopped writing—and later the answer became the truth. This time, however, he lied: "Yes, I'm still writing." And as soon as the words left his mouth, the thought came: *Now I've said it, I have to stick to it.* The lie had simply slipped out—and was it really a lie, spoken without any ulterior motive, without any calculation? The response from the poet at the wheel—not a single other vehicle on the road—"I've never written a single line of prose. All that exists for me is poetry. Descriptions, dialogue, stories mean nothing to me, not to mention plots, action, dramatic events, conflict, problems—yes indeed. Language alone means something to me. That's where I achieve my only victories. But you're a storyteller, a man of prose. And as a poet I predict that you'll write a love story, a dramatic one, a story such as only you can let others experience. I also know you're already writing it. And it doesn't have to culminate the usual way, with a revolver being aimed at the man fleeing from love as he stands on the cliffs above the Pacific. Bim, bam, boom can happen in other ways."

Juan Lagunas dropped the storyteller off somewhere in town. (Question interjected by the "spoilsport" on the Moravian boat: "In front of a hotel? In front of the railroad station? And where was the small suitcase all this time?" No answer.) A last exchange of looks, also with the dog, which had sprawled on the vacated front seat, its usual place.

Juan's eyes: still full of expectancy—then bitterly disappointed—and in the end once more expressionless. This person, too, upon their reunion after a quarter century, had failed to provide the poet with the existential foundation he so urgently needed. Existential foundation? Yes, and also confirmation of his existence. Yes, he, Juan Lagunas from the vanished town of Numancia, could receive both an existential foundation and a confirmation of existence only from someone else; another person had to ground his, Juan's, existence and also confirm it. And once more he had been disappointed by such a person.

And when he nonetheless finally spoke audibly again, the words took shape as if without benefit of his voice, simply from a flapping of his lips, like that of small children who cannot speak yet but play at speaking—except that this was no game. With some effort one could decipher what he was saying, and in the end had to read it from his lips, now moving without sound: "Home to my children, entrusted to me, my ghosts. All I want to do now is sleep, naked, without dreams and nightmares to wake me. Once I invented a secret script and went around this town from one person to the next, thinking someone could decipher it. But no one could decipher it. No one wanted to decipher it. We two have met twice over the years, *amigo lector*. And there will be no third time, and if there is, it will be in a figurative sense, in a fundamentally different sphere, whose music will perhaps be white noise."

4

~~~~~

~~~~~

~~~~~

AS THE STORYTELLER announced, getting ahead of himself during that night on the Morava, the prophecy about the "love story" made by the poet of Numancia would eventually turn out to be true, in the form of "a literally unheard-of occurrence." But for a long, long while the former writer remained alone as his journey continued. And that was how it was supposed to be. And it was to be the case—so he thought and resolved—that during this period he was moving farther and farther from the main destination chosen in advance, deep inside Austria. The more horizons he placed between himself and his land of origin, the more clearly he could perceive one vanished detail or another, from among which not a few individual destinations offered themselves within the orbit of the main destination. And from time to time he also experienced, in defiance of the laws of physics, that as the physical distance increased, the pull of the destinations grew stronger.

During this period he hardly lingered anywhere. And he gave himself time for detours and distractions. To be sure, he was heading steadily westward, toward the Atlantic. But he meandered, following the example of the rivers that streamed toward the ocean in leisurely snakelike movements. And again it was perfectly fine with him that he was putting himself and his project at risk, without specifically seeking out dangers of one kind or another. On airplane wings, toward the tips, where they appeared less massive, there was usually a line marked for the mechanics servicing the aircraft, together with the admonition: "Do not walk outside this area." At least once a day if possible, he stepped over the line, for a longer or shorter time. A kind of rejuvenating strength flowed into one from such prohibited movements. And after certain moments of terror, experienced unintentionally, one saw more keenly, or grasped what was actually going on. And because this time, in contrast to earlier journeys, he did not note down anything, not a single word, and had finally shaken off being a writer, even though his writing had never been a compulsion (?), he enjoyed a sense of freedom, far more intensely during the journey than when he had stayed put, even on the boat on the Morava—a sense of freedom that constituted for him, as it did for the rest of us, something exceedingly rare, a kind of happiness.

He remained alone week after week, paying special attention to those who were also alone, although in a different way from him. In Salamanca, let's say, down on the bank of the Tormes, he lost himself in contemplation of a young man standing there completely equipped for mountain-climbing in the high Alps: hanging from his belt he had several looped-up climbing ropes, as well as a number of pitons and rings in different sizes, also rock hammers, ice picks, flashlights, and headlamps . . . During that night of storytelling on the Morava, he left to our imagination the other items the young man had dangling from his belt, with the exception of a key ring, bristling with perhaps a hundred keys. The man stood there motionless, gazing at the river for hours, his face blank. But there was nothing contemplative about him.

He was alert, ready to spring into action, his eyes narrowed in such a way that it would have been obvious to anyone: if anything serious were to happen within his field of vision, on the water or up on the Roman bridge, he would be off like a shot, armed with his hammers, turnbuckles, and ropes, to provide first aid, or intervene, or execute a capture, or perform some other official action—indubitably as the agent in charge. And it was clear that he was not in charge of the actual people in his field of vision, those passing before him on the bridge and on the riverfront promenade. With narrowed eyes and chin thrust forward he gazed past and through them all and over their heads, his supporting leg and his working leg poised for motion. His assignment pertained to something that would take place farther away, much farther away, in an undetermined location. And even once he finally moved, heading uphill into the city, his equipment rattling and thumping around him with each of his heavy, no, powerful steps, to take up his next post at an intersection, this standing on guard, more a form of remaining alert, again for hours and motionlessly, had nothing to do with the passing cars or the crowds of pedestrians, which swelled toward evening and seemed to take as little notice of him as he took of them. But one time, when a girl brought him a cup of coffee from a shop on the corner and asked the man on guard at the intersection how he was faring, he beamed, silently, "for a fraction of a second" all over his face, whereupon he once more narrowed his eyes, all the more ready to leap into action and intervene, one hand on the ropes at his belt, the other on the key ring, bristling like a weapon.

Another time, in a bar in Ciudad Rodrigo, already close to the Portuguese border, our storyteller could not take his eyes off an old man, more enthroned than seated at a table in the rear, far from the other guests, although he was a guest himself. In spite of the sun's warmth, he had on a fur cap. The table heaped with documents, manuscripts, to which the man kept adding piles of papers that he pulled out of a briefcase leaning against a leg of his table. Black flies, large ones, buzzed around the old man, who paid them no mind as he shuffled through his papers, making notes, adding dots, always from right to left, as if he were writing in Arabic. Whenever he added dots, sometimes just one, sometimes two, sometimes three, it could be heard all through the bar, in spite of the babble of voices and the seductive melodies from the juke-boxes, and he seemed to be more in his element than when he was forming letters, all of them teensy-weensy.

When he stopped now and then, he would inspect a word or a letter through a magnifying glass. And that always took the longest time. The magnifying glass, not the gold or gold-plated fountain pen, was his primary instrument. After an expansive gesture, in which he ceremoniously shook his jacket sleeves back from his wrists, he would move the magnifying glass in circles above the page until finally it swooped down over the curlicue in question, or whatever. But then the old man devoted more and more of his time to making lines. It began with his obviously underlining things, this, too, from right to left, and later it became a crossing-out, first of a single word, then of an entire line or a whole page, with diagonal lines back and forth, and then another page, and another, the process accompanied by a snorting that swelled from displeasure to rage, then a fist pounding the table. Then came a sudden change of image: renewed silence, the pen moving quietly, and page after page receiving something applied briefly and with a flourish, like a signature. That was followed by his looking up and gazing around the room with an imperious air. Silent memorizing of the text. Preparations for his coronation speech: laying his index finger at the root of his nose, then his ring finger; supporting his chin on first one, then the other hand; both palms held up, weighing pros and cons; arms spread wide. But as soon as he caught sight of his sole observer: an instantaneous halt to all this, a blow with his fist on the table, then gathering up and packing the manuscripts into his briefcase, and hurrying out of the room. In a different era he would have had the evildoer killed. "Never again shall you look upon your king!"

Our storyteller did not avoid cities, but in them he stayed closer to the roads leading out of them than to the centers. Something new of late was the presence of more and more benches, extending all the way to the roundabouts at the city limits, and around them. He often sat there, reading, looking up, turning back to his reading. One day, during one of his far-flung meanders, he became fixated on a group of the sort of people one could count on finding in such places: idiots. No other term came to him, and he was fond of the word, one of those that stayed with one from childhood, like "gypsies," "cottagers," "path-makers," "mountaineers," "blacksmiths." The idiots were taking their daily walk, accompanied by caretakers, distinguishable from their charges, if at all, by a certain seriousness of demeanor, not consistently maintained. They did not lead the group but let some go on ahead, themselves staying more in the middle. Like him, the idiots seemed to be drawn to the outskirts and to the highways. Unlike him, they lingered for hardly a minute on the benches by the star-shaped intersections at the city limits: jumping up, they circled the roundabout, hopping and hobbling in procession as they went on their way.

On the day in question, instead of being content with gazing at and gazing after the group, he closed his book and followed them on their rounds. He stopped when they stopped, stared at the things they stared at. He made no effort to go unnoticed. He actually wanted them to know that he had his eye on them, wanted them to feel affirmed by his following. This following, like his gaze, was meant to indicate to them that they had something to offer. The very fact that he had a book in his hand, with one finger keeping his place, indicated more than just goodwill. They were the stars, and in him they had found their fan, only one, true, but he mattered.

They stopped in front of a billboard, located in the roundabout, with posters for all the films currently playing in the city. Silently they mimed in meticulous detail stories that the facial expressions and postures on the posters suggested to them. Was it more than his imagination that his engagement with them had animated them this way? Perhaps they had not even noticed him. And the two caretakers ignored him as one of the gawkers they often encountered on their excursions with the little troupe. Nonetheless, with them before his eyes, he was convinced he was acting on their behalf, in their name. He had to do so, in the interest of something higher. He had nothing better to do than to keep on the trail of these idiots, with all his senses, and not for this moment only. Rather than carrying out surveillance of pilgrims on their way to Santiago, or of anyone else, his mission was to attend to these poor in spirit.

How did it happen that, at least on the open road, human beings appeared to him almost exclusively in the form of the disturbed or the confused? Was there something inside him, in his mind or such, that merely made it seem that way? No, in this case at least, his mind, or his consciousness, or his feelings, or such, happened to be the world. He knew that, at least until the moment when one member of the group, the straggler, the only one who had not participated in the others' performances, or at most constantly whimpering, with arms dangling, was taken in hand by a caretaker as he stood there motionless, whereupon the straggler suddenly turned around, recognized the pursuer—yes, that was what he was—ran toward him and struck him, feebly, to be sure, but with a feebleness that resulted in the blows' seeming to miss the other person's chest and stomach on purpose, breaking off just a hairsbreadth before their goal, and if a blow did happen to land, it seemed more like a form of clinging, though a clumsy one, which had its own kind of strength.

And that became clear to him from the way people appeared to him after the idiot ran toward him and after this straggler there by the highway leading out of the city shouted in his face: "Make God leave me in peace! Make him stop hurting me day and night. Make him stop hanging around me all the time and wanting something of me. Make him stop thinking of me, make someone else think of me, someone other than this Lord God! God, my God, when will you abandon me? Get out of me, will you?" A strange longing seized hold of the man at whom the straggler was shouting, a longing for the idiots in his Balkan enclave and the way they hung around all the intersections, their faces turned away.

But during that night on the Morava the storyteller had no idea, none at all, what he meant to convey to us with this episode other than the event itself. He faltered, then broke off in the middle. Again he had not found the right words, the scintillating detail, the suggestive image, the illuminating comparison. Yet he had felt compelled to speak of his encounter with the idiots by the roundabout on the edge of the city, of their eyes in comparison to those of the drivers, of their voices in comparison to those that people sometimes used to call their dogs, of their movements—the way they swung their arms, raised their legs, wagged their heads—in comparison to . . . Did he miss the sense of danger he needed for that kind of pointed storytelling? Did our host need a new source of danger? The night all around the boat remained peaceful. The Morava frogs croaked. The trees in the meadows along the river rustled. The distant expressway roared. The satellites blinked. The stars gazed down.

For a long time the boatmaster kept silent, brooding, until he recognized that the danger that would motivate him was the same danger that had just threatened his story. It was an internal danger, and by remaining conscious of it as a constant threat, his constant threat, he would perhaps receive an even stronger impetus, an equally hearty incentive to keep going. And what was this internal danger? It was, as he spelled out for the rest of us, the danger of falling into a reverie, something that happened to him from time to time. And what was dangerous about that? It was dangerous in two respects: first because by now he could almost, but fortunately only almost, summon these reveries at will. The far greater danger, the real one, was that in such fugue states the world showed itself to him on the one hand as it never did otherwise, even approximately—as whole, as a whole—but on the other hand nothing more could be said to it, about it. This whole world, even when it droned, roared, and howled, as it did out there by the roundabouts, remained silent and could be greeted only with a great silence. "It" revealed itself then, silently, and that was that. It not only called for no words; words were no longer appropriate, not a single one, not even an exclamation, an *Oh!*, an *Ah!*, a *Hey there!* "By far the greatest danger, however, in my reveries," our nocturnal host continued, "is this: in the form of a detail, a street, a house, a wall plastered with posters, a person, the totality of the world appears to me, behind or beyond it, the totality of the world in the sense of something that has remained whole. Against my—what's the phrase?—better judgment, an intact world appears to me, and this intact world forces itself upon me as the superior reality, the reality that counts. Cars drive by, chimneys puff smoke, bushes sway, the grass quivers, saws whine, children cry, the blind feel their way along: that is as it should be. Everything is in order. It would take so little for the world to appear to me in my reverie as the best of all possible worlds. It would take so little for a war to fit into this state of affairs. Yes, what results is a static condition, a standstill, a dead stop, seemingly definitive, once and for all. And time and again this stand-still, monumentlike, monumental, seizing hold of me, has relieved my innermost being for the moment—each time it lasted only that long—of the burden of my self, but at the same time, as I realized almost too late, threatened me to the core, and especially during my life as a writer, a life that indeed, purely instinctively, depended on a constant rhythmic motion, even if it was teeny-tiny, in fact, the more teeny-tiny the more right, the smaller the better—depended on the succession of moments, not on moments of standstill, no matter how monumental. And although I no longer write anything down, I do not quite know what to do with my reveries, to which part of me clings, in spite of everything, because they help me get out of myself and into the world, into you over here, into you over there. All's well when I do nothing but live them, and keep them to myself—not well when I wish to impart them to all of you, a wish, which, whether recorded in writing or not, still remains a fervent one, at least as far as you are concerned. Reverie? Foolish obsession? A dreamer, a fool? An idiot yourself?" And then the boat-master added, "What seems most worrisome about my reveries is that they mean I have nothing to read anymore; that they replace reading or even make it superfluous; that the admonition 'Here, take this and read it!' no longer carries any weight."

The person among us who always broke in with questions about mundane matters now wanted to know where the incident with the idiots on the outskirts had taken place and how the weather had been at the time, and this time he received a reply for a change. The outskirts had been those of Santiago de Compostela, whose center, the destination for pilgrims and the site of a statue of the saint whose feet had been kissed until they were shiny-smooth, the zigzag traveler did not specifically avoid but never considered visiting, without giving it any thought, indeed without any thoughts, as was often the case as he continued on his way or let himself drift, roving and roaming. And the weather was just the weather. And he told us furthermore that it must have been a Sunday. For that same day, in late afternoon, still on the outskirts, he had gone to a soccer match that pitted Compostela against Numancia, teams in the Second Division. He felt a need, as happened again and again after that, to be in the thick of things, to use an expression that his brother applied to the village idiot back home, whom he described as always being "in the thick of things."

In Spain, matches between Second Division teams drew crowds almost as large as those in the First Division, and accordingly he actually found himself in the thick of things. He, the traveler from afar, yelled and whistled like the others, jumping out of his seat when a goal was scored—though in contrast to the other spectators, he jumped up for both the home team's and the visitors' goals. He shook his head in solidarity at the referee's knuckleheaded rulings at the penalty kick, and sympathized at the end of the match with the local spectators (there were hardly any others), who, with umbrellas, canes, and crutches—surprisingly many of the latter, reminding him of his Balkan homeland—wanted to swarm the referees or pounded from the bleachers on the plastic canopy under which the players disappeared into the locker rooms. Nonetheless, however much he was in the thick of things, he knew such behavior was out of bounds for him, and not because he came from neither one city nor the other. No matter how many conspiratorial glances he exchanged with those around him, he remained alone. And that was his doing, not theirs. Once, it seemed to him, remaining alone in the midst of a crowd had meant something. It had often given him pleasure. But now it burdened him, more and more as the match proceeded. In addition, he felt an increasing sense of guilt, for something he could not identify and therefore could do nothing about. By being the way he was, and where he was, even as he laughed with the man seated next to him when a player slipped and fell, he became guilty, without lifting a finger, of something that could never be set right. The floodlights came on: one was all the more alone. In the high-rise apartment buildings on the outskirts beyond the stadium, the first lights appeared: one yellow card, then another. And what a cold yellow. It serves me right. A sense of guilt at the very thought of not having to go to work the next day, unlike the locals. Leaving the stadium, alone, in the dark. And how quickly the crowd had dispersed. A gradual sensation of greater lightness. And the score of the Compostela: Numancia match? You have three guesses. And where he spent the night? In a hotel on the outskirts, as the only guest that Sunday evening, "for forty-nine euros, plus local taxes."

At this point, one of the rest of us on the boat picked up the thread of the story for a while. We had already grown so accustomed to one voice, that of our host, and to the direction from which it came in the semidarkness of the boat's salon, that we involuntarily swiveled around when, during a fairly long pause that our host took to catch his breath, from one of the small tables to the rear a second voice suddenly chimed in, its timbre entirely different from that of the other voice. But because the tone and the rhythm matched, after the first few sentences we adjusted to the change in speaker and perspective. The night, along with the Morava and its banks, constituted the third voice, in a manner of speaking, against which background the two other voices blended effortlessly.

The man who now picked up the narrative was someone with whom the former writer had crossed paths by chance during one of the next stages of his journey. "I saw you without your noticing me. And I then accompanied you along a route that happened to be mine as well, not sneakily but rather quite openly, and nevertheless unseen by you, until our paths diverged." This substitute storyteller spied his friend and ours in the early hours of the day following the soccer match, or the morning of another day, at a railroad station between Santiago de Compostela and the Atlantic—though not on the coast of Portugal, allegedly one of his destinations, the farthest westward destination on the European leg of his journey, but rather along the Atlantic coast to the north, that of Galicia. (And not for the first time, instead of the word "tour," the words "zigzag course" turned up in the story.) The station was located along the stretch between Santiago and La Coruña, and only two trains a day stopped there, one heading toward the ocean, the other into the interior. The station, far from the village whose name it bore, had been closed for a long time, including the ticket counter and waiting room, with no staff on duty, the windows and doors bricked up, a mere whistle stop, with only the platform accessible. "With your suitcase, you were sitting there alone in the sun, on the ground—no trace of a bench—leaning against the wall of sparkling Galician granite. At first I did not recognize you; that was how unfamiliar the man sitting there looked, perhaps also because he allowed himself to be seen only in profile, and did not react to my approach with so much as a blink, although I had been driven there from the village in a car." But then: was it his friend? Yes, it was. "And I heard myself shout. And no reaction to that either." After that, he could not say why, he let the other man be. "In spite of my delight at this fairy-tale encounter." He confined himself from then on to glancing now and then from a distance at his odd traveling companion: that was how unapproachable he appeared—and here the guest imitated our host's style of storytelling—"no, inaccessible."

Some time remained until the train was due, or the train was late, so the former writer began to stroll up and down the platform. Before turning and heading in the other direction he would pause briefly. He gave a deep sigh, a deeper one each time, if possible, until finally one of his sighs gave way to humming, and this to laughing, and this to a repeated cry. Was it true, then, as all the European newspapers had first predicted and then reported, that his old friend was well on his way to going completely insane? What seemed to confirm those reports was that he now pulled off his shoes and jumped off the platform onto the sharp crushed rock of the rail bed. That he then crouched down and gazed for a long, long time into the hollow space beneath the platform, where there was nothing to see but perhaps an abandoned hornets' nest, an empty cement sack, a rusting uniform button, a scrap from a shirt, a book, or a porno magazine. That he remained standing between the tracks even when the train, not yet in view, could be heard approaching from afar, as a chirping up in the wires, and kept his eyes fixed on the sleepers, still made of wood along this stretch of mine, staring at the "eyes" in the blackish wood and the oil and other droplets, shading his own eyes with one hand, as if he were looking not at the ground but rather at something far off, on the most distant horizon possible. That he sniffed, his nostrils flaring, as if there were something to smell or as if a stench were coming from the lavatory hut next to the station, long since out of commission, its door gone, with only the outline of the bowl visible, the drainpipe stopped up with crushed rock? That he— with the train in view now—in addition to his staring and sniffing raised a finger to draw something in the air (or was he writing?), as if deaf to the blast of the locomotive's whistle warning him, and then, in the train compartment, still barefoot, his shoes next to him, continued scribbling or sketching, now on the rain-steamed window, for the train and its passengers were coming from the rain, as was fitting for an episode taking place in my Galicia.

I took a seat diagonally across from him. But even if I had been sitting directly opposite him, he would not have registered my presence, as I by now realized. That my writer had gone off the deep end seemed clear from his confused scribbling on the cloudy window. With the best will in the world one could not decipher the writing. And not only his bare feet and his dirty fingernails gave me the impression that this person was not just inaccessible but had become one of the untouchables, from the lowest caste far off in India (where furthermore, after what he had declared to be his last book, many years earlier, public figures had prophesied the rest of his future). And in addition, as if to confirm my suspicion, he now stuck a dove's feather with a blood-encrusted quill in his hair, heedless of anyone else's presence, and began talking to himself, loudly and incessantly, keeping it up all the way to La Coruña. Among other things I recall the following: "Everyone is the way he is. And all the shoelaces that won't come untied. Oh, jumble of morning thoughts. My mother's singing prevented me from becoming a singer. I'm disturbing people, but I don't want to disturb them. God loves the bashful giver more than the merry one, and He loves the agitated giver most of all. How we wander about in the universe. I love too little. It's no disgrace to breathe. Green has been passé for a long time. From so much looking I no longer see anything. Actually one should die more often. No one rules the world. Worrisome that it can't be told. At least I'm alone. It's terrible how one loses track of oneself. Everything is an error. Take words, not colors! Nothing is good for you! Don't buy anything! So much time! And tomorrow it continues . . ."

Here the boatmaster interjected that of course he had recognized his Galician friend. But he had decided that during this phase of his journey he should have dealings only with strangers. "That was how it had been decided, that was how it had been conceived." And accordingly he had not let the other man get close to him, had acted in his presence absent-minded, confused, unapproachable. He even imagined that for the other man, and not for him alone, he was invisible. His idea was that if he wished, he could perhaps be seen, but perceived as a mere daydream. He had only to concentrate, and for the world around him he would vanish into thin air, as the world would for him. To overlook and make himself be overlooked: as he imagined it, that had always been his form of power. And that being the case, would he have been disappointed at being recognized this time, as his very own self, in flesh and blood, despite personifying a figment of the imagination? Not in the least: after this interjection, he urged the interim reporter to continue. "What else happened with me on the train? And after that? I trust you followed me in La Coruña? What can you report of me as I made my way through the city? What did I do there? How did I seem?" Yes, he was eager to have someone else recount happenings involving him, much as in childhood he had never been able to get his fill when his mother described what he had done or said at such and such a time. "And what else did I say, Mother? And where did I go after that? And where did I hide the next time? And who was the next person I beat up? And what was my next sleepwalking episode like?"

"When we arrived at our destination," the other man continued obediently, "I stuck to his heels for only a short time. After all, I had work waiting. But during my lunch break I ran into our traveler again, and then again after work. Or had these encounters been prearranged? Be that as it might, at noon I saw him in a funeral procession. He was walking in a long column of local people behind the hearse, completely integrated into the crowd. He had changed his clothes, if indeed it was him, which I doubted at first: a dark suit with a white shirt and a tie, and a hat. No, it was him. I became sure when, walking along like the others, hesitating at a traffic light or such, then continuing, he looked over his shoulder once, and after that again and again. I recognized him not only by his face, clean-shaven for a change; it was the way he turned his head as he walked, the gesture I most associated with him. In all the time I had known him, he had glanced over his shoulder at regular intervals wherever he went, perhaps less because he expected to see something behind him than because he hoped to sharpen his vision, his spatial vision, or for some such reason; that was my impression. But if this time he intended, as a member of the mourning party, to orient himself and gain keener vision this way, his looking over his shoulder hardly made sense, because his eyes were glittering with tears, and their source could not have been the Atlantic wind in La Coruña alone; why else, whenever he turned his head to face front again, would an unmistakable shuddering of his whole body have been visible that could be caused only by sobbing? I was standing too far away to hear it. But it was a powerful sobbing, gripping his entire body, more intense than could be observed in anyone else in the funeral procession, especially in the members of the immediate family right behind the hearse. And that aroused my suspicions again. As someone familiar with the town, I had knowledge of the deceased, and if my writer, a stranger to the region, had heard anything about him, he would have realized that this was not someone to mourn. No, he knew nothing about the dead man, let alone having been acquainted with him. So did that mean that this person weeping uncontrollably was not who I took him for? I moved in closer, forgetting my plan of spending the lunch break with a seaside sweetheart. And again I thought no: someone wearing such squeaky shoes, who in the midst of his sobbing and moaning tugged incessantly at his cuffs, who even flashed cuff links, and such cuff links, too, could not possibly be the person who had become dear and precious to me and indispensable for my spiritual well-being, no matter how nondescript, even repellent, his physical presence seemed to me time after time. And what if this was a double, one of the many who, as far as he was concerned, according to him, were in circulation all over Europe?

"After work I ran into him again, and a third time later that evening. The first of these encounters took place at dusk, in the marketplace by the ocean. He had changed his clothes again, was positioned by a fish stand, not as a customer but as the fishmonger's assistant, probably just for that one hour, wearing a rubber apron and wooden clogs on his bare feet, and stripping the scales off wolf fish for the last customers of the day, chopping off the heads, not quite expertly but less clumsily than I remembered him from before, during his writing period, and then after closing he stood there with the other vendors, hosing down the tiled floor of the market hall, enjoying himself more than I ever would have expected, with the sound of the water pouring from his companions' hoses seemingly tuned to the background noise, if one listened closely: the distant roar of the ocean.

"But that actually was his double, wasn't it? If it was, you could pick up some details with respect to the original that you might have failed to notice in his presence. The man by the fish stalls, viewed as a double, opened your eyes to the specific characteristics of the person in question. So what was he like?" "How did I look to you?" (Another question from our host, clearly eager for the answer.) "First of all, like a person without cares. Like a big child, at least so long as you were with the others. A playful person. You behaved nonchalantly, apparently not taking your companions seriously. Staying somewhat apart, but secretly the center of attention, comporting yourself like someone who, without being specifically observed by anyone, was constantly aware of being observed. If someone spoke to you, you looked past him, thinking about something else entirely. Or you failed to understand anything, so much as a single word, even when the statement was repeated, and even less if it was repeated again. In my eyes, you seemed not just slow on the uptake but simply dumb, dumb as a post, as a—what was the expression that used to turn up often in books—a doorpost, someone who spends his days staring into a corner of the room, or into the 'idiot box.' But in the very next moment: suddenly you were listening. A single word, or merely a slightly different tone of voice, and you would be all ears, completely present, with an intensity such as I had hardly ever experienced, certainly not in my romantic relationships, whether in the city by the sea or the interior. In order to be able to listen, you went so far as to turn off your water spigot. Your face flushed bright red at what was said, shared with you, told, passed from the speaker to you, and you alternated between nodding, shaking your head, clenching your fists, and splaying your fingers. And in the twinkling of an eye you regained the authority that had seemed to slip away from you almost entirely during your moments of idiocy. And when you seemed to have had enough of such thorough listening, on went the spigot again, and as if nothing had happened you went back to the motions of wrapping up the workday, having time, being in the present and self-absorbed, in the company of others.

"I decided to miss the train back to my Galician village and to continue my surveillance of my author's double, or whatever he was. (I would spend the night in the city with one woman or another, or with god knows which other one.) I waited outside the fish section until he came out, the last one, through the last open door, which he locked behind him, using a bunch of keys reminiscent of a weapon, a flail. Finding the right key took him so long that I finally recognized some of his earlier clumsiness. He was alone and, if it really was the same person, had changed his clothes; he strolled eveningward in a summery light-colored suit, worn under an open trenchcoat, extra long, with a checked cap on his head that seemed utterly inappropriate for a coastal city in northern Spain, and tennis shoes. His appearance in such a disguise was almost ghostly, though also, if I had been following him with a movie camera, several degrees more distinct than that of the person he was, or the person for whom I took him in my hallucination. Incidentally, it was generally agreed that no matter what his disguise or camouflage, those who had registered his face, or merely his way of moving, would always recognize him instantly. Even in an astronaut's suit or a Montana cowboy's outfit, no matter where on earth his wanderings had taken him, he would be greeted by such a person, who would not have to eye him dubiously for a moment, with 'Hallo, there, it's you again' or 'I see you!' One way or another, he could not be missed.

"As he had done at noon in the funeral procession, he kept turning his head to look over his shoulder as he made his way hither and yon across the city. This behavior contrasted oddly with the way he strolled along and lightfootedly snaked his way through the crowds. He must have expected to see someone behind him (certainly not me), and he expected nothing good of this person. To me he looked like someone on the run, like someone checking behind him for pursuers, no, a single pursuer. If initially he had meandered through the streets in a leisurely fashion, now he began to zig and zag, and increasingly made sudden turns. Might this still be a game, a game with himself, with his own imagination? But again no: if it was a game, then a game involving someone else. His frolicsome flight, or his performance of fleeing, was meant to catch his pursuer's attention, or perhaps turn that person into a pursuer in earnest.

"What seemed to confirm this supposition was that he disappeared into an arcade with which I was familiar. I waited to see whether someone would follow him in—no one did—and then went in myself. By now night had long since fallen. There he stood, but not alone at a game console as I had expected, but in a sort of pack with others, in front of a dart board, you know what I mean, a target like the one on the boat here, but with an electronic scoreboard, and so on. To his fellow players, who came every evening, he was a complete stranger. But despite having joined them only minutes earlier, he already seemed to fit in completely. He hit the bull's-eye again and again, and at each of his tosses the board lit up with astonishing scores. The person whose turn was supposed to come after his kept pulling the darts out of the target and handing them back to him, something that happened with none of the others. Later that night, however, when I had long since stopped watching, he lost his rhythm, his momentum. Finally he was no longer even hitting the board, or if he did, the arrows did not stick, and no one picked them up off the floor. His new pals had forgotten him, letting him continue playing out of sheer hospitality; he no longer existed for them. And was my writer—for whose sake I stuck around, even if this person was merely some unmasked trenchcoat hero—thinking himself unobserved, now showing his real face, a face, as I saw distinctly, precisely in the semidarkness of the arcade, that appeared more contorted after every missed throw, contorted with impatience, impatience with himself, with the world, with space, with time, with night, an impatience bordering on hate, a hate as undefined as it was universal? His true face? His true self? His other self? His third self? His hundredth? Or was I discovering myself in this imagined writer, my villager self from granite-bound Galicia with my not very granite-worthy, unvillagelike *impaciencia* to go home to the women, whichever women they might be! And do you know, do you all know the name of that game arcade in La Coruña? 'Saint Paciencia.' And why? Because it's located on Calle Santa Paciencia. It's a very short alley, I can tell you that, my friends. Hallowed patience. So there was once a saint called Patience. I wonder when her saint's day falls?"

In the nighttime salon on the boat, the Galician fell silent. Or was he merely pausing, hoping that one of us would ask him about the women in his life? Nothing followed but general silence. True, we were all waiting to hear at long last a story that involved a woman, but not from him. Even the croaking of the frogs ebbed away, as if to signal that something of the sort could now begin, or that a fresh beginning could be made. For a while only the Morava could be heard. Suddenly it was flowing faster, suggesting that the snowmelt from earlier in the day, coming downstream from the mountains to the south, had arrived, as if released by the opening of a lock, in a sudden surge in the vicinity of Porodin and the *Moravian Night*. What seemed like a flood slapped against the sides of the boat, and from the riverbed below came a roar. All the more silent the night sky high overhead, with the last winter constellations still visible in the west as they grew dim, and likewise silent the one falling star that shot past Orion and the Pleiades, from below to above, like matches in a Western movie being struck on a wall or on the soles of boots.

Then a sighing in the half-darkened salon, a sighing such as could come from only one person. Only our host sighed that way now and then. Early in our acquaintance each of us had asked him what was wrong. In the meantime it had become clear that the sighing held no particular significance. It was simply part of him, part of his villager's or rather family heritage. Such sighs had already been heard from his grandfather, in the house, the farmyard, the fields, and from his great-grandfather. Actually it was not so much a sighing as a snorting, sometimes turning into a moan, which, however, had no significance either, as already noted. And usually nothing followed from it. Only in exceptional cases did it announce that something was about to happen: that in a moment he would begin to speak. And during the night in question, and especially in those moments, that was the case, and exactly what the rest of us expected. It was from him we wanted to hear a story involving a woman. From him, who had never shared such a story before.

But as usual he put off starting the story, put off opening his mouth. Before he settled down to talk, he went outside and blew with all his might on the clapper of the boat's bell—but in vain: not a peep. And back in the salon he first described in great detail his wanderings in search of a church ruin, almost a thousand years old, still in Galicia, in the interior, to which he had fled from the coast, the surf, the lighthouses, the residual effects of the oil spill, in the face of which no continuation of his project—for that was how he viewed his tour—presented itself. "And there," our trusty interrupter broke in, "you came across a woman? In the rain? In a storm? What was she wearing? What eye color? Her complexion? Her shoe size? Profession? Age? Siblings? Her mother's given name? Good in bed? Can she cook? Her favorite author? Favorite tree? Favorite name? Favorite constellation? How did she smell? Did she have money on her? How much?"

He did not favor the interrogator with a reply, instead going off on tangents, more and more of them. His first involvement with a woman had not been his only mistake. All his involvements with women during his writing period—ah, if only they had been real involvements at least—had been mistakes, not to a greater or lesser degree, but all of them: complete and utter mistakes. Because he was committed to writing, or saw himself as committed, he promised one woman or another, without actually doing anything, something on which he would be unable to follow through, and on which no one could follow through in his stead. As the writer for whom he took himself, he had no right to be with any woman. He could not be any woman's man. It was a delusion if a woman thought the glow or the radiance that at times emanated from him, or more durably from his writing, was intended for her. And so both of them, as a couple, landed in a trap. She thought he was the one. And at first he believed it, too, against his better judgment—"I'm repeating myself!" he said. But then, right away, "the very next morning—no, in the middle of making love," it would fall apart. I'm not the one. I wasn't the one. He was just performing being a twosome. He performed the role, and sometimes with a thievish or robberly gusto.

It dawned on him again and again, and always too late, that with his notion of writing he was tuned differently, so to speak. His role was to be a third party, not part of a couple. Every time a heavy, heavy guilt weighed him down, and at times, with the woman in his arms, he felt a burning inside, as if of damnation ("Ah, I can't help repeating myself").

The guilt pertained only to his life as a writer. Not that this life excluded love altogether—on the contrary, as he discovered over the course of years; but it required, "on pain of spiritual death," a life beyond love between the sexes. He kept the woman secret, without the slightest sense of guilt, not merely from the outer world but also from himself. And likewise, when he deludedly saw his writer's existence threatened by her ("Oh, delusion!"), he was prepared without hesitation—a situation in which he, the champion of hesitation, did not once hesitate—to betray the woman, to deny her, if necessary thrice thirty times, to get her out of his life at any cost, so long as my life as a writer continued. During his "creative period" he had suspected an enemy in every woman. And when he shook off that enemy and put distance between them, he did so with conviction, certain he was in the right.

Whenever he suspected the woman close to him of being an enemy, she would turn into one. And her enmity consisted of becoming active, not, however, as an enemy of his person but as an enemy of his work. If this work insisted on taking precedence and induced him to push the woman away, surely the work had to have something seriously wrong with it. Instead of loving his work, he was obsessed with it, and that obsession had to be exorcised. And thus commenced the struggle between him and the woman, without ill will on either side, but rather out of helplessness, which made the struggle all the more merciless. To both of them it was a question of justice, and thus one injury led to another. He would have liked to speak about the whole thing more light-heartedly, even more humorously, but that was out of the question, unless one took his current venture into purposeful storytelling as an element of humor. At any rate, he smiled slightly and spared us further sighs as he launched into the story of the woman he had once almost beaten to death. Perhaps he smiled because of the obvious exaggeration in his very first sentence, something in which he otherwise did not indulge, or, in his own words: "not my style." It was also obvious that he intended to keep the story short and sweet—"it stands for others, is only an extreme example." Violence was apparently not his thing either. "And what is?" (A quiet question from the person who usually interrupted so loudly.)

The conflict broke out—again—when he was on a book tour. As so often before, once he set out he felt unsure of himself, repeatedly assailed by doubts as to whether he was on the right course. On some days he merely asserted that he was, and set out trying to find what was right, if only in a single sentence, and at such times he was especially vulnerable, if for no other reason than that he buried himself in his work as if it were a question of life and death. And in his imagination it literally was a matter of life and death, of to be or not to be, no matter whether the book turned out to be just another book; god—or the devil—knows why he took these things so much to heart. The woman, by contrast, did not want all this drama, the more so because she sensed that he was merely claiming to be right. No, this man was not obsessed with his project, merely weak. It could not possibly be the project. She did know about his conflict. But she did not want to know. And she attacked him. This attacking consisted of her blocking his path, the path to the book, every day. She did not act maliciously. She simply could not help herself. In the presence of this man, who treated her from morning to night as his adversary—did not even treat her but just avoided her, with one excuse after another—she had no choice. The truth had to come out: that he was doubly impotent, vis-à-vis her, the woman, and even more so vis-à-vis his supposed beloved, the book. And when he sat working on it, or pretended to be working, she had to continue the conflict, willy-nilly. This conflict had not even been declared. Indeed it was not even a conflict. It was not possible to fight this man, curled up like a hedgehog at his desk. What she did was more like disturbing him, involuntarily, compulsively, all the more mercilessly. She seized every excuse to knock on his door, or, let's say, toss pebbles at his window, or, when she had just wished him a productive workday on the telephone, she would call him right back to ask whether he was finished, and then a minute later, asking how long she would have to wait for him, and so forth. And at night, she would refuse to let him leave—him, whose motto might read, "I am the one who goes away"— even locking the outer door, and then, when he could not help staying, she would not let him sleep, not this way, not that way, him, who according to another of his sayings, needed sleep and dreams for recharging when he had a book in the works. And when, after fervent requests, even pleas, on his part, he was allowed for a change to go home to his room, to his desk—which for him, so weak in periods like this, was literally a homecoming—after he had taken a few deep breaths in his own four walls, the woman would barge into his life again, giving him no respite. He could not unplug the telephone. If he did so, in no time she would appear at his door in person. And what if he simply let it ring? After an hour of ceaseless ringing, the same thing would happen—a few moments after the telephone finally stopped, in "no time" again, as if this woman had wings, her voice, as tender as it was merciless, would be heard calling his name outside through the nocturnal stillness, keeping it up until he let her in.

And one night, when he finally opened the door, it had reached the point that he promptly threw himself at the woman, without even looking at her, and began to beat her. It almost seemed as if she had been asking for it, for she let it happen without trying to protect either her body or her face. He had never struck anyone as he struck this woman.

Even when she fell to the ground, he could not stop, kicking her without caring where the blows landed. In the middle of the fracas he almost picked up the heap lying there on the ground and without more ado skewered it on a nearby fence post with a pointed finial: *Now I'm going to do it*, he thought, as if she deserved it; as if he were acting in self-defense.

He stopped the story there, having no memory of what had happened next. But even from the earlier part nothing had stayed with him about the violence but the violence itself, no night wind, no light, no star, no tree rustling, as if that were a law governing violence. His memory remained blank until the next day, when the woman and he saw each other again as if nothing had happened: her face and her body unscathed, no redness, no swelling—this, too, suggesting that nothing had happened. "Never again a woman. Never again a book!" ran through his mind. And why was he telling us all this? (Thus our interrupter, loudly this time.) This part of the story went with his later experience at the remote monastery in ruins.

So at least our host would get to the heart of the matter, to the other story about a woman, which we hoped would be different, the story the poet of Numancia had prophesied to him, the story of being on the road with the woman. But he continued to put us off, refusing to indulge us. Was this a trick? A ploy? No. We knew our friend well enough to recognize that he could not help postponing discussion of an occurrence of burning importance to him, postponing it as long as possible, whether that was his nature or the nature of the story itself, or both. During his writing period he had no doubt missed the moment for his story by postponing it, just as his double, or whoever, had missed the moment for shooting the arrow. Whatever would come would come. It would remain his problem that, unlike the writer Heinrich von Kleist or members of a certain American school, he could not plunge with his sentences directly in medias res; as was previously the case with his writing, this problem now affected his speaking, and it actually seemed to spur him on.

Since giving up his profession, he had been in the running, and not only for a woman. Once he decided to be a nobody, he knew he amounted to something, entirely different from a certain author or another. He was in the running because he was available, and radiated availability. At the same time, that availability made him appear massive, which had nothing to do with his actual size or weight. Those around him saw him as someone who had both feet on the ground as much as anyone else, who lived entirely in the present, and embodied the present more than anyone. Thus wherever he turned up, it did not occur to people to ask about his profession. He was there, without calling attention to himself, took an interest, participated, fit in. If he had ever felt he had a calling, it was to hearing and going to hear, and in that respect he now found himself in his element. He no longer needed any special atmospheric conditions, only the ground, and he, now anonymous, rested on it with the necessary gravity. His indefinability resulted in his emanating a kind of colorfulness, a dark, earthy, peaceable, humane color and, at the same time, a music, soundless—that was how he wanted it to be heard—a music of empathy. Not only was nothing to be feared from him, the indefinable nobody; he inspired trust. Was he speaking now from experience, or was this rather his idea of himself, finally free of a profession that over time had threatened him not merely with a certain inability to function in society but also with incurable misanthropy?

"Be that as it may." After all the battles and defeats with women during his writing years, he now considered himself ready at last, having renounced his constricting profession, for a woman, for the woman. Despite his failures he continued to believe in the tale of man and woman. This belief was not an idea but rather a dream, one of those dreams that deserved to be believed, and since he still dreamed such dreams, he believed in them as he also believed in the lyrics of certain popular love songs, and not only the line "We'll never say goodbye." Actually he believed more in mutual enthusiasm than in love, or at least he avoided using that word. And as far as the tale of man and woman was concerned, he felt sure everyone on earth had to experience the same thing he did, as in general his personal certainties had to be universally valid—that notion probably a holdover from his profession?

The day on which he set out to find the ruined church, located in the interior of the Galician granite region, was a brimstone-butterfly day, reminiscent of the Numancia poet's "owl night." Brimstone-butterfly day, that meant a sky of prevernal blue, and one could expect, with a probability bordering on certainty, that on the wind, growing perceptibly warmer in the course of the day, a first little yellow fellow would come swirling along, against a sky truly bright for a change.

But hadn't he wanted to cross the border into Portugal and reach the Atlantic from there? interjected our interrupter, playing along with the delaying game. Appropriate, too, the response he received for once: he, the one setting out, had needed obstacles, particularly for this one day, more and more obstacles, before reaching his destination, and the Portuguese borders had long since ceased to be real ones, at least not the kind of obstacles he had in mind. And one could also come upon the Atlantic Ocean, together with its coastline, though in a stranger form, deep in the northern Iberian interior: the tides there—"Don't you know this, you fool?"—manifested themselves in the high tide's flowing upstream in the rivers, usually for many a mile, also spilling into the smaller tributaries, and there, during periods of especially powerful tides, even into springs, whereupon smack in the middle of the countryside the granite boulders from which the fresh water bubbled came to resemble a seacoast. "Get it?" *Ríos*, these rivers and brooks were called, which at high tide became part of the Atlantic. "Get it?"

On one such miniature fjord, a fjord in the plain, lay the ruin, his destination. And the obstacles? Of course the tracklessness, sought out where it had to be; also the willow hedges, the bulls, or perhaps just cows, that sauntered up as he slipped through. And the largest obstacle the brook itself, whose course one had to follow as closely as possible in order to keep pace with the tide surging inland. Did that work? Yes, though less along the brush-choked bank than in the actual bed of the brook. So the tide was not all that high? Yes, and besides it did not come along in waves but rather moved along more like a quiet, almost casual current upstream. And his suitcase? On his back, bulging from inside. That was how long one had been on the road.

He gladly accepted getting lost while traversing a stretch far from the tidal brook. He threw away the map he had brought. What would enable him to find his way would be pure instinct, no, intuition, which on this particular day, he felt certain, was infallible. Wasn't this an unusual attitude toward getting lost? He gave himself plenty of time, and although he constantly scanned his surroundings, he was not searching for a path, merely observing nothing, nothing at all. And sure enough, a brimstone butterfly appeared, veritably dove out of the blue sky, landed on the wanderer, squirted out its poop by arching the rear of its abdomen upward and letting the poop spray over its head and into the air—the wanderer had never seen a butterfly shit, and in that moment felt like a scientist—then swooped up again and fluttered and, yes, reeled in a zigzag course over the prevernal scrub growth, whose gray-on-gray now acquired color, and what color, from the effect of the yellow darting through it, flashed into view once more in the depths of the forest, and—or was this already the afterimage? his imagination?—appeared again, and now and then probably flashed into view again later.

He approached his destination from the back. How did he know he was doing that, lost as he was? This, too, his intuition told him. And how did it happen that on this particular day he knew his intuition to be infallible? That came from a dream he had had the night before. In the dream he had encountered the woman, and in such a way that he felt certain that what he had dreamed would occur the following day. What the dream promised would be fulfilled. He had also realized long ago, however, that it would be up to him to fulfill these promises, like the ones he had received from nature in his childhood, all of which had come true. He had to make them a reality, to put them into practice, to breathe life into them—set out to find them, fight his way through to them, through thick and thin.

And just as nature's promises had awakened his spirit of discovery, so, too, had the promising dream, the dreamed promise, awakened his boldness. Nothing could awaken one like a dream, "one like that." Even if it were a deception: the next day he felt invincible. The dream surrounded him like armor, armor without a single chink that would allow infiltration, penetration, stabbing. And it was stronger than an illusion; how else would that one feral dog, in which he recognized the one he had seen while departing from Porodin, now grown as big as a lion, after some initial growling have accompanied him peacefully, then even running on ahead through the underbrush like a scout, constantly turning to see whether he was still following? How else would the one highwayman, on the trail through the underbrush, with the ruins already perceptible, have turned upon his approach into a basket-weaver, using his knife—how could it be otherwise—only for cutting willow shoots; where willows were, there must be water?

And just as the dream provided his armor all that day, it also sent him the guardian angel, the one assigned to him personally. Time and again, as he scrambled over granite barriers, often smooth as glass, he stepped into midair and was saved from falling by the angel, who knows how? Under normal circumstances, of course, he would not have fallen far, but how would he have got out of this wilderness with a broken leg? And the word "intuition" no longer sufficed in these situations, only "guardian angel." It was his angel who restored his equilibrium at the last moment, as he began to slip, almost falling. No armor would have protected him then. And his angel had no easy time of it with him, for his boldness made this stormer of coastlines and springs impetuous. Every intervention by the angel was supposed to serve as a warning. And in the course of the day the warnings became ever more urgent. After a last warning came a very last warning. The warnings were certainly heard and also taken to heart for a while, but then forgotten every time in the constant bluing of the sky and in the brimstone-butterfly wind.

And thus at the very end, in spite of all the warnings, he was supposed to fall at the feet of the woman. Before that, however, his arrival at the ruins, alone. In their vicinity he would meet her, not immediately, but later that day. He felt torn: on the one hand he knew it, the way one knows upon shooting an arrow that it will hit the target; on the other hand, he felt the way one feels before the onset of an illness that has not recurred in a long time and has almost been forgotten: it was enough that it came to mind, without symptoms or any malaise, not even as a memory; simply hearing the name was almost a sure sign, at least for him, that the illness was just around the corner, and with it a bad time.

But first he entered the little church, actually just a chapel (its roof and doors missing), to which a network of trodden paths led through the semiwilderness. Before him in the apse, the fresco, undamaged, in the shape of an almond, from which the Judge of Mankind, his dark eyes fixed on the new arrival, blessed him, or damned him, or merely interrogated him; above him the blue Atlantic sky, and instead of circling seagulls a single red kite, flying in spirals; on the debris-littered earth—not a single flagstone left—stalagmite-like dog and bat droppings; behind him, just beyond the granite threshold, still untouched, the spring from which the brook flowed, a miniature bay far from the open sea, also both spring and bay, simultaneously, at this very moment, because the tide, having reached its end here in the interior, before retreating was holding out with its last strength against the water streaming from the spring, backing it up in a strange rocking motion, and under overhanging hazels and willows, the sand glittered with mica, out of which the spring gushed, forming a sort of beach, with fragments of shells and crabs' legs that the tide had washed up, the chapel's threshold functioning as a boat landing, without any boat, but with the smell of the sea. "Between the Waters": wasn't that also the meaning of the name of the place from which the Moravian-night narrator came? And indeed he, the man of fire, had always been drawn to water, to flowing water.

And where did it begin, at long last, the story involving the woman?

Enough delays! And he would probably have dragged it out even more and missed the moment again if, during that night on the Morava, the woman herself, the stranger, had not unexpectedly emerged from the galley through the swinging door and come to his aid. It was she who began telling their story, and at first he seemed relieved, as if he had been at a loss as to how to get started. Soon he picked up the thread, however, something she was not entirely willing to let happen. She repeatedly took the words out of his mouth, not so much to correct him—though that, too, happened once, just one time, toward the end—as to participate in the events, to repeat them for herself and recapture them, or for god only knows what reason. But at no point did a dialogue result. No mention was made of an "I" or a "you," and even a "we" was a long time coming, first occurring in the description of their parting. Up to that point, if any personal pronouns were used, they were almost exclusively either "he" or "she," with the "she" usually coming from him, and the "he" from the stranger (a stranger to us listeners in the salon), and, as an exception, the impersonal or unpersonal "one."

One of the footpaths leading away from the spring, at the same time a seashore, led to a guest lodge, located in the middle of a grove. The variety of tree is irrelevant. Or maybe not: eucalyptus—that was how far north this species had meanwhile penetrated into Galicia, which at one time had had such a raw climate. This grove appeared full of light because of the pale eucalyptus bark, and also because between the trees were fairly large gaps, in which, if anything could take root, only sparse, low-growing grasses. And thus the lodge stood in what seemed to be a clearing, without such a thing's having been created on purpose. The ground floor served as a tavern, with an outdoor terrace, which, with its tables and chairs, occupied almost the entire grove. Bordering it was the thicket surrounding the spring, crisscrossed by footpaths, on one of which he stumbled into the eucalyptus brightness, blinded by it, shading his eyes with his hand, but without showing any surprise at finding a lodge so far from anywhere: that was how it had been dreamed, conceived, planned.

It took him a long time to discover it. For such a remote location, the tavern's terrace was full, almost to the last spot, all the way back to a eucalyptus growing just before the underbrush began; at the same time, there was no noise, only a muffled, steady buzz consisting of voices and footsteps, and woven into it the rattling of dishes, pinging of glassware, even the shouts of children and the braying of a donkey, hitched to a tree, a monotone derived perhaps also from the prevernal air. A state of exception, a different one this time, for a change. And she, the woman, was seated outdoors at the farthest table. Alone? That was the idea. And he, alone as well, without relatives looking over his shoulder—two orphans—two free agents! (That being the first, all-encompassing thought.) And she recognized the new arrival, the man, from a distance. But not actually him, the pan-European writer, or former writer? Nonsense: she recognized the man in that place, about which nothing more needed to be said. And to him she immediately looked familiar. Yes, hadn't she been the third invited observer, along with him and the poet Juan Lagunas, during the—now long-ago—symposium on noise in Numancia? If so, she had disguised herself for the conference. With the exception of the black horn-rimmed glasses, she had been shrouded during the entire event, with a scarf covering her entire head and forehead, and not only during the presentations but even at the farewell party, almost like a delegate from some Arabia, inaccessible, not exchanging a word with anyone, also so unobtrusive that people looked right past her. And now: her hair loose, blowing in the wind even though there was none—"or were those snakes?"—as his chronic suspicion of women interjected for an evil moment, but that question did not come from his conscious mind; her shoulders bare, the sun on her smooth, arched eyelids—about that, too, there was nothing more to say. But why had she been disguised earlier? What had she been spying on? Or on whom?

Actually these questions, born of suspicion, came to him only much later, during her second absence. Right now the only thing that counted was to go to her and without a word—without so much as a "Don't we know each other? Where in the world did we meet before?"—sit down at her table. And what then? Consistent with the principle he had tried to follow earlier, when he was writing a book or a long story: let things take their course. With bold steps, he—who otherwise in life so often fell into the grip, if not of social phobia at least of a fear of the unknown that caused him to hesitate unduly on the threshold of a new experience—strode toward her through the trees, worried that he might miss her and find the table abandoned when he got there: a different dream that had flashed through the middle of the one that made him approach so cockily and carelessly. And later, when his suspiciousness drove him to even worse deeds, a third dream joined the others: his guardian angel, which earlier had often saved him from collapsing and falling, now saved him from meeting the woman by making him collide on the way to her table with a tree, hitting his head and falling down flat, unable to get up.

What happened next between the two of them? Had anything at all happened—that was the question posed by the rest of us during that Moravian night, though only to ourselves, with even the brash member of our group holding his tongue. The two of them, our host and the woman, offered no hints. Either they had no words to describe it, or it was not a topic they cared to discuss, cared to include in the story. At most they gave us a hint. The only specific detail they provided about each other: that later, during the night, they both fell to the ground—from tiredness, from sheer exhaustion. And because both of them, while they were speaking, kept to themselves and did not look at each other, any allusions were out of the question. But something had happened with them in that eucalyptus grove, and that they did address, speaking in turn. For the two of them, a different time calculus came into play. And when did the different calculus set in? Where? In what connection?

The new time calculus went into effect the moment their eyes locked onto each other's, simultaneously. And this simultaneity gave them both the opening for what would follow. There was no way to avoid this new calculus, nor did they want to, although he, the man, initially displayed his inveterate avoidance reflex: the moment the woman had caught sight of him he was tempted to look behind him, as if she were looking at someone else, or to look away, as if nothing were happening, whereupon the calculus might have been blocked and nothing would have happened.

The different calculus meant a transition into a different system, a transition from one world into a second world, which, for their particular time, had every right to be called a world, a transition into a different history. And now, during the night on the boat, a memory image came to him, reminding him of the way he, upon seeing her lowered eyelids in the sun, before she finally looked at him, had been convinced that she was reading a book out there on the terrace, a book, as he concluded from her motionless eyelashes, that was the kind of book he had always dreamed of in the hands of an imagined reader—and also reminding him of the way the woman's hands had been empty, placed on her knees, the palms cupped and facing upward like those of the migrants on the enclave bus. And at the same time the instant of terror. Sweet terror? One that pierced him through and through.

And the different calculus brought with it a different light, and it was not a brighter light but a markedly darker one, a dimmer one, a sort of dark light, with night breaking out in the middle of the day, the sunlight extinguished by a total eclipse, along with the accompanying gust of icy wind. The iris shot in a film, blacking out everything around the two of them and finally leaving only their two faces visible in the circle, as at the end of a movie? It was neither a movie nor an ending. And if a woman's story, one that this time did not even begin with her expecting to be rescued by him, the man. What kind, then? The kind—thus his answer to his own question during that night on the Morava—that embodied a challenge; the kind that would confront him as one would confront a fugitive or a wild animal or a crook; that would summon him to battle. How could that be? That was how it had been conceived, and that was how he saw it. Or was it a question of a rescue after all? The woman, the stranger, did have an aura of suffering, no, of some terrible deprivation. And for a second time, even sweeter and more piercing, terror shot through him.

And what about her? How did she react, standing there in the swinging door, still apart from him, as he continued to turn only to us? She did what she had done when their eyes first met in the Galician eucalyptus grove: she laughed, her laughter expressing the kind of gaiety such as we normally experienced only in certain children, but unfortunately too briefly for us to be infected by it. But we sensed that it would not be her last laugh that night.

The one word she spoke to the man outside the guest lodge, as she pushed toward him the remaining free chair, seemingly reserved for him, turned up in his version of the story: "Finally!" she said. "Finally someone suitable." Or was she deluding herself? And what if she was. And she cupped her hand to her ear to catch his reply, as if it could come only from a great distance.

In the tale of their time together—where? wherever—the two of them and what they had said, done, or left undone no longer figured, a further contrast to that iris shot in a film, in which only the couple remains on the screen. As they took turns telling the story, they kept distance between them and looked only at us. But it happened more and more often that he took the words out of her mouth, and vice versa. Did that indicate that the unknown woman and the boatmaster were a couple? Whatever the case, during their time together momentous things must have occurred, and apparently almost every minute. Even in the hour after they met, raindrops suddenly fell from the cloudless, blue, prevernal sky, but only on them and their table, came pelting down on the two of them, then stopped, then sprayed down again, a shower, also a proper downpour, though both times in small drops, one after the other, until they simultaneously discovered (how else?) that high above their heads, in a hole in a limb where rainwater had collected, an invisible bird was taking a bath, splattering the surrounding air every time it shook its feathers. That same evening a child came to sit with them and then had to be torn away from them by its parents, one finger at a time, as from a toy that a child refuses to give up. In the night that followed, the donkey tethered to a tree hooted like an owl, and an owl responded with a donkey's hee-haw. The next morning, what was in the newspaper? Nothing, nothing at all. During the next day someone climbed a ladder made of blades of straw, and it held, and on the evening of that same day someone pressed a latch and the door opened. A few days later someone played "Death and the Maiden" on a jew's harp, and someone shook his head while weeping. And one night all the cats turned green, and then the following day—or had it been the previous day?—was declared International Green Day. One time a single elderberry blossom—you know how tiny that is, smaller than any button—a white, star-shaped one, floated through the air, all by itself, without an umbel, between the bush and the ground, simply hovered there in the air without moving, attached to a spun thread, you think? not at all! it was hanging by its own mucilage, its blossom mucilage, which—you should have seen it, visible only from very close up and only from a certain angle—connected it with its umbel up above, from which this single tiny blossom had become separated. How could that be, elderberry blossoms so early?—And didn't the two of them grow impatient from being alone together? They had been impatient before encountering each other, he as well as she, and how! But in a curious arithmetic their impatience gave way to patience.

During the time when the two of them were traveling together—traveling also while staying in place—trains and buses all over the continent plied their routes without accidents for a change, no new war broke out, none of their relatives died, and those who were ill felt better for a while. It could not be otherwise; this was how it had been conceived, this was what had been determined, this was how it had to happen and be within the realm of possibility, for this period, all too finite in any case. When they set out together—set out also while at rest—the cooks' white aprons became whiter than white, whiter than in any laundry detergent advertisement; the sun allowed itself to be looked at without any risk of blindness; the steppe bordered on the Olympic stadium, the Alpine peaks rubbed shoulders with a stand of date palms; the millionaire's estate, without walls or fences, nestled against a tent city for refugees, the monastery garden hugged the international airport, the zoo bordered on the Tibetan smile center, the golf course lay adjacent to the Badlands, the noise canal bumped up against the silence labyrinth, the mine shaft plunged next to the kite-flyers' cliff, there was no distance between Atlas and Lebanon, and it was only a hop, skip, and jump from St. Jakob in the Rosental to Santiago de Chile, and hardly a leap of thought from the earth to Venus, which one evening sparkled red like Mars. And then one fine day William Faulkner's feebleminded hero panted along behind his beloved cow. And then Madame Bovary dropped her handkerchief. And Josef K. stopped in confusion on his way to the railroad station. And there stood the man who watched trains pulling out. And Baur and Bindschädler were out walking in the evening light, which was reflected by the white cliffs of Dover. And on another fine day the cherry orchard bloomed. And then the bridge arched over the Drina, even if the river was not the Drina at all. And then one time a dog barked. And then two people kissed in their stead. And then, or before that? No, at the same time a bicycle slowly tipped over, while at the same time a ball rolled out of the bushes, a spring cloud became a summer cloud, an earring rang, a runner waved, a shoelace was tied, a clothes iron crackled, a newspaper sank to the bottom of the pond, a dance floor filled up, and nowhere, "no where," was Faust to be found in the Pentecostal procession, let alone a Mephistopheles, a Nero, a Medea, a Lady Macbeth or any other witch, and certainly no trace of the Ku Klux Klan, Genghis Khan, Karla vom Bruck, Gringo Busch, Papa Benedetto, Josip Fisherman, Magdalena Ganzhell, Bernhard-Hinrich Glückskraut, Ossim Weichsohn, and all the others; even A. Hüttler was as if he had never existed. God protected the lovers, and for their part the lovers, or the two captivated by each other—or simply captivated— protected: whom? Yes, whom?

Thus, in this different dimension of time, their first time passed, the time that also encompassed their parting, without, however, the time dimension's becoming inoperative, at least initially. Parting: that was supposed to occur. That they would go their separate ways for a while, as far as possible in opposite directions, that was obvious. During that period neither of them would be heard from or would send the other a sign of life. And then one morning it was clear that this would be the day for their temporary parting; no need to put it into words. To be out of each other's sight, to know nothing about each other, that was one of the rules of the game. Game? Yes, a great game. Strange, or perhaps not: as they were leaving, putting distance between them, for the first time the word "we" occurred, and likewise later during the Moravian night, as they were telling the story or providing an accounting. "We would never have let ourselves dream, back then"—(so those events had occurred so long ago?)—"when the parting that made us both so happy took place, that war could break out between us, a war so bloody that it matched any classic wars between couples." And at this point in their mutual story the first dissent occurred. It came from her, the stranger, and as she stood there in the swinging door, she also turned away from the rest of us in the salon for the first time and faced him. And that was at the place where she, as the first one to leave—they did not need external simultaneity—looked back at him one last time, and he allegedly thought that so much purity was too much for him, and he did not deserve her, this woman: "No," the woman now said, "that is not what you thought, not in the slightest, or if you did, only for a second, and you forgot it immediately in favor of your eternal belief that on the contrary, no woman, none at all, deserved you, was worthy of a man like you, and that helped bring about what happened next, you dud, you big fish in a little pond, you mama's boy." And she laughed as she said it, but this time he did not join in.

She retreated into the galley, where we saw her through the porthole seated in the light of a neon fixture above the sink, motionless yet ready to spring into action, as otherwise only Balkan cooks can be observed. In the meantime the boatmaster continued the story alone. Where in

Europe had the parting taken place? The city did not matter, now that all the cities on the continent had long since become interchangeable. The place from which he had set out, however, deserved to be mentioned: the tunnel on an abandoned stretch of railway that in earlier times had formed a beltway around the city. This location presented itself because the two of them had spent their last time together, still their "first," nearby. And on the other hand, it had been his decision to head out through this very tunnel to seek, hm, the adventure with which he would win her, the woman. And in their parting, in their separation, reality appeared, blossomed.

The shrill cry of falcons above the former railway cut with its rusted, partially dislodged rails: "It was a falcons' cryday." The cries outside accompanied him partway into the darkness. Similarly the low-angled rays of the sun, whether of morning or late afternoon, lit up the tunnel ahead for a short distance. Their yellow reflection off the concrete walls, off the rails, off the rotting wooden sleepers, off the sandy ground, had something inviting about it, making the tunnel, not only its entrance, appear inviting. Walking along was a pleasure, albeit a somewhat uncertain one. The tunnel occupied a longer segment of the former beltway than could have been anticipated. Ahead of him only blackness, no light from the end, not even a small bright dot. He had neither a flashlight nor matches on him. ("That was how it had been conceived.") Soon he found himself walking in a complete absence of sound, the din of the city having died away, leaving not so much as a faint roar, and inside the tunnel he heard not even the occasional drops of water from the ceiling landing in a puddle on the ground or the scuttling of rats, such as would have accompanied a corresponding scene in a film. Was the rest of the tunnel even passable? He had not inquired— that, too, as it had been conceived, just as it was out of the question to turn back to the stretch where at first, when he looked over his shoulder, he could see the sun shining through leaves stirring in a semicircle that moved farther and farther back, and where then, from a certain point in the underground curve that traced the periphery of the city above, the entry behind him appeared only as a dim shimmer of gray, very far back in the tunnel, and then no longer visible at all.

At least the tunnel's ceiling had, at intervals, something like air or light shafts, or what remained of them and had not been blocked by falling debris or whatever or completely covered aboveground by high-rise apartment buildings on the outskirts of the city. But even where a little light still penetrated, it must have come from far away, that was how weak it was. And no air to speak of. The ground with the rails seemed even more bottomless, if possible, in the few places where light entered from high above. A blackness seemed to rise in front of him from the ground such that one raised one's knees with every step as if one were walking on quicksand and had to expect that at any moment one would sink in, or even fall into a pit.

Still: light now and then? Yes, except that these extremely rare spots seemed dimmer each time—which reminded him, as he told the story, that the time of day at which he had set out to traverse the tunnel contributed to the effect, and how. It was the late-afternoon sun that had lit the way for him at the beginning, and in the meantime the sun must have been going down outside, up above. Soon night would be falling, and he would have to grope his way forward in total darkness. Along some stretches with blocked or covered-over light shafts he had already seen himself in such a situation, or rather not seen himself, and with arms outstretched had navigated through the pitch blackness, placing one foot right behind the other, expecting at any moment to be dealt a literal deathblow or devoured by the man-eating giant into which the darkness would coalesce.

Then night arrived: even from the light shafts—if there were still any open ones up there—came not another drop of light (he thought and said "drop"). "At least" he had his mobile telephone on him, and its keys lit up and let him see his own hand, or sense it. Obviously he had no reception down there. And that was all right by him, whether that is obvious or not. He no longer cared to find his way to safety, as had earlier been the case. And he most certainly did not want to be someone who had been rescued. Upon entering the tunnel and plunging into the first dark curve, he had still been on guard against human beings who might be squatting there, the homeless, fugitives, drug addicts, lying between the rails, leaning against the walls, cowering in niches, silent and ready to pounce, along with just such dogs or the devil knows what other creatures that might jump him out of the black-on-blackness. Then later, with the disappearance of the bit of light in the accursed tunnel that refused to end, he had longed for people, any people. And in the third phase he simply groped along, without thinking how far he might have to go or whether he had at least reached the midpoint, teetering onward, ever onward. Before he summoned us to the boat for the Moravian night, he had considered whether he could introduce into his story phosphorescence, for instance from the rotting railway sleepers, as something that had helped him keep going from time to time. But there was no phosphorescence that would have allowed the entire episode to appear less monotonous, so he had dropped that idea.

Instead he had: the sound of his own footsteps and the rhythm, determined by the invisible cross-ties themselves, even where they were dislodged or missing altogether. He began to count, and in the process of doing nothing but counting he moved ahead, now beyond any earlier hopes and fears. He counted and counted, and counted. And imperceptibly he began in the silence to describe, no, merged into telling the story of what he was experiencing just then in the present, but using the past tense. No, it was not he who merged into storytelling, but rather it. It told the story in him. It began to narrate inside him. And the storytelling was not addressed to some undefined listener, and certainly not to the rest of us—the desire to gather us around him did not arise until much later on his tour—but to her, the woman from whom he had just parted. To her alone the story was told silently, continuing after the darkness in the tunnel into the time that followed, from time to time, no, not merely from time to time but from step to step. And clear as daylight, and without need to invoke a fairy tale and fairy-tale powers: in this way he finally made his way into freedom, now no longer a traveler and not even a former writer anymore, and especially no boatmaster, only a simple creature. When he reached the end of the eight-mile tunnel, night had fallen long since. But having scrambled up the embankment, he found, right there on the edge of the city, a bakery that was still open, brightly lit amid the darkness of the outskirts, and without needing any prodding from us during that night on the Morava, he repeated what he had already told her, the stranger, in the bakery, simultaneously with becoming a customer—"the last customer of the day": he bought a small loaf of bread with olives baked into it, heavy ones, and also an almond roll with raisins, as well as a cruller with plum-jam filling, and consumed all of them outside on a bench by an arterial road leading out of the city.

5

~~~~~ ~~~~~

~~~~~ ~~~~~

~~~~~ ~~~~~

HE HAD NEVER known his father, and during the man's lifetime he had never felt the urge to make his acquaintance. Nor was it to see the grave that he set out now. His intention, rather, was to get to know the area where his progenitor had been born and died, and if possible also the areas adjacent to and beyond it. The plan had come to him a while back: if he was to undertake the tour he had in mind, this area would be one of his destinations. But after his time with the woman, this somewhat vague plan had become a powerful drive—an idea that pulsed within him. If earlier he had perhaps needed an excuse, once the two of them had been together that necessity vanished. He would go to his father's and forefathers' region just for himself, and for her, the woman, as indeed everything he experienced and took in during her absence was also for her. And what was the idea? What was he burning to experience? (In actual fact: he was burning.) To roam hither and yon and, especially, to snoop around. Yes, snooping around would be his principal activity there, and he felt certain there was something to ferret out in the paternal landscape, whether involving the deceased or someone or something else, though not a crime? One could never know.

He could not bring himself to utter his father's name, just as he concealed from the rest of us the name of the town. It was located in "Germany," in the southern foothills of the "Harz Mountains"—to pronounce those place names he had just enough of the energy that he lacked for saying the town's name, and also, unlike with the Dalmatian "Cordura" that came up earlier in the Moravian night, for inventing a place name. In the case of places in Germany—towns as well as villages—he lacked the capacity. But "Harz" and "Germany" he mentioned, even repeatedly, with a storyteller's gusto.

The only somewhat more precise indications of the topography: the landscape forming an arc around the town was karst, of the sort otherwise encountered primarily in our Balkans, with subterranean limestone and dripstone caves, fields covered with knife-sharp white scree. Dolines, visible as darker green hollows in the grasslands, and watercourses that suddenly disappeared into the ground. And the former border between West and East Germany was nearby; the town was located in the area where the two zones touched. One mile farther east in the *Mittelgebirge* his mother had escaped without being shot at, crossing the border, which at that spot ran through a hilly evergreen forest that provided cover. She had begun her escape just as the sky began to lighten on a morning in early summer, the huckleberry bushes wet with dew, the berries still small and green, here and there with a hint of blue, and the bottoms of the two cardboard suitcases the very young woman was dragging became soggy, that was how dense the dew was by the end of that night.

At that time he had not yet come into the world; he was conceived only later in the town in the Harz region, or wherever. But when his mother talked about her escape, he felt as if he had been present. He saw the dew-drenched cardboard suitcases with his own eyes, smelled the air, fragrant not of pine pitch but simply of the cold in the mountains before sunrise, felt the chill brush cheeks and temples, his own as well as the fleeing woman's, heard a plane's engines, not far off—the military?— heard a stifled cry—what was that?—and then another, ah, a pheasant, its rustling high up in the crowns of the pines creating the illusion that one was not merely safe and out of danger but already somewhere else entirely, beyond all sorts of borders, at home, near a village; and heard the heart pounding, no, "pumping," not only in his ear but in his entire head. Did his mother tell him this story? No, she did not take on the role of storyteller herself or attempt to become one; she simply let herself be heard, with the words welling up involuntarily; they had been gathering inside her for a long time, and now the moment had come, probably also because her son was a listener who could not get his fill, and not only of happenings and situations but also of pine-crown-rustling, rain-drumming, snowflake-crackling, cricket-chirping, swallow-screeching, train-thundering. And it was not only the young woman's border-crossing that remained intensely vivid to him but also everything she described to him from her life and also that of her ancestors, and with all kinds of details that she had not experienced herself.

He reached his father's town in early or late afternoon—in this case the time of day certainly had no relevance. Or did it? Hadn't he preferred, and described it this way during his writing period, to reach an unfamiliar place toward evening, when, as film terminology had it, the light was already breaking, or, better still, here and there in the dusk a lamp was already lit? Accordingly he got off the local train as dusk was falling, and, after inspecting the station, this one, too, located far from the town, a mere whistle stop, with the toilets bricked up and graffiti on the passenger shelter, headed north with his suitcase/backpack, made of fabric, not cardboard, toward the town, hidden in the hollows of the Harz foothills. And where was the dog from Porodin? There it was, running alongside him for a bit in the roadside ditch in the form of a pied wagtail that had a white bib, like the dog "back home," he thought involuntarily.

No one else was on the road. And if the region was karst, no sign could be seen of the characteristic jagged forms. It was an ordinary German and European landscape, possibly even more ordinary or undistinguished than your usual point of the compass. Yet he was filled with quiet enthusiasm as he walked toward the gloomy Harz Mountains and the still invisible town. For once he paid no attention to the cars, the standard makes, that passed him and for some unknown reason revved their engines and seemed to grind their gears. Enthusiasm: the effect was that everything seemed equally large. Or: nothing seemed large, nothing seemed small, and as he made his way toward the town, going overland, he engaged constantly in a process, without conscious thought, of taking in sights, sounds, and smells (including stenches, also the smell of decay, suddenly emitted by a dead stag in the ditch, its eyes wide open, mirroring the sky, still bright).

Then the impressions he absorbed, step after step, formed a silent monologue, not a conversation with himself but one directed toward the distant "person of reference," the woman (whose name we would really have liked him to share with us by now). Not that she accompanied him in her thoughts; she remained far away, and he reported to her from afar, transmitted to her his visual and auditory images telepathically, so to speak. Accordingly the sentences in his monologue usually began with "You know . . ." or "Picture this . . ." or "Let me tell you . . ." or "You can believe me . . ." So something like an imagined reportage? If so, not a live one, but, as already mentioned, in the past tense: "You know, on the access road to . . . there were potholes, not at all typical of Germany, but just like in the Balkans." "Imagine, the first person I encountered in the Harz was really old, pushing a walker with wheels, whether you believe me or not, and it was the same with the second person, and, much later, the third . . ." Not to forget the archaic use of "hear this" in the middle of the monologue: "On the road, hear this, there were potholes." "And I'm telling you, in the entire town, hear this, not a single evening church bell tolled."

Arrival during the second phase of dusk, the dark one, made even darker by the location of his paternal town in a bay formed by the Harz Forest, with the two sections of the town branching along hollows carved out by brooks, and the rows of rather squat houses extending like fingers into those spaces. Apparently the town was a health resort, complete with a "Spa Center," a "Casino," guesthouses clustered together; a scattering of mineral springs, thermal springs, mud baths, alternative therapies for god only knows what ailments. And if he encountered anyone in the gleam of the antique streetlights, in fact it was almost exclusively old and/or frail people who gazed right past him, seemingly focused on nothing but their troubles with their bodies and dragging themselves along. Likewise stricken with years were the dancers he could see through the floor-to-ceiling windows of the casino, against whose panes and walls were propped all sorts of appliances to aid mobility, not only crutches but also cross-country ski poles and wheelchairs— metal reflecting metal—surrounding the shadowy faces and bodies of the dancers, who, however, as they waltzed and played ring-around-the-rosy, radiated a carefree and almost a joyful air, at least for as long as they were dancing or being swung around by a partner. A health resort? His mother had not mentioned anything of the sort. Only that while she rested there briefly during her escape she had met his father. How? Not a word about that either, as indeed she had said not a word about herself and the stranger except that they had loved each other. Had he loved her? "What a question, you fool. Of course you're a love child." And then he did recall a word she had used in connection with his father: he, a good dancer, had "swooped" over the dance floor with her—that kind of outdoor platform must have been popular at the time in the town in the Harz—and the word she used seemed rather daring, given her own birth- and death-place with its somber Balkan mood.

He spent day after day in the central German town without—what was that formula used in old novels?—experiencing anything worth mentioning. (That was not entirely true, for, toward the end of his stay in the Harz, this much he revealed to us in advance, one small event or another did occur, but no, there was nothing external happening there; see the previous reference to large or small.) And nevertheless he was amazed, constantly amazed in this place where there was hardly anything to be amazed at, and until he resumed his journey, much later than planned, he did not cease to be amazed. He was amazed for the first time, and not only for the first time on this tour but for the first time since way back, "since time immemorial." Who would have thought that in Germany of all places, in a remote part of the country, where from beginning to end one was not entirely sure where one was—at least nothing reminded one of Europe or of any other continent—this particular, long-lost capacity for amazement would turn up, even if perhaps only for the time being?

But was this really Germany at all? And if so, was it the West? Was it the East? No, he realized as he roamed in ever-widening circles through this town in the Harz: it was neither/nor. It was a chronic border region, through which his mother had fled right after the war; perhaps it had been such a zone even before the war, had always been one, possibly as a result of the mountainous mass plopped down in the midst of the German provinces. If what Hugo von Hofmannsthal had described a century earlier, or had experienced as indescribable, still held true— that in Germany even objects, such as a washbasin, an apple, a floral bouquet, lacked reality, lacked thing-ness—then the region around his paternal town did not belong to that Germany. Did it have to do with the aura radiating from his mother's escape routes and ramblings, as he imagined them, or from his unknown progenitor, or in general from the not even legendary ancestors on his father's side? He, one, had no explanation, and no desire to find one.

Amazement and reading. For the first time on his journey he got around to reading, became capable of reading and had need of it. And as he read, the zonal area expanded after all into something that might be called "Germany," though only because, and while, he was reading the one book he had brought along on his tour. To be sure, he had opened it earlier at random but had been incapable of letting the sentences sink in, skipping them as he also skipped individual words, as if he could anticipate them like phrases in a newspaper, and that did not qualify as reading; it showed disrespect for the book, at least this particular one. He did not want to reveal the title to us. Only this much: it was not a volume of Heine's *Journey Through the Harz*, neither the one taking place in winter nor one from any other season. Amazement and reading and thus feeling that he was in Germany after all: double amazement. It was unlikely that he would have traveled through a more peaceful region than this, either previously or later. Yet in this area he encountered no one else who was reading. Either this fresh-air and mineral-bath resort had no bookstore, or, if it did—and that seemed more probable— he gave it a wide berth, as he had done with all bookstores for a long time now. And yet, in one of the many side streets of which the town largely consisted, he had come upon books, a large pile of them, amid the bulky waste put out on the sidewalk, and among them, no, right on top, was one book whose author was—guess who.

Reading and a Germany in which objects said to be inanimate filled one with amazement, as if they had been resurrected after a century in an antechamber to hell devoid of form and color. Objects, meaning, hear this, not the omnipresent crutches, wheelchairs, ambulances, and burial racks but rather the things that blossomed in the interstices still open and probably also opened up as a result of the reading, objects that blossomed without actually blossoming, billowing, arching, asserting themselves, surviving, which included the interstices as well. Such things, for instance, could be a wooden hunting blind in the forest no longer in use, or a portable typewriter in the bulky waste, bright red, or a napkin ring separated from the rest of its set, or a bench—or was it a seat from a movie theater?—deep in the underbrush, black and shiny after the rain. And in the surrounding area such things always turned up singly—strange, strange—just as he later noticed that animals and the residents of this zonal area also appeared singly. On one of the numerous sylvan ponds near the town floated a single, solitary leaf. In the one jukebox still in operation in the zone, in a tavern that looked more like a barracks that had once housed border guards and was located in a nearby village, a single record perched in the otherwise empty carousel—"Only You"? no, you wimp, "Love Me Tender." A single horse grinned in an apple orchard. A single window still showed a light after midnight. He saw just one person using a phone booth to make a call, just as any schoolchild on his way home was always by himself. He saw a solitary workman in one of the stone quarries on the karst, a single lumberjack in the spruce forest, a single policeman in his patrol car, one female clerk in the post office, one cashier in the surprisingly large supermarket, one old lady innkeeper and one young male innkeeper in one or another of the village taverns, along with their one patron, one man on a harvester, one female engineer repairing a waterline halfway up the mountainside, one individual, believe it or not, attending Mass in a church, in addition to the priest and the acolyte, a single surveyor on the arterial road, one ballplayer on the field, one chess-player in the senior center.

It goes without saying that time and again people also appeared in crowds, even en masse—though each time only after a fairly long uneventful period. But he did not really pay them any mind, consistent with the reputation he had acquired during his days as a writer, namely, that he tended to portray both things and people singly. And couples? No matter how he kept his eyes peeled for them in this border zone, he saw not one. Not even the magpies formed a couple, not the ducks with drakes, not the mourning doves with cocks. Even the hedgehogs, supposedly in their mating period, encountered him only singly, and when he came upon one, in the wooded area along the border, and heard from a distance its unmistakable courtship snorting and saw leaves and needles flying in all directions, it turned out that the animal was tangled in a rusted chain-link fence and was trying with its last strength to free itself—so at least once on this journey our host could play the rescuer? That was so. And yet there were some couples after all: the small, reddish-brown butterflies with dark spots that constantly circled each other in the air, so close that their wings occasionally brushed, and whose swoops made them appear like three, not merely two, which is also characteristic of butterfly pairs here in our Balkans.

He felt safe in that region where his mother had once met his father, or vice versa. He did not see himself as threatened, either by his reveries, from which it was difficult to find his way back to the everyday common sense of time, or by any Germans. At least as far as the people in that zonal region were concerned, the individuals, there was no German people, had never been one, nor, he thought, had there been one anywhere else, or at most as an impudent fiction. (However: could impudence possibly have a more harmful effect than in a fiction?)

He could have stayed longer in the Harz, continuing to narrate silently moment after moment to the distant woman. Safety also meant the following: for now he and time were in harmony. But precisely the sense of being in safety drew him away from there, if not immediately back to his Balkans then at least in that direction. The quivering second eluded him in Germany. The country or something else blocked it. Or kept it at bay? In this Germany he did not need his guardian angel.

He used the last few days in the southern foothills of the Harz to prepare himself for a struggle. Some such thing awaited him, of that he was certain; what remained uncertain was only the form it would take. This struggle would demand the utmost of him. And thus he trained in every way he could, undertook what had once been called forced marches, all night long, in the rain, which he welcomed. He became a cross-country runner, sprinted up and down mountainsides in the steepest places, swam in forest ponds that had obviously been frozen over only a short while earlier, scrambled across the jagged limestone cliffs of the local karst, cut a succession of hazel branches, sharpened each one to a point, and hurled them like lances across clearings. In the town itself he hired himself out to one solitary old person or another—everywhere posters proclaimed the "Senior Spring"—to push a wheelchair, also to haul coal and chop wood (yes, in this zonal region they still had woodstoves). And above all he read, and read, and read: this constituted his primary form of preparation for the struggle, breathing practice without a specific exercise.

Meanwhile his thoughts dwelled on the absent woman, and he conveyed to her, always in the past tense, what he experienced in the present. For instance, hear this, on a woodland path he suddenly came upon a solitary hiker, an elderly one, what else, poring over a map, but a map that showed not merely a different region but a different country in an altogether different part of the world. And in one of the abandoned quarries in the Harz's karst, hear this, he found a similar old man standing in front of an easel and painting in oils, but the picture, almost completed, represented not the quarry directly before him but a coastal landscape, with the ocean stretching all the way to the distant horizon.

Toward evening on his next-to-last day the town suddenly filled with young people, and then only they seemed to count, until late at night. They were very young, the majority of them still children, and they were hauling suitcases and backpacks, an endless, silent procession heading uphill. They had arrived on the last train from, let's say, Göttingen, and they were not setting out on a hike through the Harz but were rather returning, at the end of the holidays, to their boarding school, as he realized while following them. He had overlooked this institution previously, although it was almost the only larger structure in town, located along a hollow branching off another hollow in the foothills, remote not only from the town center and the grounds of the spa, but remote from everything. One after another lights went on in the building's hundreds of windows, several at a time on the lower floors, one at a time on the upper ones, where the windows were much smaller and correspondingly more numerous. In the courtyard in front of the building, school staff members sat at several tables in the near-darkness to check in the students, who formed long queues. Hardly a sound to be heard, let alone laughter, or had he, watching from a distance, decided it should be that way? He remained in position until the wee hours, watching. The silhouettes in the upper courses of windows did not always remain single but sometimes moved back and forth together, and it was not until late that, if any were still visible, they were by themselves, with hardly any movement to be seen. For a while the clatter of Ping-Pong balls could be heard, alternating with a flute, and very briefly a harmonica, and then only the tac-tac-tac, as even as a metronome—or was it actually one?—and later nothing at all, the windows dark without exception, the night wind around the long building carrying the smell of the communal evening meal, or was he merely imagining that? And when he finally decided to leave, as if he had seen enough, "as if one can ever have seen enough," a pupil appeared at his side, another near-child, with a bag slung across his chest and a bulging knapsack on his back, the one straggler, or one who had postponed his arrival to the very last minute. He paused in front of the almost entirely dark school building, which stood on a slight rise. No, he hesitated, and from his mouth burst a very soft but also very shrill exclamation: "Oh, no!" He had no eyes for the adult next to him. Not a moment later this same adult called attention to himself. And how? By taking hold of the boy's shoulders in such a way that he did not even jump, and after exclaiming "Come along!" led him away, where to and to whom he did not say, just away, away, away from there for good! But wasn't this clearly taking place only in the narrator's imagination? It was true, he informed our interrupter. Imagination? And what if it was? And why "only"? One quivering second had apparently manifested itself up there in Germany after all, in one way or another?

On the morning of the last day he would be spending in his father's hometown, he finally went to the cemetery. It lay on the edge of a forest beyond seven ridges belonging to the foothills of the Harz, and the spruces, which were very tall, seemed not to have been planted specifically for the cemetery but to have been left over from what had once been a spur of the forest. It was a repetition of the brimstone-butterfly day in southwestern Europe—this species had reached the interior of the continent. His father's grave and those of his forefathers were not easy to find, so he inquired in the nearby flower shop. The woman alone there behind the counter had an immediate explanation. Because the maintenance contract for the grave had expired and no one had taken the trouble to pay for further care, the grave had been emptied, though only recently; the spot was still free, and she showed him on a diagram the row and the (former) number of the grave, for which she had been the caretaker. A perfectly flat rectangle, not all that small, with grass growing up through the gravel and flanked on both sides by burial mounds: there it was, that was where it had been. All that remained was the empty rectangle with a stone coping. In the middle of the rectangle a blade of grass with a fluffy little feather clinging to it, still damp with dew. And the sand and gravel inside the rectangle matching those on the cemetery paths, though one shade lighter.

No name, no burial mound, nothing to remind one of the departed. He would not have known in any case whom to remember, had no picture of his father—at most one of his father's father that his mother had passed on to him; he had never once asked of his own accord about these German ancestors. And this picture? It showed his father's father, unknown to him and nameless, out sledding with his wife and children, somewhere on a hill in the southern Harz region, perhaps similar to the one where the rows of graves marched up a gentle incline, and his grandfather, still young, was pulling the sled with his son and daughter uphill, stopping suddenly and saying to his wife—the only German to whom the former writer gave a name during that night on the Morava— "Lina, I'm dying," and almost at that very moment falling into the snow. And what was strange: he now repeatedly found himself talking spontaneously with his deceased mother, whereas with his vanished father it was not possible to speak, although he felt the urge to do so.

He squatted down beside the empty enclosed rectangle, and it was astonishing, or perhaps not really, how he felt the presence of his grandfather, or, as he involuntarily thought, "ancestor," in all likelihood dead for almost a century, but not that of his father, to whom he partially owed his life after all, did not feel it even here before the clear, bare geometric void, which otherwise could embody one absent and vanished person or another as little else could. He should have asked his mother after all. Now he had questions upon questions, and he had missed getting them answered, which caused a wave of bitter guilt to seize hold of him, and an anger with himself, accompanied by the thought, "Ah, my damned fatherlessness! Without a father: an outcast."

As if it had read his thoughts, at that very moment the awaited yellow butterfly floated down out of the blue sky above the cemetery, the brimstone butterfly of the Harz, as if just born of the air. One of us on the nocturnal boat, allegedly an expert on Japan and on Noh theater, predicted at this point in the story that as it fluttered closer it would assume human form, just as on the Noh stage, and exclaimed, when the boatmaster in fact described this very thing, "Exactly! Just as I said!" in a booming voice. Before the metamorphosis occurred, however, the butterfly fluttered up and down for a long time as the embodiment of the middle ground, though weightless. Forming a similar middle ground were the white sheets flapping on a clothesline in a garden that bordered on the cemetery and likewise, as a sound, the whistle of a train far below on the plain that stretched out from the Harz range.

The butterfly, more yellow than ever against the brown background of the spruce trunks, worked its way from its seismographic dance to a straight line heading directly for him, and by the gravel rectangle transformed itself—"Exactly!"—into an old hag. She was ancient and heavy, and at last not a visitor to the spa but an indigenous inhabitant of the Harz region, with a walking stick, a hazel branch—what else?—which she brandished in the air instead of using it to lean on. And she promptly began to speak, roughly following the rhythm of her blows on the air, a confused babble: "Ah, yes, you damned man without a father! You think you're invincible because you never had a father. You keep all eyes fixed on yourself, for better or worse. Make allowances for yourself, as a man without a father, that no one should make for himself. Think no rules apply to you, and if any do, then only very special ones. Rid of your father: the freest of the free? No, no, my dear fellow: no-father's-child will never become an adult, will never ever, not through any number of forced marches, pinnacle conquests, desert crossings, become a complete man, at most an eccentric. You're not above the law, you who thought you never needed a father; you're an outlaw. You've been banished, banished not only from your father's town but from all towns; you have no home. You put on princely airs, you fatherless man, with open space around you, but if you were a prince, then only the Prince of No Land, a prince without a country. You, fatherless one, were bound and determined to hurl yourself as a knight into the fight for an ideal, and when the moment came, you betrayed the ideal, failed to take responsibility, just as you betrayed your father from the very beginning, claiming to have no responsibility for him. As a lover, you dreamed up . . . You saw yourself as unique . . . You presented yourself as the one who . . . even in private, even when no one was there . . . Away with you, you fatherless fellow. You have no business being in your father's town, not even here by the empty grave. You'll never belong to the human race. If seven—or was it nine?—towns all claimed to be Homer's birthplace, in your case nine times seven will deny that you come from them. You'll die as an enemy of mankind. You'll perish at the hand of a woman, an unloved woman, a hater of men. Too late will you call out for your father, asking why he abandoned you, when it was you who . . . Oh, dear, if only it were that simple. Maybe you can't help it? Maybe you did search for your father at one time, here and there, with this person and that, but couldn't find him, not to this day? And are still searching for him? Is that right? Or not? Away with you, my good fellow. You have no business being here. *Srećan put.* Safe travels."

6

IF ON THE previous leg of his tour the former writer had given himself time in not merely princely but positively regal fashion, as he now set out for the country of his birth he suddenly felt in a hurry. He was drawn less to Austria than to what lay beyond, his home, yes, his home in the Balkans, to that boat on the Morava. He felt? thought? no, knew he was bound to the river and to the town of Porodin, knew he had an obligation to the place, even if almost no one there gave a damn about him, let alone needed him. With Austria, however, nothing in his thoughts linked him now, and that had been the case for so long that occasionally it struck him as almost sinister. His brother, to whom he felt somewhat close without their being in contact, and likewise Gregor Keuschnig, who had recently fled home from the no-man's-bay, and Filip Kobal: these two did not constitute Austria for him, any more than did a couple of other acquaintances in that country. His native land—to which he had once been attached, which then, in a transitional period, had become his enemy, and to which he had once more become attached, and ready to defend it like a true patriot, if it happened to be attacked again, tooth and nail, from the outside, though in a way different from past attacks—this homeland had slipped out of his consciousness, for better or worse, and he did not feel altogether good about that. Not even in his dreams did his native land turn up.

On the other hand, when he thought back to the period, mercifully short, when as a young writer he had been assigned the role of representing his country and had accordingly sometimes acted in that capacity, even today he was flooded with embarrassment, and at least it had given him a sense of freedom when he had subsequently ceased once and for all to be the spokesman for anyone or anything. Oh, not to be a public figure, not even of the sort he had sometimes been in those earlier days, more in jest than in earnest, and certainly not as a "national author." He had escaped from all that not only by moving to the Balkans, a region under a cloud, and not only by renouncing any form of publishing. He still thought he had incurred guilt by playing along, if only halfheartedly, with the idea of being a national writer—lasting guilt. And why had he played along? Perhaps because at the time he had actually believed for a short while in something like another kind of nation, in fundamentally different nations, and had thought he could help to embody them. Fool. Village idiot. Housepost. ("Let me explain, for you houseposts," the boatmaster interrupted his nocturnal narrative, "housepost is the Austrian expression for the feebleminded or hopelessly retarded person on a farm, someone who in every sense will never get beyond the house and barnyard but simply remain just that, a housepost.")

Recently, however, dreams about his native land had returned. Every night a birthplace dream, lasting all night long, with an epic breadth new for such dreams (if also with less content). He explained this phenomenon to himself, and later to us, his audience in the boat's salon, thus: during the time he and the woman, the stranger, had been together, he had talked to her constantly about his childhood village and his ancestors, without being asked, as if this sharing, including the fact of his not being asked, were a necessary component of his enthusiasm about her and him, about the two of them. Even in her absence he continued telling her, silently, about the escarpment behind his house where on Easter eve the ring of fire, visible across the entire valley, formed by oil-fueled torches—or was the oil burning in tin cans?—glowed, and where Jesus's resurrection was celebrated with fireworks, in the course of which an operator had once had his arm blown off, and he also described the bend in the brook where one summer he saw, could not help seeing, his mother naked for the first and last time—the last time, Mother!—as she bathed there with several others, and he described the barn out in the fields, from which he heard, as he passed it one day, the voices of a man and a woman ring out, no, sing out—and those voices were so calm, so melodic in their alternating singing, with equally calm and melodic pauses in between, the voices of two people invisible behind the weathered gray planks, a dialogue that he could not make out, but more tender and intimate than he had ever heard anywhere, and not to be jolted out of this particular calmness by any incident; he went on and on, describing how things were back home, by preference talking about nothing of moment, nothing at all.

But why was he looking to explain the reappearance of his village in dreams, he of all people, who normally shied away from any kind of explanation and responded to anyone who began offering explanations with a blank if not withering gaze? Since when did he need explanations? Since he had stopped writing? Since he no longer wrote sentences, one after the other, linked by "because," "as a result of," and "due to"? Ah, wasn't this precisely an attempt on our part to come up with an explanation? Since when did we, his listeners, his friends (more or less), need explanations? Since we had ceased to be his readers? Ah, isn't that precisely . . . Enough about explanations, now and forever, amen.

Furthermore, his recent dreams were terrifying. The terror, or rather the horror, came not from the fact that his birth village no longer existed, which was quite natural, so to speak, but rather from the people there, the ancestors, who, actually dead long since, in his dreams were initially still alive, but soon fell into their death struggle, as ferocious as it was monotonous, and in the end, still dying ferociously and not wanting to die, departed from the scene of the action, leaving from then on only the former site of the village in a void as gloomy as it was poignant, nothing but the geologic formations there, or—how did one put it?—the topography, the hilltops, the gulches, the bends and three-way intersections of former roads, without the roads themselves, the circle of the tree stump in the middle of the village, without the tree, and above it the dome of the sky, without the sky.

Now our interrupter wanted to know whether this explained why the traveler had been in such a hurry to get through his country of origin—of course he was asking only in jest. For wasn't it clear that these dreams pertained only to the village and its surrounding area and in no way to all of Austria—that had never been the subject of earlier dreams either? And besides, during his passage through the country he was soon not in such a hurry after all, as would become clear in the course of events.

Heading southeast from Germany, he traveled by plane, an exception on his tour, and however quickly it took off, it flew much too slowly for him. With every glance out the window it seemed as if the aircraft had hardly moved. It was a clear day, and the flight passed over the Alps, covered with snow, as white as snow can be, all the way down into the valleys. Each of the valleys, dark, narrow gashes, had more the character of an inhospitable trench, an uninhabitable ravine, a cold spot. And this desert of blinding snow below, without a single sign of life, stretched on endlessly. The pilot came on the loudspeaker to recommend looking down at the Sea of Stone, and an eternity later the Death Range. The two sights hardly differed, however. The plane merely pretended to be moving. In reality it had not "budged from the spot," the expression he involuntarily used during that night on the Morava. Never would it land, and he would have to remain forever staring out the window, stuck at ten thousand meters, at the unchanging, glittering white mountains, which, whether the Sea of Stone or—six of one, half a dozen of the other—the Death Range, provided no variations in contour. The cloud cover in between was welcome—then furrowed by the tailfin of another airplane, otherwise invisible, like that of a shark.

And the greater his hurry to get away from there, not merely away from the mountains but to a different country, the more time seemed to drag. The plane was supposedly zipping along at a speed close to the sound barrier, and at the same time he experienced a kind of impatience that he took for the symptom of an illness, a particularly malignant one, which he dubbed "time-sickness." He wondered whether this sickness belonged to him alone, as something unique, his being the only case. At any rate, being time-sick expressed itself—if one was in a rush—in physical terms by squeezing the air out of one's lungs, air that in any case was hardly breatheable in a plane jetting along, and by exacerbating ordinary everyday afflictions such as a rapid pulse, a scratchy throat, fatigue, or also merely chilled or burning feet; and as for the soul, this time-sickness that broke out as a result of excessive hurrying suggested that one's destination was not only not closer but was rather receding farther and farther, from heartbeat to heartbeat, and above all, that it was not a destination worthy of the name, and that the people and landscapes awaiting one there, even the most beloved ones, were alien in the sense that they meant nothing—that the destination itself in that sense was alien territory.

When the plane, after an evil eternity, landed after all, he welcomed being shaken by the bumpy concrete runway and would have been glad to be shaken even more roughly. Nothing against haste—it could be pleasurable at times and mobilize one's vital spirits, especially if one could concentrate intently on the haste itself, have eyes and ears for nothing else. But rushing, being in a rush, should be avoided wherever possible. For the rest of the tour he had to see to it that he would never again stumble into the kind of excessive haste that came from within and inflicted an acute sense of having too little time. He reached that decision as he stood motionless for a long time outside Schwechat Airport, off to one side, as a woman's voice repeated over and over on the public address system, "Attention: this is a tow-away zone!" Earlier, as the plane approached his Austria, flying in a wide loop over Lake Neusiedl, close to the Hungarian border, before heading west again, he had already decided to rescind the cuts he had been planning to make in his itinerary; while approaching solid ground and experiencing the plane's deceleration, one returned to time, settled back into it in a presumably innate system, all within the space of a single second that restored one's soul to health. And that meant that the earth below could be seen, and soon also felt, without one's needing a bird's-eye view: looking down, one caught sight of the reeds forming a belt around Lake Neusiedl at the same time as one felt them tickling one's cheeks as they had long ago, and as one gazed down at the expanse of fallow fields bordering the runway, one recognized the former cart tracks, long since plowed under or leveled, and the filled-in brooks as darker strips, welts, hairpin turns, and meanders inscribed on the smooth, pale surface, went walking along one of those tracks or along one of the brooks, holding an ancestor's hand, barefoot on a summer day before dawn, ankle-deep in the dust of the path, which shimmered in the dim first light and was still cool from the night, with scattered raindrops falling, large ones— the size of a schilling!—that dug schilling-sized craters in the dusty sand, one crater after another, and connected the cart track, the two people walking on it, and the summery predawn landscape for another eternity, with the moon above, whether visible at that time or not. No, abbreviating the itinerary "homeward" to the Balkans was out of the question. Being on the road, the expedition, had to continue in the rhythm that had guided it up to that moment. No leveling, no infilling, no beeline, no speed-up, no time-lapse effects. The round- and zigzag trip had to continue as it had begun, as a long-drawn-out tale.

It was already long, and as he arrived in Austria it was a day shortly before the onset of spring, like the day on which he had set out from the enclave on the Morava: last patches of snow here as there, gray grass, with single fresh shoots, few and far between. It was still the middle of the day, and the sun was shining, the sun of having time. To enjoy the sun he decided to set out on foot from the airport, heading into the countryside, without a predetermined destination, letting himself be led by the roads, the paths, the shortcuts, the horizons—and of course the sun of having time—all the way to Vienna, for all he cared, though not into the heart of the city, the inner districts.

Not that he had any specific objection to them. It was involuntary resistance. In the past he had been in his capital city often, very often, and each time it had presented itself to him as a labyrinth, unlike any of the other great metropolises. And the center had been where he completely lost his way. If occasionally he thought he finally knew his way around, at the very next narrow side street, or after taking the covered passageway from one palace to the next, he would have no clue which way to turn. That was during the period when passersby still recognized him as the person who . . . and when he asked someone for directions, the person would be surprised that he of all people, in the other person's eyes a public figure, a representative of the country—for that was how a writer was viewed in those days by not a few—could get lost there, in the very heart of the country. And it seemed inevitable that in the inner districts of Vienna he would lose his bearings from one moment to the next. Even if it was his hundredth time in a certain location, even if he had a map in his hand, he would strike out in the wrong direction and eventually be unable to find his way out of the labyrinth, or at least not without someone's help. And in the government district he invariably mixed up the ministries and the buildings in general and introduced himself to the concierge of a theater who he thought was the concierge of the Hofburg; tried to enter the Hofburg, or whatever it was called, through a delivery entrance, and finally fled from the kaisers' crypt, which he had never intended to visit, to an ordinary sausage stand, where he breathed a sigh of relief.

So all that was left of the once great empire was the labyrinth in its center? No, with the newly realigned Europe—was that the right term?—some of the old grandeur seemed to have returned, at least for certain of its citizens, especially the younger ones. Gone was the imperial mentality, if it had ever existed (he as a villager had hardly come in contact with such a thing), replaced by an openness to the world of the sort that he as a young person, having left the cherished village behind, had found sorely lacking in most adults. Although nothing about the borders had changed, the country no longer appeared so small. Strange, or not really all that strange, that the empire seemed to have returned, if only in certain hints and trace elements, presenting itself not boastfully in its—somewhat ethereal—representatives, but, on the contrary, quite modestly. No actual features of an empire could be seen. And the country would never again degenerate into an empire. Or maybe not? How about the unspoken aspirations of some older folk? Be that as it might: the younger folk from this country whom he saw as reviving some aspects of the former empire appeared to have no unspoken aspirations, to be immune to anything imperial. The reinvigorated trace elements of the old empire would remain just that, or was he mistaken? "Or I'll eat my hat."

And how did he know all this? He knew it first of all from the flight, during which the natives among the passengers had behaved in a manner fundamentally different from that of, let's say, two decades earlier. Even when one of them spoke dialect, it was just a coloration. Their eyes no longer "gawked," but simply "looked" or "gazed." And above all it was their voices, if any at all were raised—but was he hearing properly?— that projected matter-of-factness, together with a calm, sovereign confidence previously unfamiliar to him among his own people ("which would take us back to the empire after all," he said during the night on the river). And he also knew it from all his time in our Balkan enclave, where his younger fellow countrymen stood with the encircled residents of the enclave, unostentatiously, quietly, attentively, egalitarian in spirit, eager to learn. These young and not so young people—even if some of them slipped back into the old familiar braggadocio—reminded him of a Europe, a unitary one such as had probably never existed except in propaganda (and never would?), and which he called "the third Europe," without being able to tell us anything more specific about it that night—it remained as hard to pin down as the memory itself. "But," he said, "all hail to this memory!" Did he simply want to see everything—the airplane, the enclave—in this light? "No, this memory meant: I saw it that way. I see it that way." And if—and if he wanted to see it that way? Wasn't this how he had also written his books? "Never heard of Utopia?"

It turned out, you know, easier than he had thought to get away from the Vienna airport on foot and reach the open, more open countryside. For a while he continued walking along the shoulder of the access and exit road, being honked at now and then by one of the cars in the bumper-to-bumper traffic. In most of the vehicles, the occupants did not even notice him. A child had once urged him to look closely at people in cars, saying it was "so interesting to peer in." He had tried it many times as he walked on the shoulder of highways and byways all across Europe—one of his specialties—but his head always began to spin and it left him disoriented.

On this particular day he finally succeeded. It happened because he paid no attention to the faces, which in any case could hardly be decoded, and concentrated on the hands on the steering wheels. How differently each of the drivers held the wheel, or did not hold it. The classic model, with one hand on the right and one on the left side of the wheel, marking its diameter, so to speak, was more the exception than the rule. It was more common to see both hands resting at only a slight distance from one another close to the peak or divide of the wheel's circumference. If the first-mentioned placement of the hands suggested an image posed for a movie close-up being filmed in a studio, with the driving merely simulated, as became most pronounced when the driver kept turning the wheel slightly back and forth without having to negotiate a curve, the second placement suggested a film being shot on location, as did all the other hands glimpsed on steering wheels.

What all the hand positions had in common was that despite the distance from which he was viewing them in the steady stream of heavy traffic heading toward the airport, each and every one appeared as a close-up. The most frequent hand position, as he recognized after a while, was probably the one in which both hands rested close together near the bottom of the wheel, and the champion was the woman who grasped the wheel at the bottom from behind, in such a way that her fingers, except of course for her thumbs (how else?) pointed toward her, while the second-place winner was the woman whose two hands held the wheel at its lowest point from above, so to speak, which looked like fists clenched around the wheel, with the knuckles—in a close-up within the close-up—appearing most prominently, paler than the rest of the hands. Not infrequently he also saw a single hand on the wheel, sometimes a right hand, sometimes a left, preferably when the wheel had a spoke to hold on to. This one-handed steering occurred more often with men than with women, and then exclusively young ones. Only once did he see an old man driving along casually with one hand, and when he looked closer, the man turned out to have only one arm.

The drivers more advanced in age either kept both hands in the classic position at the wheel's midpoint or, and these constituted a slight majority (he counted them), higher up on the wheel, and almost one hundred percent of them held their arms out straight, with the seat pushed back, looking as if they had sunk into it in such a way that only their arms and hands were visible, seemingly stretching toward the distant wheel from somewhere underground or from a different horizon. Some truck drivers also did out-of-the-ordinary things with their hands, sitting either with their torsos leaning toward the wheel, no matter where their hand, fist, or just the fingertips rested, or with their elbows braced against the wheel. No matter what their position, most of the drivers were alone in their vehicles—except for one time when the car was "packed" with passengers, "as in our Balkans."

As he strode along the shoulder, away from the international airport and into the countryside, a film unreeled rapidly before him, which, hear this, almost appeared to be in slow motion. This film did not tell a story. It amounted to nothing, yet as he deciphered one image after another and placed the images in relation to one another, he felt himself to be temporarily, yes, temporarily, a researcher. It was as if simply from observing he were discovering a secret writing that was revealing itself to him, or a tiny fragment of one. And what did this writing signify? Nothing, nothing at all. But researching, studying, learning, even if it was only imagined: it soothed him (again our story-teller invoked Flaubert for us), and initially, even without soothing, it had a cushioning effect, cushioned the roar there on the highway, made walking along pleasurable, in short, made him fleet of foot. Someone in one of the cars finally noticed him as he walked along the shoulder in the opposite direction, and, instead of honking at him or honking him out of the way, waved to him out there, raising his hand from the steering wheel, raising both hands. Did he envy him for walking along the road, just as he, the one now walking, had at one time, very long ago, envied a pedestrian while he himself had to drive? No. Not yet. But once again he, the walker, resolved that since he was already walk-ing, he would walk in such a way that someday he, too, would awaken envy, if only in one person, preferably a young fellow such as he had been. Envy? Longing. *Čežnja.*

It was afternoon when he turned off the highway heading toward the city to take a road that he imagined led north through the mead-ows to the Danube, the Danube in the area where it has left Vienna behind and flows freely through what is already the Pannonian plain. He was familiar with that flat countryside from way back. Whenever he had been in the capital, he had felt drawn to the region, and accord-ingly had stopped by to see Joseph Haydn's birthplace, had undertaken a pilgrimage from Petronell across the fields to the Pagans' Gate in the late Roman town of Carnuntum, and had nonetheless cast to the un-ceasing wind the admonitions about the beggar's mentality formulated by the writer and emperor Marcus Aurelius, who had held the fort there in the wilderness; intrigued by its name, he had "checked out" Fischa-mend, where the small Fischa River flows into the Danube . . . He knew some things about the area, extending beyond Maria Ellend, Hainburg, and Mannswörth. But on the day he arrived in his country of origin he wanted to know none of that and to avoid anything he had yet to learn. He decided, as he took a shortcut through an uninhabited region of grasses, already more like the steppe, to turn a deaf ear to any knowledge, especially knowledge of names. Feeling crowded by names such as "Vienna," "Austria," even "Danube," he thought this approach would give him some flexibility.

A hefty gust of wind from the east buffeted his side. Where was the dog from Porodin? For a moment the dog crossed his path in the form of a raven, large enough for two and almost silent, accompanied by nothing but a rushing sound from far away in the east, and whisking by so close to the ground that it looked as though it were running at greyhound speed through the faded grass, a deep black gleaming pelt storming through the fronds. The many hollows in the meadows along the Danube had to be avoided. These were branches cut off from the main river, dried-up streambeds or ponds, which did have life in them after all; how else to explain the omnipresent fishermen on their banks? Often, as he forced his way through a dense old-growth forest, he would find himself in what looked like a New England vacation spot, where, however, not a few of the white wooden cottages appeared to be inhabited year-round, with smoke billowing in a westerly direction from the chimneys, laundry fluttering on clotheslines strung under porch roofs, next to rocking chairs, clothing enough for entire families, even several generations, mixed in with dishrags and bedside mats, or whatever. Here and there gardens carved out of the overgrown floodplain were being raked in preparation for spring, with some of the rakes sounding as if they were striking ground that was still frozen solid. Some of the gardens were being not merely tilled but also expanded: the clearing continued. Trees were being felled, whether legally or not, less often with chainsaws than with axes, which was also more practical with such scrawny saplings. The roots—most of which spread horizontally— were dug out with shovels, picks, and mattocks (old terms came back to him) and heaped up for what he pictured as an Easter bonfire—the dried fungi on the trunks would serve as tinder. And every time, from garden colony to colony, all of which soon had nothing weekendish about them, hear this, he would encounter two or three people sawing up trees, splitting firewood—as if winter, Nordic-style, lay just around the corner—whitewashing the houses, or digging trenches for water lines, probably the most strenuous of these labors. Whole swaths were being cleared through the underbrush, and the gardens, unfenced here, were visibly making inroads into the wooded areas. No flowers or even decorative shrubs would be planted there. That meant these were not ornamental gardens but arable land. The inhabitants of the settlements, starting with what had been weekend cottages (in the Balkans we called them *vikendice*), were engaged in wresting land from the over-grown floodplain. But what did it mean that boats, not simple fishing skiffs but proper houseboats, were up on blocks in many of the yards, and like the houses they were being scraped, sanded, and painted, though not white? Were they intended for the next hundred-year flood, now to be feared every decade, or every five years? Heavy though the settlers' heads might be from all their labors, when he greeted them as he passed by—and he felt compelled to greet them, an urgency that had overcome him since he entered the country—they looked up, hear this, including those wearing earbuds as they worked, and returned his greeting as if it were the most natural thing in the world. Likewise they struck up conversations with him about the wind and the weather, about the right times to sow and plant, without showing any surprise at seeing him out walking by himself (a rarity) with a suitcase that he car-ried as a pack, wending his way among their clearings. It happened more than once that he was invited to pitch in, for pay, of course, and when he could do so in passing, so to speak, he helped out with moving a sofa, pushing a truck that had got stuck, and one time he did accept payment, though only in the smallest of small change. On these occa-sions it occurred to him that he had expected these people to speak a different language, not German, and if German, then a strange, unfamil-iar, perhaps archaic form, a kind of Volga, Amazon, Mississippi, Yukon, or, why not, Congo German. But all of them spoke Austrian, even Viennese, dialect, you know, whether it was the variant from Erdberg, Kaiserebersdorf, Simmering, Siebenhirten, Hietzing? no, not from there, from Liesing? no, not that either, from Hütteldorf? no, from Ottakring? no, from Grinzing? from Döbling? no, from the inner district? oh, no, heaven forbid, from Lower St. Veit, yes, from Upper St. Veit. Nonetheless he could guess that among them were some of the émigrés from the enclave of Porodin who had started out on the bus with him: they had put down roots here in the floodplain and in no time had picked up the local language, at least superficially, not that difficult with this dialect. Among all the new and resettled inhabitants, it felt odd to encounter weekenders, as one thought one knew them or who fit the stereotype to a T: they were mowing their lawns even when there was not one blade out of place, grilling fish they had caught themselves, finger- or palm-sized, and when one of them was sitting indoors, his presence revealed itself in the billowing of a lace or not lace curtain, in a voice booming from a radio, and when such a person could be glimpsed through a window, one saw only two hands—again, only hands—holding up in one way or another a small newspaper, seemingly meant for dwarves. And likewise this person could be felt by virtue of his absence, as a silhouette in the gray east-wind air, guessed at from a flowered or not flowered enamel coffeepot on a windowsill, a porcelain or ceramic cat on a roof, also an ibex of the same material on a ridgepole, from a mousetrap left on a porch railing, from an oversize thermometer on the side of a house, its mercury column missing, and especially from a crawl space under the porch, from the junk accumulated there, including a weather-beaten broken paintbrush in the dust, its bristles stiff with dried residue, a chopping block without an ax, its surface scarred and worn as only a chopping block's can be, the cover from a shoe-cream tin with the little lever that pings, and, weighted down, seemingly unintentionally, with a rock, a page ripped from a book, darkly yellowed but with some sentences still legible, if one went down on one's knees: ". . . thyme and poppy. / Ah, from them the heart receives / a distant intimation . . ."

Out of the floodplain forests, and after another stretch of steppe, a broad one, where the east wind blew even more fiercely, sometimes blowing a leg out from under one as one walked and one sometimes had to stand still, legs braced to steady oneself: the Danube, or as we call it in the Balkans, the Dunav, a masculine noun, whereas the German name is feminine. Here, just east of Vienna, it appeared to him as a mighty stream, whereas he had previously seen it in this area at most as "a fairly wide river." The river's altered character could probably also be attributed to its flowing here through open countryside, with flat steppe on either side. True, here and there huts perched on the bank. But these resembled hunting blinds or guardhouses, with a single room high above the ground, to be reached by means of a ladderlike exterior staircase or sometimes only by a ladder. Fish traps hung outside, and the huts themselves looked like fish traps, larger ones. The stream was as deserted as its banks, except for a single freight barge as long as a train, which one imagined as being on its way to the Black Sea; the next evening it would already be passing the mouth of the Morava.

But no more jumping ahead! One step at a time! Now, despite his reservations, he headed west, toward that capital he had never been able to view as his own. Moving against the current, upstream, had a bracing effect; so he had observed. Besides, if he had to proceed alone, it did him good to do so in the vicinity of a metropolis, holding a steady course toward it, and then, time and again, fixing his eye on its skyline, skirting around it, avoiding actually entering it. One of his earlier resolutions: to circle all of Europe's metropolises on foot, wherever possible, for days at a time, for weeks, for a month—and a couple of times he had come close to pulling that off, around Paris, Madrid, Rome, or even just Dresden ("just"?). If he felt drawn to people at all, it was to people in multitudes, where they gathered in large numbers, anonymously, which meant he was drawn less to villages and towns, but usually it satisfied his need to sense that those were not far.

It also made him feel good, quirky walker that he was, to have the wind not at his back but blowing toward him, in his face. And thus he now wished that the wind would shift from east to west. And his wish was fulfilled, except that the west wind brought rain. He could have taken shelter under one of the cottages on stilts located on the towpath atop the dike, but he let himself be rained on as if that were fitting for the day of his arrival. And what if the things in his pack got wet, especially the book lying on top? Let them. Let it. For him the adventure of reading had always been enhanced, you know, if the book had suffered some external damage—was singed, mildewed, had pages stuck together, had a pungent, perhaps mushroomy, odor. When he had new books waiting to be read, he would sometimes leave them outside on purpose until they started to yellow from exposure to the air, the paper became wavy from the dew, or, why not, from light rain showers, and then, before he began to read, would bend the book till the covers almost sheared off, strike it against a wall, play football with it, hurl it at the ceiling, and in the middle of the most enjoyable reading, if it was snowing outside or, even better, hailing, it could happen that he went out and let the pages he was reading be covered by drifting snow or properly pounded by hailstones, after which the reading became more enjoyable by several degrees.

It was a bumblebee-dying day, characteristic of the season between winter and spring when the weather turns so warm toward noon that the bumblebees come thundering in from somewhere or other, perhaps searching for even greater warmth, staying close to the ground rather than up in the air, down in the grass, through which their heavy yellow and black bodies wend their way, not at all numerous and each one by itself, but with its sonorous buzzing creating the impression of several, or a whole swarm of, bumblebees—do bumblebees actually swarm? Then, however, when toward evening the late-winter chill returns, the buzzing and the sonority fall silent, or instead, here and there, even deeper in the grass, an abrupt hissing becomes audible, breaking off just as abruptly, a whimpering as if from a prisoner, and when you look down, you see, littering the towpath up on the dike, bumblebees on their backs, their legs still quivering and flailing, or already cricked and motionless, and the two pairs of wings drawn in against the body, with perhaps one of the transparent wings sticking out a little, these little puffed-up creatures that but an hour ago were so full of life now shrunken, a couple of them lying on their backs or, more often, tipped on their sides, uttering one more cry of alarm, but most of them already dead, dead as bumblebees, which is perhaps more vividly *dead* than dead as doornails, more graphic, with the cricked legs, their antennae extended rigidly into the void, their proboscises expired in the middle of sucking, and above all their bumblebee posteriors with their furry covering, meant to warm what, and how? The rain may cause the various parts of the bumblebee anatomy to glow in fresh colors, honey-yellow and bear-black/brown, but no amount of placing you bees in one's palm and blowing on you will save you from death or bring you back to life; that was already true in one's childhood, and nevertheless, I tell you, it was tried again and again, back then on bumblebee-dying days as today.

Was it his imagination that he now heard the great bell of St. Stephen's Cathedral booming in the distance, ringing in the evening and reaching him from the heart of that city of which he could glimpse only a few warehouses far off, while at his feet the rain slapped the deserted surface of the Danube, which seemed to flow faster while swooshing by smoothly? No, it really was the bell, and so three sounds mingled, the distant booming combining with the rain's slapping and the river's swooshing, almost roaring for moments at a time, and he then noticed a fourth sound, that of his footsteps on the path along the dike, which blended with the others. And in this way he finally found a name for himself in the story of his journey through Europe: not as a traveler, tourist, or former writer would he henceforth be known, but? as a wanderer. Yes, he was a wanderer, the wanderer. And wasn't there a song about that? "I am a lonesome wanderer"?

Beyond the warehouses, hundreds of years old, towering skyward, and seemingly long since out of use, there now appeared through the rainy haze a similar structure, which, instead of towering skyward, walled off the entire horizon. This was the former Kaiserebersdorf juvenile penitentiary, or whatever it was called, stretching for miles along a ridge, its thousands of windows now only gaping holes, which they might have been even when the building was still occupied, and above them a roof as massive and heavy as if from another planet, made of the heaviest material possible and itself a part of that planet, a structure such as the world, the earth, had not yet seen, which probably also explained why this bulwark against delinquent youth was still standing and not to be torn down, and high up he recognized, by an opening just under this roof, his own cell in the boarding school, recognized all of our cells, and he felt a powerful urge to go where he could be among human beings.

Away from the stream and across the steppe toward the warehouses. Upon approaching them, in the rain, which in the meantime was pouring in classic rain style, he saw that the warehouses had once formed part of a gigantic mill complex, to which and away from which ran rusted railway tracks. In the lee of the mill towers, a rail yard for freight containers was in operation, with neon tubes gleaming in front of the two concrete barracks for the workers, but without a single human being anywhere in sight. Making his way along the sleepers, and seeing, as was always the case, bird skeletons between the ties, while the rain drummed on the metal containers, in many pitches, up and down the scale, as it were, now and then on just one note, which sounded massive and frenetic, according to the containers' contents, whether they were more full or empty, or entirely full or empty, a jumble of colors at any rate, and with point-of-origin stickers from all corners of the globe, and correspondingly in a variety of scripts—not even the Armenian, Georgian, Thai, Malaysian scripts were missing. And on the edge of the container depot, where, after the stretch of steppe the floodplain forest resumed, appeared the inn for which he had been hoping. It had to be there; its presence had announced itself while it was still out of sight. And the name, too, could have been predicted: "Floodplain Inn, formerly Inn of the Unknown."

A sort of garden bay, bordered on one side by the floodplain forest and on the other by stacks of containers, surrounded the inn, with trees that were neither alders nor poplars as in the forest but were left-overs from an old orchard. They were still bare but could be identified by their bark as apples, pears, plums, cherries. Old, much older, was the house, long and single-storied with a row of small windows, all of them with their sills almost at the level of the lawn, as if one were supposed to climb in and out through them. The steep roof, as high again as the building, was covered in slate, with dormers that mirrored those of the juvenile penitentiary, if only for an alarming second. The building's stucco was pale yellow, freshly painted, making it look more like a farm-house than an inn. Yet it was a quintessential inn, as became clear from the smoke puffing from the chimney with such force that it pushed aside the rain, and indicating, even without cars parked among the trees, what destination one had reached; the lettering above the rather narrow front door seemed almost superfluous.

Entering, soaking wet, or, to use a somewhat older expression, drenched. A dark, empty vestibule, unlit, reminiscent after all of an old farmhouse, and cold like one besides. Not a sound. Where to enter? Ah, there it was: Dining Room. And unexpectedly he found himself, just as he had wished, among people, among many people. Too many? No. At first the wanderer thought he had stumbled into a refugee camp—that was how self-absorbed each occupant of that one room appeared, also lost in thought, or rather simply lost. Hardly one of them looked up as he entered, except for the innkeeper, if that is what he was, you know, behind the bar—if that is what it was, you know. Occupants of a refugee camp? Reinforcing that impression, many of the many in the room were not sitting at the long tables, on the benches provided, but on the bare floor, or were even squatting there, on their heels. Packed in, al-most like sardines. Contributing to the image of a reception center was the composition of the crowd, in which all races, or whatever they are called, were represented, Mongolians with Africans, among them Zulus and—or was he mistaken?—pygmies, Eskimos, unmistakable, with equally unmistakable Indians from the Andes, Tibetans, though not displaying that world-famous smile, with—was this possible?—yes, Australian aborigines, though here not wearing loincloths but suits and ties . . . But how to account for the presence among the refugees of one-hundred-percent-native Austrians, they, too, there on the bare floor, some of them in traditional peasant costumes—from Styria? from Carinthia? had he been away so long that he had forgotten? And what about the tall Irishman there, in an elegant ankle-length duster, red-haired, of course, who at that moment worked his way out of the crowd and mounted a previously unoccupied platform by the wall in the back of the back of the room? And how about the naturally snub-nosed, naturally Viking-blond Scandinavian in a fur-lined parka, who now followed the Irishman? And in the meantime had Japanese, North Americans, Germans, even some of us Austrians become refugees? At any rate, one after another, clearly identifiable individuals now stepped onto the stage, a beautiful Mongolian woman, a suntanned Uzbek, a Galician from the north of Spain (so here we met again).

No: these were not refugees. If the many people, whether in the dining area or on the stage, were lost in thought, at the same time they were paying attention; they were lost, as one could see on closer inspection, not in their own thoughts but in something outside themselves that they all had in common. Did such a thing exist? Yes, it did. It was anticipation. Any moment now, it, whatever it was, would begin. That impression was reinforced by the innkeeper—or organizer?—who, from his spot behind the counter turned toward the new arrival and placed his index finger over his mouth. With his other hand, however, he energetically waved the drenched traveler—with such a welcoming, veritably Balkan-style hospitable smile in his eyes—over to the granite fireplace, not at all usual for a farmhouse, where a fire blazed like that of a blast furnace, sending out so much heat that in no time one would feel "dried through."

The lights in the dining area went out. But above the stage, over the heads of those standing there shoulder to shoulder, floodlights came on, powerful ones. A concert? But where were the instruments? None to be seen. A choral performance, a cappella, so to speak? Given the variations among the people up there, hardly to be expected. Or perhaps after all? A song cycle from around the world? *Urbi et orbi*? Heaven preserve us! And suddenly he knew, should have known from the moment he approached the front door. Bolted to its wood was an iron shape, not a horseshoe such as one would often find, but rather something that had to be mysterious to an outsider, though not to him, the wanderer: it was a jew's harp. And unlike a horseshoe, this jew's harp did not have its normal dimensions. In its natural size probably the smallest instrument in the world, this jew's harp appeared on the door in monumental proportions, and that perhaps explained why he had not recognized it instantly.

Who would begin, start playing the jew's harp? Not likely that it would be the two Austrians in their traditional brown loden suits with horn buttons, the buttons on the lapels in the form of skulls. But why not? Their faces, in which their eyes were screwed up with concentration, hardly differed from those of the Mongolians and Yakuts; their foreheads and cheeks gleamed just like those of the Zulu, the Indio, the Athabascan from Alaska. All of them up there on the stage had positioned their "gewgaw," "guimbarde," "buzziron," "thoughtcrusher," or "khomus" between their lips, and one had to be familiar with the instrument to recognize them as such and not mistake them for metal toothpicks or who knows what. Who would begin? The white American from Bay City, Oregon, let's say, in the cowboy hat and Oregon boots? No, he edged unobtrusively into the background and made himself invisible. The young woman struck the first note, the one in a white fur cap, who had eyes that looked inward yet at the same time took in the entire dining room, and menacingly flared nostrils, the Mongolian woman, come to the world jew's-harp convention from Inner Mongolia.

She played alone. From time to time she also sang, a vibrating that could hardly be distinguished from that of the instrument that had half disappeared into her oral cavity and was also almost covered by the hand holding it, a vibrating that responded to the instrument's, only pitched an octave higher?—but such numerical indications did not do justice either to her voice or to the sounds produced by the jew's harp. How long did the Mongolian woman play all alone? As long as she did, and could vary the pitch of her breath. And if initially she was perhaps performing an established, traditional tune from her native region, from the arid steppe or wherever, she forgot the tune even before it was over, abandoned the familiar song right in the middle, quite decisively, and began, equally decisively, using her breath and her finger on the trigger, to express in vibrations and sounds what was inside her at that moment, as well as in those around her—see above, her eyes taking in the entire room.

It was as if this decisive abandoning of what had been in her head, or wherever, from long ago, or whenever, of oneself, of one's people or tribe or anyone from before, and moving on to a different kind of playing, one without signposts, one that could be either free or also misleading, was in the nature of performing on the jew's harp, regardless of what part of the world one came from, also regardless of the variations in the instrument from continent to continent, where it could take very different forms and be made from different materials—the vibrating tongue could be made of twisted animal sinews rather than steel. The players who followed the Mongolian woman—the Sicilian, the Turk from Konya, and so on—if they even started playing anything from their own countries, as their signature melody, so to speak, all broke off in the middle and moved on to something that could not be characterized and certainly not captured in musical notation. Even the two Austrians, who fell in at the end, together, unisono, in the rhythm of a *ländler*—or was it a polka?—gleefully abandoned the rhythm after the first few measures and, with eyes gleaming like those of the players before them, took up a kind of call and response consisting simply of each breathing toward the other through that one steel string between his lips, a sound beyond, or rather before speaking and music, just as the jew's harp, if an instrument at all, was one that preceded any kind of speaking and any kind of music, a sort of tuning fork, though a very special kind, its particular sound produced not by means of striking a dead object but by activating sustained human breath.

Yet even without a signature melody, usually struck up more in jest, one could hear an entirely different country from each performer, no matter how unself-consciously he plucked his string and breathed on it from deep in his chest. His own, his native environment, his ancestral land? Not necessarily—rather an indeterminate one—but definitely a country, a hinterland, clearly distinguished from that of the person playing before or after him. The feature common to all these very different countries turned out to be the way in which each individual performance evaporated so suddenly after it ended. How so? Listen, listen: it seemed to be a further part of the nature of playing the jew's harp that it resisted coming to a harmonic close, a finale. If it ended harmonically, with unmistakable concluding notes, as was traditional here and there not only in Central Europe, one had the impression, as with no other instrument, of some kind of betrayal, or at least a trivializing. The secret and also obvious law of the jew's harp went this way: there is no ending, only breaking off. A good ending is a false ending. And: the performance time must be brief, from performance to performance, from player to player, with a long gap before the next performance, that, too, in distinction to every other instrument. The jew's harp's time is soon up, often after just a few notes, even after just one note. But what a note that could be. What a vibrating, so long as it sounded at the right moment, beginning without end, and instead of an opening measure, just an initial sound.

No question about it: these laws were suspended for the duration of the international convention in the inn's dining room. Once returned to his or her part of the world, each of those gathered here would be playing alone and would continue to do so for most of the following year—except perhaps for the Central Europeans—and would observe those laws strictly. Here, however, for the few days of the meeting, of which this was the last, and their last evening together, different rules were in force. Although the players had come from all corners of the globe as individuals, not as representatives of those corners, now, toward the end, each of them struck up a melody from his or her land of origin, plucking, striking, pounding out, not just any tune but one that stood for that country, such as a national anthem, from "The Star-Spangled Banner" to "Deutschland, Deutschland . . ." to "Allons, en- fants de la patrie," from beginning to end, through all the verses. Played on the jew's harp, the buzziron, the thoughtcrusher, the guimbarde (its first meaning: accompaniment for the country dance), all these anthems at first sounded ridiculous, but that changed, even when eventually all those on the platform were playing simultaneously, anthems and popu- lar songs all mixed up, you know: the Indio playing "Guantanamera," the Irishman "Two for the Road," the Italian "Azzurro." To a man, or woman, they all looked frightfully ugly, their faces twisted and the jew's harps between their teeth. But to hear them . . .

The only person in the dining room of the Inn of the Unknown who took this final performance by the international jew's-harp players at face value was the new arrival, the wanderer. When he described the rest to us during that night on the Morava, he could not say whether he had actually experienced the event or had merely dreamed it. If it was a dream, it nonetheless filled him with a feeling stronger and more lasting than almost anything experienced while awake. Going off on a tangent, he remarked that more and more feelings of great and persis- tent happiness, gratitude, affection, and love of life came to him only in dreams.

And what did he feel upon hearing the medley played on the jew's harps? Rage. A rage this overwhelming he definitely experienced only in dreams. And what did he do in this rage? Or what did he dream about doing? He jumped up from his spot by the fireplace—or was it a smith's hearth, left over from an earlier blacksmith's shop?—and has- tened in long strides to the players on the stage. While still moving, he fumbled in his hiker's jacket and pulled out a jew's harp, his old travel- ing companion, which, when he pressed it between his teeth, tasted rusty. He aimed single notes, first from below and then up on the stage, at eye level, at the miscreants, isolated notes full of rage, at intervals calculated to disrupt their melodies and rhythms. Abusing the jew's-harp to play mendacious harmonies: that was impermissible. The jew's-harp players had no business representing the globe, *urbi et orbi*, but rather, if anything, the back of the world, the backwoods, the stubborn, proud, mournful backwoods existence. Wasn't Abraham Lincoln himself, at least in his youth, the epitome of such an existence, with his own kind of jew's-harp playing, one note after another emanating from his reflections, as he scrupulously avoided any kind of melodic demagoguery, listening first to the echo of each note, each thought, for a long, long time, and only then testing the next one in the wide-open spaces, and listening as each thought note, each sound thought, died away? Yes, indeed! Or had that not been Lincoln in person but rather the actor who played him, Henry Fonda, in *Young Mr. Lincoln*? So what if it had.

But that must have been a dream, no? dreamed by the wanderer as he dozed off while drying his clothes by the inn's fireplace, the smith's hearth. Yes, it was a dream. One of us in the boat's salon who had participated in the international convention of jew's-harp players—the second convention in this story—took over for the faltering boatmaster and narrated the actual course of events. Unthinkable that the jew's-harp players on the platform should have struck up any national anthems— that would have been a nightmare. Even anything resembling a jam session was out of the question for that humble instrument: for heaven's sake, no jew's-harp jazz! Each performer played alone before parting. And more and more guests joined in, on and in front of the stage. Soon there was no audience left, only players, each awaiting his turn on his pathetic breath-vibrator, then harping, or drumming, or droning, or sending out into the air what he had inside him or around him. And he did as well, the man the rain had driven inside, whom rage had startled out of his dreams.

The sounds he produced, as the other narrator described it, were unusual. "Unusual in what respect?" the wanderer asked, seemingly eager to learn how he had played that evening. "Less self-confident than the tunes the rest of us played, in which each took full responsibility for his tone." "So I didn't perform with full concentration?" "No, you did. But as if you were somewhere else. With a different sound space surrounding you." "A smaller one?" "No, and also not a larger one, more an unfamiliar one. Perhaps that had to do with your having been fast asleep. It was a dream-sound, one from the boundary between sleeping and waking, a threshold sound. Earlier, when you entered the room, all of us except the innkeeper had simply not noticed you; that was how nondescript you looked, like someone from the cleaning staff, perhaps, arriving by bicycle in the rain. At any rate, no one was surprised to see you come in or thought it was worth asking about. *Aiylgy*—that was the motto of our annual gathering, from the Yakut, supposedly meaning 'middle world.' And God knows, we had conjured it up all these days with our harping, drumming, and plucking. But you, with your sound from a different realm, gave our middle world, *Aiylgy*, a different form."

Here the interim narrator turned away from the host of the Moravian night, who apparently could not get enough of this account of himself, and addressed the rest of us on the boat, describing the ending of the jew's-harp episode. The meeting ended in general astonishment, "between heaven and water," as one of the wrap-up speakers expressed it. The instruments were pocketed, in cases that looked positively precious, in contrast to the little harps, which at rest resembled frozen, shrunken praying mantises. Just before this they had been passed from mouth to mouth, to allow them all to be touched by everyone's lips, being dunked each time in a glass of brandy. Just as people had previously shown considerable amazement, now they ate and drank until far into the night on the banks of the Danube, with considerable gusto, the wanderer included, without anyone's getting drunk. But intoxicated some of them certainly were. The rain pounding on the roof tiles, the fire hissing in the forge, and the imminent departure were all they needed. One person held up his jew's harp and snapped it in two, bending the steel tongue until it broke off. But that was no misfortune, because the inn, as it now turned out, was also a workshop for making jew's harps, and the innkeeper was also the blacksmith, and close to the forge stood his work bench, where he fabricated a replacement, using his metal file and a soldering iron—the intoxicated player stopped just short of putting the new instrument to his lips while it was still red-hot.

When the playing had finally ceased, storytelling took over in full force. There was a connection between the jew's-harp playing and the storytelling—"jewish harp and storytelling!" (as the American from Bay City, Oregon, exclaimed)—and not only in the speaking voices, modulated from days of playing, using the breath and the instrument. Playing had filled people with a desire to tell stories. How could that be, after performing on such a small, humble instrument, after such monotonous buzzing, barely capable of variation? Yes, desire, more pure than after any playing of the flute or the saxophone, not to mention the piano or the organ. Pure in what sense? In the sense that the most incidental detail appeared worth telling about, in fact precisely such details. During that night in the inn it then seemed as if their days of playing the jew's harp had been only a prelude to the final night of storytelling. Did the beautiful Mongolian woman also tell stories? Yes, with her eyes and with her neck.

But something was not quite right. Even earlier, during the farewell performances, something had been wrong with the picture. The jew's-harp player who was standing on one leg? The woman performing virtuoso-style on two or three harps at once, alternating between the left and right side of her mouth? She was the more likely source of the problem, but her performance was probably less showing off than high spirits and self-mockery. And then it became clear what was so jarring. It was the watches on the players' wrists. No objections to the clock on the wall: it told the wrong time as if on purpose, or had stopped altogether. But all these watches offended the eye, even if one was set to the local time in Cancún, another to the time in Palermo, and yet another to the time in Kuala Lumpur. In addition, they created a melancholy mood. Catching sight of them made one feel as though the storytelling time and the performing time could not hold their own against real time, as though both, one as much as the other, were a futile illusion, smoke and mirrors, and also the wrong form of measurement. It did little good that all those present, as if by previous agreement, removed their time-measuring devices from their wrists, one after another, or hid them under their sleeves. Even without visible clocks, normed time was taking over, and more menacingly the closer the festivities came to their conclusion. And what threatened those celebrating? Isolation, an absence of future. Ah, time as prison. Come back, stuff of dreams, stuff of play.

All that was left was defiance. That was what the inhabitants of the Balkans had once been criticized for, as the worst of all our bad characteristics. And we are still criticized for our defiance, and today as in the past by foreign powers, part of the problem being that the most common word for defiance is not our own but a loan word from the vocabulary of the power that occupied us the longest, a loan word and a curse word. But such defiance was perhaps the only meaningful attitude and not something bad at all, but rather the last means we had to assert ourselves and radiate something beautiful, and that meant something moving and unifying, and such defiance could thus be transmitted from the Balkans to all those on earth living under the dictatorship of normal, real time and threatened with isolation? This much maligned defiance: could it become a source of strength? Give rise to action, all in good time?

Our host had forgotten to mention that children were also present in the inn's dining room. Only now did they occur to him, during the night on the Morava, and the fact that the last episode of that other night, the one with jew's-harp players from the five continents, involved them. He could not say whose idea it had been to bring the children up on the stage and have them try plucking the instruments. At all events, one child after another mounted the platform. They all held the steel instrument, or whatever it was made of, to their mouths and clenched the frame between their teeth as they had seen the grown-ups do; plucked with their thumbs or index fingers the narrower trigger or loop, standing out from the flexible tongue at approximately a right angle, set the tongue to vibrating, then breathed as hard as they could. They were one and all dying to have their turn and be allowed to play. But most of them, no matter how hard they plucked and blew, could not coax a single note out of the instrument; their attempts at playing produced nothing but a tinny rattling and a snuffling, puffing, and groaning, reminiscent of the sounds children make when a doctor instructs them to breathe slowly in and out. Some of them managed to produce at least the beginning or a suggestion of a sound, if so soft and with so little range that even in the room, which was quiet as a mouse, it could be heard only by the person closest to them, or remained purely imaginary. All kinds of instructions and suggestions were offered to the children by the "world champions" present, as if they had not realized that playing the jew's harp was not something that could be taught. There was no such thing as technique.

One child, a single one, finally managed to send a droning sound into the room, which—have you ever heard anything of the sort?—provided redemption and made all further attempts unnecessary. For a long time this child had resisted mounting the stage. He was chubby, freckled, and snub-nosed, wore glasses, and had a side part in his hair and a clip holding the hair out of his face. Truculently, his face screwed up as if he were blind, the boy stood there, holding at arm's length the instrument that had been almost forced on him. Only with someone else's help did he put it up to his lips, and the harp was more pushed between his teeth than placed there by him. He barely had it positioned before it boomed forth, through the whole room, louder than an electric guitar. Altogether involuntarily, without intention, without any preparation, the chubby child had made it produce sound; he had not even taken a deep breath on purpose, or if he had, not for the purpose of playing the instrument. For a moment he was startled by what had happened, and went rigid with fright, and from this very rigidity another note issued forth, powerful in a different way, transcending his fright or any other feeling. And now the chubby boy beamed at last, somewhat embarrassed, somewhat shamefaced, and then continued playing on his own. He refused to stop until a different redemption was demanded of him who had previously redeemed the gathering. And who managed to interrupt him? It was our wanderer, imagine that, who raised his voice and invited the jew's-harp players to attend the following year's convention in the Balkans, along with "you, my child!"

7

~~~~~~~~
 ~~~~~~~~
~~~~~~~~

WHEN HE HAD brought the story up to this point, the sound of a jew's harp made itself heard on the nocturnal boat, as if he had planned it as the finishing touch, the same note several times, at the same pitch, and only gradually did we realize that no one was plucking away in the semidarkness; no, it was his mobile phone's ringtone. He did not answer it. Instead the frogs answered, in a sort of chorus, from the belt of reeds along the Morava. And how did they answer? Their monotonous croaking modulated into an unmistakable droning, an angry drumming, half underwater. Was the enclave threatened again? Did the spot where the boat was moored have to change again? Or did the storyteller, as suggested by the index finger he put to his lips, want to create the kind of tension of which we, the audience, had no need? Only after some time had elapsed and the ringtone had finally fallen silent did he resume the story, his detour to the playwright Ferdinand Raimund in

Gutenstein at the foot of the Schneeberg—Austria's Mount Snow—but he was immediately interrupted by our fact hound, who wanted to know where the jew's-harp players from all over the world had gone when they scattered in all directions.

But that episode was rather mournful, and sad things, even if they had appealed to him all his life, were not exactly what the storyteller wanted just now. If the parting took the form of an episode at all, it was a minor one, not enough to fill a chapter, at most a gloss, a paragraph—an intermezzo. So they set out just as dawn was breaking. The rain had stopped. They stood outside, under the trees, in a triangle between the inn that had hosted the convention, the Danube, and the cemetery from which the inn had received its former name, the Cemetery of the Unknown. This cemetery had much earlier provided a final resting place primarily for unidentified corpses washed up by the river and for suicides, and old headstones from a period between wars were still tended, headstones with inscriptions such as "Unknown—Unforgotten!" As they stood there in the grayish light of early dawn, the mournfulness assailing each had less to do with the cemetery or with lack of sleep, also less with the necessity of parting—they all felt lastingly enriched by each other and were looking forward to the next year—than with the fact that after spending this time together with the jew's harp, the khomus, the thoughtcrusher, they now had to return—"to their countries of origin?" broke in the interrupter, getting ahead of the story again—no, to their respective jobs there. Each participant in the international jew's-harp convention had a proper job back home, you see. And they all came from different lines of work. One was employed near Paris as an "experimental physicist," another as a "linguist" in Kyoto, and yet another as a "roofer" ("That's where my loud voice comes from, from constantly shouting down to the street or to the opposite side of the roof") in Lima. A "home economics teacher" was among them, a "master tailor" ("a soccer referee on the side"), a "laundromat attendant" ("ah, all that steam"), a "professor of church jurisprudence," a "shepherd" (another one), a "bus driver" (another one), a "professional fisherman" (on a lake in Austria), a "pharmacist" (one of those wearing a peasant costume), an "opera singer," a "beekeeper," a "tax auditor," a "hunter (and game warden)," a "sanitation worker," a "dentist," a "hair-dresser," a "model" (male), a "disc jockey" (female). And on this particular morning they all felt disgruntled, almost disgusted, at having to return home—wherever that might be—to their jobs. And there was nothing more to be said on that subject: end of paragraph, end of explanation. "Which was not really all that mournful": thus our interrupter, who could not contain himself.

So the former writer, glad to be rid of his profession, subsequently found himself outside the country estate that had belonged to Ferdinand Raimund. Did that literary figure actually exist? Had he ever existed, and hadn't the writer and actor occupied only a rented room in the tiny village of Gutenstein, near the Schneeberg, and only during the summer weeks dedicated in the nineteenth century to seeking "fresh air"? And even if that were perhaps true: from the village in the shadow of the mountain, filled with the sound of rushing brooks, yet quite close to the capital, a city of theater, Raimund's spirit wafted toward the new arrival. He had expected no less, and that was why he had made his way to Gutenstein in Lower Austria, and his expectation was fulfilled the moment he took his first step past the sign marking the entrance to the village. The same thing had happened every time he had sought out the haunts of his predecessors, or rather path breakers, as whose successor, or more like a slowpoke follower, he had seen himself during his earlier life as a writer. The spirit of those who had put him on this track could be counted on to waft toward him, surround him, dance around him, speak to him, whenever he sought out their favorite haunts, even if those places existed by now in name only, with nothing left but overgrown fields, stagnant creeks, tree stumps—Vergil's "Andes" near the banks of the Mincio River, or a cul-de-sac ending in a tangle of brush on a mound of rubble from which Sophocles' "Kolonos," let's say, had received its name: right there, in the middle of nowhere and nothing, without any memorials, the spirit probably spoke to one most powerfully, and in smaller places, like Oxford, Mississippi; Višegrad, Bosnia; Cleversulzbach, Württemberg; and yes, Gutenstein, Lower Austria; more clearly than in large cities—where, whether in St. Paul, Minnesota, in Taganrog, in Oslo, in Lüttich, it spoke to one, if at all, at most in a seemingly deserted side street.

It was not curiosity that drew him to the realms of those who had become most near and dear to him in the course of his life. Or rather: in such places he wanted to know not anything specific about the place itself but about the person whose spirit, he had no doubt, resided there. For that, however, he had to go to the actual place. Only there would he learn what he wished to know. But these were probably not conventional pilgrimage destinations? And for heaven's sake, not oracles' lairs. What could be more perverse? No. Those oracles, those emanations, were not something he, not something anyone, could possibly— no, not believe in—trust. They offered nothing that merited belief. And also nothing one could understand, whether unambiguous or ambiguous, leaving one simply and solely none the wiser. But how did he happen to feel that he was on intimate terms with these other spirits, and after his visits to them constantly kept his ears cocked for what they would say to him? He had encountered each one back in the day when he still wrote everything down. In each case the connection occurred only once, for the duration of a sentence perhaps, or at most a paragraph, sometimes just for the instant of an exclamation that he jotted down; that was probably the most common form it took. For this one, more or less lengthy, moment, he felt at one with them. And he did not need anything more than that one moment. It allowed him to experience the presence of his predecessors, from the earliest times to now. Now! and now! he was with them, was the twin brother for the moment of John Cowper Powys, of Cervantes, of Patricia Highsmith, of Katherine Mansfield, of Eduard Mörike, of Georges Simenon, and this now, although it flitted by faster than a falling star, for instance, would never be gone for good. It could not be destroyed by calendar time. He would share a space forever with those writers, or would occupy a room next door to theirs, something like a chamber, a *morada*, a cell, in the "castle of the soul" described by Teresa of Avila.

Thus he had experienced an atom of time like this, a second in a writing expedition, with Ferdinand Raimund. Unexpectedly, engrossed in a dialogue, or rather a two-sided monologue, or, even more accurate, a dual, daydream-like, aside, he had been sure that he felt the presence at his side of the author of those magic plays, and had seen himself as the one chosen to carry on the tradition, as a second voice, a repeater?—a recapitulator. And thus he had come to Gutenstein to commune with his comrade and followed the brook upstream through the village, located in a valley that narrowed as it neared the Schneeberg. And lo, the *spiritus loci*—of its own accord the village would not have radiated any spirit—not only became eloquent and spoke continuously to the new arrival but also showed itself to be receptive, loosened his tongue, involved him in a dialogue. The *spiritus loci* spoke above all of Gutenstein— how matters stood and lay there—to be precise not so much of matters connected with nature, such as the brook or the trees, but of things made or produced or manufactured, fabricated by hand, crafted, but never of those mass-produced, such as cars (those drove around as they did everywhere), television sets (not even ancient models discarded behind houses), or the like. And on the other hand no *spiritus loci* spoke from obviously older manufactured goods, from handcrafted objects from past eras: the nineteenth-century wooden galleries remained mute, as did the garden bowers from the same period, the painted marksman's plaques on the verandas, the old horse-drawn carriages parked in the remaining sheds or placed in front gardens as flower containers, or on terraces. Likewise silent were the Biedermeier wardrobes, chests of drawers, and armchairs glimpsed in the houses as one passed by, indeed every object from Raimund's period, whether an oil painting or very early photograph (?), as were the writer's personal possessions, let's say the bed he had slept in during the summer holidays, his writing desk, his quill pen (?), his bed (probably child-sized), for which reason the wanderer making his way through the village avoided from the beginning any spot designated as a memorial. What spoke to him and sparked the dialogue, one more lively, more spirited than almost any he succeeded in having with a living person, were inanimate objects almost exclusively, along with the stones in the brook and the breeze from the brook that blew up at him from below: timeless objects along the road, such as a crudely knocked-together bench, a chair of indefinable style in a front courtyard, a beehive that was neither clearly old nor freshly painted, a wooden ladder, even a bicycle from some time in the past, a hazel stick leaning by a front door, a flower box filled with nothing but sand, a mailbox for complaints that would not be emptied until the following fall, if at all, a dusty cap on a windowsill, a row of gray, weathered clothespins on a line, a so-so gazebo, a so-so support for a fruit tree, a privy in a rear courtyard with a heart sawn out of the door, or maybe not.

Wherever he looked, Ferdinand Raimund spoke to him in his Gutenstein, and then spoke not merely through objects in that place but also through the occasional cat lying quietly on a shed roof—not, however, through any dog, no matter how sound asleep: "Caution, risk of rabies"—and likewise through the inhabitants' eyes, cheek-lines, shoulders (often slightly stooped like those of mountain folk), primarily the older ones—odd in light of Raimund's rather early death—and especially the dangling arms and, if possible even more distinctly, through the cowlicks of children, more straggling or dawdling home after school than hustling, and often going out of their way to accompany one another rather than heading straight home.

And how did the dialogue go between these two, yes, old comrades? More or less as follows. Ferdinand Raimund: "Greetings to ye, friend. High time you showed your face in Gutenstein. What brings you to me? What would you like to know? Ask me everything—except how one can become happy and contented." The man seeking insight from the oracle: "Are there still fairy tales like yours to tell?" "No. Or at most in fragments. Fairy tales that last only a second." "Should I have continued writing instead of giving up?" "No. For you are incapable, as I was, of speaking of evil and describing an evil person, someone rotten to the core. And devils exist, as they did in my day, and worse now than ever. In my time, I could banish evil by invoking fairy-tale magic. But you, nowadays—and besides, I also practiced magic as an actor. When I played on the stage, the audience erupted with enthusiasm. But you— you may be a player, but not a winner. And as a writer, too, you would in the meantime be a loser also. For in your case, as in mine, the good would win out. And unlike in my case, no one would be willing to believe you anymore. For what wins out everywhere can only be evil, the devil, I mean, with his saccharine grin and his malice—who wants to sow dissension, between individual human beings as well as between peoples." "Can't you be less unambiguous, Ferdinand?" "Then don't ask me so specifically, brother." "Why am I so reluctant, since my arrival in this country we share, to strike out directly for home, for the village I come from, or what's left of it? Why do I take detour after detour, go off on tangent after tangent, to postpone stepping into the house where I was born? Why do I have the sense I would be approaching a forbidden zone there? A death zone? Warning! Death zone!" "Ask me something else. In a house where someone committed suicide, there is no room for an expression containing 'death.' And besides: yes, dear friend, don't you know that it is characteristic of rational people not to think about death but only about life?" "And likewise about love? For a time, while I was on the road, that was my only thought. One thought led to another, and accordingly one sentence, addressed silently to the beloved, gave rise to the next. But how does it happen, magician, that since I have been back in our shared country I have had to make more and more of an effort to summon these thoughts, that the corresponding words and sentences become more and more theoretical—not innately theatrical as in your case—and they are hardly directed to a distant reality, the distant proximity, but no longer have any direction, are incapable of flying, if indeed words of love don't fail to materialize altogether? How can this be: homecoming and threatened with lovelessness? Or worse still: heading home and having ulterior motives?

Homeland and distrust?" "Ah, speak not to me of love, little brother, not to me. Love, especially love for a woman, does not belong to my vocabulary, any more than homecoming and homeland. True, I am an illusionist. But I know my limitations. And they are called distrust and suspicion. Or you might call it mistrust, healthy mistrust? Unhealthy, fundamentally unhealthy. For all my days I lived with the thought that a woman would save me, who else but a woman? And I needed so badly to be saved, my friend, time and again. And then, time and again, Beware: woman, beware: betrayal, beware: death zone. And then time and again a period in which I was not close to Antonie even in writing. And then I was with her. And then we quarreled. And then again. And then we were on good terms once more. And then we swore eternal faithfulness to each other under the column with a statue of the Virgin Mary in Neustift am Walde. And then we quarreled again, and for a long time she did not come up to see me. I had terrible headaches. That time was not good. Evil absence. And then we traveled to Gutenstein, where I was very sad. And on the way back I put the pistol in my mouth and fired, not out of fear of rabies but because of the woman. Nothing is free in life. A great deal is free in life." "What to do, Ferdinand?" "No danger is ever past. Even hunger cannot be relied upon anymore. Why do human beings turn up only in the newspapers nowadays? Nonetheless you should write, write it all down. There is much to be seen in a village. You are in foreign parts here; be peaceable! Is all this surviving worthwhile? No one will save you. In the end it all comes down to grace. Much still takes place. No cause for rejoicing. Do not call me an inspired writer; call me a collector of material from the air. An ashman. Ashes to ashes, air to air. I am puzzled by everyone who is merry. Keep to the truth, and seek it. Actually one should do nothing all day but sharpen pencils. All have found a safe haven, only we two have not. Nothing, yet again—and everything splinters. Run to the lilac bush. Today is Monday, and Monday is a good day to go up to the mountain. Parting should be tender. The sun is friendly. Continue not calling attention to yourself, you hear? Once a day you will experience something new.

Or perhaps not. There are no heavenly days. And in the end no one knows anything. Parting must take place without answers."

Even once he had long since left Gutenstein behind on his way to the Schneeberg, the wanderer remained under Ferdinand Raimund's influence. He thought of himself as not merely invisible in it but also invulnerable. "Nothing can happen to me!" Furthermore he felt as if it lent him wings, so that he veritably flew up the mountainside, although the path grew increasingly steep. Beyond every bend and boulder their dialogue, or rather their chaotic, stammered exchange, resumed. It was the kind of ecstasy of which lifelong experience really should have taught him to be wary. But right now that did not concern him, and it also did not count that after a while he had no path to follow; as he progressed up the mountain, sometimes walking, sometimes scrambling, feeling his way across scree or pulling himself up a fissure in the rock, in his imagination he created his own path. And in no time—or so it seemed to him—he found himself in the snow, still far from the snow-covered peak, the various peaks that gave the mountain its name, but in the brilliant blue it appeared to be only a stone's or a snowball's throw away. Setting one foot directly in front of the other like a fox, he was proceeding without pausing across the high plateau near the tree line, seemingly covered evenly with crystallized snow, when all of a sudden he tumbled into a crater, a sinkhole in the karst that had been almost impossible to see because of the lack of shadows and because of the snow that had blown into it to a considerable depth. And there the wanderer lay. Struggling to his feet, he stood there down in the crater, up to his hips in snow, and—he saw himself from the outside—looked around, at a loss. "Damned snow!" At that a chamois, a real one this time, came to the edge of the depression and, with its head turned to one side, stared at him out of one black eye. And after it had gazed at him from above for a good while, using its rump as a sled, it slid down to him in the sinkhole, stood up on all fours, and conveyed without beating around the bush, without stammering, unlike in that earlier dialogue down in the valley: "Enough of avoiding the beaten path!

Enough of going it alone! Leaving others in the lurch! You're the traitor; you're all traitors. You're a wild creature, I say. But an aging, decrepit one. All your phony ecstasies. Now you see where they get you: into a snow pit, into snow-blindness. Back to the realm of the living, of the modern world, of pairs of eyes. I'm not going to rescue you, not I. But I also have no desire to see you perish poetically up here in white and blue, over the course of days. Up with you, you stupid flatlander." And did that help him get out? How else would he have been able to tell us the story during the Moravian night?

After that, for a while he was no longer a wanderer. He allowed himself to be transported, by train, if you really want to know specifically, and if you want to know even more "precisely": once he had made his way with bag and baggage to Puchberg on the Schneeberg, he took the late-afternoon local east to Wiener Neustadt and there changed to the express heading south to Carinthia and Styria; he was not yet sure in which province he would get off that night. But only briefly did he enjoy the sense of security that came with being transported. Soon he found himself missing the awareness of danger. What comforted him somewhat was the thought that it was probably enough that his life had hung in the balance for a day. Besides, he told himself, if the danger did not come from outside him, it could be counted on to come from inside. He personified the danger, was his own threat to himself, especially since he had let his profession go—and was no longer working. So during his time on the road he had survived a danger each and every day? Yes. And why had he not mentioned this to us? "Nonsense: I haven't concealed a single danger from you—you haven't been listening properly. If my tour had been a boat trip, I would have been telling you about the hundreds of ways I came close to capsizing every day."

This run was one of the last times the train would traverse the more than hundred-year-old stretch over the mountains, the Semmering Pass. Very soon a new tunnel would be opened. Did that explain why the compartments were so full? Not another seat available, and even the corridors were crowded. That was fine by him, and not only because he had been hiking alone for so long. It felt to him as though it had been even longer since he had been seen by anyone, at least any living human being. He had no memory of a human eye observing him, even with a fleeting glance, and he was beginning to miss being perceived by others. Looking at himself in the mirror no longer sufficed, and besides he tended to avoid mirrors, or ignore them. There was another odd phenomenon: he, who during his period as a public figure had felt awkward at being recognized on the street or wherever, now wished that someone, even just one person, on the train would recognize him, specifically as the one who had published this or that work, no matter that it had been some time ago. If in the past he had been recognized by someone or other "in my own country"—these words came to him unbidden—at most it had been as someone vaguely suspect.

This wish, too, finally found fulfillment during his tour. He did have to wait a good while, and as usual contribute in some way to the fulfillment. He squeezed past those standing in the corridor and sitting on the floor, making his way from the end of the train to the locomotive up front and then back. Along the broad and then unexpectedly abrupt switchbacks on the Semmering route, he was constantly thrown against the bodies of the other passengers, and he allowed that to happen, almost luxuriating in the contact and thankful to feel himself integrated into the crowd, even enthusiastic when, from time to time, it was impossible to get by, and he stood there in the mass, compressed by another curve, his arms close to his sides, unable to move a finger, and forced, like the others, to "breathe lightly." It goes without saying that in such close quarters, eye to eye, no one recognized him. But neither did he expect anyone to. Being seen, yes. Yet even in this situation, that did not happen. He looked expectantly at the faces of all those around him, no farther away than a hand's breadth, a nose's length, the distance of a toothpick, of an eyebrow, of an auricle, of a hasty glance, but far and wide there was no one who returned his gaze for even a second. Was that a function of excessive closeness? Was it impossible to register anything at such close range? No. Even once the people in the carriages had long since been distributed more evenly, his gaze at their faces was not reciprocated, and no one perceived him. And he was not the only one to go unseen, to not exist, as it were. Even among themselves, even in cases where their clothing, age, or other features suggested that they belonged together, formed a group, they did not relate to one another. No one had eyes for anyone else. Yet almost all of them, from one end of the train to the other, were very young, and without exception—what was the expression?—good-looking. Entire classes from Carinthia or Styria returning home from a school trip to the nation's capital?

And he in their midst, so needy of faces, having needed faces for so long. Nothing meant more to him, when the time came, than a human face, nothing in nature, no sky, no book. And now was that time. Looking out the train's windows, he saw snow again, that was how high the train had worked its way up the mountain, and, poking out of the drifts, the back of a bench meant for hikers: if only he did not have to see any more snow, any more objects. Faces! One face! Give me one human face, and my soul will heal. But these thousand faces crowded together now offered nothing to see. Or rather: they did not allow themselves to be seen, intentionally, and that had been the case for a good while—even if, according to normal time measurements, it had been only a week ago, only a month ago, only at the beginning of the school year, that that had happened or been decided on. All these young faces, most of them female, which had doubtless once been quite diverse, revealed an almost worrisome uniformity—to which the earbuds here and there and the pale complexion repeated in face after face contributed only slightly, certainly not the decisive aspect—a twinlike? a doll-like uniformity, certainly not a family resemblance anywhere. And it would not have taken much for him, as he squeezed between them, to pick one of the young women, for whom he and no one else existed, one standing in for all, and shout at her, berating her, calling them monsters, zombies, troublemakers, holy terrors of the last days, scouts from the Planet of Blind Souls, would-be masters of the universe. If he had berated her, it would have been less out of rage than—to be honest—

out of fear. And his shouting, if like anything, would have been like the shouting in a bad dream, coming out wordlessly as pathetic croaking, or remaining stuck in his throat.

So he literally fought his way through to the very last car in the excessively long train, from where he had first set out, hoping to find a face—as if one human visage, even one bowed or turned away, would suffice to let him feel that he was being seen. There, with a view out the back, onto the tracks, would be his spot. Time and again someone jostled him, unintentionally. Did no one see him, then? Did he in fact perhaps not exist at all? In the end he almost jostled someone in return, simply to prove that he was really present among all those young people. And then, at the very end of the train, the girl sitting on the floor and reading, her back against the glazed, sealed rear door. The steeper the climb up the mountainside, the slower the train moved, taking the turns almost at the speed of a walk, with the result that the landscape behind the glass door receded in slow curves, offering each time a changed perspective, while also seeming to recur, like the backdrops in a play or in an old film.

At first glance, the girl looked hardly different from the other young folk on the train: leather jacket, jeans, ankle boots, a fake diamond stud in one nostril. But what immediately set her apart from the others was the way she sat there and the way she was reading. Initially he saw her only through the legs of those standing all around, and caught only a glimpse of the book on her knees, without its title. But the way she was reading: that was a reader for you! She was visibly living in the book, spelling it out, interrogating it, interrogating herself, connecting with it, becoming and being one with it. In reading this way and obviously having a book that lent itself to being read this way, this young person showed herself to be transported out of her surroundings—in another element altogether? No, in contrast to the others, she was actually in an element, her own, the only one appropriate to her, the one in which she could be herself. And yet she was not lost to the world; being transported did not signify being lost or sealed off: she could also take in whatever was happening in the corridor and outside the train that was worth taking in, *vide* the way she periodically raised her eyes from the book and looked over her shoulder through the glass door, both actions apparently motivated by her reading, nothing but her reading. And he could not get enough of watching this young woman, almost still a child? no, no longer a child, read and read and read. Concentrated solemnity radiated from her brow, her lowered lids, her flattish nose, her full lips, which at times seemed to be humming along with what she was reading. A solemnity that radiated—really? yes, Mr. Know-It-All. And although he was gazing down at her as she sat there, legs crossed, it seemed to him, the more he immersed himself in this reader, that she was floating, weightless, above the ground, and he with her. Part of her solemnity was that now and then, even though she was clearly not reading anything comical, let alone humorous, she would smile or grin (quite a rarity, a grin on such a young face), or, most frequently, would shake her head after every paragraph—indicating her astonishment, her surprise, her inner eye-opening, venting itself in a barely audible sighing and/or giggling. Everything, everything about her, no matter how still she sat, harmonized with the book, and if the book facilitated such opening-up and becoming beautiful (but wasn't openness already in itself beauty?), it indeed deserved a name, or maybe not? A reader like this, male or female, sensitive through and through, he had imagined in the past for his own books—a being like this; from that kind of reading he would have recognized her on the spot, "with hundred-percent certainty." Even supposing the book being read had not been one of his: he could have been its author, judging solely by the reader's eyelid movement, a movement free of all reflexes, an eyelid movement that marked a conscious pausing—dawning awareness as pausing. "His" reader instilled patience in him; and accordingly the conviction came to him that her reading was tantamount to protection; by reading as she did, she was helping someone in danger. Such reading provided protection, giving and maintaining safe conduct. This reader came across as motherly, though she was still partly a child, and would remain so all her life. "Yes," to quote his exact words, "I esteem my readers more than myself."

Again she raised her eyes from the book. But instead of looking over her shoulder as usual, she gazed at him, through the legs of her fellow passengers. That happened after they had already reached the summit of the Semmering Pass, and through the train's rear door the tracks no longer ran valleyward but rather, in the fading light of day, up the mountainside, quite steeply, appearing at certain moments like a ladder leaning against the mountain. What about him disturbed her so? Perhaps that he was so battered from his solitary journey to Gutenstein and up the Schneeberg? He stepped to one side so as to remain unseen, his heart pounding at the same time like that of someone caught in the act. And at that she had already jumped to her feet and stood before him, her large eyes ringed with dark makeup. So she must have recognized him after all? She, the tenderest and loveliest of beings, not only in the train here, and he, long since rejected, even by himself, cast off into an almost longed-for state of oblivion, and for the most part also feeling at home in that state? Yes, she had recognized him, and his first thought was: *Oh, no!* And what happened next was described during that night on the Morava not by him but by the stranger, the woman, who as if on cue emerged from the galley to join the rest of us again. He seemed to have told her the rest of the episode so often that she knew it by heart. (Or had she been present? In secret?) Did the boatmaster wish to avoid the appearance of vanity? But in listening to an account of his own adventure, didn't he increase the likelihood of seeming vain? On the other hand, what came next had hardly anything to do with him.

The stranger told us the following story: The beautiful young thing had not only recognized the man (she did not say how, whether from some old photo, or perhaps from a caricature?—probably the most likely to remain recognizable over time). She was his reader. "I know your books," was her second statement. Almost involuntarily his eyes came to rest on the book she held in her hand. No, it was not by him; it belonged to a long-ago century. But for moments it could have been by him. She stared at him in amazement. That he was alive. That he existed in flesh and blood. That he was on a train. That he was there, not somewhere inaccessibly distant. She plucked at him, at his coat, his pack, and pulled him to the rear door of the train. They stood there together and looked out at the tracks curving away from them. She knew nothing about him, nothing personal, and also did not want to know anything, either where he was coming from or where he was going; she also had no idea that he had long since and consciously given up writing books—he was and remained the writer, here and now. Likewise she did not tell him what she thought of his books, did not judge them, did not even mention specific ones, and at first he wondered whether she hadn't mistaken him for someone else. But no: he was the one, that was clear from what she said, which, or so he imagined, would never, never, never have been expressed so frankly and straightforwardly to another member of his guild (or what should he call it?)—downright trustingly, an impression reinforced by the way she continued to touch him, without any inhibitions, putting her hand on his shoulder, punching him on the upper arm and chest in her excitement at being able to speak her mind, picking a hair off his coat, twirling one of its buttons, and one time, completely caught up in the subject or her views on the subject, unconsciously bumping him with her hip, like a stray animal that had adopted him, like his pet. True, he had to keep asking questions to make her go on speaking. But he sensed that she wanted him to ask. Could he have asked her anything, so to speak? Asked until she had told him everything? No, only harmless matters were permissible, or what passed for such. And this very asking and refraining from asking helped light a fire under him, in the past always deeply resistant to asking questions. An animated give-and-take developed between the two of them as they stood by the glass door, and viewed from the outside it looked as if all the people here and there, sometimes even in large numbers, lining both sides of the tracks, who in reality had come for the train's last crossing of the Semmering, were their spectators, forming an aisle of honor.

During the Moravian night, the former writer picked up the narrative thread at this point. Yes, the girl, the reader, the "creature," as he thought of her, was still in school. Yes, she got along well with her parents. With her father, at the moment out of work and getting trained for a new job, she often went mountain-climbing. She had a more than fifty-kilometer bus ride to school. In the wintertime she walked the last three kilometers home in the dark, without being afraid. Yes, she had a brother, with whom she sometimes had fun. Her mother was a teacher, for special-needs children, also far from home, but in the other direction, so the evening meal was often prepared by her grandfather, who still lived with them. But she did not care for his cooking. During the holidays she earned money as a swimming instructor at the community pool on the river, and by offering tutoring in math, Latin, and even Russian, becoming increasingly important in her area, and on weekends she played the piano in the town where she went to school, in a blues club, really? Yes. She sometimes felt sad, though not often. What did she plan to be when she grew up? She did not know. Go abroad? She did not know. To her, reading was simply essential. It was the drive train, the engine, and the fuel all in one. The blues on the piano came later, inspired by her reading. Some guests at the club thought her playing resembled a lament. "Such a tender lament," one of them had remarked, "impervious to any comfort, and also not needing any." Someday she would sing to her own accompaniment, but that day had not yet come. She would probably never write, at most a song now and then—again, when the time came. Her parents did not read, at least nothing worthwhile. The daughter had reproached her father and mother for that, and not only once. Her brother did not read either, but for him there was still hope. Her parents, on the other hand: what a disgrace. She had never seen either one of them with a book. In their spare time they rattled around the house doing the most inane things, and very noisy things. Only if it made a racket did it count for them. But yes, she was fond of them in spite of everything, and it was not her father's and mother's fault that she, the sixteen-year-old, despised the current era, the time in which she lived. Her reasons? None. All she could say was that some of her male and female friends—so she had some? yes, of course—felt the same way: isolated, filled with an enthusiasm that could never find expression through a larger movement undertaken with others; they disliked the present, they rejected it, excluded as they were, and were prepared to fight it, each in his or her own way. Not even rap offered any hope these days. And if she, the creature, wished she were living in a different era, it was not one in the future—she could not imagine one she would like—but in the past, and in a different place. She would have liked to live, for instance, in America in the forties and fifties of the last century, or in Russia during Dostoevsky's time—despite the nihilists? precisely because of them—or in pre-Christian Greece, in the days of Pythagoras, whom she, the only girl among the students at her school to do so, pictured as a teacher, one whose mathematical principles not only taught one to calculate and measure but also guided and disciplined one to understand the logic of language, of speaking and writing.

What a creature. And to think that such a creature was growing up in the country that had epitomized for him, at least during one period in his life, the hub around which his prejudices revolved. The disappearance of prejudices: worth narrating as hardly anything else could be. What would be more fruitful as a narrative subject? And that such a creature was confiding in him, of all people. What a gift. One he did not deserve? His heart, he said, using this exact word, was ready to "burst" in the presence of such "innocence," again his exact word. And receiving once again, certainly not by any means for the first time in his life, receiving such a gift, which he thought he did not deserve, became too much for him, and at the station where some of the cars were uncoupled to continue on to Styria, he abruptly said goodbye to the young reader, the "tenderest among thousands," as she appeared to him, and got off the train. To be alone, with the afterimage of the creature.

If he could still imagine a painter for his times, it would be a painter of afterimages. That was the role he assumed during our night on the boat, though merely with one finger in the air and a few evocative sentences. With the afterimage of his fellow passenger before his eyes, he sketched out for us how he pictured her at the moment. Although it was night, he saw her in daylight. As we sat in the boat's salon here on the Morava, each of us at his table, she was climbing with her grandfather to a mountain pasture, far off beyond the Karavanka range. They had slept in the hay loft of a barn belonging to the last active farm on the southern slope of the Sau Alp. She had scratches on her legs from the hay, cut years earlier, and dust in her nostrils—but those features were not significant in this afterimage. What was significant? What was going on inside her; the interior of her exterior. And the girl seen against the glow of mica flakes along the trail, which now narrowed to a cow path in the first light of day. He saw her beneath the last flickering stars, which she pointed out to her grandfather, but he was too bleary-eyed and also too preoccupied to look up. He saw her between two boulders at the entrance to a hiding place once used by the partisans, with nothing there to serve as a reminder, no grenade fragment, no shell casing, no ring of ashes, no pieces of a cot, no scraps of a pamphlet, not one piece of type from the printing machine the Allies had dropped by parachute—perhaps the most important of all: with only the grandfather remembering, reminding himself as well as his granddaughter, and suddenly no longer feeling tired. He saw her with glowing black eyes, holding in her hollow fist, no, not bullets but rock-hard blue juniper berries. He saw her darting up the mountainside, far ahead of her grandfather, letting out a piercing shout, then another, until finally she heard the echo. He saw her waiting for the old man, squatting on her heels, then going back downhill toward him, and forever going toward him, or also no one, at least no one specific, simply all her life going toward, not allowing anything or anyone to get her down, filled with sadness from time to time, but externally invulnerable, protected by herself, by her nature, by her being, forever free, forever young. And in the end that was what he wished her from afar.

And he? After the meeting with the young reader, he remained alone again for a long time. He wanted that, too, avoided any encounter, decisively, with conviction. Yet upon getting off the train he had ended up in the town where he had perhaps the most acquaintances of anywhere in the country, not from his profession but from his time at the university. How to avoid running into them? Simple: by staying well away from the center of town, which also, in contrast to Vienna, soon and without clear markers merged into nondescript areas. But why not head straight for home, his birthplace, as he wished to, or as the chamois by the snow pit had ordered? What took you instead to G., of all places? It was a dream, another dream.—A dream?—Yes, hasn't a dream ever made you go somewhere?—Not me. Me, never.—What kind of a person are you? You should be ashamed of yourself, forgetting your dreams. Or even worse, being embarrassed by them. Listen to my dream—all of you have already dreamed it, each of you, again and again; otherwise I wouldn't tell it to you. It has to do with the back side, a back side. What kind? The back side of a house, for instance where one spent one's childhood. The back side of a mountain that one has seen or hiked only from the front. A dream, as you recall, never has a subject. It has no action, ever. All it enables us to see, as we cannot when awake, is the back side, an empty, seemingly lifeless sphere that can nonetheless make itself felt in our innermost vein and heel bone. The back side of the mountain lies there in a clear haze. One step inside and down into the sphere takes me to a different planet. In a moment I have landed in an invisible, immaterial spaceship on a foreign, distant star, where everything, except for the light from the sky, is exactly as on earth: the varieties of trees, the topography, the air currents, the bodies of water (except that those on the brother or sister planet are omnipresent—water wherever one looks). Once a small bird there perched on my hand. A hummingbird? I asked. Yes, a hummingbird— it had the same name as on our planet. Everything, almost, looks the same and has the same name as here, and yet my innermost vein, or someone, or something, knows that it is different, starting with the first step into the realm of the back side. Different how? Simply different. Fundamentally different. Overwhelmingly different. Persistently different. Wonderfully different. Worrisomely different. Investigation-worthily different. Systematically different. Systematically? Yes.

8

≈≈≈

≈≈≈

≈≈≈

DURING THE YEARS when he was at the university in G., he had lived on a hill, on a slope that faced the city and the buildings where he had classes. The path he took had run along the ridge of the hill. But either the side of the hill facing away from the town had been obscured by houses or he had never consciously looked down in that direction, let alone been tempted to step off the path on that side or venture downhill; during all his years as a student the back of the hill was not even terra incognita to him, it did not exist. In a dream, in his dreams, however, much, much later, that side of the hill, as well as the landscape down below—dizzyingly far down—appeared to him as the Different Planet, also under a Different Sun. And to this dream he gave credence—a rare enough occurrence. And so he set out for this overlooked area, full of curiosity, positively driven by the spirit of discovery.

He had little to report from this part of his expedition. (On the other hand, during that night he really had little interest in giving a report.) If he made discoveries, they were fairly ordinary ones. The sense of the uncanny that had underlain the dream—that the Different Planet could lose its atmosphere, its airspace, at any minute—dissolved. The day on which the wanderer turned off the road along the ridge and ventured onto the back side of the hill was a bright, sunny day like any other. On the winding streets and alleys leading downhill, he felt he had particularly firm ground underfoot. A draft wafted up toward him, strengthened further by the breeze his own movement generated. Spring sunshine lit the way ahead, mild in a way that one could imagine only for one's home planet. What remained in effect from the dream: the sense of having plunged into another realm. From the moment he stepped off the ridgeline, even his own circulatory system seemed to take a different path. The back of the hill, in contrast to the side facing the center of town, the north side, turned out to be thickly settled, this, too, contradicting the dream, in which it had been unpopulated. The houses were rather small, often having only one story, more frequently older rather than newly constructed, and all of them of different heights, at varying distances from one another, also with a variety of roof styles, in a nice jumble, and set in equally small yards. And this for as far as his eyes could see, and they could see far, all the way to the opposite slope, the antipodes, so to speak, not merely thanks to the landscape but also just because they could. With every step he saw new territory, and, alien and familiar at the same time, it showed no trace of dream-gloom—this was not his city, to be sure, but his country. You heard right: he caught himself, no doubt about it, saying to himself in quiet amazement: "That's my country. That would be my country. That would have been my country." And in that respect perhaps he could speak of a discovery after all. It fit the circumstances that, although the houses were almost exclusively private dwellings, they appeared to him as small businesses, here a mill, over there a carpentry shop, in between a distillery, a cobbler's, a sawmill, a stonecutter's, a master mason's, a laundry, not to forget one or two farmhouses and inns, and also one or two small factories for all sorts of things (no weaponry, however), and in particular a research center, and next to it the house of the town clerk. That business about "my country," however, he forgot almost immediately. In silent amazement, yes, without words. If, as he had done earlier, he had been writing down everything that went through his head and opened his eyes, or the opposite, he would have written that as one word: silentamazement. The sounds, the noise, the racket were the same as everywhere in the world, that, too, in contrast to the completely soundless dream; let everyone come up with his own soundtrack. But during his descent, this time at least, he listened in silent amazement to the whistling and whirring, the pounding and banging, the barking and meowing; or: the types of noise were pretty much all going at once, but with him they went in one ear and out the other. The amazement occasioned a type of concentration more involuntary yet also more complete than one could wish for. It involved admiring, concentrating exclusively on one object, one happening, one moment. And it involved learning, enjoyably, in a way that made him wish he could continue learning forever—but only in this way, and never again in the way he had learned in the old days, during his, oh well, his student days on the other side of the hill, in his narrow, dim garret there without a glimmer of larger understanding and without a breath or whisper of the present, of relevance, of the significance for the world of what he was studying. Amazement and learning, now, and now, and now. But what specifically did he learn on the back side of the hill? "Concretely?" What earthshaking things? What, for instance? For instance, a sparrow, no bigger than a hummingbird, was bathing there in a dust-filled depression. Two men were standing at a garden gate, one of them inside, the other outside. On a windowsill stood a saucepan. A bicycle tipped over. A woman had gray-green eyes. A man had a scar on his cheek that was not from dueling. A branch bounced from a bird that had just taken off. A scrap of newspaper poked out of a catch-basin grating. The sun shone. A jackhammer pounded. A black man was sticking advertising leaflets in mailboxes. A Turk and an Asian were talking, in Austrian dialect. The engines of an airplane that had landed screamed far off on the plain. The sky was the way it was. But below him different people were moving around, and he, too, as he made his way along, was a different person. If all this was learning, at the same time it was unlearning, a no less enjoyable process. And the danger again of taking leave of one's senses and not finding one's way back to the old earth, to life, from the New Planet? This danger did not exist when one was silently amazed, or hardly. And what, and where, was life in this case? And if so, what preserved the sense of equilibrium was, for instance, entering a shop somewhere and buying something, almost anything, naming numbers, supply and demand.

And thus the wanderer, when, after much crisscrossing, he had finally by the end of the day reached the bottom of the hill, promptly turned into a customer, purchasing a small carpet that he wanted to give, as quickly as possible, as a present to someone, anyone, in the spirit of the day, and sticking it under his arm, he then wandered around the base of the hill toward town, remembering a drawing class in boarding school in which he had drawn a house with only windows, no door. And when the teacher asked him where the door was, he replied, "In the back"—whereupon the teacher turned the paper around and, holding it up to the entire class and shouting, "Where in the back?" poked a very sharp pencil through it.

Later, when? later, as he was marching day and night along the Old Road to get to his birthplace, and confided to one of the people he met along the way his experience on the back side of the hill, this other person unexpectedly turned out to be a journalist and explained to him that this was not appropriate material for an article, and that it was especially not considered proper nowadays to describe such a thing or such an absurd thing the way he, the wanderer, had just done. But this will be discussed later, and in more detail. For now and henceforth, one thing at a time.

That Old Road had long since been off-limits to vehicles. It had been used for vehicular traffic before the war, before the wars, a light ribbon of gravel snaking its way across the countryside. Later it ran parallel at varying distances to the more or less straight paved road. The latter served as a highway, while what was now called the Old Road, whose many twists and turns made it somewhat longer, had always had the appearance of a local road, composed of a hundred and one smaller segments. In the meantime it had become usable only as a hiking trail, and even that only in some stretches, for not all of them were still passable, although those that were were generous. When one reached the gaps, one had to keep one's bearings as best one could, and even the remaining passable sections of the gravel road were often overgrown with brush—the Old Road did not attract many walkers (especially since it was not marked as a hiking trail anywhere), and for this very reason some found it even more attractive.

Beforehand, he again took a plane to get him to the place from which he had always set out for home. It was a domestic flight, the route between G. and K. just being inaugurated that day, and the flight plan indicated that they would be flying almost directly over his village. He sat in a small aircraft that flew at low altitude, not much higher than a helicopter, perhaps also because it was the maiden flight and the passengers were supposed to be offered something to see. As if in answer to his wishes, it was clear, calm weather, and he sat, again as he would have wished, by the window that afforded a perfect view and then saw below, very close, every detail sharply defined, the region he knew from childhood, which he had never seen from a bird's-eye perspective, and especially not in such proximity to the adjacent areas: now, from the plane, or the flying carpet, he saw the village in relation to them, and beyond that in relation to the whole country—even if what could be seen this way did not all belong to that countryside. And at the same time he recognized the tree in the center of the village, the cherry tree that was probably dead by now, along with the spring house of rough concrete at its foot, and next to it the abandoned village tavern, which still glowed in rich yellow, and across from it the wall around some-

222

one's orchard, which he and others had scaled more than once to steal apples and pears. And there, the wall of the barn belonging to his grandfather's place, his birth house, with the vent cut into the boards in the form of a cloverleaf—four-leafed, of course. Or was that another fata morgana, a hallucination from a long-ago time? And over there another barn wall, with movie posters advertising coming attractions, one poster for every month, small white sheets with nothing but the films' titles, nothing but writing, pasted on top of each other as thick as a book after all the months, years, and decades, and then the end, the last sheet, the last of the screenings. And now the cemetery with the wall as high as a house to protect "against the Turks," where a cat was just darting along the shingled roof. And now the lake, silted up? no, not that bad, not entirely, one watery eye still open amid the jungle of reeds, the stalks rising from black mud, which oozed refreshingly between one's toes, and the leeches in the black mud, and, and . . .

From the airfield directly to the Old Road. It was also high time; time to go; time to "drop by at home," perhaps for one last time. And soon the first encounter. A man was standing there by the road, close to the stinging nettles, in front of an easel. He was outfitted with an enormous paint box, an equally enormous palette, a white painter's smock, from whose numerous pockets poked brushes in every size, and so forth, like a so-called princely painter, also wearing a fur cap, adorned in back with a foxtail. But when the wanderer answered his wave and came closer, the canvas turned out to be bare, with not a single dab of color, also without any preparatory sketch. The man, who had apparently been here on the Old Road for quite a while, had not yet begun. It looked, however, as though he was close to starting, so energetically did he gesture with first one of his brushes, then another, next with the palette knife, using it repeatedly to measure something, something different each time, something near, something far, at his head, by his feet; what could it be? He closed his left eye, then the right one, suddenly exclaimed, "Ha!" then "Yes!" then again "So!" (with a short *o*), yet nothing happened, and besides, the paint squeezed in huge blobs onto the palette had dried up and was hard as rock. He seemed to be a wannabe painter, not a proper one, or at least not yet, not for the moment. In reality he came from an almost opposite world, or this world had once been his, as the gesture with which he urged the approaching stranger to come closer betrayed, more an imperious gesture than a wave, just one brief, lordly, no, constablelike beckoning with his index finger, his body otherwise motionless, the eyes and the entire face rigid, the legs splayed.

Just as with all the subsequent individual encounters on the Old Road, appearances proved deceptive and everyone was sooner or later revealed to be someone else, so, too, here: Oh, dear, wasn't this the politician who had once been in power in the country and on whom a person described as mentally disturbed had made an assassination attempt? Yes, it was. "Yes, I'm the one." He said it softly, in a completely unrecognizable voice. It was a gentle voice, yet it carried, as it once had on the radio or elsewhere, perhaps carrying even farther now. His beckoning had been an illusion, he had probably made the gesture by mistake, or he had been playacting. His eyes were also gentle, eyes such as one seldom saw in his day, and large, as if opened wide, pleading, almost dry, the pupils intensely enlarged like a child's, as if he were gazing into darkness. And he talked incessantly, without asking the other person where he was coming from and where he was going. He had waited so long on the Old Road for another human being; no one had been attracted by his getup, or had no one else happened by? At intervals he showed off the scar on his abdomen from the gunshot and gave himself an insulin injection: in the shock of being shot at point-blank range he had become diabetic from one second to the next. He had turned his back on politics. He was nothing but a disabled pensioner. A widower, without friends. He had not had any friends earlier, either, but that had not mattered to him at the time. How pale he looked, although he was out in the fresh air all day. For a while he had still gone to the marketplace, making his way from booth to booth, also to the soccer field or ice-hockey rink, had mingled with the crowd when one of his successors presided over the opening of a bridge somewhere, laid a cornerstone, put the first shovel in the ground. In the meantime, however, he spent most of his time on the Old Road. Not that he wanted to get away from people. On the contrary. He could cry every time someone so much as noticed his presence, let alone recognized him. It was the masses he could not bear anymore. Even just a few, more than two or three, scared him off.

First of all, only one person at a time came along the Old Road. And besides, in his painter's disguise he could think so wonderfully, so wonderfully painfully there. More and more ideas, not for himself but for his country and its citizens, were spawned there. If he had the chance to do it over again, he would still become a politician, but a politician such as there had never been in these parts since the kaiser's time. One who was not indistinguishable from the others, one whose person, his very person, was sorely needed. And first and foremost he would speak a different language. Everything else would flow from this different language. And on the Old Road a new language came to him, but only individual words that did not fit together to form sentences. It had not reached that point yet; he had not reached that point yet. But just you wait. And he stretched out his arm toward the distant city. How his hands shook. He could hardly hold the brush, which in fact dropped into the stinging nettles without the former politician's seeming to notice. He did not take his eyes off the other man. He did not want to let him leave, blocked his way, stopped just short of lying down in his path to keep him from moving on. And then he suddenly let him go after all, wished him "safe travels," wanted only to be looked at once more, which actually brought tears to his eyes?

Some time later a voice called out to the wanderer on the Old Road from behind, the voice this time not gentle but grating, a scratchy voice that drawled out the sounds and swallowed syllables like a drunk. He turned to look, and what he saw seemed to confirm that impression: a man he did not recognize staggering along and babbling at him, so unceremoniously that one wondered where one had met him before and whether one hadn't known him for a long time, or whether one had been on the road so long that one had lost one's memory, and even old friends had become strangers? And he let the stranger catch up to him, thinking that might help him remember. Apparently he was not a drunk after all but a vagrant. Did that mean someone he had known in his youth had gone downhill or, as the expression went, taken a wrong turn, like his first love or also that schoolmate, the brightest boy in the boarding school, whom he had run into again in Athens, busking on the slope of the Acropolis, his flute so shrill it made one want to cover one's ears, and the performer not wanting to be recognized? (His dialect alone would have given him away there, below the Parthenon.) No, this man who then walked beside him, moving and breathing with difficulty—or actually forcing him to adjust his pace to the stranger's scuffing along—was no old acquaintance who had degenerated into a vagrant. He was not a vagrant at all. The first impression of wild hair down to his shoulders had been deceptive. It was a headful of tightly curled hair, and it belonged to—what was the term—a black person? And likewise his outfit revealed itself upon closer inspection to have nothing clochard-like about it. No trace of its being matted. All the materials were choice, without exception: worsted, cashmere, silk, "pure cotton." From close up the garments did not appear sloppy or tattered in the slightest, but rather capacious and flowing, the thick-soled shoes suitable for hill and dale without being actual hiking boots. They gleamed on the ribbon of gravel as if this were London's Bond Street or such. This person was completely unknown to him, a man who despite his shortness of breath talked without pause to him, or rather to himself. But in the process he revealed himself to the other man. Had he lost his way in the area? Not in the slightest. He had settled here on purpose, near the Old Road. He had had pulmonary disease for a long time, was mortally ill, and once a day he struggled out to the Old Road to get fresh air. Walking there, slowly up and down, refreshed his lungs, or what was left of them. He had been a professor of "world literature" in the capital city, and every third or fourth sentence he spoke was a quotation from Homer, Shakespeare, Keats, or from his own father. Yes, his father was a world-renowned poet, "from the Caribbean, from Nigeria, from Madagascar—as you wish" (the storyteller put it this way during that night on the Morava). He quoted his father and hated him. So was this father still alive?—And how! He was in much better shape than the son, fighting death every day here on the Old Road, far, so far from home. Had his progenitor disowned him, then?—No answer. It became clear that the poet had never hesitated to sacrifice anyone for his goddess, poetry. It was not even so much sacrificing as ignoring. It cost him nothing; to drop the other person or to lose sight of him created no conflict in him, no reflection, no self-doubt, let alone inner conflict, that conflict that one world religion calls great. He viewed himself as consecrated to poetry from birth, poetry's deputy on earth, and thought he had every right to walk over dead bodies for his goddess's sake, or to banish from his poet's life those who should have been his nearest and dearest—to let them die as he had his parents at one time, then his wives, and now his son, Isaac and Ishmael in one person. Goddess? She had long since shriveled to an idol, to a stuffed bugaboo, without air in her lungs, as had the poet, his father, her embodiment. It had been a long time since a poem had come to him on wings of inspiration and had gone flying from him into the world. For a long time now he had merely performed a public role wherever he appeared, had become a circus barker among thousands of barkers, including on those occasions when he recited his poems in a whisper, presented himself, spoke, sat there as a celebrity even in the most private moments—but what could still be private about that kind of professional poet? He did not merely have an opinion on anything and everything but also constantly broadcast it to the world, his eyes darting around, demanding attention, representing poetry, even when he was alone for a change, in the men's room or wherever. And instead of his having run out of breath, that had happened to his son, as a sort of proxy. So had the father completely forgotten his son, now so ill?—For a long time that had seemed to be the case. But now that he knew the end was imminent, he called him almost every evening, across several continents, and asked for an update.—And what did that mean?—The father planned to write a poem about his son after he died, and was collecting from afar his penultimate, last, and perhaps this very evening his very last words. He had a plan, but it did not mean that on the telephone he had ulterior motives. The plan had been explicit from the beginning; it was consistent with his profession and did not prevent the father from caring; his voice, after he had listened to his son's report on his condition, uttered with much wheezing and panting, sounded different from his usual proclamatory voice. It sounded stricken, as if he was choking back sobs, stricken by the other man's pain and suffering, but by the same token inseparable from the thought that this fate cried out for a poem, yes, cried out for a long poem, an epic one, such as he, the poet-father, had dreamed of all his life, a Caribbean or a Nigerian epic, an epic about a new prodigal son. And a little while ago his father had actually burst into tears, in the middle of a long-distance telephone call, and had not stopped sobbing, had only sobbed louder, despite, as almost always, being not alone but surrounded by other public personages like himself who, as could be heard through the satellite transmission, were turning away, even lowering their eyes, each for himself, and removing themselves from the room with the telephone, softly, softly, let's leave him alone, and in the end the two of them, the son on this end, the father on the other end of the line, had simply sobbed, bawled, and whimpered at each other—which one was the father, which the child?—without words, which on him, the one who was ill, had the effect of carrying oxygen to what was left of his lungs to a degree normally achieved only by his walking up and down the Old Road all day. And with that his story ended. He continued to walk beside the homeward-bound wanderer for a while, but without uttering another word. Toward evening he turned back, for a telephone call? It was he, the temporary companion, who received the small carpet as a gift. Gazing westward over his shoulder after the forgotten son, our host saw smoke eddying from his head: was he smoking? The sky above him seemed vaulted (not often did it appear that way). The sun, almost down to the fairly level horizon—the mountains lay in the opposite direction—cast lance-length shadows over the innumerable rock fragments on the road. The son's wheezing could be heard almost all the way to that horizon. He was wheezing hard enough to melt a stone, as if he were bearing his father on his back.

The other man, "I," walked on all through the night. The former politician had given him a handful of nuts "from my own garden," and the former professor had given him a piece of chocolate "from my homeland," and those were his provisions. The night on the Old Road was bright, thanks in part to the gravel, still white, possibly bleached by the weather. Even where the material had sunk into the ground along some stretches and had been covered by layers of postwar fill, even when it was out of sight, the road retained a certain incomparable firmness due entirely to this gravel that did not let one wander off course, even along the stretches that were almost pitch-black, where the road led through woods, usually a dense spruce forest. During the night he still had quite a few encounters, each of them only in passing, for a couple of minutes, merely sensed yet leaving no less of an impression, encounters moreover affecting only him, the walker, whereas some of those encountered by him that night on the road did not so much as notice him, perhaps on purpose. As our host for the Moravian night described this to the rest of us, it seemed as though the night of storytelling—already far advanced—was reinforced by the night he was telling us about.

For a long time all he registered of the nocturnal figures on the Old Road was their gait. Depending on how they came toward him, despite the darkness distinct gaits could be recognized. Those who bustled along wanted to call attention to themselves, but were harmless; there was nothing to fear from them; as was always the case with vain people, one was perfectly safe in their presence. On the other hand, some of the walkers were dangerous; their very gait spelled danger, just as the running posture of certain dogs signals danger even at a distance: one had to reckon with the possibility of being attacked. The peaceable walkers were something else again; one could count on being greeted as they passed and receiving good wishes for the rest of one's journey. And it was something else, yet again, with the peacemakers among the walkers, not that they meant anything by it: completely preoccupied, taking no notice of the world around them, let alone of the person observing them, they infected that person through their casual art of walking, which forestalled any warlike thoughts, and involuntarily, like any art—or perhaps not?—offered a liberating example, lighting up the road in the darkness. On the other hand, there were the warlike walkers, tromping loudly but not really dangerous, at least for the moment, dangerous only by virtue of their numbers, albeit during that night on the Old Road dangerous also as individuals. And then the desperate or despairing walkers, their heads and shoulders drooping, their steps ever so small, hardly raising their feet off the ground (but walking nonetheless, whether alone or in clusters, or at least still walking). And the ugly walkers, each of whom, instead of moving in one piece, with legs and brow in sync, as they were supposed to be, or perhaps not, after all, had his limbs all in a jumble, dangling, bobbing, not head over heels but heels over head, and altogether full of ill will— otherwise it would not have looked so ugly—not a walking but a seemingly vengeful, intentionally offensive letting himself go, which created the impression that the person in question wanted to show the world that the only real thing, the only thing that would remain in the end, was this kind of scornful refusal, absolute refusal, to budge. And even more insulting were the self-consciously attractive walkers who mistook the Old Road for a running track and while passing an imaginary reviewing stand gazed into the distance, a distance they merely feigned to see, and with their rolling shoulders and vigorous gait conjured up an élan that stemmed from the devil only knows what but definitely not from their style of locomotion, which seemed utterly fake and at most made one want to crawl on all fours in front of this type of walker or creep forward on one's stomach. But then the opposite occurred with the walkers whom our host placed even higher than the peaceable and peacemaking walkers: he called them "the imagination-sparking walkers" and varied or corrected that moniker to "the inspiring" ones. Their characteristics? (the interrupter)—he did not want to mention any except perhaps that the inspiring walkers, Old Road be damned, moved along beneath the heavens, Kant's starry ones as well as the starless ones; and he added that during that other night there, in some cases, the walker types had switched identities in midstep, like chimeras, so a peaceable walker might turn in an instant into a desperate one, a pseudoattractive one into a truly attractive one, an order-loving one into a dangerous one, and so forth.

Things were really hopping, or hopping in a different sense, on the Old Road in the hour after midnight—how should it be otherwise? Action! And what, specifically? Flight and pursuit. The country's past returned, in scenes of war, in life-and-death situations. Some time ago the silence had become sinister. Soon blows would fall. And then, without warning, a little squad of partisans emerged from the underbrush along the road, soundlessly, and one felt no surprise, either at what had occurred or at what happened next. The partisans had several children with them, were leading them, hand on shoulder, and the children walked with their eyes closed, in their sleep. No one spoke. Get off the road—you've been betrayed! one wanted to shout, but could not get a word out. And in fact a moment later, at the next bend in the road, people jumped out of the ditch, with only swastikas and gun barrels visible, and, and? and? See above. And suddenly a church bell pealed, and after midnight at that. But just as suddenly a third group came into view, on a sort of reviewing stand, made of steel, new, and plainly not belonging to the Old Road: a camera could be seen there, the kind that can also film in the dark—the whole thing was a scene in a film, the action belonged to a film, bodies hurtling to the ground, blood spurting, eyes breaking, one child diving back into the underbrush, the sole survivor—who later, when he was grown old, would say, "We always walked at night. I gazed at the stars until I fell asleep. When a

231

partisan's child survives—the fear stays with him all his life. A child fears for his life much more than a grown-up. Only now do I know that. All I knew was fear. A life in fear, and in my fear I felt like a stone. I did everything possible not to be a stone anymore, to feel myself. But I was a stone—that was all there was to it. And something else stayed with me: that I never again trusted anyone enough to talk about my feelings, and not only those about the war. That stays with me."

And look at that! Who was the director, who was making the film? Wasn't it Filip Kobal, the writer from the neighboring village? Yes, it was, and he had also written the script, which he let the wanderer glance at, with a flashlight. Did he even recognize his old friend and onetime rival? Did Filip—who had gained weight and spread horizontally, he who had once been so gaunt—realize with whom he was speaking? Pointless questions—such things did not count during that night there on the Old Road, where everyone could speak with anyone, spontaneously, without needing to be introduced. And thus Kobal opened up to the other man, friend or not, without any preliminaries, during the brief interval before the next scene had to be set up, perhaps also out of tiredness. For a long time now he had been writing only film scripts, and because they were "hopelessly personal," he filmed them as well, not without passion, and above all free from fear, in contrast to the days of his novel writing. He was also always elated to be working with others. In his eyes, literature had lost its luster, only for this era? forever? It no longer had anything to offer, not even the stars, for it had no glow for the glow of distant parts? And yet, and yet. Franz Kafka was not dead. Franz Grillparzer and Adalbert Stifter still lived, in our midst in the next room. Samarkand was no less legendary and real than before, had even moved closer, to this side of the border, if now it had shrunk to the size of a village, to the neighboring village beyond the neighboring village, and was located no longer on the Silk, Salt, Pepper, or some other road but not even half a day's walk away on the Old Road here. And there was so much pleading in the world, silent pleading, in so many eyes, perhaps more than ever before. And so much sighing, to be heard by anyone who had ears to hear, embarrassed, wordless sighing, as never before. Only the bold ones, the inwardly cold ones, the shameless ones survived? No, the shame had also survived, though in a form different from the one described of old. And the silently pleading ones and the wordlessly sighing ones demanded, yes, panted to be asked and likewise to receive an answer. They wanted to be preserved and written down, but not necessarily in images, and certainly not for television. And look, the child here, the children: in them is concentrated, far more purely than in us big folk, us grown-ups, the secret of the times, and this secret cannot be filmed. The secret of the times in the children? What did he mean by that? Without any external happening or action, and also without any outward sign on the little one there, on his little body, a single moment determined in him the entire future course of his life. A single moment, not anything lasting, decided what time would be for the child from then on, and also how this time would be for him. The one decisive moment struck the defenseless little body like a bolt of lightning, going straight to its core—unlike with me, the adult, who, on the contrary, has become more or less immune and would have to search for a long time to find anything resembling a core in myself—and the secret of it was that this lightning moment passes the child by seemingly without a trace. The one who caused the lightning, who lit and tossed the bolt, I, the adult, the father, the mother, saw the child continuing to play as he had been playing the moment before—if only he had at least paused or looked up at me—and did not notice, or noticed only long afterward, when it was already too late, that that one moment would remain branded onto him, irrevocably, hopelessly, for eighty, ninety, even a hundred years of time-sickness. But someone else was to write that story, or perhaps it had already been written, and not only one story?

Kobal was called for the next scene—the child lying among corpses as the sole survivor—and the nocturnal wanderer continued on his way, having been given a salami sandwich from the film crew's field kitchen. He could now cancel his plan of visiting Filip Kobal in his

Rinkendorf, close to the Old Road. And that was fine with him. It still did him good to be among his own kind—that was how he felt, strange, even now, when he was out of the game—but for as short a time as possible, just in passing. Once there had been three of them in this area he was passing through, who had—what was the expression?—made a name for themselves as writers. Ah, names. Oh dear, names. How comforting it was now to go through the night as a nobody, in a darkness that in this hour along some stretches on the Old Road veritably solidified into something material, a material so soft and cloudlike that one had the sensation of being lifted off the ground and becoming disembodied, without worrying about losing one's way—hoisted under the armpits by the darkness and made to hover, at least without the earlier strain of walking and without the slightest resistance from the air. Names, oh, names. He had hardly been able to invent names and write them down—as if for him and his writing they were taboo. And yet there were certain names that had kickstarted him. Nebuchadnezzar. Maracaibo. Tatabánya. Kristiania. Fyodor Mikhailovich Dostoevsky. Joseph Conrad. Joseph Cotten. Elio Vittorini. Galicia. Dolina. Gariusch. Fontamara. Providence. Lind. Dob. Himberg. Matthias Sindelar. The impetus for one of his first stories had come solely from such a name, the name of a murderer: Geronimo Benavente. Praised be names, in spite of everything!

He thought of Gregor Keuschnig, the third person from that region, together with Filip Kobal and himself. And then, not for the first time, someone whose name had just come to mind showed up in person within the hour. At any rate he saw the figure he encountered next during that night on the Old Road as that very Gregor Keuschnig from yet another neighboring village—their villages formed a crook-angled, very sharp triangle—who, rumor had it, had turned his back on his French host country and his no-man's-bay to return to his native Rinkolach, whose only resident was now him. But the man standing at a bend in the road shining a flashlight (another one) into the woods, which, at the spot in question, was a pine forest, was not Gregor Keuschnig, although he resembled him so closely, especially in his posture, that the wanderer, who had stopped behind him, could not help seeing in the stranger his erstwhile friend and almost-relative. He contemplated, measured, and studied in a stranger one of those to whom he felt closest; recognized perhaps more clearly who that person was than if he had had him actually there, with all his idiosyncrasies and identifying features. And this was not the first time he had had such an experience.

The night was no longer so pitch-black, and the contours of "Gregor Keuschnig," the stooped shoulders and the rather angular head, seen from the back, along with the "lost profile," became increasingly distinct. The night wind already felt somewhat like a morning wind, wafting up from below, from the ground, changing directions. The man by the side of the Old Road seemed not to feel the gaze on his back. He had eyes only for the cone of his flashlight, which he moved pouce by pouce—so this old measurement unit still existed—over the litter of pine needles. At the same time he offered himself for viewing, as if intentionally, showing himself not to one person in particular but to his surroundings, the gaps between the tree trunks, between the leaves on the occasional bushes as the wind blew them apart, between the stinging nettles and the blackberry brambles. At his feet a basket, filled with what he had gathered during the night: dandelion greens, feathers, snakeskins, a mummified fire salamander, pieces of birch bark, white, with lines that made it look like natural writing paper, and—how could it be otherwise?—among the other odds and ends a goodly number, and numerous types, of mushrooms, spring morels, wood ears, dottles, arranged and exhibited as if to prove to the world that it was possible to gather fresh mushrooms all year round, and it was these he was after above all, these he was hunting for—which showed that the rumors about him were true—these days even at night.

So who, as what kind of a person, did this "Keuschnig" reveal himself to be? Engrossed in studying his contours, the nocturnal wanderer gradually formed an image, no, not just one, but rather one image after another, more and more visual atoms in succession, which yielded a story, though not the kind focused on "what happened up to now" from the past of this "Gregor"—but one that began effortlessly in the present, now, in the course of his being observed, and flowed equally unobtrusively into the future, into "what would come later." It was a pessimistic story, without malice aforethought: it took shape all by itself behind the observer's forehead. A poignant story. And here are a few atoms or elements from that story: gathering mushrooms was not the escape Gregor Keuschnig hoped for. Neither was returning to the area around his native village. Driven out of the no-man's-bay by the noise, sooner or later he inevitably found it catching up with him on his home turf. After half a day, the silence under his grandfather's linden tree was already gone. He needed earplugs to block out the night wind, even here along the Old Road, as well as the music of the wind in the trees, the flute, cello, viola, and saxophone notes that sounded when the trunks, thick ones, thin ones, rubbed against each other, now below, now up above. The noise was there, all over the world, unceasing. That which seemed ugly, those who seemed ugly, could be thought of as beautiful, or reconceptualized, if one animated them by writing about them, but not in the presence of noise. The noise he had in mind could not be thought of as beautiful. (This Gregor Keuschnig could have delivered the keynote speech at the world symposium on noise . . .) And his escape, his return to a gatherer's existence, would not turn things around. On the contrary: as a gatherer he would lose the rest of his soul. More and more the world around him would narrow, and, with his greed to gather, eventually disappear, and he would be so caught up in gathering that he would become incapable of thought, let alone more elevated thought. What would not disappear would be the noise, until one day the final metamorphosis of Gregor Keuschnig would take place: he would run amok from sheer defenselessness. Armed hunters, defenseless gatherers.

To be sure, our host told us during the Moravian night, it was important to add that at the end of his fantasy generated by the contours of this "Gregor Keuschnig" during the night on the Old Road, the person in question turned toward him, his smile revealing that he had been aware all along, gathering or not, not merely of his surroundings but also of the gaze on his back. Viewed from the front, the stranger in no way resembled the Keuschnig the wanderer knew. What appeared in that hour between night and day was a human face, wide awake, calm, open. And at that sight, the thought, again, that nothing could be better. It went without saying that—for a price—some of the booty gathered during the night changed owners; he would not arrive at his brother's empty-handed. Defenseless gaze of the gatherer? On the contrary: armed? Ah, the disappearance of prejudices.

In classic on-the-road stories, the account of yet another adventure would be followed immediately by the sentence, refrain-like, describing how they, the heroes or some others, rode on for a while, across La Mancha, the steppe, or the prairie, "without encountering anything worth mentioning." As he now resumed walking along the Old Road, or what was left of it, heading into the morning, toward the sunrise, for a while nothing more happened, and perhaps for this very reason various things happened that did seem worth mentioning, at least to him. One after the other, his forebears came toward him in the early light, reached him, went by him. He encountered some he knew only by hearsay, mostly from stories told him by his mother. One member of the family who had emigrated to America, almost a century and a half ago, and had disappeared there, trundled past with his possessions, a few bundles knotted together, in a one-wheeled barrow called a *carriola*, and spat out a wad of brown chewing tobacco, his pale blue eyes open wide, unblinking. Then his grandfather, still young, came along, pulling a small ladder wagon behind him in which his mother's older brother was sitting, as a child, one eye covered by a blood-soaked bandage, father and son on the way to the city to see a doctor, who would say they had come too late. Where the bridge over a brook was destroyed, with only one wooden girder left, on which one had to balance to get across, the young man, one-eyed yet able-bodied, as they classified him, was marching off to war, weeping with rage, and later his mother's younger brother caught up with the wanderer, a duffel bag on his back, he having run away the previous evening from the municipal boarding school for future priests, and as day was breaking the boy approached the family farm with nothing in mind but never again to leave home (he, too, soon to be declared fit for service—may the soil of the tundra weigh lightly on you!). On this stretch of road all his absent relatives could be felt; where there was nothing, where nothing else was happening, they formed a procession, no matter in what direction they were going; they wafted toward him, wafted over the wanderer, wafted through him, not just one of them gone forever—all of them gone. Only his mother did not make an appearance. And that was fine with him. True, with the passage of time he had rid himself of his fundamental sense of guilt toward everything and everyone; he owed this reprieve in part to the fact that the primary source of his guilt, writing, or even the mere compulsion to write, no longer existed. But toward his mother he still felt guilty. He thought he had failed her, telling himself that he was already too caught up in a "life of his own," or he had stayed away while she, clinging to her pride in her loneliness, died by slow degrees. Without his apparent assent to what was happening to her, he thought, the woman could still be alive today, even displaying her characteristic cheerfulness, not at all motherly, flicking the ash off her cigarette, taking his arm (which nowadays he would tolerate), tossing her head over nothing at all. And instead she lived only in his dreams, in which time and again death was imminent; in which she lay dying, over and over. If only he could have at last shaken off this final remnant of his fundamental guilty conscience, or could at least blame it on original sin or something.

After sunrise, about a mile before the Old Road met the New Road, he came across a person of flesh and blood again, a living soul. It was no longer far to the next settlement, from which he heard, coming over a rise, a jumble of noises, astonishing for this rural area, the noises themselves astonishing, and smelled more and more smoke, streaming from still invisible chimneys, and the wanderer noticed behind him a man who was walking very quietly, noticed him probably only because he had the habit of turning in a circle a couple of times to rest and refresh his gaze. The second wanderer was practically on his heels, walking quietly, quietly, and barely avoided stepping on his foot when he paused for a moment. But not to worry: Everything about the man behind him seemed made for reassurance. Everything about him looked friendly: the eyes, which shone at "me"—"I" was the one meant, "I" alone—the voice that emanated from way down in his chest without his drawing a deep breath, a sonorous voice with a confidence-inspiring timbre; the firm yet not too firm, warm yet not too warm handshake, the spread of his legs, wide yet not too wide (unlike those of soldiers standing their ground), and above all the thick lips, looking as if naturally pursed in a dreamy smile, the kind of lips that in a classic story would have bespoken devotion and bliss, and which reminded him, the wanderer, of the lips belonging to the three kings from the Orient as portrayed in statues back home on the village church, the three of them offering their gifts of gold, frankincense, and myrrh for the newborn babe in Bethlehem, and the sight brought back the names of the kings, which in turn suggested the name of his amiable fellow walker, "Melchior," and that was the name he bore during the future course of events.

The two of them continued along the last stretch of the Old Road together, as if it were entirely natural. Hadn't he run into this Melchior time and again during his journey, at the jew's-harp players' festival, on the maiden flight from G. to K.? Indeed, his companion played a jew's harp for a few paces, the newest model from Sardinia, not exactly impressively, but nonetheless. And the former writer then told this Melchior various things about his European tour, long before the night with the rest of us on the Moravian boat. That, too, came about perfectly naturally: Melchior appeared so eager from the first moment; he was all ears even before he had heard anything. And how he then threw himself into everything he heard. A laugh at every other sentence. If he had been seated, he would have slapped his thighs; if another listener had been beside him, he would have poked him in the ribs; and in fact he kept gazing into the empty space beside him, nodding in that direction, as if to say, "Will you listen to that! Isn't that just too much? So true! So true!" And in that way he gave the storyteller the feeling that his tale was something very special, unique, as if every little episode were an unheard-of event, and as if the individual words and phrases were precisely the right ones and above all occurred at just the right moment—why would this Melchior otherwise have kept repeating them or commenting "Exactly!" "Right you are!" "That hits the nail on the head!"? And finally he threw his arm around the storyteller and walked alongside him, shoulder to shoulder, matching his steps to his, his chubby-cheeked face turned toward him, so close that it made the wanderer feel almost uncomfortable after a while, reading his sentences from the wanderer's lips and thus progressing from repeating after him to speaking in unison with him, although what came out was mostly a meaningless gibberish, similar to what results when one sings along with a song, trying to guess the words by looking at the singer's mouth.

Eventually Melchior slapped him on the back and let go of him. There followed a seemingly contemplative silence, during which they walked along side by side for a while. The last segment of the Old Road was laid out as a fitness trail, for the inhabitants of the town on the other side of the rise, waking up with a racket? For Old Road nostalgics weary from the long journey? The only person at the moment who paused briefly at the stations along the trail and followed the instructions on the sign boards was Melchior. He danced, hopped, crawled on his belly, turned somersaults, clambered up a pole with footholds, and when he came upon a sign saying CROSS THE DITCH AT A RUN, he obeyed to the letter, and likewise with TAKE YOUR HEAD IN YOUR HANDS AND PRESS IT THIRTY-SIX TIMES BETWEEN YOUR KNEES! People came toward them from the town in increasing numbers, each by him- or herself, simply out for a morning stroll, leaving the fitness trail to its own devices, and from afar he greeted each walker, waved at all of them with the broadest smile, which was returned rather shyly, also with a surprised expression. At the same time, he made room for each of them, moving to one side, letting the other have the right of way in the narrow stretches with a politeness that could hardly have been outdone. His demeanor as he walked signaled that he was the opposite of one of those space hogs now so common all over the world: he made himself skinny, moved forward in a sort of sideways gait, leading with his hip, as if he were snaking along very cautiously to avoid bumping into anyone, prancing from gap to gap, also hopping now and then like a child, making himself not only skinny but also small, and unmistakably eliciting the sympathy of all those he encountered, of young and old, men as well as women, and dogs as well, all of which made a point of seeking to be stroked by this man, who could have nothing but benign intentions. And at the end or beginning of the fitness trail, with the New Road already in view—the heavy morning traffic almost at a standstill there—he threw himself on his knees, as the pictogram instructed, remaining that way as if in a place of worship, bowed his head, and at intervals touched his forehead to the gravel remaining from the Old Road, his body facing to the east, which could be a display of reverence, probably no longer feigned, to Mecca as well as to Jerusalem.

Melchior remained in that posture for a long time, hardly visible anymore among the luxuriant weeds that had sprung up amid the gravel. No, this was no longer playful; something was happening inside him. And when he finally stood up, it was a veritable leap. But after that he did not continue along the road. What he said to the wanderer, not to his face—he no longer cared to look directly at him—but looking past him, came bursting out of him as he stood there, moving neither foot nor hand. And he said, among other things, "Let it go, my friend. I know who you are. I write, too, not only newspaper articles but also books, even novels from time to time, *à mes heures*, as the French so beautifully put it. I've been following you and your literature for a long time. Your aesthetic literature, your aesthetic books have had their day. Poetic language is dead, it no longer exists, or only as imitation, as posturing. Didn't you yourself proclaim that you weren't worthy of your noble profession? So why would you reproach the rest of us for our lack of dignity? We've had enough of you writers and your dignity. Any writer today must make a point of being undignified. Yes, those of us writing today have jettisoned dignity once and for all. The Holy Ghost no longer has any part in what we do, and no subject is sacred anymore, and for us no word and no subject is taboo. The dream of the writer as an originator is dead. If only you had learned the art of adaptation in time. Long live the literary adapters; we're it, we alone. Adaptation is all, I'm telling you, man. Only my language, the language of journalism, still lives. It alone hits the target, nails down the facts, doesn't put you to sleep. The book about your European tour: I'm going to write it. Most of it's written already, was already written, finished, before you set out from your *Moravian Night*; I need only add the names of places and persons; everything was laid out long ago—the plot, which is different from the one you just hinted at to me, the situations, dramatic in a different way, the characters, yes, real ones, not the stuff of dreams, and also the way the characters are characterized, their psyches and also the way their psychology is worked out, the current reality, and also the way it is realized, the climaxes and the elements of surprise, and also the way the ground is laid for them—all that can be learned in any creative-writing program. I was born into money—my private jet is waiting on the other side of that hill—and the most beautiful women in the world caress my chest, which is bare under the white shirt I always wear, unbuttoned down to my navel. But admittedly the only thing that turns me on is literature. I haven't succeeded yet, despite my books, despite my novels, despite my plays—I've bought up the publishing houses and theaters, of course—in making literature my own, mine alone! But now it will become mine, and no deus ex machina will tear it from my grasp! And you, my man: off with you to the ash heap of history. You've already lost the last shreds of your dignity by living in the Balkans, and loving the Balkans. What may have been special about you and those of your ilk, the—listen to me, you wannabe!—creative aspect is no more now than an aberration. The couple of you who still insist on aesthetic qualities aren't even a minority among those writing and publishing, you who see those qualities as the essential content, in contrast to the majority, engaged in the dominant forms of publication—technical, legal, journalistic; you who think you come closest to the language of nature, of human nature, as allegedly the sole natural and appropriate way of expressing matters of the soul. You're nothing but dead letters, desperadoes, standing on lost ground. 'The writer's profession, a noble profession': what impertinence, and no wonder you eventually overreached, betraying your principles. Speaking on behalf of noble souls is no longer a profession, no longer fills a book, not even a page. Noble souls exist as they always have, but more among the illiterate than among readers, hardly among readers of books and even less among readers of the press, not to mention writers, wherever they may be. How I know this? I know it because I myself was a noble soul at one time. And those highbrow books were the ultimate, they meant everything to me. Then I lost my soul in midstream, don't ask me how—if anyone is going to do any asking, I'm the one. It was a gift, a relief. That soul was heavy, you see, so much heavier than the twenty-one grams it allegedly weighs, a burden time and again. Having a soul meant feeling pity, hesitating, being stumped, lacking language, stammering, seeking the magic word, and—as I experienced daily—not finding it, over and over. Getting rid of the soul: no more problems. Especially no problems with language and writing. Adapting means: we already have the words available to describe any circumstance as well as any person, along with that person's psyche, on hand from the very first sentence, which—no need for hesitation—is not an opening sentence but, short and sweet, an attention-grabber, to the last. If anyone starts nattering on about the soul, the wind, love, the essence of something, I not only laugh in his face but cut him dead. I don't believe him. He's lying. Is that clear? Clear. And because I simply don't believe him, he himself thinks he's lying. Of course I know from earlier that poetic language is natural, appropriate. But only if there's real feeling behind it. And none of the writers has real feeling anymore. Didn't one of your ancestors say long ago that he had to hunt for a whole year to find a feeling in himself? And in the meantime all that's left is the vocabulary of feelings. And the vocabulary for the soul, and thus also for the feelings, belongs exclusively to those of us without souls, finally and, ultimately relieved, rid of the soul. In the meantime we are the sole proprietors of words and sentences and fill the press with them, as well as books. If at one time being a writer meant creating images, today the language of books is the language of journalism. Otherwise there's no truth, no reality, no forthrightness. Poetry equals floridness, equals not hitting the nail on the head but taking refuge in flowery sentiments. I'm a rotten person, I know. But at the same time I'm clear about it, so I live with my rottenness and enjoy it. Being clearly rotten gives me power. And I know the others are rotten, too, just like me, and you, too. But you don't admit that to yourselves, and therefore I have power over you, have an easy time of it with you. By being clearly rotten, I'm right for our time. I'm the monster that dances for joy. When I followed you on your journey, to do research for the novel about you, I already knew what you were like, in what direction to look and how to judge the things I saw. And likewise I already knew how to work the people from your native region into the book. It's true that I haven't spoken with any of them, but in my tale they will all appear as hicks, peasants, village idiots, drunks, ex-cons, revisionists, future terrorists, reactionaries, anti-Europeans, eccentrics, and so on. Doubtless I will come across one or two who confirm all that, someone who moved here years ago from another country and 'still can't go to the village pub,' a woman who 'wants to remain nameless for fear of some act of reprisal by the locals,' a method I regularly use in my work as a journalist, which I pursue parallel to my novel-writing, as an author should. And if I can't find the 'two reliable witnesses,' I'll simply invent them, using—what's the term?—novelist's license. I've envied you for a long time, my good fellow, less for your books—though at one time they spoke to my soul, if I may—than for your being a writer: back in the day, you were considered the gifted one, and I was considered the phony. But now, in my day, you're nothing but a character in a novel, and perhaps not even that. And nonetheless I hate you, even if the Internet confirms that you don't represent any danger to contemporary literature. You aren't writing anymore, or you aren't publishing, keeping your convulsions and your ecstasies, your quivering seconds—which at one time (see how much I know about you) provided the starting point for your books—to yourself, thanks be to the devil. I hate you because you still stand in my way, and more than ever. You break into my circles and force me to run in circles, without beginning or end, circles that are less a pleasure than sheer hell. I'm going to tear you to shreds, you can count on that, my esteemed gentleman. You will neither return to your village nor to your boat in the accursed Balkans—certainly not there. And thanks to my power, what's left of your books will go up in smoke this very day, faster than you can look, in the smokehouse behind your ancestors' farm or somewhere. You wanted to become pure spirit as a writer, and what did you become? A ghost! True: your quivering writerly language came from wordlessness, a primal wordlessness. Without this primal wordlessness, there would be no writing, or so you believe. (And your writing, then, between guilt and elation.) But wordlessness today? As the basis of a writer's existence? Old hat, snows of yesteryear, not worth mentioning. Every word and every sentence is available nowadays in advance, as prefabricated components, so to speak. Enough of your guilt and also, granted, your elation. The quivering is over and done with, my friend."

All this and more Melchior brought forth calmly, in his trained voice, with his glowing eyes and his telegenic smile, uttering now and then, without altering the gently oscillating tone, a heartfelt welcome to occasional passersby on the Old Road, as if he owned it. "And how did you get to the village after all and back to us in the Balkans?" the interrupter of the Moravian night asked at this point. "How did you rid yourself of the monster?" "I wished the Wild Hunt on him. I wished him to the devil," our storyteller replied. "And did the wishing help?" "Yes, for the moment. But he'd keep turning up, in different guises. There's an infinite supply of his type." "And how did he go to the devil?" "He shrank instantly into a hedgehog, whose spines shot off in all directions as poisonous arrows, and his face became a grotesque caricature among the grotesque graffiti faces on the wall of an old barn out in the fields."

The next monster in the story turned out to be the storyteller himself. Before he got to that subject, he asked us, his audience on the boat that night, whether we had noticed that as he continued narrating his experiences from the journey he had been addressing the woman less and less often as he continued. That his "Listen, I saw..." or "Just imagine, two lizards were mating in the spring sun..." had recently ceased altogether. Just as he was asking us these questions, we could see, through the bull's-eye window in the galley door, the woman, the stranger, jump off her kitchen stool and throw open the door. She hurtled into the salon and out the other door onto the deck, where her silhouette could barely be made out way back in the stern. It was unmistakable, however, that as the boatmaster resumed his story her back did not stop shaking. Was she crying? Was she laughing? Or was she just shivering out there in the night on the river? And before her man—if that was what he was—continued, he hemmed and hawed for a long time, shaking his head, as if at himself, biting not only his lips but also the back of his hand (one of us cried out in pain for him), and striking his skull with his fist, so hard that he swayed to one side.

During their period of separation it had become clear to him that he had been mistaken about himself. His notion that all his previous failures with women could be ascribed to his profession, which demanded exclusive attention, had been wrong. He had fooled himself into believing that if he gave up his life as a writer he would perhaps be free at long last to commit himself wholly and lastingly to the being who his dreams had always promised would be the one who... He still considered these dreams truthful. But they applied to everyone else, not to him. With or without his profession, he was meant to be alone. This was not his calling; it was almost a sickness: he had fallen victim to being alone. When had that happened? He could not say, at some point, certainly long before he became a writer, perhaps in his childhood already, when he ran away from his grandfather's house, from the family, from the village, crossing the steep meadow to the edge of the pine forest, to sit there alone, to listen to the trees' rustling, alone. And how had he come to recognize during his journey that he belonged to the species of those who are by nature unalterably, incorrigibly, hopelessly alone, the aloneness-idiots, aloneness-lunatics, independently of his writing, which, he had thought, had prevented him from realizing his dreams—from "living," others would have said—by demanding all of him? He had recognized how things stood when in her absence the woman, who unlike any woman before her corresponded to his dreams and the intimacy they portrayed, man-woman intimacy, had come more and more to seem a threat. A threat to what? A threat to his being alone, to his experiencing things alone, altogether to a way of experiencing things that with her at his side would become impossible. Increasingly from station to station, merely imagining that she was there with him, or he with her, would cause all perceiving or experiencing to break off, and so long as he could imagine her gaze resting on him, he would merely go through the motions, perceiving and experiencing himself as his own marionette. He almost saw the distant woman as his antagonist, as, to quote him, his "interferer," almost. And so he turned, in the moments of experiencing something, away from her, abruptly, instead of toward her as he had done at first, constantly.

He saw the woman as his enemy in the very second when they met again after the long separation. This occurred at the end of the Old Road, at the entrance to the town there beyond the rise. The plan had been for them to travel the last stretch to his birth village together. That the danger he constantly sniffed out could equally well originate with him would prove to be true there. For quite some time he had thought of the woman with mistrust. His suspicion had been reinforced by the encounter with the person he was calling Melchior, who had appeared at first sight to be the soul of likability and human kindness, but then—see above. However that might be, when he then saw the woman for whom he had been longing all this time waiting for him, still at a distance, at the intersection they had agreed upon, a bolt of lightning flashed through the wanderer, blinding and at the same time clear: she, who presented herself as his beloved, was in reality the woman who had been persecuting him for years, the one who fought him, the writer, even now that he was a former writer, beyond all reason, eventually not even refraining from dishonoring his deceased mother, imputing things to her that would not have occurred to one of Shakespeare's witches, the woman he had sworn to see killed for that, if not by his own hands then by a—what was the expression?—hit man, anything not to touch her himself! And now he had touched her, in a way so different from what he had imagined. She had ambushed him, there by the clearing under the eucalyptus trees, and he had fallen into her trap, the trap of that most evil of witches—there were also good witches, angelic ones!

Should he turn on his heel? And already he was running toward her. At certain moments in his life he had seen himself from the outside, as if he were watching a film in which he was also acting. That was what happened now. With his pack on his back bouncing with every step and producing a rhythmic rustling, pounding, rattling music. Although he had eyes for nothing but the woman at the crossroads, he leaped over every puddle and skirted the boulders that marked the beginning and end of the Old Road and prevented the vehicles on the New Road from turning onto it. Thus his running—he saw himself from above—looked playful, high-spirited, and as he ran he was also picturing a film with the title "The Gentle Run," and he was also silently humming along with the music of his pack and of his footsteps crunching on the gravel. But primarily he was intent on striking a blow, and, if it came to that, why not, a death blow, and what was going on inside him at the same time, the remembering, the silent singing, did not clash with that intention, it was in harmony with it, was even clarified from one step to the next by the mounting impulse to violence in the core of his body, his consciousness. And she? She understood his running, and above all the way he ran toward her as his way of greeting her. In a moment they would have each other back, and this time for good, and no words would be needed between them, not now, at least, and then not for a long time, perhaps never again. A word, whatever it might be, even the tenderest, would shatter the morning dream, which, as long as they both just gazed in silence, meant more than any other reality, would destroy it. But then the runner spoke, his voice becoming louder, shouting, in a way completely at odds with his running. And what did he shout? "I know who you are. I've seen through you. Get away, you she-devil. Go to hell."

She responded with a smile, thinking he was speaking in jest and that his words actually meant the opposite. But already he had hurled himself at her and struck her, just once—just?—so hard that she fell to the ground, into the tall grass around a tumbledown milk stand at the intersection of the Old Road with the New Road, and did not move. Hadn't anyone witnessed the act of violence? Wasn't there a lot of traffic on the New Road? It had happened so abruptly, so fast, and the woman had disappeared into the grass so fast, all of it so unbelievable that no driver, including those who might have been startled for a moment, believed it had really happened. There were no eyewitnesses. Or rather there was one, and that was him, the perpetrator. And what did he see? (As he told us about it during the night on the boat, he held his hands over his face, no, had already done so when he mentioned the blow.) He saw himself at the moment of the blow, and this moment would continue to pop up in him at least once a day for the rest of his life, and no amount of sharing the story would heal or absolve him. He saw his own face as he struck, and it was not as dehumanized as it perhaps should have been, it was the face of an avenger, of one who had lived year after year in anticipation of the moment of revenge, calm and handsome, the face of a hero in a film, if not exactly that of Gary Cooper or Marlon Brando, but of one suitable for him, his true face, undistorted.

And the woman? Out of sight. Vanished. And besides, after the blow he had continued on his way without stopping, away from the Old Road and the scene of the crime by the milk stand on the side of the highway, heading toward the town beyond the rise, briskly but without running, and without looking back. He had done the right thing. Victory!

9

~~~~~~~~~
~~~~~~~~~
~~~~~~~~~

IF HE HAD known the place at one time, he did not recognize it on this particular day. He did not recognize anything for a whole long hour, although this had to be his native region, very close to the village where he had been born and spent his childhood, over the next rise, or perhaps not after all? The sky-high mountain chain on the southern horizon, craggy limestone, should have been the Karavanka range, behind which his Balkans began—but it was a different range, an unfamiliar one that seemed to have been moved there from somewhere else entirely, and he had the same impression of the rounded ridge to the north, it, too, almost sky-high: it was not the Sau Alp familiar to him from childhood, with veins of iron, a great crouching animal of granite and mica that attracted lightning. And the river below, hardly visible as it flowed along in its trough, was not the Drau, but also not the Ebro in Spain or the Silver Bow Creek in Montana. This river was as unrecognizable as the mountains, coming from an unknown direction and flowing in an unknown direction; impossible to locate it and this entire landscape, and foreign, so foreign, the village when he reached it. Where am I? Good heavens, where am I? The only halfway graspable feature of the village was the name Filip Kobal had used for it the previous night: Samarkand—although that was not its name, but rather? Nowhere a sign, and if there was one, smeared over, blackened, the letters riddled with bullet holes, illegible.

Samarkand? For an entire hour nothing homelike revealed itself to him, not in the dwellings and especially not in the inhabitants. On earlier visits he had seen only familiar faces, even if he was not personally acquainted with them individually: he saw features passed down from great-grandparents to great-grandchildren, the same features appearing through the generations. These features, as well as the traditional dress, including chamois-horn buttons, the groups of hikers with ski poles, the mud-spattered backs of mountain bikers with piercing voices and screeching brakes, the black cassock of the local priest, the old wheel-barrows planted with pansies in the front gardens, the local dialect—all these he could have done without, not necessarily with heavy heart. But this village seemed to be inhabited by people of all human races except the one native to the region, so to speak. And the majority were—well, see "Samarkand"—people who were, as would have been said at one time, "from the Orient." They were alien to him not because of their dress and appearance but because they were strangers to themselves in the region. True, the houses, almost all of recent construction, could have been found anywhere. But the network of streets and alleys still typical of that country was thronged with numerous residents who apparently had not been settled there long and appeared out of place in an almost ghostlike fashion, and not only at first glance, also ghostly for the town, with its relatively few quarters, by virtue of their numbers. The Arabic signs on the shops—those in Roman script, here and there, were in the minority—the minaret and the women in head scarves, whom he at first mistook for nuns from the nearby monastery, also the few in veils, were not the decisive features, more an accompanying phenomenon.

Where was he? Good heavens, where was he? Upside down, that was how unfamiliar the presumed landscape of his childhood appeared, and he felt as though the next time he attempted to get his bearings his insides would be pushed to the outside and he would become part of the chaos that was closing in on him from all sides, wherever he looked. He wanted to move on, get away from there, get home to his village. But no matter in what direction he turned: the way was blocked. No entrance. Could he have used his guardian angel now? Too late. Earlier, before he entered this "Samarkand," the angel could have helped, as a warning angel. And though he kept looking behind him for the woman he had struck, he could not catch sight of her, but he felt her behind him, now pursuing him in earnest. Where was she? Where was he? And who was he? No longer a wanderer—he was being pursued, hunted, by himself as well. Not even the dew, deposited during the night on the saplings that had obviously been recently planted along the streets and now spraying off the leaves like a blessing, creating a wreath of sparkling rays in all colors of the rainbow, gave him refuge or waved him on.

Day had long since arrived, and a bat zigzagged across his field of vision, teasing him. Or had it been a swallow, announcing a thunderstorm by swooping close to the ground in the sudden burst of mugginess? No, the swallows were flying around as if nothing were wrong, very high in the air, while already it was thundering and lightning: the swallows were teasing him, too. A camel ambled past, belonging to a traveling circus? No. But probably the lion did, which he heard growl just once? Or had that been a person, behind one of the closed window shutters? A cat jumped up on him, and, believe it or not, the cat crowed. A viper whipped across the road, actually a dead branch. A brake squealed, and he leaped to one side, but it was his shoes squealing. Likewise the hail of stones that made him duck came from the stones he had collected during his journey, jostling one another in his coat pocket. By a grassy patch he bent down to pick up a copper coin, which turned out to be a dewdrop, glittering bronze or copper-colored. Next he took a single red flower petal on a sidewalk for a shred of plastic and wanted to toss it into a trash can, likewise a longish, rough rock he mistook for a broken mobile telephone someone had dropped, and when he picked up a metal pin it turned out to be a fat earthworm. In general, things he thought would be hard turned out to be soft to the touch, and vice versa, which was comparatively reassuring; things he had seen as fluid turned out to be solid when he touched them, in contrast to things he thought were firm and dry, which turned out to be disgustingly moist.

Never had he passed through a less familiar place, with less familiar people, than here in the region from which he came. Was he passing through? He wandered around, not even in a circle, which would also have been comparatively reassuring. During the hour of his wandering around, he never came upon anything he had seen before. The traffic mirror that reflected the landscape around the bend was followed by one that seemed identical but this time reflected his image as he roamed aimlessly, making him recoil, and not just one step, as if before a stranger threatening to strike him dead. Even things that seemed unquestionable filled him with uncertainty, doing little to mitigate his vertigo, his sense of not knowing what was going on. In a parking lot, a perfectly ordinary parking lot, someone was sitting on a stool behind his car and playing a tuba, one prolonged note, which echoed off the walls all around like an alphorn. Another person was sitting on a bench by the road that looked as though it had been left over from an earlier era and was painted with a half-weathered edelweiss emblem. He was reading the Koran, his back held very straight, or maybe something by Ibn 'Arabi, probably a treatise on *M*, *W*, and *N*, the secret spiritual and ontological meanings of the letters of the Arabic alphabet. He was wearing only an undershirt, which revealed his naked arms and shoulders, completely covered with tattoos, none of which represented the sacred letters, however, and that, too, like the tuba player, was no hallucination, any more than the third person he saw standing in front of a closed door, as large as that of a former barn, and pleading with someone, or rather no one, behind it, then cursing, then falling silent and getting ready to move on, then turning back and resuming his pleas, which gave way to curses, then to silence, and leaving anew, then promptly turning back again and screaming and waving his fist at the barn door, and so on, and likewise it was indubitable that one of the resettled or refugee residents, in the midst of the crowd, which paid him no mind, was trying, with a rug spread before him, to pray, gazing into the distance, which did not necessarily indicate the direction of the Ka'aba in Mecca but more likely the hinterland behind all other hinterlands, and he was failing in his attempt, no matter how tightly he balled up his entire body, not just his clenched fists, failing each time he was about to merge with or disappear into the one god, a failure that each time brought the bitterest tears to his coal- or kohl-black eyes, and when one watched him, one knew that sooner or later, this man, missing his goal time after time in his fervent praying, would pull out a submachine gun or, no, more likely a scimitar, and fall upon the disrespectfully indifferent crowd. And the one who was taking all this in? He would be the first victim, calling attention to himself not only by his gaze: as in some nightmares, no, nightmarish moments, he had the sense he was moving in broad daylight, filled with shame as otherwise only in a dream, barefoot through the huge crowd, or perhaps almost naked, wearing only a skimpy T-shirt that was not long enough to hide his nakedness, no matter how hard he tugged at it.

At last another grassy patch, and there he crouched down. And finally something appeared there that he could recognize. He saw a familiar form covered by the grass: a triangle. From where did he know the triangle, this particular one? And—quivering moment—now he knew: the grassy triangle, surrounded by sheds, barracks, sandy stretches, marked the place where the road branched off from the Old Road to the Old Village, his Old Village, marked its threshold; the two branches, equal ones, formed the merges on the left and the right onto what had formerly been the artery, long since built up and incorporated into the village. And the village itself was his village, in the meantime sprawling far past its original limits. Without his becoming aware of it, he had reached his journey's main destination. With the grassy triangle, greening as it always had, on which he was squatting, began the original territory (was that the term?) of the village where he had been born. The wanderer now had only to continue straight in the direction in which the triangle's apex pointed. The road to the village center still existed, now a tarred alley with apartment buildings, stores, also a bank with a sign saying WESTERN UNION instead of the orchards where pigs had grunted and turkeys had gobbled. And he walked along, slightly uphill as in the old days, looking back again and again, but no longer checking for a woman in pursuit. A dog ran toward him, the one from Porodin? his brother's? No, the mutt did not recognize him, or did not want to recognize him; instead of licking his hands and face, it growled, backing away step by step into the village, or what remained of it. Samarkand, the would-be homecomer realized, had the same vowels as Stara Vas, the village's name, and just the same number of them: *a-a-a*. So perhaps it was possible to go home again after all?

As time passed, the racket from the new settlers' district on the outskirts receded, or did he merely imagine that? At any rate, the closer he came to the former village center, the more dense the silence seemed. Aside from him there was no one on the path he had once taken to get home, transformed into an alley almost urban in character. Hardly a tree was left, and nonetheless he heard a rustling, as if high in the air. Suddenly a large limb broke off and came crashing to the ground near him; it missed killing him by a hair. And after another bend, it, too, familiar, the alley turned back into a road. It was laid with wooden planks, slightly elevated above the ground, with a hollow space underneath, and the sound they made as one walked on them was like a ship. And again he was probably imagining that he had already seen this boardwalk, from the plane. Had his gaze been so intently focused on the village that he had not even registered all these new features? And along the road he then discovered other traces of the old village. Of one house all that remained, if anything, was a blank window, perhaps merely painted to look like a real window, complete with crossbar, and in the window a painted geranium, carmine-red, and next to it the upper body of a child leaning on the painted sill, welcoming him with large, pale blue eyes? or rather fixing him with a Medusa-like stare, which, like the dog's intermittent growling, was supposed to force him to back off or leave altogether. And the ladder leaning against another house, which at first also seemed painted on, then turned out to be real and seemed familiar. He climbed up a few rungs: yes, it was the one he remembered. One plank, much longer and also broader than the others: left over from the bowling alley? Yes, it was. And in a ground-floor window a real carmine-red geranium, and behind it, her head and toothless jaw wobbling, the face of an ancient crone he did not recognize, although she apparently recognized him. Glowering at him over the leaves of the potted plant, she cursed him, without words, simply with her eyes.

There it was at last, the cemetery, with the church next to it. At one time both had been freestanding, but so much building had taken place around them that one had to be almost on top of the gate to be halfway sure of being in the right place. But was this really the graveyard? The voice of the muezzin calling to morning prayers was so close that it seemed to ring out from the old church tower. Or was that merely the echo, greatly amplified by the new buildings tightly packed in on the edge of town that bounced the sound from the minaret from one angle to the next? This was the cemetery after all, and this was the old gate leading to it and the church, with the stone bench built sideways into the gateway, and on it the weathered, indestructible wooden plank—ah, how wood guided him from place to place, wood upon wood—and the still mysterious dip in the plank, a narrow spot, just large enough to accommodate a child's backside, where a child could be enthroned now and forever. Yes, this was the cemetery where his ancestors lay buried, and this was the proper gate leading into it, and if the gate, as an effect of the muezzin's voice from the mosque in the new district, for the moment received an Oriental name, wafted there, so to speak, from Samarkand, namely Bab el Mandeb, or Gate of Mourning, this effect strengthened the sense of being in the right place, the consciousness and the certainty that that was really true here.

How many things, to be sure, seemed to want to prevent him from entering, not to mention the in-house dog and the death-wish gaze of the old woman, whose last day on earth this one almost surely was. How many things assailed him physically as he stepped through the Bab el Mandeb: a butterfly that jostled him from the side with an unexpectedly hard body, a dragonfly whose knife-sharp wings scratched his cheek, a hummingbird, or was it a wren, in Samarkandian a *minmina*, that beat its wings around his ears? to say nothing of the swarms of black flies, not necessarily from the Orient, that zoomed from all sides at his eyes, heading directly toward them. Even the harmless bumblebees, which really ought to have been grateful for his taking such sympathetic notice of them earlier, surrounded him on left and right with buzzing so loud that as its volume increased he was reminded of the droning of hornets? no, of something else, something seriously threatening. No, of the threat itself.

So was everything ganging up on him? Did every object and every being oppose his entrance into the place he sometimes in his own mind called his "center," at other times his "sanctuary"? Did nothing welcome him, provide an escort? Even the gate's threshold, paved with round river rocks pounded into the ground, had tried to block his way by making him slip on their smooth humps, damp from dew. A wind gust came along, and a clump of shoulder-high stinging nettles by the gate whipped him in the face. His gaze sought out the trusty three kings of the Orient sculpted in stone in the arch above the portal of the thousand-year-old church: Hello, old boys, here I am again, here we are again!—and the round-heads' response? An unmistakable triple turning up of noses (odd, given the flatness of those noses), a gazing past him, a refusing to recognize him, not only from Melchior in the middle, who turned into his adversary from the Old Road, but also from Caspar and Balthasar flanking him, and the gold, frankincense, and myrrh in their hands turned into rotten apples. There, in the nook in the high, thick wall built to keep out the Turks—they, too, from the Orient?—was the bumped-out sexton's house, whose darkened wood and light-colored window frames had always exemplified coziness; but on the sills of the grimy and in some cases broken windows, instead of flowerpots there perched doves and more doves, all of them looking mangy, an indication that the place had been uninhabited and abandoned for years. And as abruptly as the wind gust earlier, after the homecomer's first steps into the cemetery grounds, the earth under his feet quaked for a moment, during which the sparrows present everywhere scuttled back and forth before him like rats, and the gaps, otherwise outlines of a still possible and different world, took on the form of pursuers closing in on him.

When the ground shook, he almost fell down flat. But he stopped the fall, quivering in the aftermath. At the same time, as was usual after a near fall, he saw everything around him more distinctly, each detail as if enhanced by a postfright magnifying glass. And through this glass, between the blades of the cemetery's grass, a very strange migration came into view. He saw tiny frogs, not much bigger than ants, making their way along. A short while ago they had been swarming, still black, slippery tadpoles, in the village pond that bordered the cemetery, actually more like a large puddle, and overnight they had metamorphosed into fingernail-sized pale gray frogs, each with the most delicate four legs in place of its tail. Four legs? More like a pair of legs and a pair of arms, which made the animals resemble tiny humans, also in the form of their heads. The impression that one little human after another seemed to be moving through the grass was reinforced by the way they did not follow close on each other's heels like ants in a procession; instead each made its way alone, at a slight distance from the others, yet taken all together they constituted a people on the move. They lumbered and wobbled awkwardly along, zigging and zagging, out of order, sometimes veering to the side; crawling, groping, scouting their way

259

forward, away from the water in which they had been born and toward the forest, where, if there was any forest left, they would live for the time being and mature. Again and again they stopped in their tracks, as if exhausted, and finally dragged themselves onward, their arms pulling the rest of their bodies along, which gave them the appearance, although they were moving on a flat surface, of mountain-climbers extending one tiny arm after the other. Thus each one reminded the viewer not merely of a human being but of the very essence of a human being, and if this impression stemmed from the gaze through a magnifying glass, it was through one that magnified and reduced the image to the same degree, and to the degree that here and now, on this particular morning in this particular place, it had this effect, at the same time reaching retroactively into the night of time, and illuminating it for the moment. A new rapture was occurring, yet another, that constituted a form of repair. Even if the procession of protohumans in the grass was headed in an entirely different direction, he allowed it to lead him, and at last he reached, without encountering further obstacles, the grave site that had been his destination. Day of the first brimstone butterfly. Day of the falcons' cries. Day of the bumblebees freezing in the cold wind. And now the day of the miniature-frog migration.

The rapture, and the peace it brought, did not last. "Why, oh why?" the storyteller on the nocturnal boat burst out, while the woman, the stranger, now dashed from the prow, where her presence had hardly been detectable, to the stern, taking herself completely out of our line of sight, as if what came next in the story should be crossed out, as it were, or blotted out. The hour of insanity that had seized hold of the wanderer upon being reunited, at the spot where the Old Road met the New Road, with the woman intended for him was apparently not yet past. One indication was that he remained silent as he stood before the grave of his ancestors, just as they, the ancestors beneath, above, and behind or around the gravestone, did not speak a single word to him. On earlier visits there had usually been a lively exchange between them, lively and silent, as silent as lively. A round dance consisting of statements and replies, replies and statements, lipless but all the more impassioned, had occurred, and in the worst case he had at least greeted them, and they had responded to his greeting. In this hour, however, he did not manage so much as an inner greeting, although he acted as though he were formulating one and bowed his head. Instead he was thinking that it was high time he cleaned his hiking boots, muddy from the nightlong tramp, that he needed to find a cash machine as soon as possible, that after the meeting of the noise victims and that of the jew's-harp players and before his return to the Morava—"Ah, if only I were there already"—a third meeting was scheduled, that . . . All he registered of the grave was the faded inscription, with one or two letters missing and whole names blocked by the beech sapling that had shot up in front. And he was distracted by every trivial thing: by the sound of a water spigot squirting in one corner of the cemetery, by a contrail in the sky, by a molehill. Finally, by his mother's grave, he ate a few blackberries he had picked earlier.

The old woman who had emerged from the sexton's house, as if out of the massive defensive wall itself—so the house was not abandoned after all?—then undertook a not-at-all-trivial task. She had with her a cauldron-sized pail, apparently filled to the brim with water. This she hauled with both hands back and forth along the rows of graves. And in front of each she put it down, and with the help of a spray of beech leaves she sprinkled the grave, likewise the ones that had been cleared out and the spaces between the grave sites. The same thing happened with the plaques for suicides in one corner of the cemetery, where the ground was not consecrated. Soon she could carry the pail with one hand. And when she paused at the grave of his ancestors and sprinkled the holy water over it, she greeted him as the neighborhood child who, on his way home from school, had come into her house almost every day—like all the houses in the village, it was never locked—while she was out working in the fields with the other villagers, and in the front room had read everything he could lay his hands on, the newspaper, the farmers' almanac, the Holy Bible, paperback Westerns, and whenever they returned from the fields or elsewhere, he would be sitting at the table in the front room, so lost in his reading, whatever it might be, that he did not so much as look up when they came in, let alone wish them a good day.

He did not recognize her, any more than he had recognized a soul in his childhood home up to this point (and had also not been recognized by anyone), as if such nonrecognizing were part of his hour of insanity. As a distraction, a diversion, the wanderer overcome by insanity brought the conversation around to what the former neighbor, now transformed into a sexton, was doing in front of the graves. Her sprinkling would not have been necessary. As if of her own accord, while she was already bestowing consecrated water on the next grave, she explained: the dead needed this, expected it, were veritably panting for the few drops, indeed daily, and she made her rounds daily, directed to do so not by the village priest, certainly not by him, but by the dead themselves.

Once she had disappeared back into the house in the wall, he thought he had been freed of the insanity. Insane: at the moment of his outburst at the end of the Old Road, part of him had clearly understood that the violence the other part of him was perpetrating was an act of insanity: the woman he was stomping on there was absolutely not the one he thought he saw. It was not the woman who had been pursuing him all his life but rather the love of his life. But the other part of him remained all the more blind in the face of this certainty, all the more insane, and he lashed out all the more mindlessly. And now, in the cemetery, alone? What had the old neighbor just said about the dead and the daily water? They "panted" for it. And in the same fashion he now panted for her, the love of his life. He thirsted for her, was starving for her. Outwardly motionless, silently engrossed, he was consumed with longing for her. He veritably begged, in silence: "Come. Come back. Come back to me." And, as once upon a time, one neighborhood child would say to another: "Let's be friends again."

As he turned around, there she stood, smiling, to all appearances unscathed, as if nothing had happened. For a moment he smiled back. But then: the insanity surged through him again. Or wasn't it real after all that at her side, also smiling, was the evil one, the pseudofriend Melchior from the Old Road, his mortal enemy, and not only his? It was the very one. And she was in cahoots with that Old Nick. Two devils were standing there, a devilish pair lying in wait for him. And again: part of him threw itself into her arms and remained forehead to forehead with her, once and for all. And the other part, which he clearly recognized at the same time as by no means part "of him," did the exact opposite and resorted to violence again. And how? The former writer had forgotten to tell us how, during the night on the Old Road, he had cut a hazel branch and sharpened one end to a point, for walking and perhaps also for self-defense. Now he hurled this stick, the sharpened end pointing away from him, as a spear at the satanic pair. Nonetheless: he was aiming not at his love but at her evil twin, whom he of course struck directly in his artificial heart, whereupon the specter pierced by the hazel stick dissolved as intended with a bang into thin air.

But she, too, when he finally opened his eyes after hurling the spear, had disappeared, through the door in the wall into the area behind the village cemetery. Her response to his spear-toss nothing but a wail, which still rang in his ears as he described it during that night on the Morava, as if she were the one after all whom he had struck in the heart—a sound so piteous and at the same time so gentle, between weeping and coughing, that it would have brought anyone to his senses, except him in his hour of insanity. And at the same time a thought, a single one, in the form of a question: "Who will save us?" And as he described the scene to us, we heard this question repeated in the voice of the woman, the invisible stranger, now at the bow, but no lament, no pleading tone accompanied the question, or if it did, then only as we reflected on it later.

Like her, he made his way out through the door in the wall at the back of the cemetery. But he did not follow her. Much time was to pass after her disappearance. Just a short while ago it had been morning, and now the bell of the church in the Old Village was tolling for vespers, with evening around the corner. And in between, very far off, the muezzin of New Samarkand had summoned the faithful, the *muminin*, to five o'clock prayers. Had the wanderer fallen asleep on his feet in front of the ancestral grave? The vesper bell tolled as he had never heard it before: each time two notes, first high, then low, a diminished fifth apart, an interval that was actually proscribed, that was how mournful and inconsolable it sounded, beyond the familiar clanging for someone who had just died, not a death knell but a tone of general mourning and inconsolability, the two-tone sound more penetrating because of the unaccustomed interval of silence between the ding and the dong, in which the inconsolability intensified. This bell had usually reverberated across the landscape, far and wide, all the way to the horizons. But on this late afternoon its two notes remained each time confined within the circular patterns of the stone latticework high up in the church's façade: they no longer let anything through, screening the sound in rather than sending it forth.

Was it a rule that after an action like the mighty hurling of the lance, which really should have thrown him off course and could have made events take an entirely different turn or made the story break off altogether, instead plans and projects perhaps worked out long before were now implemented with all the more determination, also more attention to detail, as if nothing at all had happened? At any rate, as if following such a rule, he made his way to the door in the wall and out into the fields behind the cemetery, heading toward the orchard there, it, too, enclosed by a wall. The fields seemed unchanged at first, except for an irrigation pipe cutting diagonally across them. But no, it was a pipeline, and the fields lay fallow, the patches of green on the bare earth actually more rust-colored. Climbing over the orchard wall had also been part of his plan, and accordingly that was accomplished, in no time flat, without the need, as in childhood, for a young partner in crime to give one a leg up. Crime was the right word, for the orchard in those days was forbidden territory, and the children scaled the wall specifically for the purpose of swiping fruit. From early on and to this day he had disliked thieves, except fruit or orchard thieves. All his life he had been a fruit thief, and freely admitted it. Stealing fruit was part of his self-image, far more so than wandering or writing. As a child he had already known when the first fruit on every tree in the area would ripen, and . . . he had called his first book *The Pear Thieves*. And to this day he could not pass someone else's orchard without at least making an attempt, even if only in his thoughts, to nab some fruit. The fence or wall around the fruit trees, whose crowns beckoned invitingly to him, had to be scaled, called out to be scaled, admitting him to the forbidden realm, to the heart of the real. And no matter how much of a hurry he was in, nothing, however urgent, would deter him from making this crucial detour.

So now over the wall, just as long ago—mission accomplished. But where were they, the apple, pear, and plum trees? A wild forest had sprung up, one without fruit trees. Here and there amid the underbrush some were still standing, but they had been dead a long time. He came upon one living apple tree as he forced his way through the thicket, and it was in bloom, with white blossoms, and at the same time was already bearing some apples, little ones that would never get any bigger: it had reverted to being a wild apple tree. And it was dark in this forest that had returned, dark as night. And wasn't it actually night already? Single lights could be seen, flickering through the tangle of brush and vines, which came—was it possible?—from tents, yes, tents, and a few voices could be heard, isolated and scattered, like the lanterns and the tents, actually all shelters made of plastic, some of it tattered; they were occupied by the homeless, who did not even have dogs. Yet in some places a doormat lay in front of a shelter; or what looked like a genuine kilim, strawberry red, peeped out from under a sheet of ragged plastic; or a beeping could be heard, as if from a battery-operated computer; or a flowered porcelain bowl stood on a tent's proper threshold, crafted out of pieces of bark and ceramic, and the bowl was filled to the brim with shimmering reddish-black Chinese morels that had been peeled off dead elderberry branches, not from China but from the surrounding area, mushrooms that the long-standing residents of the Old Village had called wood ears, while those in the bowl were labeled with their Asian name, "Mu-Leh," perhaps to be sold to the other homeless people. And farther on by a few steps—also leaps over, scrambles up, slips through, head- or feetfirst crawls—he came in the near-darkness upon an actual Asian. He had encountered the other inhabitants of the forest only with his ears, hearing them talking from time to time behind the mostly blue sheets of plastic, talking to themselves. The Asian, the Mongolian, was the only one to show himself, and indeed as one without any roof over his head, not even one made of sticks. He sat there, clearly alone, in the wilderness in a hollow that the wanderer recognized as the crater from a bomb that had landed in the former orchard, his head and bare torso erect and motionless, his face in profile, as perhaps only someone from Asia could hold it, so absent, ghostly, out of this world and almost in the beyond, and at the same time entirely present and drawing a circle around himself merely by the way he sat in the hollow, a throne circle, as it were. No, this person could not be described as homeless. This was beyond all homelessness. A hermit of the hollow. Beware of disturbing his circle! (Indeed it was marked off all around with piles of files, pages clipped together, all of them numerical tables.) Tiptoeing around him in a large arc, and, as in a night scene in a Western, heaven forbid one should step on a dry branch! And somewhere on his journey he had encountered this particular "homeless" person before. But where?

The rear wall of the former orchard: caved in. Picking his way through the rubble. There: his grandfather's house, now his brother's, all the windows lit up, no more forest flickering, and on the roof the neon sign with all its letters: OLD VILLAGE INN. It was the only property in the Old Village that had survived the years and the times. And it had also, at least to judge by the outside, largely preserved its original character as a farmhouse, including the stable wing and the wooden hayloft above, the latter with a wooden gallery, where bundles of dried corncobs hung as in earlier times, or still. Even the stable lantern below them was the same, and the white enamel shade over the bulb looked as if it were spattered with fly droppings, even if it was perhaps pure white. Not a trace of other properties. The farmhouse, which his brother had converted to an inn, stood all by itself, the vegetable garden with the grape arbor—there it was, wasn't it?—now a garden for the inn, the site of the manure pile now a parking lot. Cars could reach the lot from the expressway that had been constructed in the meantime, its lanes disappearing not far from the house into the tunnel under the mountains that formed the southern border, the traffic swallowed up suddenly, along with its roar.

The way he approached the house, however, in the last daylight, was by one of the many intersecting footpaths that led from the forest in the former orchard to the inn—no upgraded route; so the path appeared to be available to the homeless, or whatever they were. How brightly lit the house was, and how quiet. No trucks in the parking lot. No silhouettes in any of the windows. A single person sitting on the long bench by the stable door, now the main entrance, in the dim light of the lantern and the residual glow of the sunset, blocked by a small birch like the ones traditionally set up at Pentecost to the right and left of the front door. Was it Pentecost already? No. The figure sat so motionlessly that as the leaves of the birch sapling fluttered in the evening breeze the figure seemed to have blended with the tree, as its reinforcement and human protector, while the birch, fluttering and fluttering, seemed to remove the human figure from its time and its story, it, too, serving as reinforcement and protector. Who was sitting there? Surely not the woman? Don't let it be the woman—or do? It was not the woman, it was his brother. The dog that had followed the wanderer for days finally caught up with him, and its constant growling gave way to joyful barking, directed at the person seated on the farm bench, up on whose knees the dog jumped; by contrast, however, the dog lunged at the new arrival. No longer just threatening, it uttered a howl of rage, signaling that it was ready to bite: the family dog did not recognize him even there, in front of his birth house, did not want to recognize him.

And his brother, too, did not recognize him. It would not have taken much for his brother to sic the dog on him. But no, that was not his brother's style; he called the dog off. So had the wanderer become that unrecognizable overnight? He was standing in front of the man on the bench, had greeted him, had let his voice be heard. The greeting was returned, but directed at a stranger. So had his voice changed overnight? Did he have to explain to his brother who he was? "Don't you see? Listen: it's me!"? That was out of the question. Explaining, much less proving his identity by showing his passport, for instance, or something else, or calling his brother by the name known only to the two of them, or speaking the magic word they had come up with an eternity ago: that would ruin the moment of being reunited after long years of absence, would suck the air out of it, and not just for that moment but for the entire episode of their reunion. How could he clue his brother in as to who was standing before him without being explicit but also without engaging him in a guessing game (this was not the moment for games)? Inspiration: did such a thing exist? The concept had never been part of his vocabulary. "Intuition," yes, and then, as had become his standard practice with words during his writing period, not in the form of a noun but in the form of a verb: not "intuition" but "to intuit."

And thus the wanderer intuited in this second that he should recapitulate a scene from one of their mother's stories, a scene that both of them, his brother and he, had carried with them since childhood as revealing one of the characteristic behaviors, if not the fundamental behavior, in their family's and clan's history. The episode involved their mother's youngest brother, who was supposed to become a priest but was overcome with homesickness at the diocesan boys' seminary, could not take it anymore, and ran away one night, heading home by way of the Old Road. He arrived as day was breaking, but did not dare to enter the house. It was a Saturday, the day on which every week the courtyard in front of the house was thoroughly swept in preparation for "the

Lord's day." Sweeping up chicken shit, cow manure, or chaff, or just sweeping the bare ground, leaving broom marks in the sandy courtyard. With the sky still dark, he took the twig broom from the wall of the stable and began to sweep. The sound of the broom outside gradually woke everyone in the house. Without looking out, they realized who had returned and was signaling that he would not leave home again, at least not voluntarily, would never go so far away again, and never be absent for so long. The twig broom was still leaning against the wall of the former stable, the very same one, even if it was not the same. Picking it up. Sweeping. Being recognized after only two or three passes with it. Laughing on both their parts. "Ah, it's you. I must be blind and dumb. Come into the house, brother. Wash up; you need it—you smell. And put on some clean clothes. I'm not exactly going to slaughter a fatted cow for you. Or throw a party to celebrate your homecoming. I know you'll be pushing on tomorrow. But come in and stay the night, in your old room, in your old bed, as you've been wishing you could do for a long time now, right?" They were only "half brothers," with different fathers? "Only"? Hairsplitting, and not just for the moment. How old his brother had become! And he put his hand to his own face. How old had he become himself?

In the taproom, formerly the stable, he was alone at first, at the smallest of the tables, in a niche. His brother had not forgotten how he liked to sit and what he liked to eat and drink. The dog stretched out peacefully at his feet. Chains clanked as the cows munched their hay. Bats swooped through the open stable door, even though it was closed and was no longer the stable door. A clear evening, with the moon shining through one of the windows, and on the wooden gallery on the upper level it was broad daylight, with rain spraying in under the roof, a summer rain, onto someone who was sitting there cross-legged, with a book. Later that night the tavern filled up: closing his eyes briefly— or had they closed involuntarily?—he opened them to see the room full, with forest dwellers in their Sunday best on the one hand, with long-distance truckers on the other; among the guests some residents from the new district, New Samarkand, if you will. Only men in any of the groups, and not much to observe; at most that the new settlers sat at a right angle to the tables, according to Oriental custom, and did not drink, did not even smoke a water pipe. But no, one woman was with them, heavily veiled, but seeming to be in disguise, in truth a man, Melchior, the journalist and writer? who was photographing them all surreptitiously and had secretly switched on a tape recorder? Let him be; he did not exist, had never existed.

Later all three groups gathered around one of the Orientals, the oldest man present, who sat there very erect and received one after another, as if he were holding court. He was something like the local oracle, giving each person a few words to take away with him, not prophecies but rather transmissions, articulations, and illustrations of something just then happening inside the oracle, as yet unspoken and unvisualized. And inside him something was always happening. What was it? Where others perhaps heard voices, he heard sounds, in his head, in his ears, ever changing, sounds that had nothing to do with those in the taproom or the kitchen; and where others might perhaps have suffered from these sounds as a constant, indistinguishable, tormenting noise in their heads, he had the ability to separate the sounds and keep them apart. At the same time, he listened to them as if they had been sent to him from a distant place where inner and outer merged. And translating these sounds, simultaneously, into words, sentences, auditory and visual images, made him in the eyes of the people of New Samarkand a medium, or simply an oracle, and that was also his profession, which he practiced with natural dignity, unapproachable, unsmiling, or at most smiling with pleasure at his translations and at passing them along to those assembled.

What oracular sayings were these? Anything unambiguous was of course not to be expected, but neither did his utterances sound classically equivocating or even ambiguous. They issued from him without interpretation, defying interpretation, on the one hand in complete, syntactically correct sentences, on the other hand quite meaningless, yet also not posing a riddle but borne by the rhythm of the noises in the translator's head and his voice, shaped by what he was hearing. And that seemed to satisfy those who gathered around the oracle, consulting him without posing questions. Each man nodded in response to the saying he received, seemed to be enlivened by it, lastingly, then went on his way, so to speak, the couple of long-distance truckers as well as the forest-dwellers and those who had moved there from Samarkand or elsewhere. And the sound-interpreter made each of them pay, more than a regular soothsayer.

Later the soothsayer joined the wanderer in his niche, did not let him out of his sight, and then began to speak, with the roar from the expressway in the background, muffled by the windowpanes: "Blue eyes need not be a misfortune. Uproot yourself even more, my friend. It can't hurt to chew on the other side of your mouth for a while. Ah, all those who wave around their roots like whips. There's nothing but rest for the wicked. You can't have more than you have. And sometimes the way it is isn't the way it is. And at one time God was on the side of the long-suffering. That time was long ago. It is rare to be saved. If only one could disappear, you think—but one can't. The word "night" grunts deep in one's heart. And the Babylonian welter of opinions. An attraction is no attraction. The spirit travels nonetheless down the road of darkness, man, and leaps out of one's mouth for joy. The devil can't rob you of the light. Nothing is not as bad as the farmer thinks. Go as a stranger. Destiny never comes from without. Each person is timid in a different way. You contemplate your mistakes too little. All is iniquity! And all is frazzled, and that was life. And somewhere someone is always laughing. And anyone who contemplates human beings dies of grief."

And even later the wanderer and his brother sat alone in the half-darkened taproom. At one time the brother had been the black sheep of the family. And who was he now? They played cards, and as in the old days neither wanted to let the other win. In the old days? "In the old days" also meant walking along the Old Road, arriving in "Samarkand," standing in the cemetery, passing through the overgrown orchard. The brother had seen the world, from the pipeline construction in Alaska to the rail-line-laying in Mali, and every place he had visited had lent its name to a hill, a brook, a road, a forest in this region. He would never take a single step to leave again. The steep hill above the tunnel, where primarily birches, ferns, and, in the gaps, brilliantly red strawberries grew, he called Bosnia Slope. The grassy expanse between their parents' house and the virgin forest was the Virginia Meadow. The brook that curved around the Old Village was Elk Creek, flowing into Alaska's Yukon River. Where the sunken road up into the foothills of the alp turned to yellow clay, it led to the Dogon area in Africa's Mali. The frog pond belonged to the Danube delta. He had also worked in Arabia for many years, and accordingly his whole native Carinthian valley was called Wadi al-Yawm, or Valley of the Day.

As he pictured it, the members of the clan to which he and the wanderer belonged had been from the beginning and through the generations secretly mad, not seriously so, to be sure, but still . . . "We all have a screw loose," as he put it, "including you, and each of us in his or her own way." And what was his own loose screw? The brother could have mentioned all kinds of things, but he left it at one harmless delusion: he thought that all the places on the planet where he had ever spent time were stored inside him, not in his memory but in his body. The world he had experienced during his years as an itinerant worker, along with all its parts, even those of which he had hardly or only fleetingly been cognizant, even the most trivial ones that had made no impression on him when he was there, had been inscribed on him. The sites of his past had bonded with his flesh and blood. There was no part of his body to which a place did not belong. No cell, he was convinced, that did not harbor a place name. Except that the places around the world and their names in the cells of his body remained hidden most of the time. They were asleep. So did they emerge in dreams? Not in dreams, and not during the night, but exclusively by day. Then often but a single movement was needed for one of those earlier places, along with its name, to wake up inside him, for example in his knee, glowing or smoking quietly, and then quickly extinguished, though the flickering could continue for a good while. He might raise the ax, for instance, and his armpit would recall a particular village in the Himalayas. He might heave a kettle onto the stove, and a spot in his stomach cavity would promptly embody a particular highway barracks near, let's say, Regensburg. He would jump off a ladder and his ankle, or his hip, or his scalp would open up to—"Well, fill in a place yourself." No reliable method for awakening all the places in his body existed. He knew only that stretching helped, and likewise exercising caution in his movements, one movement flowing smoothly out of another, and especially that the former locales stored in his body came to life only when he was engaged in his daily chores—he had to work them loose in his cells. But how alive they could become retroactively, in his neck, between his ribs, in his temples, more lively than they had ever been when he experienced them externally. "If you only knew how many places I revisited inside my body just this evening, while I was busy in the kitchen."

Even later that night nothing happened except that the two brothers sat side by side in silence. If one of them sighed, their ancestors would sigh in response, only more loudly. A brief moan, and the ancestors would moan back, and then did not want to stop. A soft laugh, and in reply the ancestors' peals of laughter. And then a cry from the depths. Who was that groaning? At least there was no echo, no one groaned in reply. An air hug, arms reaching into the void, as a child had once been observed doing. Why couldn't they sit this way in the dark forever?

Still later that night the brother led the wanderer down to the former apple cellar, and behold: it had been turned into a meeting space, but a very special one: wasn't this an underground church, or at least part of one? And hadn't they always been told, and seen it confirmed in old engravings, that the ancestral property had been the site of the first little village church? Yes, this was it, the sanctuary, which over the centuries had sunk deep into the ground as a result of the rubble piling up around it. The brother had discovered it one day while digging out the cellar and had secretly cleared it out: the vaulted ceiling of the fruit cellar had once been the church's roof. And now it was serving once more as a house of God, but rather secretively, at least not officially, and not advertised anywhere, a sort of crypt or catacomb. Some long-distance truckers would come downstairs from the bar, using it as their highway chapel; some old-timers from the village—of whom there were still some left, and they were the brother's regulars—would recite the Rosary and the Litany of the Blessed Virgin or the All Souls' Litany down there after work before they began drinking upstairs (or not); and the new settlers from "Samarkand" used the cellar for their communal Friday prayers, at first just a few of them, but in the meantime more and more (who had gradually become tired of the mosque, which for their taste had grown too visible and ostentatious); in the small space, unlike in the mosque, they could easily crowd in so close together that, as their religion demanded, there was no room for shaitan, the evil demon, to slip into. And more and more often the three groups, the long-distance truckers, the locals, and the new settlers, met downstairs in the catacomb just as they did upstairs. And? That was all. Just goodwill, and people of goodwill. Not only goodwill but also a will to change! And the barriers? None. There was no such thing in the catacomb, or the barriers were no obstacles. Benches were positioned along the walls where once the fruit bins had stood, and the niche where the cider kegs had been kept was now the apse and the *mihrab*, with a long oval table; the entire crypt under the tavern was brightly lit and quiet, with no noise penetrating from the expressway, and the most prominent impression the smell: of cider and apples, apples and cider. And in one spot the echo underfoot. Long may it echo there.

Did the wanderer, even later that night, find his way upstairs to his old room? There, too, his brother had to show him the way. In the doorway—the walls were so thick that his brother could stand there sideways, legs splayed—the wanderer heard from him how the whole family had trembled downstairs when he, still an adolescent, had been engaged in his first attempts at writing up there in his room. They had not been allowed to make a peep. If one of them so much as coughed or scraped a chair on the floor, he would yell for quiet. And from time to time he yelled without provocation, into the silence, as if angry with himself. They had also been afraid of his facial expression when, after many hours, often an entire day, he came down to the living room, now the inn's parlor: either his eyes shot bullets, with which he wanted to mow them all down, or he looked around as if not just asking for forgiveness but begging for mercy, or he stared wide-eyed at nothing at all, as if expecting to be confronted by an execution squad. Even when he smiled—which happened seldom enough—as if nothing had happened, as if he hadn't just been ranting over their heads, and without missing a beat read aloud what he had written, forcing them to listen—their mother was the only one who did not need to be forced—he seemed uncanny to them, especially because his smile had something menacing about it, was a smirk, a villainous one, as if he had committed some evil deed. His brother had not read a single one of his books, had not so much as opened them. And nonetheless he thought he knew them all, each of the long stories in detail. He had experienced them, and the other had written them down, in a way that matched their separate realities, of that he was convinced, and so he had no need to read the fraternal books. There were not many books in the house, and most of those had been read, but not one from the family writer, and both of them found that completely natural. And before saying good night in the doorway, his brother returned to the subject of the family: with his attempts at writing the boy had not merely interfered with their domestic life but had furthermore thrown the rest of them into confusion, if not sown dissension and possibly destroyed the family. At least, he said, certain things might have turned out differently in their home without that initial writer's tyranny. It had contributed to the split in the family. But that was not what he was getting at. This was not a night for settling accounts, and besides it would be the last time the other man spent the night in his ancestors' house, in his old room and old bed. So what was he getting at? That the two of them, the sole remaining members of the family, only now constituted a family. That altogether it was only now, with the two of them alone, that one could speak of a family. And what did his brother mean by family? He could not say. "Family is family." Or perhaps this: "Something nice . . . something heartwarming . . . something lasting . . . a rock of Gibraltar . . . an air-raid shelter . . . a border station, unarmed, at the same time a border-crossing . . . a round dance while sitting quietly around the table . . ." The family had grown smaller and smaller. And now, with only these two left from the entire extended family, the family was most present: a strange arithmetic again.

If the wanderer had harbored expectations for his night in the house where he had been born, none materialized. First he sat down in a chair by the window and tried to retrace the landscape lying there in the moonlight, inscribed on him since childhood, whereupon his eyes closed almost instantly. And when he got into bed, intending to stay awake as long as he could and to try to be conscious of where he was and of all the specific things he had experienced, suffered, done, neglected, done to others, and done wrong, he had hardly curled up under the covers as in the old days when he not only fell asleep but, so it seemed to him, lost consciousness. He fell away, as though a trapdoor, and the ground along with the trapdoor, or the universe, or whatever it was, closed over him, and he no longer existed. It was a voice then—but what did "then" mean? and what was "later"?—that called him back into the present, but into a different present. The voice belonged to his mother. Was he dreaming? No, it was no dream, even if he was sleeping, and deeply.

He had learned to distinguish between dreams and apparitions. Both occurred during sleep. But he experienced an apparition entirely differently from a dream. Dreams were the usual occurrence, so to speak. They turned up, both nightmares and pleasant dreams, as happenings, as things taking a certain course, as precipitous events or long-drawn-out ones. Apparitions, on the other hand, took the form of intrusions, abrupt ones, images shooting into his heart and disappearing just as abruptly, but leaving an image burned into his consciousness. He often dreamed about his mother: that she was still alive, though always tired to death, wearing herself out for him and the others, exhausted to the point of collapse, her eyes bleary from exhaustion. But she had appeared to him only once, and that was in the weeks after her death. Abruptly she had flown to him from the night, the night of the universe—that was how he experienced it—no, had assaulted him, had taken possession of him at one blow, and had promptly zoomed back into the darkness where she belonged. And what had impressed itself on the sleeper from that one monumental second? Only his mother's face, surrounded by darkness, and in her face her pitch-black eyes (not their actual color on earth), and these were against him, but did not express a reproach, certainly not a curse: they were simply against him, against the way he was, or the way he had been, but that with all the fire that could blaze in his mother's otherwise gentle eyes, and even more fire, beyond that.

During his last night in the house where he had been born, his mother did not appear to the sleeper—she spoke to him, invisible, without face or eyes. And she did not speak to him from the darkness; what she said was accompanied by light, or provided light, or was itself the light. And to her sleeping son she said approximately the following: "You with your eternal sense of guilt and your seeking of guilt in others. You're innocent, you silly boy, as innocent as those of whom you were suspicious, a bad old habit of yours, not congenital and not inherited, when you and they were absent. Just as you suspected me: suspected me of having given up on you from the beginning; of not believing in you; of not tolerating any woman at your side; suspected me of having lived an unhappy life, or of having loved only your father, of having despised your brother, and of having not told the truth when I wrote you that I was happy to die. Listen, son: I did love several other men. I loved your brother, even if differently from the way I loved you:

whereas you intentionally brought tears to my eyes, they flowed by themselves when I thought of him. No doubt I feared that both you and your brother would go astray, but I could never quite picture the way that would happen with you. And if there were times when I couldn't believe in you, didn't that spur you on all the more? And it's not true that I wasn't happy when I was finally able to go to sleep for good, just as it's also not true on the other hand that my life was unhappy. Some of my wishes were fulfilled, and more than that I never expected. And some unexpected things also happened, and there was never greater joy. No one in the entire extended family could be joyful as I could, there was no one who could infect others, except maybe you, with my pleasure as I could. My name should be Herzefreude—heart's joy—not Herzeloyde—heart's sorrow—you spoilsport. So get up this instant and bring that woman intended for you to your bed. The night is cold, and she's been waiting under your window for an eternity. Do you expect her to serenade you and climb up to your room on a ladder, you fool? Enough of guilt and looking for guilt in others. Enough self-martyrdom and making martyrs of others, who were always those close to you, are those close to you. Why do you make a martyr of only yourself and those close to you, you lazybones, you village idiot, you last remaining know-it-all and phony sympathizer. No love without mercy."

In this manner or one very much like it his mother spoke to him in his sleep, and he did as she ordered. From the depths of sleep he had wanted to reply that what she had corrected in his version of herself, her life, and her death was even less true than his version. She had said those things merely for form's sake, for the sake of this story—but as always when he was sleeping he could not get out a word. And then he woke up with a jolt and in fact heard noises down in the courtyard. No, it was not a broom. It was footsteps, in the depths of night, and they were peaceable, in the gravel and the sand, also as if determined by the gravel and the sand, guided by them. And in fact he found the woman, the stranger, at the gate to the courtyard—which was not locked—why had she not simply come into the house? Had she wanted to summon him with her footsteps alone? How patiently she was walking up and down, back and forth in the moonlight, the very soul of patience, and her walking was a game of patience, following a pattern invisibly inscribed in the sand. Nonetheless she was startled when he appeared, held up her arm to shield her head, backed off as he strode toward her, the creature. He caught her, or it, brought her, or it, home (only James Stewart, Joseph Cotten, and Matthias Sindelar could have done it better), carried her up to the room (not even Lancelot and Gawain would have had stronger arms in that moment), and then lay down beside her.

At long last he understood her as she understood him, and laughed; it was rare for him to laugh that way, and as he was telling us this part on the boat there in the night we would never have believed our host could laugh that way, and the woman, the stranger, laughed back at us from the stern. Back there, beyond the mountains, she had joined in his laughter, also laughing at him, but benevolently, face-to-face, until both of them turned serious and that turned into a trembling, on her part also a delayed effect of the night out in the open, a trembling on both their parts, until they did not tremble anymore. And again they fell out of bed together from exhaustion, but not only that. Land of two rivers.

When the wanderer introduced the woman the next morning to the homeowner, he did not show a second's amazement, as if he were accustomed to such things, from his brother and others as well. If his eyebrows rose for a second, it was at her beauty. And what else? He arranged for his brother's chosen one to hitch a ride in a tractor trailer. She wanted to go on ahead, in a southeasterly direction to the Balkans, to the boat on the Morava, and prepare various things for his return and for the night of storytelling. The wanderer still had one more stop on his tour of Europe. He had toyed with the idea of skipping it. But no, that was out of the question, just as with the previous stops. And why?

As much as he longed to go back, he had to face the enclave and the river, the one he had imagined and that had engraved itself in him as his route and his plot. Abbreviating, skipping, avoiding would have not done justice to the story. Ah, justice! And the woman and he: what did they picture for the future as they parted again? To work together. (For the moment the interrupter had no further questions.)

10

~~~~~~~~~
  ~~~~~~~~~
~~~~~~~~~

IN THE TIME when this story takes place, there were still a few people left from a different time who clung to the idea, or the pipe dream, of a large unified country in the Balkans, in a different kind of Europe. They certainly could have known, and probably did know, that there was no way to alter what had happened, or been planned, or set in motion and implemented. But nonetheless this handful of people, or dear folk, stubbornly or obstinately held fast to the notion that one aspect or another of what had been put in place could be adjusted, especially if it were recognized that the former unified entity had perhaps stood not so much for something imposed as for a sense of belonging that had developed over time and with the generations. For a while one or another of them had even imagined that history, or whatever it was called, would one day prove him right. Meanwhile, however—with the exception of one or two incorrigible believers in history in their midst—they had long since ceased to believe in the allegedly decisive and final word of history, or of the historians, as the case might be. Or if they did, the decisive word did not absolutely have to be right, and those who had the last word did not for that reason necessarily have a monopoly on the truth. Wasn't having the last word suspicious in any case? The last word: was such a thing even permissible?

The few holdouts used sophistries of this sort as a pretext for coming together now and then, and then one last time, and then one absolutely last time, and so on, to talk about the large country and what had happened to it. Initially they had formed quite an impressive group. By now only a few turned up. The reason was not, however, that they were tiring of the subject, let alone changing their minds and coming to their senses—none of them, not a single one, would ever give up his so-called convictions voluntarily or revise his opinion one iota—but an entirely different reason: the dying off of the group's members, an almost strikingly frequent phenomenon. These people usually did not live to be very old. One of them had his heart stop as he was walking along the street. Another, driving while intoxicated, crashed his car into a bridge railing, which, together with the bridge, which had been destroyed by bombs, had just recently been rebuilt. The third had disappeared hiking in the mountains. Some of the deaths were also remarkably violent: one woman's dress—polyester; what else would one have expected of a Balkan woman?—caught fire from a candle in church, an Orthodox church, of course, and in a flash she was totally engulfed in flames, beyond saving. One lost his life when he was struck by a ridiculously small rock, not even a stone, a pebble, that happened to hit his temple right in the spot where . . . One drowned while swimming in the river that formed the border, the river famous for its ever-green water. Quite a few suicides, too, of course. And even if they did not all die violently, they all died abruptly; their dying happened suddenly: heart, stroke, aneurysm, suffocating during an asthma attack . . . And those who did not die instantaneously—have you seen the like?—went mad from one moment to the next, in the wink of an eye, so to speak, just as all those around them had been constantly predicting, and anyone among them who had not gone mad yet was bound to do so soon, *je lui donne au plus un ou deux ans*; in one year or at most two. Their deranged state had started with the conviction that they were being watched by the secret services of the whole world, not just by the CIA but also by al-Qaida, by the Mossad, and so forth, and the letters they sent each other were taped together so firmly, for the sake of secrecy, that the recipients were often unable to open them.

The little (nameless) posse of true believers, or screwball believers, called their periodic gatherings "conferences," in reference to the secret "conferences" held in the woods by partisans during the world war, and it was not entirely certain whether the choice of this term was made only in jest. For like the partisans in their day, each of the participants, wherever he might be located, received instructions in code telling him to appear at a certain time in a certain place, and each traveled to the spot under cover of darkness, if possible, disguised as a lumberjack, as a nocturnal pilgrim, as someone looking for a lost pet, or whatever; approached the conference site alone, by back roads; used a false name such as Desanka, Varvarin, Kravica, Kolubara, or Ohrid. And the place itself always had at least the appearance of a hiding place—an earthen cellar, a cave, a ruin; and once they had even met at the bottom of a dried-up cistern, probably in memory of the resistance fighters who long ago (or only recently?) had installed their secret transmitters in such shafts.

The current conference was really supposed to be the absolutely last one—which it turned out to be. And it took place in a doline, a round, deep depression in the karst. What do you mean, another doline in your story? The karst again? Yes, but this one was in our own country, and besides, the doline was a field, a garden, a paddock, a stable, a playing field, a dance floor, a bake oven, a Red Cross post, a fishpond. It was that large? That large. And built up and furnished with all these resources, a *delana dolina*? Yes, a doline in the karst above Trieste, the one from which every karst in the world, including the ones in the Yucatán and Minas Gerais, take the name—the mother of karsts. And in spite of that, secretly there in the Delana Dolina? In spite of that, secretly.

The wanderer had not been in the karst for a long time. Without the "conference" he would hardly have gone there anymore: the place had had its day. And besides, it had changed markedly. True, everything was still there that made it unique: the updraft from the sea below that fanned the high plateau with incomparable gentleness; the big sky; the brightness of that sky, reflected on the ground by the porous limestone used in the construction of village houses and the stone walls leading from the fields into the wilderness, or by the fields themselves, formed as the underlying limestone weathered; the silence, of a sort possible only in an out-of-the-way location; the far-flung villages, out of sight of each other and recognizable only at night, and then only when cloud cover hung low over the plateau, from the reflections, usually round, here and there on the underside of the clouds; and of course the dolines. But the silence of the karst was no longer its only distinguishing feature, and the area set apart from the surrounding countryside, as well as from the sea, held its own at most for moments at a time, among many others of a different character. It may be that even in the past the karst had been an area fairly central to Europe. In the meantime it had explicitly become part of something—first a feeling, then a conception, then an idea, and finally a norm—known as "Central Europe," right? Over time this norm had become dominant—well, more or less, but more more than less—and according to this dominant norm the karst belonged, without any special status, to the unit called Central Europe, or to what else should it belong? Perhaps even to the goddamned Balkans, consistent with a previously prevailing norm? The newly introduced norm of "Central Europe" was in any case hardly less potent in the karst; omnipresent at the very least in the language. There had never been as much "center" in the region as now. One "Center festival" after the other. The small main town of the karst received a new name, in translation "Centertown," and a group of villages had themselves renamed into what would translate as "Central Village One," "Central

Village Two," and so forth, in the same way that many of the old wagon roads were turned into hiking paths with informational signage, part of the "Great Central European Hiking Trail Network from the Bohemian Forest to Dubrovnik," as "Central Trail Red," "Central Trail Blue," "Central Trail Black-and-White," and so on, marked as such on the "updated official trail map of Central Europe."

And so the dolines of the karst had been declared "Central European Natural Monuments," and the largest and most beautiful of them, the Delana Dolina, close to one of the Central Villages, had received the status of a national shrine in Central Europe, a "shrine of the Central European Nation." Not only down there, in the expansive earthen depression—but also in the entire karst and the surrounding area everything Balkan or even distantly reminiscent of the Balkans was frowned upon, from foods to clothing to music (music especially: only Central European melodies and instruments were allowed, preferably Viennese waltzes, and the radio stations from Central Village to Central Village to Central Village set the tone, day after day). In the Central Doline, as the Delana Dolina was now officially known, the Central European regulations were enforced with particular strictness. Unthinkable that a Balkan clarinet or trumpet would have been heard, that a lamb would have been roasted on a spit (not to mention a suckling pig), or that anyone would have eaten onions raw. Day and night the plateau and slopes of the karst basin witnessed Central festivals, solemn Central masses, readings by Central European writers, matches between Central European teams, Central European congresses.

None of this did any harm to the "conference." Precisely amid the welter of celebrations, the unbroken succession of public events, the few attendees could preserve their secrecy unobserved (though not entirely so). Besides, there were only three of them left, three who had been scattered to the winds, who, as they came together down in a quiet corner of the doline—such a thing still existed—already had a premonition that this would be their last conference, their final farewell. So as they sat on the shore of the man-made lined pond—the dolines, like the entire karst, were otherwise extremely water-permeable—and looked up at the round horizon of the depression, they filled each other in on those who had been unable to join them. A man and a woman, he from France, she from Spain, had been the group's trophy couple. They had met during the divisive Balkan wars and had thus become a couple, both of them dedicated for years to aiding the affected peoples, all of whom, as they always said in unison, were "walking barefoot over thorns." After all these two had been through, they could only stay together forever, right? And now it was reported that the woman had left the man, feeling that she was locked in a relationship with a "cold cadaver," whereupon the man had gone after her and shot her, and then himself. Another person had become convinced that the principal blame for the smashing or falling-apart of the large country rested with a small Buddhist country on a South Sea island, and accordingly he made his way to the island and in a suicide bombing blew up the one-story structure that was more like an administrative building than the seat of government. And another one crisscrossed for months the former country, from one statue representing a hero of the Second World War to the next—not many were left—demanding at the top of his voice that they restore the country to its former glory, until one night, when he was running back and forth between hero sculptures in the Kalemegdan Park in Belgrade, falling on his knees, embracing and imploring them to intercede for him, he was taken away to a locked mental institution, with not the faintest hope of ever getting out. All that had been reported long since in the newspapers, but apparently none of the three were keeping up with the papers?

Who were the other two, along with him, the former writer, the remnant of the minority of the minority? One was the former minister of justice of a country not only very large but also extremely powerful. Now he was an old man and long since retired. He occupied himself primarily with traveling the world and representing the losers' cause, a self-assigned mission. Without going to the courts, the national as well as the international ones, to plead his case—they would not let him in, even as a witness—he viewed himself as the lawyer he had been at the beginning of his career, and presented himself as such in the environs of the tribunals, almost unnoticed or at most smiled at pityingly. He thought of himself as a successor to the criminal defense lawyer Abraham Lincoln, and was coming to look more and more like him, especially with his bushy eyebrows and deep-set eyes. But had Lincoln also been so gaunt? And certainly Lincoln had seemed less rickety, being nowhere near so old. It was quite possible that Lincoln had also had very thin legs—but they had not been clad in jeans like those in which the former minister traveled tirelessly from continent to continent. The wanderer had never seen him in anything other than work boots, a plaid shirt, and those everlasting blue jeans. Out on the street one could mistake him for an elderly vagabond. What strengthened the impression was that he always came alone and that his luggage never consisted of more than a bundle. Even at the "conferences" or as a member of a "delegation" he seemed solitary, the others avoiding him a bit. And he was definitely alone once he had made his presentations and intervenings: alone at the end of the table, alone on the top step outside the entrance to the tribunal, alone also the next morning at breakfast in the hotel on the outskirts, usually more like a flophouse; while his colleagues of the previous day—if there were such—still huddled together, he sat, quiet and forgotten, almost invisible, in the darkest and farthest corner of the breakfast room. He booked all his own flights and train rides, washed his own laundry on his travels, darned holes and sewed on buttons. Yet this "lonesome hobo" was always approachable. If someone spoke to him, even abruptly, he showed sovereign presence of mind, like someone who is prepared for anything and has thought through every contingency in advance. That the current world no longer took him seriously seemed not to trouble him. That was how it was, and it was all right, that was how it was supposed to be. He at any rate would have represented a different system of justice, would have presented himself as a different citizen of his country, would have spoken a different language, above all in a different tone of voice, not at the top

287

of his lungs like most of his fellow citizens, and not with sounds suggestive of bugs being squashed. And indeed, for someone in the role of a lawyer, his voice, in harmony with his body, while clearly audible, at the same time sounded dreamy, also intimate, as if he were speaking, even when several people were present, to only one, a high-pitched quavering singsong. But that impression was misleading, as was his fragility. He, this American who over time and in these times had become more and more quiet, would not die all that soon, and also not suddenly. Or might he after all? And never, ever, would he, was he allowed to, lose his mind. Or perhaps after all?

The other participant was a former motorcycle racer, a woman from Japan, who had gone on to study Slavic languages and was now a professor of Slavic literatures in a provincial university located in southern Japan. A soccer star from the Balkan former country whom she met while his team was competing in Japan had been the love of her life, and that had inspired her academic studies. Since her lover's death she made a point of flying to Europe at least once a year and crisscrossing the Balkans by bus, train, and also on foot. She was still young but did not ride a motorcycle anymore, let alone take part in races. It was hard to imagine her ever driving one of those huge, heavy machines, a Kawasaki or a Honda: this Japanese woman was so tiny, almost dwarflike, and so thin. She must be, and have been, far too light for the mass of steel beneath her, although that could be deceptive: upon any attempt to heave her playfully off the ground—her fellow conference attendees were tempted to try it because she looked as light as a feather—she always backed away as they approached, with a sound of dismay. She did not allow anyone to touch her, let alone hug her, not even as a greeting or farewell. Each time it was more than mere avoidance; she shied away from the other person. Instead, when they were apart, she wrote letters full of warmth and expressions of gratitude at having been welcomed as a participant in the conferences, with all kinds of enclosures: flower petals from her garden and, especially, photos she had taken in the Balkans, always of a place she had sought out after reading a book set in the former country—and there was no place described or narrated that she did not, "like a typical Asian," track down in reality, no matter how hidden or remote it was, or how encoded or fundamentally altered it appeared in the literary descriptions. Writers such as Ivo Andrić, Miloš Crnjanski, Miroslav Krleža, Ivan Cankar, had they still been alive, would not have ceased to be amazed at seeing the Japanese woman's photos of the Balkan places they had had in mind when they were writing. Might she not someday mount a motorcycle after all and reveal herself to be someone else entirely?

So the three of them sat there, the sole survivors, in their quiet corner at the bottom of the doline, and in memory of their lost colleagues moistened the ground, according to Balkan custom, with a few drops from their glasses, while between them, on a cloth, lay the provisions they had brought along, including one or two items that were frowned upon. Strangely enough, people who passed by on their way to a game or a festival did not look askance at them, even at the sound of the allegedly highly unpopular traditional Balkan music that one of the three played on a minirecorder—instead, a brief pause, a recollecting, an approving smile, even from the constable of the Central Doline as he made his rounds. Strange in another way were the fish in the man-made doline pond, in water so calm and transparent that it might have been frozen. So was it that cold at the bottom of the doline? But when the three of them now got to their feet, a summery wind wafted over them from above, bringing a warm gush of fragrance—new-mown hay and grain, such as one would expect at the height of summer. Ah, summer! And a tree above their heads had a ship's bell hanging from its lowest limb that had both Latin and Cyrillic lettering, the bell rusted, and likewise rusty and stiff its clapper.

Was this not the last time in the karst after all? Was this perhaps still the old karst empire, independent and free as no other great empire had been, allied with no one but itself? Would they all see each other again someday, the madmen no longer mad and the dead no longer so dead? And as if on cue the three survivors blew with all their might on the clapper, rusted to its bracket—without, however, getting it to swing, let alone strike the bell. The former writer, at one time described as bringing a breath of fresh air to literature, also had no luck . . . But at least they had tried. And when, after one last attempt, they turned away from the bell, they heard behind their backs something that sounded like a clang after all, more a pitiful tinkling, or a mere rustling, probably only in their imagination? Only?

II

~~~~~ ~~~~~

~~~~~ ~~~~~

~~~~~

THEN BACK AT last to the Balkans deserving of the name. If the vast majority thought of that name as a swearword, to him, and also to us, his audience during the Moravian night, it represented something else. Where had they begun, his and our Balkans? Long before the geographic and morphological border. The Balkans, for example, had been momentarily the steppe around the vanished Numancia in Old Castile, when a torn blue and white plastic bag caught on a purple thistle flapped and crackled in the wind. Balkans: the tiger-striped falcon's feather next to the dead roebuck that had broken its neck falling off a limestone cliff in Germany's Harz Mountains. The pole dwellings along the Danube to the east of Vienna, with fishing nets hanging outside, and under the houses all kinds of junk lying around between the poles— discarded refrigerators, gas canisters, automobile tires: the Balkans. The wood and coal smoke from the chimney of the jew's-harp house and the apples there between the inner and outer panes of the windows that came down almost to the floor. The sawhorse next to his grandfather's and brother's house, tipped over, half-buried among beverage crates, piles of rock, tar paper, cabbage stalks, withered and freshly shooting onions. The whistling of a train echoing from a distant gorge in the karst. The pairs of butterflies in the sun, fluttering around each other in a narrow space wherever he came upon them during his travels through Europe, hardly larger than a thumbnail, reddish-brown, with Oriental rug patterns on their wings, circles and triangles, and always appearing to be three, if not more: all of that anticipated the Balkans.

Those had been traces in time and in various spaces, anticipations, islets, isolated moments. Now, however, he set foot on the Balkan mainland, on terra firma, far from any kind of coast and ocean. Back also in the interior, with rivers flowing through it, all aiming for the Danube and the Black Sea. Standing water? Hardly any. And all the dugouts on the rivers.

He set out on foot, downriver, downstream, cutting across fields in a southeasterly direction, over hill and dale, through the Pannonian lowland, over the one ridge plopped down on it, the Fruška Gora, which took two days to cross, and from there down in serpentines past the monasteries on its southern slope and toward the White City, or rather to the central Balkan bus station in the spandrel where the Sava flowed into the Danube, where buses still departed in any direction one could desire, and from there home to the enclave of Porodin, to the Morava.

Upon his arrival in the interior and continental Balkans it had been a day of mayflies; wherever he went, they were out on their short-haul flights during the morning, began to reel in the afternoon, and roosted in the evening to die; by the next morning at the latest they were dead, without having fallen over, either to one side or onto their backs; they stood still and stiff but not quite deathly stiff on their long, sharply bent legs, on windowsills, on television sets, on cement mixers, on watering cans, their transparent little wings displaying something like a delicate letter, thicker in one spot, resembling a *W* or an *M*, their posteriors slightly raised as if prepared for flight. They allegedly lived only one day, but during this day no one could touch them; they escaped from everyone, could not be caught. So why, then, their daylong panic, their constant leaps through the air? And how weightless they then were, as cadavers. Cadavers?

Then came the day of the ladybugs, each displaying Balkan ostentation with at least fifteen or twenty black dots on its red-star-Belgrade shell. After this came the day of the vineyard snails, which left the wanderer's pack studded with shells whenever he put it down upon stopping to rest and eat along the way, like the scallop shells on a pilgrim's knapsack, except that the snails were alive, and how! all jumbled together, and their shells, unlike those of the scallops, rubbed against each other almost silently, without rattling, and by god he was no pilgrim, and if he was, then one going in the opposite direction from all established pilgrims' destinations.

Then came the day of the emerald lizards, golden-green, some lying motionless in the sun at the base of monastery walls, others skittering ceaselessly back and forth until sundown, darting in front of him across the country roads in the lowlands, as large as dragons, especially their heads as they scuttled away, flat as a frog when they had been run over. Then the day of swallows, who, hear this, appeared unexpectedly way up in the blue of the sky, having flown there from nowhere, as if called forth by the blue of the sky itself, and in vast numbers, in a second filling the sky, which just a moment before had been empty, swooping, sailing, curving, fluttering, flitting. And then the day of bees in the white clover blossoms, which trembled as they landed. And then the day of mating dragonflies, which then continued their flight conjoined. And then the day of the Balkan horses, leaping and galloping up almost vertical banks, like chamois. And then the day of the jewelweed, which popped, softly, softly, in the wanderer's palm. Then came the day of the "real" Balkan butterfly pairs, fluttering around the hiker's wrist like a moving bracelet. And then, listen to this, the day of the first linden-blossom fragrance, a gust from the interstices, with a suddenness that did the opposite of startle him. The day of getting lost. The day of sleeping in a barn. The day when he sat by the side of the road and drew, before a thunderstorm, and when the lightning struck nearby, listen to this, lost control of his pencil, which traced a thick line across the page. And in between, the day of high summer, with crickets chirping from all the horizons of the earth. And the day before that: formations of wild geese, as in late autumn.

So was there nothing else he experienced? (Our interrupter could not control himself.) No, there was: when he stopped for lunch one day, the impoverished innkeeper, hear this, was deaf and scraped the last crumbs together for him: so delicious! And one time, hear this, all of you, he sat for an entire day at a crossroads. And? In an abandoned garden gladioli were growing. And the clouds mostly came from the east. In the school buses the children sat crowded into the back. The election posters, even the newer ones, all looked faded. Nut trees and plum trees also far outside the villages, and he assuaged his hunger with the previous year's nuts, lying in the grass, and with plums that had dried on the trees. Clouds of dust preceded him along the side of the road or swirled on the ground. And the path that unexpectedly led through a remote cemetery. And in one of the monasteries, let's say the one in Grgeteg, the fresco showing Jesus having the Last Supper with the disciples outdoors, under trees, with fields in the background. And everything greening in that incomparable Balkan way. And the bluing. And the nightingales singing in the sun. And for a day he pitched in on a field, as long ago in boarding school, planting potatoes. And daytime began as soon as he started to hear, or when shadows started to play. And in the course of time and his walking, hear this, his shoes turned into footgear, and his clothes into garments or "hose," and the old young Europe awakened in his moving body, in its interstices, and less countries than various obscure corners, and the corners joined together as limbs of a sort, without borders, without a border.

And encounters with human beings? A long pause for reflection. No one? No one encountered anyone? On the contrary: one time he fell into conversation with someone, or merely listened to the other person. That was the day of getting lost in the area called the Balkan Desert. From the highway all sorts of paths or trails led into it. But, hear this, they all terminated somewhere in the middle, at the end of one last field, usually planted with corn, beyond which stretched in all directions an endless, arid, slightly hilly landscape of sand and clay, where from one horizon to the other there was nothing more to harvest, at most, perhaps, as in the taiga, things to gather or to hunt. And here, after a meander in the bed of a brook that had probably dried up ages ago and looked deceptively like a path, he came upon a very old man who, hear this, all of you, was squatting in front of a clay bank pocked with birds' entrance holes, as if serving as the watchman there; the place looked like a burial site for urns. And without returning the wanderer's greeting, he promptly began to explain that he was a refugee from the other side of the Drina, from Bosnia, and had been searching since the end of the war, now almost two decades ago, for his son, who had gone missing. In the meantime he had combed through almost the entire Balkans without finding a trace of his child, and many, he said, were out looking as he was, usually the fathers, while the mothers stayed home to take care of the house and wait, if they had not died. And the old man told him where the lost son had been seen last; described him—eye color, the shape of his ears, scars—and traced a picture of him in the air, especially his shoulders and head, all this more for himself than for the other person, who merely offered him a pretext to utter out loud the conversation he had been having with himself for decades. He wanted to bring home at least one bone belonging to his son. The bone he measured in the air, however, stretching out both arms, was that of a giant, as long and as large as an entire person. And no one else? No. Or rather, yes: all the ferrymen who took him across the hundred and one rivers. And the other old man, the other refugee, the one with eyes like a child's, once condemned to death in the former country as a such-and-such dissident, who had become a philosopher in the course of fleeing the country, and who now, shortly before his death, still wanted to rethink the entire world: "We must come up with a new way of thinking!" And the woman with eyes like cherries. And the sunburned Coptic pope, out on the road with nothing but a toothpick between his lips. And the general ducking at the sound of planes high overhead, peaceable though they were. And the secretive old lovers, both of them white-haired, with flushed cheeks. And much seemed simple. And then nothing was simple. These were wounded peoples, from one remote spot to the next, knowing peoples, wise ones.

At the bus station in the White City. (On the latest maps it was once more called, as in the time of foreign rule, "Weissenstadt"—how had Belgrade of all places come to have this name?) Waiting for the bus to take him back to the enclave. Only one bus a day went there now, and so the homecomer, or whatever he was, had plenty of time to sit and look. The sun at his back was a help, as was a certain weariness and the spot he chose, the terrace of one of the many restaurants surrounding the large bus station. And as it happened, his field of vision was confined to the bays where the buses pulled in. Had the country become small? Not to judge by the sight of the buses here at their last stop. Not only did one arrive right after another in an uninterrupted change of scene: one bus, empty, heading off to the depot, and already the arrival, or appearance, of the next one, filled with passengers. Also each bus offered a different image, starting with its markings or body style, its age, its color, or, as was understandable, given the many peoples of this country, unique within Europe, even or precisely in its truncated condition, the variations among the passengers getting off—a different image, however, from that presented primarily by the bus windows, and a particularly clear one once all the passengers had left the bus, in the brief moment before it drove away. The sun, shining through the empty space inside, made the glass more visible and lent contours to the traces remaining on the panes from the trip. Bus windows without traces, or with old traces, possibly there for weeks or months, encrusted, hardened, would have evoked thoughts of a trip from not far off, from one of the suburbs. But such buses never pulled in. All the buses, including their windows, had obviously been washed before setting out, and the traces on the windows were, without exception, fresh, left over only from the trip just completed and now at its destination. And all the trips had lasted more or less long. The traces were fresh, that they had in common, but how greatly they differed otherwise from one another. How differently the windows had been breathed on: over there a child's breath, over here an old person's breath. Sleep breath. Fear breath. Observer breath. Rage breath. Hesitant breath. Abandonment breath. And most of the windows in one bus showed the imprint of noses, in another more that of foreheads, in a third more that of cheeks, in a fourth more that of hands. The buses could also be divided, just from the outside of the windows, into those that had only a day's journey behind them and those that had traveled through the night; those coming from mountainous regions and those from lowlands; those from dewy regions and those from rainy regions; those from landscapes with hailstorms and those whose windows had been covered with frost that morning—the traces were still there—or which had gone through a snowstorm; those traces, too, though long after the snow had melted, clearly inscribed on the windows, like those of a sandstorm, a shower of blossoms, a wave of mosquitoes, a swarm of grasshoppers. Maps of the country on the bus windows, unusually detailed. But were they accurate? Yes, for the moment, and for a good long while to come.

And so he then sat on the bus taking him back to Porodin and to the Morava. He had set out heading in a southwesterly direction and was returning from the northwest. The circle was closing. Did it close? The bus home to the enclave, unlike the one on the morning of his departure, was almost empty. Still, a passenger had sat down next to him in the rear, as if looking for company. He did not speak after all, but unfolded a newspaper, and as always the homecomer could not stop himself from reading along, in violation of his resolve to read no newspaper during his journey. New popes, new world champions, new heads of state, new stars, new volcanoes, new epidemics, a new planet, a new variety of wine, a new painkiller, a new mathematical puzzle: so he had been away that long? Halfway down the page a headline with his own name: it was a report, initially called a "tale," about his, the former writer's tour, written by the journalist and writer with the lovely name of Melchior. He was known for publishing each of his articles in all the countries of Europe simultaneously, translated into each country's language, and so, too, here, in the former country, whose—what was the word?—leading newspapers had long since been taken over by foreigners. His seat neighbor soon turned the page, but he had already been able to skim most of the article, also because it was written in a language that made it possible to take everything in almost at a glance; transparent language was probably the right term, with any need to continue reading obviated after the first few sentences—which spared one from wasting time on reading. And what was it that caught his eye? That he, as was already clear from the headline, had undertaken the tour just to get away from himself. That he had willfully sought out only the weird and out-of-the-way. That he had closed his eyes to reality. Serious writers were passionately concerned with current problems—and he? At most he brooded over them, hadn't a clue. Destinies, characters, actions: not for him. Climate change; the hole in the ozone layer; the old and new primitives; the mass die-off of penguins; the Iroquois' fear of heights, where at one time they had been able to build skyscrapers without vertigo; night-blindness increasing among cats and even owls; nuns getting married; genetically modified sorrel; amphibians turning back into fish: all of no interest to him. Nowhere did he show any compassion for his contemporaries. Instead he waxed enthusiastic over a glow worm, a hedgehog, a brook with a flake of mica at the bottom, an old road, a cow flop, a child's cowlick, the red of clay, the white of quince blossoms. And as a person he was equally weird. Yet he had eyes everywhere, especially when it came to women's posteriors. On the entire journey he had expressed himself vehemently and shown some feeling only once: when his cell phone fell in the ocean. Weird also in his religious observances—a regression to animistic practices: what else should one call it when he constantly turned around and listened to the faintest breath but was also constantly breathing on inanimate objects (for example: the rusted clapper of a ship's bell). He apologized to a table he bumped against, to a stone, even to his own hand when he jammed it. And another time he threatened a creaking door with "Shut up!" while a broken shoelace was called "You no-good! You filthy pig! You wimp! You looney tunes!" and he shouted "Silence!" at a ringing telephone. A feral cat that he stroked he addressed as "whore," and to a daddy longlegs he said, "Hey, doggy," while he always addressed stray dogs with "Well, you old dodo bird!" And more than just a couple of times he was observed breathing with all his might on dead animals—flies, spiders, beetles, bees, even moles and mice, as if he thought he had the power to revive them—and that was the only time he showed passion.

The author of the article was already informed about the end of the journey, as could be seen from subheads like "Returning Empty-Handed" and "Even Well-Wishers Concerned About This Knight of Ill Fortune" and "Closest Friends See Through Him." (Directly below the article the day's horoscope, with a sentence that applied to him in quite a different way: "Work for peace.")

When the homecomer looked up from the paper, his gaze caught that of the third passenger (there were no more in the bus). The third one was—what was the expression?—a mere child. He was sitting way up front and had turned to face him, apparently not just that minute but some time ago. And it seemed as though that boy there, almost a child, knew what the man behind him had been subjected to by the newspaper his neighbor to the rear was reading. It seemed that way? No, he really did know, knew literally, from A to Z, and he confirmed that during the night on the Morava boat, for he was among us in the audience, the last one to have been invited, the mystery guest. And he took over the storytelling from our host for a few sentences: upon reading the article, our host turned into the person the article portrayed, or played that role, trying it out—nibbling his fingernails a bit, closing his eyes (not completely), glancing, as the bus passed a traffic accident, with his mouth open like an idiot's, back and forth between the tips of his shoes and the bus's ceiling, as if it were the firmament, puffing out his cheeks by the bus's window curtain, and so on. He leaned with the bus as it went around corners, and without regard for his neighbor threw his arms in the air as if about to take off and fly into the wild blue yonder; and finally he did nothing but smirk, meanwhile moving his lips, from which the boy could read the shortest of all the Balkan curses: "May the mouse fuck you!" Where had this curse been heard earlier on his journey?

This was not what mattered to the boy as he told the story. Time and again he had become completely entangled in something he had seen. The crown of a tree stirred out in the schoolyard, and as he watched it he was up there in the treetop. A sparrow bathed in a hollow in the sand, and he bathed along with it. A pebble rolled with the current along the bottom of a brook, and he rolled with it. Was this actually a case of being drawn in, of losing himself? It was more a kind of seeing in which, little by little, he merged with the thing seen—in which he did not lose himself, on the contrary: the thing became part of him. Up to now, to be sure, he had hardly experienced this kind of transference with people, at most with his younger siblings, and only when he watched them sleeping. The man behind him was the first stranger with whom such a thing happened, and the boy could not even say why he was filled with empathy in the case of this particular person, when there was nothing to empathize with, least of all in his gestures and facial expressions. However that might be, in the moments of transference, in which the near-child finally became the other person entirely, he felt something wash over him that in one way or another would determine the course of his life.

As the night sky over the river gradually brightened, the boatmaster had obviously resumed telling the story, a few sentences back. He had interrupted the boy, but lovingly, with enthusiasm. And so he continued: in the way the young person on the bus had looked at him, in the "osmosis" taking place, body and soul, he, the abdicated writer, had recognized the future writer. The person who became so engrossed in looking, to the point of complete, self-forgetful participation, all of it unintended and involuntary, showed himself to be a worthy successor. A successor in the profession: so such a thing existed, who would have thought it! Make way for the successor! And how amazing that the boy did not try to duck what lay ahead, and not just for one or two seasons but for his entire life! Any escape to a different profession, no matter what, was senseless: if anything he could only become, practice, and continue practicing what he was made for, or, to paraphrase Jakob Böhme, his primal condition, or, in still other words, his beautiful yet terrible problem. Welcome, successor, repeater, message-bearer. Greetings to ye, little brother, maternal child. Hallo, new writer-in-the-air, new die-tosser, fresh-speller, old boy. And fear not: you are it. And be afraid: you are it.

12

~~~~~~~~~~~~

~~~~~~~~~~~~

THE ENCLAVE OF Porodin no longer existed. With it the last enclave in
the Balkans, and in Europe as a whole, had disappeared, or "disen-
claved." Only he, the homecomer, had not known about this—the rest
of us had long since adjusted to the changed situation. It had had to
happen. It was how things went, and as far as Porodin was concerned,
it had even happened peacefully for the most part, and the changes had
not taken place all at once but very gradually, almost imperceptibly.
Only at him, after what some of us considered his "unforgivably" long
absence, did they jump out.

It was a warm summery evening as the bus rolled into Porodin, and
it would stay light for a long time. He noticed right away that the sign
at the entrance to the village was in Roman script, no longer Cyrillic,
"PORODIN," not "породин." Another writer had said once, responding to a newspaper reporter's question about things he disliked, that

among others it was the Cyrillic script, and one could sympathize with him after what had been done to his people and his country under the banner of this script. With Porodin, however, it was different, wasn't it? The Cyrillic script did mean something, but not what one might assume, right?

The other thing that jumped out at him upon his arrival was above all what was no longer there and had previously given the enclave its character. A welcome change: no more rolls of razor wire marking the town limits and surrounding the fields and vineyards that belonged to the town; also the absence of tanks in a semicircle on the hills, their guns pointing in all directions, of surveillance aircraft thundering overhead—hardly above the tops of the poplars—of signs with crossed pistols at the entrances to taverns. The whole village unarmed and unguarded, freely accessible, no more rocks being thrown at the bus's windows as it entered town, at most a few kisses being blown, more for old times' sake than with hostile intent. Had he mentioned vineyards? They no longer existed either. They had become superfluous; there was no one to take care of them; the few remaining grapevines had dried up or been burned; or the vineyards had been bulldozed to make way for a golf course—the many hollows that had protected the vines from the wind were ideal for golf. Besides, the wine they had made, heavy and naturally cloudy, had been good only for domestic consumption. And the sheep grazing as far as the eye could see? Not a trace of them, not even their hoof marks. And the village idiots? Out of the picture.

Every enclave, including that of Porodin, to which he had allegedly at one time "linked his fate" (Melchior) meant nothing to him by comparison with the unknown. To stumble into a region in which every step led deeper into the fairy-tale-like unknown: nothing could top that. Ah, the great unknown, with colors never before seen, with noises never before heard. What he saw on his way through the village, beginning with the new bus station, all glass—for one arrival and one departure per day—with bird silhouettes pasted everywhere on the panes, seemed fairly familiar, however. A strange sight in enclave times would have been the many runners, all with name badges, as if for a permanent conference, wearing the track suits now worn all over the world; if a single runner had swerved around the slow-moving or seated enclave folk, that would have been strange—but no longer. The footgear and clothing and not just that of the runners: internationally known brands (although they might be knockoffs). The former chicken pens had become bright green lawns, the grass scalped even shorter than at Wimbledon, and here and there in the middle a marble fountain. A single turkey strutting over the bare ground in what remained of a farmyard, around and around in a circle, but silent, not gobbling; all that could be heard was his stiff feathers, which hung down and brushed the ground with every step, making the sound of a leaf rake. The enclave sounds and especially the smells? Once upon a time? Instead the constant racket of alarms from parked cars, factory-new. All that was missing was a pedestrian zone and smiling Tibetan monks. Were they missing?

At one time he had thought all these "new folk" came from another planet, were extraterrestrials. But no: they came from here and were firmly anchored in the here and now. The planet belonged exclusively to them. The ones from another planet were him and his kind—"You, my audience!" And those who were holding the fort now ran and ran, and continued holding the fort. If they were to stop running, not only their name badges, complete with photos, would promptly fall off.

He did come upon a few of the original inhabitants. They were all old, and they had all been old acquaintances—except that on the evening of his return they looked right through him. It was not only that they did not recognize him. They had no eyes for him. (The only one who had greeted him had been one of the runners, who shouted in broadest German or Danish, "Welcome to Porodin!" adding considerately, "Beware of strangers' looks!") The couple of natives sat huddled together at a small table in a former transformer hut, which, emptied out, had been made into their clubhouse, among them the friend who, way back when, had driven him on his tractor to the bus. And for that friend, too, although he looked in his direction, he did not exist in his hour of return. To be sure, the oldsters were busy singing their enclave songs at the tops of their voices, fervently yet so preoccupied that what was taking place around them probably did not enter their consciousness. A new song had been added to the repertoire, up to then just a saying, and this saying and the new song were "*To je to!*" ("That's that! And that's that!") And so forth—that was all there was to the lyrics.

Who had died in his absence? In earlier times one could see who had died from the house façades, where black banners would be hung bearing the names and the dates of death. Now: not a single banner, neither a new black one nor one of those from the enclave period that were left hanging for several years, to be used the next time someone died, becoming faded and eventually almost illegible. And the cemetery? In the meantime it had been surrounded with a high wall, which reminded him of the rampart in his Old Village, erected to keep out the Turks—but here, according to the posted Internet link, protecting a "European Cultural Monument."

More and more abandoned houses, only gradually revealing their presence between and behind the new construction. The shutters closed, the hooks that secured them when open dangling uselessly. Luxuriant blooming in the equally abandoned gardens behind the houses—a lilac bush amid tangles of weeds, known by its Balkan-Turkish name as *jergovan*, and a single peony glowing amid stinging nettles, with all the colors in the world gathered in its center, glowing its heart out. And all the fruitfulness, the trees laden with apples, plums, apricots in the gardens of those who had been gone so long, or were dead? He did not ask, did not want to hear the word "death" right now. And the ringed dove in the crook of a tree, with no letter in its beak, or was there one after all?

Whooshing back to the living. Where were they? There: on a bench by a wall, sitting in the evening sun, were a few, this time old women, and for them, too, he did not exist; they had eyes only for the mobile telephones they all held in their hands, waiting for their children and grandchildren, the emigrants, to call, from Canada, from Australia, from Brazil.

Outside the former enclave, making his way to the *Moravian Night*, to his boat: no danger anymore? But he still felt it, from the years of being surrounded, or imagined it, as an element of his life, or an element of his story. The sense of menace remained. He almost hoped for an attack that would prevent him from returning, there, at the crossroads between the fields. The sound of a shot, coming from a balloon bursting or an automobile tire popping: disappointment. A wild boar, snorting, lumbered out of the underbrush behind him, coming closer: unfortunately just another runner, dripping with sweat, self-absorbed. The figure by one of the huge oaks on the edge of the Morava meadows (let's hope he's lying in wait for me): another lone wanderer, leaning against the tree, as if trying to draw strength from it. And another figure at another crossroads on the riverine plain, holding something metallic with noticeably sharp edges that glinted ominously in the setting sun, with everything else already in shadow: just a third solitary wanderer, reading a book as he stood there. And the black great Dane that hurtled toward him from the green meadow rose into the sky and turned into a raven—he had rejoiced too soon. And the person yelling clear across the fields, still fallow even in summer—"O old man, O rage, O despair"—was an actor, not even all that old, in fact very young, practicing for his role as an old man in *Le Cid*. But then, finally, someone who was not just playing at being in despair: a man who was lost—a native, in his familiar region.

No more walking backward in his usual fashion—only forward now. Finally dusk, and with it the smell of the river, and through the aspen and poplar trees the neon sign from his boat, no, his hostel, flickering on, MORAVIAN NIGHT, with some of the letters hidden by the trees, more the consonants than the vowels. Smoke: black and strong from the funnel. Fire? No such luck. A surge of joy, and at the same time he delayed his return. That was how it was, or that was how the story wanted it. Or perhaps he really could not find his way, on a stretch

he had traversed hundreds of times before. Passing through bomb crater after bomb crater—the last section of his journey: a trip through
bomb craters, left over from the Second World War, from the Thousand-
Year Reich's assault on the country, which in those days became former
for the first time. And since he was thinking of numbers: the craters
came from the first of three bombardments the country had endured
in the twentieth century (in the twenty-first century since the birth of
the Son of God, who became a man for us and died, that we might live
in him, bombardments had not yet been necessary).

The craters were not large, but instead came thick and fast, one after
another, in a fairly straight line, as the bird flies, so to speak, across the
meadows to the Morava, and in this way they marked his route for
him. This hike was a pleasure, with its gentle up and down, which created a rhythm, and that rhythm possibly enhanced even more the pleasure of walking. And besides, the bottoms of the bomb craters were
firm, yet at the same time soft from the dead leaves that had collected
there over the course of the almost seven or eight decades since the
bombs were dropped, with the result that one bounced along. There
could be no more harmonious and peaceful up and down than this
walking from crater to crater, the leaves at the bottom so thick (and as
fluffily soft as otherwise only the pinfeathers of birds of prey) that one
involuntarily began to walk like a crane. One was almost tempted to
use endearments: "Dear little craters. Sweet little bomb craters!" The
evening dew collected at the bottom much more plentifully than elsewhere in the meadows, began to flow, forming little roundish puddles
in the gaps among the leaves, good not only against thirst, and there he
again found the human frogs from his Old Village; scores of them were
crouching on the edge of the evening-dew puddles, their teeny-tiny
human fingers stretched into the water to moisten them.

An interruption of the rhythm then occurred only with the last of
the bomb craters: this one much larger and above all deeper than the
248 previous ones (with the rhythm he had started counting, and 248
had been his laundry number long ago in boarding school); it was a

true crater, more than a mere hollow, extending way down to the water table, dug by one of the mother bombs from what had been the last war, for the time being, against the country, dropped by no one in particular, and at least without the intention to kill—enough of that had been done already—but rather to get rid of the extra weight still on board after the successful attack farther south on the Varvarin bridge and the civilians on it celebrating Christ's ascension. Naturally—according to what nature? (our interrupter, once more after all)—acceptable pretexts had been found yet again for the solicitous release: necessity as the mother of invention.

Not a good idea to cross this crater, in which, after the mother of bombs detonated, there were still some son and daughter bombs, small but—oho!—waiting to explode. The impact had hurled clods of clay from inside the earth against the most distant tree trunks, where the clay still clung to them like cement, and the fractured rock that had pierced the bark to the core had in the meantime been encapsulated by the wood, also growing with the trees, so that rock after rock was trapped in the forks of the trees and way up into the crowns. He made his way around the crater, seeing a bronze reflection on the forest floor—although the sun had long since gone down?

And also bronze—where was the light source?—was the reflection on the water, flowing silently and rapidly along, when at the end of this hike he stood on the bank of the Morava. At his feet, in the grass that grew along the bank, the familiar hedgehog, it, too, with a bronze glow on its spines, and what did it say? "I'm here already!"? No, it said, "I'm still here!" And that now the ship's bell tolled: for real? And the scent of honeysuckle, which he otherwise knew only from books. But what did "only" mean? He tossed his pack into the river, together with everything in it (not much). Yes, he would return empty-handed. And that was as it should be.

13

~~~~~~

~~~~~~~

~~~~~~

THE NIGHT WAS at an end. The writer opened his eyes. Broad daylight. Morning sun. He pulled the woman, the stranger, to him, but no one was there. Yet they had just embraced each other as no couple had ever done before. Love? The woman had let him feel that she was there for him. What was so special about that? To him it was a miracle. And now, in the morning, he wanted to snatch her, was panting in empty space for her body. Yes, did the woman then not exist? On the contrary, she did exist, outside of the dream, and how, but she did not belong to him. Ah, the pain at her absence. He was at odds with himself, for good.

And where were the rest of us, who had listened all night on the boat, the friend from Porodin, the dentist from Velika Plana, the former officer, now a mushroom grower, the successor writer, the unemployed lawyer, the unemployed teacher, the night porter? No trace of us either;

no question of a "we"; the writer was alone in the salon, with not even the bus-chasing dog at his feet; looking around for "us": again nothing. Yet the thought had been that the story would end with all of us on deck, under the awning, and also no longer on the Morava but farther north, past its mouth, in the middle of the Danube, ten times wider, heading toward the Black Sea, toward which we would have chugged in the gray of dawn, once again fleeing. Nothing. Ah, such pain, so great: separated forever.

Not even a river, not even the Morava outside the windows, which certainly were no bull's-eyes. Striking, the harsh light in the cracks of the swinging door, with the sign KUHINJA, kitchen. Pushing the door open—and again nothing, again the void. Standing, blinded, in the sun. No trace of a boat, of the *Moravian Night*? What had just recently been a boat had shrunk into a dugout, and now the dugout sank. And the river, the Morava? The Morava dried up. And Porodin was no enclave after all, had never been one. The Balkan enclaves were somewhere else.

What had he been seeking among the lost souls in the Balkans? Why had he not left them to their fate? And was it even the Balkans anymore? Wasn't that the rattle of suburban trains rather than the roar of the Balkan expressway? Still lingering, the echo of the night, like the roar of the tractor trailer trucks and the rushing of the Morava, of the bellowing of the chamois, the croaking of the frogs in the reeds along the banks. And like the echo, the residual images. The one who was lost, wasn't that in reality him? Had the night's undertaking been nothing but seizing a handful of dust?

Now a third angel put in an appearance at the end of his story: after the guardian angel and the warning angel, this was the reassuring angel. And it reassured him. And he allowed himself to be reassured. That's that. And that is that. *To je to, I to je to*—geography of dreams, stay with me now and in the hour of my death.

All his life the writer had worked on a book at night. And it was during the night that he had always finished it. Except that in the morning the book was no longer there. It had even appeared at night as a book, been published. But in the light of day: gone, vanished. Reaching out for it: into empty space. It had happened again and again that the writer could close his eyes and still have the book before him for a while. Just one page, a single one, showed itself to him this way, handwritten. The writing, however, was not his own. It was legible, yet he never succeeded in deciphering it, not a word, at most a letter here and there. It also seemed as though the book was not written in his language. So in another one? Which one? In a foreign one, no, in an entirely unknown one. And nevertheless it was one page of the book he had written during the night! He was still utterly exhausted from writing, his heart racing, his writing hand aching and cramping.

And each time this writing remained visible for an amazingly long time. And when at last it began to flicker, flickering apart and fading: what emptiness, what blackness. A planet all its own appeared in the blackness, scarred, craggy, with occasional bright spots, a chaos, pulsing, and accompanying it a music so quiet and fragrant that its like would never be heard again. Accompanying it the wing beats of an enormous bird, invisible, the sound almost identical to that of a cloth being shaken out and spread.

In the course of his life the writer had written not a few such nocturnal books, which had been dissolved into nothing by the light of day. Into nothing? Really? Something remained inside him from all of them, something tangible, so much so that he could not believe they had really disappeared, that these one-night books had never existed. And how did he define what remained, was tangible? What remained to him from every nocturnal book was a taste. The book existed somewhere; it was no nocturnal fata morgana; it had something durable about it, something he could taste. And the taste always had a foretaste as well. And something else remained with him from the night: a word from the writer's Arabic period, which meant to "pass the night in conversation," and the word was *samara*. Again, after Stara Vas and Samarkand, the threefold *a*.

It was a dark, clear morning, as if made for setting out—and for staying put. The forest outside the window here: not a riverine forest? The Morava River near the village of Porodin in the depths of the Balkans: swept away? The boat called *Moravian Night* rocking no more? Hauled ashore?

And a fourth or fifth angel grabbed him by the scruff of his neck, the scruff-of-the-neck angel: the rustling in the treetops now; listen, just think, here just as there. And then look, imagine, the cherry tree, turned red overnight: the night of the ripening cherries. And the swallows, look, here just as there in our Europe. And the quivering, rippling seconds here just as there. And the clouds here just as there. And the mosquitoes here just as there. And the people out on the street, hear this, all of you, really were those of Porodin, and I greeted them, hear this, through the window in their Balkan language, and—they greeted us back. And the morning bus driving by was a Steyr diesel, and the silhouettes in the windows were familiar to me.

Light streaming diagonally out of the clouds, look, that was how life sometimes was. May you be the son of your moment. And may the moment be your breath.

The writer had invited us onto his boat, saying, "Come along, all of you, I must tell you a sad story!" A sad story? That remained to be seen.

—January to November 2007